La Playa de Los Muertos

A Corsair Novel
Douglas Pratt

MANTA PRESS

For Ashlee

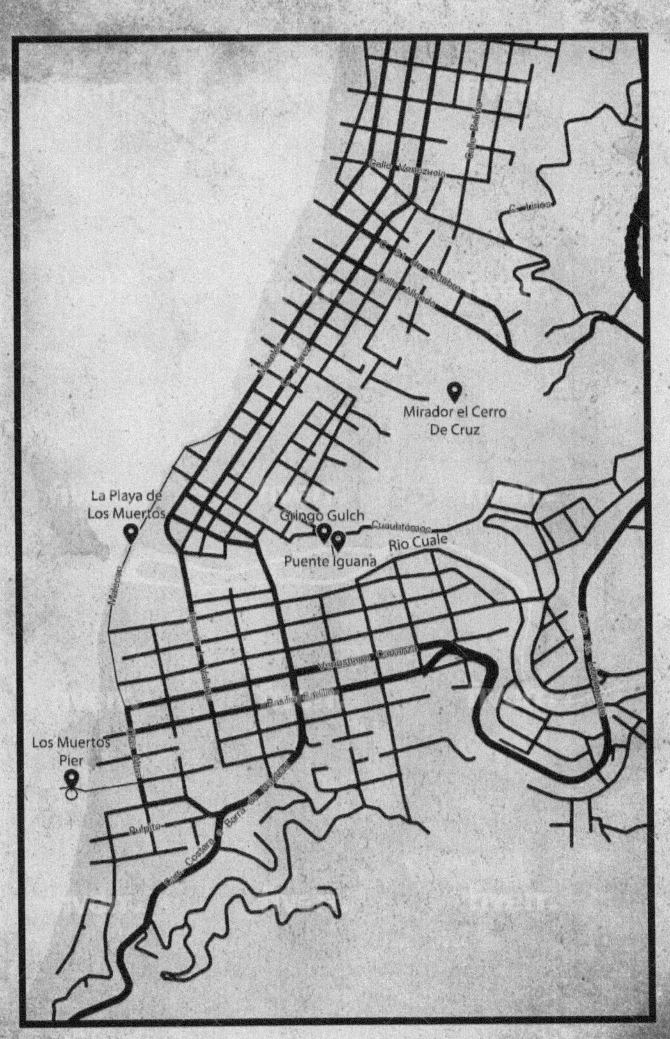

Calle Bolivia
Calle Venezuela
Guatinos
Mirador el Cerro
De Cruz
La Playa de
Los Muertos
Gringo Gulch
Cuauhtémoc
Rio Cuale
Puente Iguana
Venustiano Carranza
Los Muertos
Pier
Pulpito

1

The spray spewed almost fifteen feet into the air as the surf rolled into a curl nearly that high. White foam slammed against the sand, and the bubbles raced up the beach toward the umbrellas and lounge chairs filled mostly with Canadians, something Caleb wouldn't have guessed until he'd been here for a few days. He wondered if everyone in Vancouver picked up in January and moved to the western coast of Mexico. Given the perfect weather in Jalisco, Caleb couldn't blame them. Why stick around some place with negative temperatures?

He'd never been to Puerto Vallarta before he and Amanda traveled across Mexico. When he found out so much of the tourist and ex-pat population was from Canada, he was relieved. In fact, he had an alias that fit right in. Roland Bryer of Toronto. The passport was virginal, but the conditions offered a perfect reason to break it in. It would be easier to pass Amanda off as Canadian than it would most other nationalities. With any luck, as she grew up, her speech would develop just enough of an odd accent to throw off most people. And as long as she didn't sound like she was born in Augusta, Georgia, he felt she'd be safer.

The breeze came along the beach, passing under the pier as he carried a large wooden tray through the crowded waterfront. Mounds of oysters and ice piled up on the platter. A leather strap wrapped over his shoulders, helping him carry the nearly seventy pounds of shellfish.

"*¡Ostras! ¿Quién quiere ostras frescas?*" he called in Spanish before repeating in English, "Oysters! Who wants fresh oysters?"

An older fellow with an Ernest Hemingway beard and a stiff, tan Panama hat waved. Three women, evenly bronzed by the Mexican sun, stretched out in lounge chairs around him. None of them seemed as if they should be with the man, except for their age. They were all fit, thin, and surgically enhanced. He, on the other hand, sported the same deep brown skin, but beer crafted his gut. Caleb lifted an eyebrow at the tiny pink swim briefs the man wore which left nothing to the imagination and little for the guy to show off.

The water is cold, Caleb considered.

"*Dos docenas,*" Hemingway said.

Caleb seemed to drop the salver, but he jerked it up suddenly. Two legs flopped out from the bottom as he rose. His right foot adjusted both braces to hold the table, and Caleb pulled a small, dull blade from his waist. The oyster knife was practically homemade.

More like home-repaired, Caleb thought.

The round metal tip jutted from a handgrip fashioned from melted acrylic. Caleb assumed someone along the way created a mold for the thick bulb of a handle and heated scraps of trash until it liquefied. It would be easy to set the alloy blade and pour the mixture into the cast. Whatever they did, it made a serviceable shucking knife.

With his left hand, Caleb snapped a towel off his belt and wrapped an oyster before nestling the tool into the hinge. He rotated his wrist, gently opening the crack slightly wider. A second later, the metal edge pried the shells apart. Caleb scraped the side of the tool under the muscle to sever it from the bottom shell. He repeated the process twenty-three times, dropping the top shell into a bag hanging off the table and setting the half filled with meat on a paper dish. Before he handed Hemingway his oysters, Caleb pulled a whole lime from his pocket, slicing it into quarters and adding two pieces to each platter of shellfish.

"Hot sauce?" he asked, pulling a small vial of red liquid from a makeshift holster on his belt.

"Yes, please," the bearded man agreed. Caleb spun the bottle, passing it to him, watching as Hemingway doused the oysters with the spicy red liquid. He handed it back with four hundred pesos.

"*Gracias.*" Caleb responded with a nod.

Hemingway returned the gesture as he lifted an oyster to his lips and slurped it out of the shell. Caleb holstered his sauce and knife, looped the towel on his belt, and hoisted the table up. The legs sprang up, and he used his knees to push them against the bottom of the tray.

Caleb wondered when his skin would brown as much as Hemingway's and his ladies' had. He spent six hours a day lugging oysters up and down La Playa de los Muertos, which translated to "the beach of the dead." It was an unusual name, but it stemmed from when the city's earlier inhabitants built a cemetery somewhere on this stretch of coast. The graves had long since vanished, although Caleb wasn't sure if it was intentional or simply the fact that building a graveyard in the sand along the Pacific Ocean was a terrible idea.

The weather in Puerto Vallarta had one setting—unless it was hurricane season—sunny with about seven puffy billows in the sky. Caleb instinctively glanced upward at the three clouds drifting behind the Los Muertos Pier, a strange-looking spire sticking up from the concrete platform. The structure reminded Caleb of an art deco fan, and he half expected it to rotate every time he looked at it. The edge of the pier remained crowded at almost all times. He'd never been down here after midnight, but he suspected that like the rest of the city, it never really slept.

The sun glinted off the sand, and despite the cheap aviator shades he got from Carlos, the sunglasses man who peddled his array of eyewear along the shore, Caleb squinted. These aviators might not have been of the highest quality.

It's what I get for 120 pesos, Caleb considered. He had grown accustomed to thinking in terms of the Mexican currency instead of dollars. It was an old habit—blending into whatever culture in which he was located. It almost surprised him how easily he reverted to operational mode.

Maybe, he contemplated, he never left it. Although, after a few years with Audrey, he felt more at ease. Caleb convinced himself he'd let his guard down. Perhaps it just never needed to rear up.

He lowered his head, letting the brim of the straw hat shade his face as he scanned the crowds for more customers. Most of the beachgoers held a special tolerance to the many vendors, hawking everything from massages and hair braids to dresses and artwork. Caleb noticed that while the guys traipsed up and down offering stuff, most took being turned down pretty easily. When someone wanted something, they learned to seek out the vendor with it.

He was an expert at watching mannerisms, anyway. He knew which tourists were interested in buying and which weren't. The ex-pats and visiting Canadians loved supporting the vendors, and those were easy to spot. The cruise ship people, on the other hand, held their wallets tightly, afraid the brown folks might make off with their cash. Of course, he figured that was part of the cruise ship warnings—don't take all your money ashore because it's safer to spend it on board. The same was true for the all-inclusive crowd that sneaked off the resorts to dip their toes in the culture. They bought nothing outside of a taco or some weed.

Sand shifted through his sandals as he shuffled along. He paused when he saw the man in the baseball cap.

It wasn't the New York Giants hat that caught his eye. He slouched in a plastic chair with a can of Pacífico. Everything about the man screamed "American," and to Caleb, everything about the man also screamed "killer." If asked what caused him to classify the character that way, Caleb might not have been able to pinpoint the details. The knowledge was innate—an uncanny sixth sense.

He rotated around and walked back down the beach. Caleb used the edge of his sunglasses as a mirror to study the man. The angle distorted the reflection, but it provided him with the detail he needed. He wore a typical tropical-style button shirt with shorts. Caleb put him in his thirties, closer to thirty than forty.

He was by himself, and while that wasn't reason enough, it set off a few alarms. Very few travelers visited Puerto Vallarta alone. They came with friends, spouses, significant others. Or they met people here—too many friendlies to leave a stranger sitting by themselves. It was the bane of the place for Caleb. A man who wanted to go along in life unnoticed didn't do so well when every day someone tried to strike up another conversation.

This guy avoided that. There wasn't an extra seat for a friend to come later. He also positioned himself so he could watch both the shore and the walkway leading back to Basilio Badillo, the closest street feeding directly to the sand.

He was on the prowl. Caleb knew the look of a hunter—he'd been one long enough to know the telltale signs.

"Can I get a dozen?" A voice interrupted his thoughts. He glanced up to see an older man and his wife reclining in the Adirondack chairs under an umbrella. This wasn't a local tourist, as Caleb came to refer to them. Those were the ones who were here for months on end. This guy was only here for a few days. Neither he nor his spouse had the tan of weeks on the beach. Instead, both were pinkish from a few too many hours in the sun.

Caleb dropped his table down and started shucking oysters. He glanced over his shoulder as he worked. The Giants fan turned his head toward Caleb for an instant. If he hadn't been wearing the cheap shades, Caleb would have locked eyes with the man. They held the gaze for less than a second, but to an operator like Caleb it was an eternity.

The man stood up, dropping a small wad of colored bills on the table. He moved in Caleb's direction, and every fiber in Caleb's body tensed up. Past training ignited, and Caleb's breathing steadied as he moved. The eyes behind the tinted glasses narrowed, and Caleb prepared.

The Marine Corps and, ultimately, the Office of Compliance instilled that preparation in him. They trained it into him as a kid. A lifetime before today, Caleb Saunders departed Parris Island to be recruited into the Office of Compliance. He had an innate talent for killing, and the United States government didn't want to waste him in the Marine Corps when they could wind him up and aim him to the targets they wanted eliminated. Caleb knew he had a gift for it, and he considered it part of his civic responsibility. At eighteen, he took a Greyhound from the tiny burg of Clayton, Georgia, with every intention of fighting for his country. At the time, Caleb only wished to follow in his grandfather's footsteps by joining the Marines. From his perspective, being a Marine meant he only had to kill out of duty. When Carl Winston gave him the code name

Corsair and put him to work for the Office of Compliance, he thought he was still doing just that.

Until Turkey.

Turkey changed everything.

The information his handler passed along to him stated the apartment was the headquarters of an Al-Qaeda cell. The mission was almost rote work, simple compared to others he'd accomplished—set off an explosion to make it look like they'd accidentally blown themselves up. Fate forced his hand. The device malfunctioned, and Corsair never left a job unfinished. He moved inside the building to take out the cell, only to find the targets were a twenty-nine-year-old woman and her seven-year-old son. At first, Corsair thought it had been a mistake, but somewhere deep in his gut, he knew otherwise. The boy had a bounty on his head. He was the illegitimate son of a Turkish leader whose enemies targeted the kid to scare the Turk into a political deal.

Caleb sent the woman and her son running before blowing the apartment up. His bosses in the OOC presumed he died in the explosion.

Ten years passed, and he enjoyed being dead.

Until one day, two thugs resurrected Corsair.

Right now, Corsair stuck his head out of Caleb's subconscious. He studied the Giants fan as he moved toward him. Caleb's grip on the oyster knife shifted as he finished up the dozen oysters.

His mind played out six different points on the man where he could kill him with one jab of the dull blade. The neck—stab into the jugular. Either eye. The back of the skull—right into the brain stem. The liver. Worst case, he could put it into the man's leg, rupturing the femoral artery.

The New Yorker came closer, but he had made no threatening moves yet. Corsair waited as Caleb plated the oysters. When the American passed him without glancing his direction, Caleb handed the shellfish to the tourist and his wife. Before the couple could pay him, Caleb popped the legs up on the table and turned to watch the Giants fan as he walked off toward the wooden walkway that led to the pier and street.

Caleb paused, watching the individual he knew was a killer trail behind a young woman strolling along the road.

2

Not your business, Corsair warned himself. *Keep your head down*.

However, the face of his daughter flashed through Caleb's mind. This girl was someone's child. The gut-wrenching dread crippled him for a second as his memory sucked him back to the gas station in Southern Florida where he straddled the lifeless figure of his only son, Jackson. Throughout his career, Caleb witnessed more atrocities than most people can imagine, but the seared image of his son who didn't even have time to bleed out—in fact, the boy was dead from a gunshot wound to the head before his body hit the ground—burned its way to the surface at least twice a day.

The girl strolling away from the Los Muertos Pier wasn't older than twenty-two. A baby compared to Caleb. Her dark brown hair pulled back in a ponytail with a red ribbon pinching the strands together.

Someone's baby, he reminded himself.

"Fuck," he mumbled, walking toward the restaurant where Félix, a server with whom he'd become friendly, stood.

"*Félix, tengo que irme,*" Caleb told him. I have to go.

Without waiting for a response, Caleb dropped the legs on the table and slid the leather strap off his neck. The towel whipped off his belt and landed on top of the pile of oysters. The oyster knife, however, slipped into the pocket of Corsair's shorts.

It was early afternoon, and while historically most of Mexico took this time after lunch to rest, Puerto Vallarta long ago left that tradition behind as it tried to accommodate the thousands of tourists filling its streets every day. If the foreign visitors intended to spend their money during *siesta,* then the businesses of Puerto Vallarta would make it work.

That meant right now visitors crowded the sidewalks, moving either from one bar to the next or from their hotel to the beach. Or vice versa. It didn't matter where they were going, it only seemed important that they went.

Whatever the Giants fan intended to do, it was a safe bet it wouldn't happen in a crowd, especially among the Saturday afternoon activities. Although that was not a guarantee. Corsair recalled three kills he made amid a thick throng of people. Anything was possible. However, Corsair considered himself an aberration. A flick of the wrist allowed him to drive a blade into a man's jugular without losing a stride. By the time the wound sprayed blood, he'd be ten to fifteen feet away and never look back. As he reasoned this, he remembered each of those three hits. He donned a pair of headphones—obvious ones, not earbuds—giving him every appearance of oblivion to everything that happened in his vicinity.

In contrast, the football fan spent a lot of energy swiveling his head as he watched the surrounding crowd. Perhaps he was used to New York City, where pedestrians actually noticed others when they were different. It seemed the opposite of what most people would say about New York. They'd call it impersonal. It was easy to get lost in. That was true, but strangely, Americans judged things that didn't fit their mold. Caleb's experience had been that not only did people notice dissimilarities from them, but they didn't like them. Well, at least the outspoken demographic vocalized that.

However, in Puerto Vallarta, it was a unique environment. With banners hanging from every light post in the Zona Romántica [GD1] advertising the drag revues and the heavy population of foreigners, most people seemed to realize that nothing was unusual in PV. Motorcades of heavily armed police forces might roll down Olas Altas followed by a parade of goats. It might draw a curious eye, but that would be all.

Caleb assured himself that this hunter would not act until he isolated the girl from the crowd. If the Giants fan cornered her alone, then Corsair's reactions would draw no attention to himself.

As a predator himself, Caleb wondered what the man's reasons for targeting the woman were. A thought like that would never have occurred to him before he met Audrey. He wasn't a psychopath, although he assumed he had some sociopathic tendencies. Probably most professional soldiers did, to some extent. Otherwise, the faces of the dead would render many incapable of further action. To Caleb Saunders, it was duty to country.

But his wife brought out more from him. She understood what he was. After the second date, Caleb realized he wanted to be with her, and he didn't want to keep any secret about himself from her. Not if he ever wanted her completely.

Thinking about their second date spread a smile across his face. It didn't linger because, like any fond memory of Audrey, the grief of losing her followed with a sucker punch to the stomach.

Corsair pushed the sorrow away as he focused on the man seventy-five feet in front of him. Was he a professional? Or was this some impulse brought on by whatever feature the girl was unlucky enough to possess?

He supposed some serial killers had a similar mindset to assassins. A hired hitman killed based on orders without respect to the individual. They were basically decrees, therefore, they were to be obeyed unequivocally. Perhaps a serial killer obeyed those impulses the same way Corsair followed commands—unquestioningly.

His attention shifted to the girl who had turned north on Olas Altas, walking toward the Malecón. A brightly colored sundress hung from two straps off her shoulder. It was common attire for almost all women he'd seen since arriving in Jalisco. It seemed to fit every daily need, from strolling on the beach to working in a shop. She wore sandals that Audrey would have called "cute." It was odd how at one time he'd only notice the shoes based on their ability to help his target run from him. Now, he recognized the style, too. He'd long determined that "cute" didn't mean practical, something he would warn Audrey about every time she brought home a new pair of shoes.

She continued past Basilio Badillo, where vendors set up stands lined up on the north curb so that the diners at the restaurants across the street stared at carts filled with the same goods someone else sold along the beach all day. Surprisingly, most of the things were made in Mexico, although Caleb doubted they were local. There was probably a factory in Mexico City churning out leather commodities and decorative table coverings that ended up in places like Cancun, Cabo, and Puerto Vallarta.

After the following block, she veered into Cárdenas Park. The New Yorker picked up the pace as soon as she vanished from his view. He tried to close the distance between them without her noticing him. It was a sloppy execution as he almost sprinted forward through the people. Caleb locked his eyes on the bright blue cap as he zigged around the individuals massing along the sidewalk. Corsair would not run yet. One person dashing down the sidewalk would attract some consideration. Two people became a chase, and that was worth pulling their phones out to catch what might happen next. The last thing Caleb Saunders wanted was to be the center of someone's Facebook feed. That kind of attention would be pinged by whatever software the CIA and OOC currently used to hunt down assets like Caleb.

Nowadays, it was damned near impossible to elude cameras. Facial recognition software had reached its pinnacle, and based on the way technology evolved, it was only going to get more precise. The only defense for some-one hiding out like Caleb was to avoid places where the OOC focused their attention. If any excitement occurred, Caleb would cover his face and vanish in the blink of an eye.

The first week he was in Puerto Vallarta, he mentally mapped every visible camera within a six-block radius of his flat. Should he need to make his way home, he had a route to his apartment that never offered a clear image to a single camera. At least in theory, that would work. It was impossible to predict when Becky from Kansas State would snap a selfie on the street ahead of Caleb. At the end of the day, safety measures only protected him so much.

Lázaro Cárdenas Park occupied an entire block along the Romantic Zone's section of the Malecón, a pedestrian walkway stretching a little over a mile from the Los Muer-tos Pier north to *Calle 31 de Octubre,* or, as the visitors not-ed, the McDonald's. Every Saturday, Cárdenas Park hosted the Farmers Market[GD2] , filling with tents and tables offering fresh food, crafts, and artwork. It also brought in scores of shoppers. If the sidewalks on either side of Olas Altas were knotted on a Saturday afternoon, the park resembled a wad of Celtic knots as lines formed for warm tortillas, street tacos, marmalades, and fresh bread.

Caleb lost sight of the girl in the crowd, but the blue hat bobbed past an array of strawberries and blueberries. A raised gazebo sat in the center of the park, and Caleb squeezed behind a table where a woman with jars of home-made jellies stacked them in pyramids.

"*Perdón,*" he said to her. Pardon.

She glared at him as he climbed the four steps to stand for a brief second above the crowd. He located the girl as she turned north on the street just west of Cárdenas Park. Caleb continued through the gazebo and made a beeline to the next road.

In less than a minute, he wriggled through the Saturday afternoon throng, but he reached the corner of Lázaro Cárdenas and Pino Suárez streets just as the New Yorker came out of the park. Corsair brushed against him. The Giants fan never felt him pick the knife out of his pocket. Caleb didn't feel a gun, and after he took ten steps, Caleb spun back to follow him again. He examined the four-inch blade. The man bought it somewhere in Mexico, likely from a street vendor. It had a small leather sheath designed to attach to a belt at the waist. Obviously, the man didn't want to draw any attention. Most tourists didn't walk around brandishing weapons.

The crowds thinned as they moved away from the park. The girl made a right at the next block. She slowed in front of the boutique at the corner. Caleb wondered if it was part of a surveillance detection tactic. The man ahead of him hesitated a step, but Caleb continued at the same pace. He pulled his most recent prepaid phone from his pocket, lifted it to his ear as if he were engaged in a conversation as he passed the Giants fan.

3

Khloe Evans didn't notice the man in the New York Giants hat right away. She'd just worked a short morning shift at the Silver Unicorn. Alejandro, her boss, asked her to open up for him. He was coming in late—something to do with his mother-in-law, who lived with him. Happy to do it, she offered to cover all day for him. That was out of the question. Saturday mornings were the busiest time of the week, and Alejandro, as nice as he was, couldn't relinquish control of that.

She understood, grateful he found enough tasks to fill forty hours. She always loved jewelry. If she'd chosen a smarter path out of high school, she would have gotten into the diamond industry. Unfortunately, despite all the strides in equality made over the years, people in Kenwood, Ohio, thought girls were only good for one thing. Her mother never worked outside of the home. None of her mother's friends worked outside of the home. She grew up hearing "You're just a little girl," or "Girls don't do that." Her favorite was "What will people think?"

Even when she went to college, her family all but encouraged her to rethink her goals. Sadly, she listened to them. She transitioned from the girlfriend of Billy Kewer in senior high to the girlfriend of Kelly Fabbon in the summer after she graduated to the girlfriend of Jake Gibbons. Through all of those characters, she never had an identity to herself. She was forever going to be "the girlfriend of." Well, she realized, not forever. Eventually, Khloe would become "the wife of."

That never happened—now it never would. The nail in her coffin seemed to be when she became the girlfriend of Dominic Deluca. Nic ran numbers for Sonny Departi. In the scheme of the mafia, Nic hadn't reached middle management. Still, he earned good money. At least once a week he'd promise Khloe he was on his way. "Babe Sonny's my cousin. Being family is better than being made."

Khloe never understood the difference, really. Sonny and his upper echelon sent Nic on the shitty jobs. She never asked, but somehow she figured he'd killed a couple of guys. Khloe remembered that Tuesday. Later on, it dawned on her. That was probably his first. He left the apartment with pent-up energy. When he returned, he forced her into the bedroom. After that, this sullen mood sank over him.

For a while, Khloe thought it was her. Until she overheard one of the wives comment offhandedly about a girl who wouldn't be around because her husband, Johnny, was "taken care of."

Her life became like one of those images that made no sense until you stare at it long enough to distinguish the face of Marilyn Monroe or something. Once the hidden picture popped out, it was impossible not to see it. If you didn't look directly at it, the visual mishmash seemed to take over. But it was inevitable—the brain picked it out.

After that, so did she. Every time Nic told her he had to go out, she realized he was doing something illegal. When he came home sullen, she worried he killed someone. Those ideas scared her. She didn't want to stay. But how could she leave? Would he let her leave? Nic never raised a hand to her, but she assumed he might resist if she packed her bags.

Even at that, where would she go? Home to her mother and father?

They'd judge her as a failure for not making it work. Khloe never told them what Nic did for work, either. If Nic didn't have a problem with people knowing what he did, certainly his cousin Sonny would.

And Sonny downright scared her. Upon meeting him the first time, she saw he was evil. It oozed out of his pores. That man would kill everyone in the room if it put him on top. No remorse. No empathy. Nothing.

It took her a couple of blocks to notice the stocky figure behind her. It was the Giants hat in a reflection that caught her eye, triggering some recognition.

At first, she hoped it was a coincidence. Anyone could be a sports fan.

That quickly turned to wariness. She stole a glance over her shoulder, searing his face into her memory.

Khloe didn't know the man, but she felt as if she recognized him. She'd seen plenty of Sonny's guys at different family affairs. Oddly, they all looked alike. Not in their appearance, although almost all had that olive Italian skin tone and dark hair. It was more like something in their eyes. The robotic stare when no one was looking at them. As if there were no commands telling them what to think or do. More frightening, though, was the laser focus their eyes had when they received their orders.

He had that mindless dogmatism. Khloe suspected she was the bullseye he was targeting.

How did they find her? She'd changed her name, gotten a new passport, and hadn't even emailed anyone. As far as her mother or father knew, Khloe Evans vanished from the face of the earth.

But someone had found her.

Her wooden flats clicked against the concrete faster as she quickened her pace.

I could lose them in the crowds, she thought.

It was almost noon on a Saturday. The normally busy streets were filling, not just with vacationers, but also with locals enjoying their weekend. Kids weren't in school, and while they were almost invisible during the week, come Saturday, the streets and beaches filled with them.

Saturdays also meant the Farmers Market opened up in Tile Park. The park was a popular weekend gathering point for artisans, cooks, and farmers to display their wares. Tile Park wasn't the actual name, but after an artist worked to refurbish the entire area with murals formed from tiles, the nickname grew up among the younger crowd. In reality, it was called Lázaro Cárdenas Park, named after a former president of Mexico.

Lines of people, trying to get fresh tamales and tacos for lunch, would pack the park. She was at least half a block ahead of Sonny's guy. When she saw the corner of Olas Altas, she sighed with some relief at the crowd in the park.

The intersection of roads was really just one turn. Olas Altas ended at the park, turning into a pedestrian path and was something of a break in the Malecón, the walkway built along the waterfront. Technically, the Malecón started at Calle 31 de Octubre, translated simply as October 31 Street, and ended two kilometers south at the pier on La Playa de los Muertos. The Malecón replaced the avenue as a walkway to this point, when it turned toward the ocean and followed along a smaller path to La Playa de los Muertos.

Khloe crossed the street to the sidewalk and hurried into the park. She could lose Sonny's man in here and hurry across the river. The one thing she didn't want to do was lead him back to her apartment.

If she alerted the police, they would discover she was technically an illegal immigrant. There was no way to know how the Mexican authorities would treat her. Worst case, at least as far as she was concerned, was that they would ship her home to Ohio.

Her mind worked as she climbed the steps to the park. How did they find her? What mistake did she make?

As soon as they killed Nic, she wasted no time running. Maybe they never expected that. Otherwise, Sonny would have had someone grab her as soon as Nic's body hit the ground. There was no way they knew she witnessed Vincent kill Nic. She wasn't supposed to be there.

I suppose I wasn't yet, she thought.

She saw Vincent, Sonny's number two, enter the apartment. Nothing unusual about that. She'd seen him come by to pick Nic up. Usually it was for something big. At least, that's what she surmised. Vincent came by for Nic, and when Nic returned home, he'd have that gloomy mood. The dots connected with little difficulty. Vincent did the heavy work—or ensured someone did.

Before she made it to her door, the gunshot sounded. It was a silencer, but like most people who'd been around that world knew, it wasn't silent. Khloe wondered why they didn't call them something else. It morphed the noise more than silencing it. But the distinctive *pfft* remained instantly recognizable.

As soon as the sound came from the apartment, Khloe knew what happened. Her gut nearly emptied in the hallway. Instead, she hid in the mop closet at the end of the corridor.

Vincent stayed in her apartment for twenty minutes before he came back out. Cowering in that supply room, she cried quietly. Partly for Nic, although she didn't think that she would miss him, really. Khloe might not have loved him anymore, but she liked him well enough.

Nic always told her he had a parachute. That's what he called it, a parachute or an escape plan. He kept a duffel bag of cash in a vent in the boiler room downstairs. He'd even arranged for each of them to have a fake passport.

Khloe never bothered going into the apartment. Anything she had in there was tainted. Part of her often wondered why she didn't at least confirm that Vincent killed

Nic. Of course, that wasn't necessary. The news reported it as a home invasion.

The passport.

Nic never said how he got them. Obviously, it was through illegal means. Someone Sonny knew? That was the only way they could track her.

She had realized the identity wouldn't last her. As soon as she settled, she began searching for alternatives. It wasn't all that difficult, although the process wasn't cheap either. But now she had two passports in her safe deposit box at the bank. Along with the hundred thousand dollars Nic collected.

"*Disculpe*," a woman apologized as they ran into each other. The fault was entirely Khloe's. Her mind remained jumbled with fear and confusion.

The man was still in the back of the crowd, but now she could tell he was looking for her. His head strained and twisted, scanning ahead.

She cowered slightly, trying to shrink.

He intended on killing her. No doubt about that, she convinced herself. It would be just as easy to do it in a crowd. Bump into her like she did that woman, and a knife to the heart would drop her to the ground. By the time anyone realized what happened, he could vanish in the streets. Hell, he might be back at the airport before the cops arrived.

Suddenly, the surrounding people crowded in on her. Khloe gasped for air as she scurried past a line of senior citizens sloppily eating street tacos. As soon as she reached the opposite side of the park, she sprinted down the steps to the sidewalk.

Every muscle in her body wanted her to run, but she took a deep breath, stepping at a brisk pace that fell short of a jog.

Don't look back, she told herself.

She needed a second to think. Seeing a boutique on the corner, Khloe stepped inside. From the window, she saw the man move to the far side of the intersection. He tried not to linger too close, but he wanted to see her come out.

How many blocks to the bridge? She couldn't remember. Not many.

If she lost him in the river park, she might take the back roads back to her apartment. Isla Cuale, the small island in the middle of Rio Cuale, housed a park much bigger than Tile Park. It remained equally crowded, depending on the time of day, with the stands of vendors filling the artisan flea market set up there every day.

She just needed to get there. It offered plenty of places to hide.

She picked up a simple dress, wanting to look like a woman on a shopping jaunt. The buy took over half of the pesos she had on her. Hopefully, she could make a quick change if she got the opportunity.

4

They were only a block and a half from the beach, but the cinder-block buildings cut most of the breeze off, and the afternoon sun beat down. Caleb watched the New Yorker remove his hat and wipe the sweat from his forehead. Without the cap, Caleb noticed the man had a seriously receding hairline. He replaced his hat as the woman exited the boutique with a small paper bag bundled under her arm.

Caleb sighed as he realized she'd only stopped to shop, and there was no hidden agenda. For a minute in the Farmers Market, he thought she appeared scared. She rushed out of the crowd. Her speed picked up on the street, but now, nothing she did seemed to indicate she knew she was being followed. By the time she strolled by Caleb's location, her tail closed the distance between them.

She continued down Madero, where she crossed the road to head north again on the intersecting road. When Caleb first arrived in PV, he memorized the streets throughout the Romantic Zone and into the next barrio, *5 de Diciembre*, in case he needed to leave the city quickly. This highway, which cut right through the old town, intersected Rio Cuale and ended up running parallel to the Malecón and the shoreline.

Most of Puerto Vallarta was a pedestrian city. Even though it spread over five hundred square miles, most of the residents stuck to their neighborhoods. If they couldn't bike or walk it, they might take a car or ride-share to the big-box stores close to the Marina District. The city built large sidewalks along the bridge, with stairwells leading down to Isla Cuale, a municipal park constructed on an island where the waters diverged around it on both sides before it came back together and fed into the river.

The girl took the first set of steps, descending into the park where rows of makeshift stands combined with permanent structures made up the flea market. Most of the trinkets were identical to what vendors sold elsewhere.

When she reached the bottom of the concrete staircase, the woman walked west through the crowded booths. Shopkeepers called to her as she passed, begging for her to look in the shack. She'd been here before, Caleb noted, watching her ignore the constant beckoning directed at her. Unlike a lot of the long-term visitors, her demeanor glazed over, where many offered polite shakes of the head and even a few terse conversations.

Those were mostly Canadians, Caleb thought. This girl seemed American, even if the color of her skin left it in question. She carried a "don't give me shit" scowl that didn't seem to hinder the shopkeepers from hounding her with masks and beaded bracelets.

Caleb often brought Amanda down to this section of the park. It was off the beaten track, but his daughter loved walking through what she called the "cat garden." They had designated the park as a hub for art, in part because of the role it played in the most famous movie filmed here, *The Night of the Iguana*. The film, starring Richard Burton and directed by John Huston, seemed to put Puerto Vallarta on the map with Hollywood. Puerto Vallarta prided itself on the movie, honoring Huston with a sculpture in the park. As Caleb passed the director sitting perpetually in his director's chair, he saw Amanda's "cat garden," which was a flower garden amid an array of sculptures under the canopy of trees. Feral cats wandered the plot. Most dropped off by individuals Caleb considered heartless—a serious indictment from a man who once killed people without mercy. The animal problem grew large enough that the city posted signage in English and Spanish warning of fines for disposing of animals there.

Through the maze of trees, Caleb caught sight of the woman again, but the blue hat was gone. She'd changed dresses. No, she just slipped one over the top of her other dress.

Smart girl.

But not smart enough. The Giants fan was still on her tail. Now he knew she was aware of him.

As they continued deeper into the park, the crowds thinned. If the New Yorker planned to make a move, Caleb guessed it would be soon.

As if he read Caleb's mind, the man picked up his pace. The Giants fan pulled out his phone, tapping out a quick message as he pretended to stroll casually. Caleb knew the direction the woman was going—Puente de la Iguana, the stairway bridge that crossed over the northern branch of Rio Cuale.

Caleb took the right fork at the next intersection. He'd walked along here with Amanda plenty of times. Like the rest of the streets of PV, he committed the paths to memory. This one circled around the trees and connected back with the other sidewalk. It was a longer route, but he broke into a sprint, charging past the tiled mosaic path to get ahead of the girl.

When she walked past him, her eyes locked with his for a split second, and she smiled warily.

"You're being followed," Caleb warned.

The smile disappeared. "What?" she responded with a look of surprise.

Caleb continued by her, and she turned to watch him. If Caleb looked back, he might have seen the sheer terror crossing her face when she realized the man in the Giants hat wasn't the only one following her.

The man was searching his pockets.

"Looking for this?" Caleb asked, lifting the knife he'd pickpocketed off him on the street earlier.

Turning to look at him on the steps, the New Yorker's face twisted as his brain registered recognition. He stared at the knife in Caleb's hand. The blade remained sheathed, and the man considered for a second if he could overpower Caleb. Footsteps clipped along the pathway as she ran toward the bridge.

"Fuck," the Giants fan cursed, and he charged through the trees around Caleb.

Corsair's wrist flicked, and the knife whipped through the air as Caleb unsheathed it and hurled it in one motion. When the blade missed the man by inches, Caleb bolted after him.

Puente Iguana didn't have the steepest stairs in Puerto Vallarta. The architects designed them for more casual walking. Each stair was about a foot and a half deep.

The girl had a head start. She was in good shape with long legs, and she ascended quickly. As the man in the blue hat struggled up the steps, he lost ground. He wasn't in the best condition, and Caleb caught him by the waistband of his shorts, jerking him back. Shocked, the New Yorker fell onto his ass before rolling down one step.

"I'm pretty sure I can outrun you," Corsair pointed out, as he grabbed him by the shirt and lifted him up against the rail.

The American scowled at Caleb. Indignation seethed from him. Most people must treat him differently.

"What the fuck do you think you're doing?" Corsair demanded.

"I'm just walking," the other man lied. His head twitched as he glanced up the stairs to see the girl vanish over the top into Gringo Gulch.

Caleb twisted around, carrying him by his shirt in a circle, and tossed him to the ground. "Yeah, I'm calling bullshit," the former assassin declared. "Who have you been texting?"

"Nobody," he denied, as he pushed up to his feet.

"Give me your phone," Caleb ordered the man.

"Or what?"

"Or I throw you off the bridge," Corsair explained matter-of-factly.

The New Yorker's face flashed concern. This man just threw him around like he was luggage, and he'd lifted the knife off him expertly earlier. Still, the man carried a brashness with him. He wasn't accustomed to people on the street confronting him.

The Giants fan whipped a small chrome Ruger 22 pistol from his pocket.

"Couldn't bring your gun down, huh?" Caleb questioned. "You had to have flown down from New York, right?"

The man didn't respond.

"I pegged you as some kind of hitter, aren't you?" Corsair asked. "Mob or something. Not military for sure. Where'd you get that piece of shit?"

"What do you want?" the man asked, wondering why Corsair got involved.

"Your phone."

"Asshole, I have the gun," he snapped.

Corsair stepped forward, swifter than the man expected. His hand caught the barrel of the gun, swinging it down. The twenty-two fired, and the bullet chipped into the concrete step, spewing grains of concrete up.

Corsair rammed his forehead into the man's face, shoving him back against the railing. The twenty-two tumbled from his grip into the gorge.

Resignation creased over his brow as he realized his weapon was gone. He stared at Corsair, waiting.

"Your phone," he repeated, and the man pulled it out reluctantly. By now, he figured the girl had escaped. He needed to get out of this situation before it got worse.

Caleb took the iPhone and glanced at the screen. It tried to open, but the facial recognition didn't respond. He rotated the screen toward the New Yorker. The cellphone chirped as the camera captured the man's features, matching them to its memory.

As Corsair turned the phone to him, the man lunged forward, driving his shoulder into Caleb. Both slammed into the railing as the hitman was obviously attempting to shove Caleb over the edge. Corsair dropped the phone and drove his right elbow down into the man's clavicle. The New Yorker grunted as the point of Caleb's elbow connected with the muscle in the man's thick neck. While the blow stung, it did little to hurt him. Caleb reached behind his attacker with his right hand, grabbing the hair on the hitter's head.

A flash of blue flew through Caleb's peripheral vision as the Giants hat dislodged from atop the man and, caught in the wind, tumbled over the edge of Puente Iguana. Caleb wrenched the man's head around as he jutted his right foot between the man's legs. The swift motion to the right coupled with the sweeping of his legs twisted the man away from Corsair. In the split second that the burden lifted off Caleb, his fists moved like lightning, striking the man in his solar plexus and throat nearly simultaneously.

A guttural grunt emanated from the hitter as he tried to charge forward. The next punch from Corsair slammed him against the rail, and the man toppled backward over the metal barrier.

Caleb peered off the bridge below, but the trees hid the body of the Giants fan. As he glanced up the stairs, he saw no sign of the woman. With a swooping arm, he scooped up the man's phone and jogged down the stairs.

5

Lee Hubbard rubbed her eyes. She shouldn't be here on a Saturday, but the forensics just came back from the boat.

It had been a nightmare coordinating a thorough search of the vessel. The Mexican government didn't like the idea of the United States shipping a couple of lab personnel to scour the yacht. Hubbard assumed there was concern that there might be some backlash from the Mondal Cartel. The cartel ruled the area around Tampico, where the boat turned up. Lee presumed the six men on board when two operatives of the Office of Compliance found it were associated with the crime syndicate.

Unfortunately, her boss ordered the hit on the yacht with an assault team. Carl Winston didn't have what one might refer to as restraint. He made the call to take the vessel, assuming Corsair was still aboard, and the agents complied, killing all but one seventeen-year-old boy. He probably wouldn't walk again, according to the after action report Lee read, but he was alive.

As Lee expected, Caleb Saunders wasn't on board. As she reviewed the forensics findings, it appeared he had either never been on the yacht, or someone scrubbed the decks with every cleaning chemical known to man. The latter seemed less likely given the amount of DNA they'd found. Lee struggled to understand. While the official reports indicated Corsair and his daughter capsized in a fishing boat in a storm off the coast of the Everglades, Lee, and more importantly, her boss, didn't buy the tale. Further investigations suggested he fled the western tip of Florida on *L'étoile,* a yacht once owned by Libyan arms dealer Awan Khaled.

Lee read through all the witness statements. Although there were very few surviving witnesses who claimed Khaled, a suspected human trafficker, actually had Corsair's three-year-old daughter. Those few reports indicated Khaled had plans to take the girl to Africa. By the time Lee tracked down the alleged story, the *L'étoile* was gone, along with Corsair. Khaled either vanished in the wind, or he was dead. Lee guessed if the man attempted to scurry off to the Mid-East with Corsair's child, he didn't survive contact with the former OOC operative.

Carl Winston was desperate to eliminate his once pet assassin. He pressed her and her team to scour the globe for Khaled's boat—a daunting task. Boats were often the most difficult to track because of the ease with which a vessel could make landfall. While they were required to go through the immigration process in nearly every country, it was a simple task to pull along a stretch of shore, far from any immigration office.

Despite those concerns, Winston persisted in driving Lee to find Corsair. Lee Hubbard wondered why.

Winston was a weasel of a human. Perhaps it was something as simple as pride, but she didn't think so. Corsair proved he was dangerous, but so far, he hadn't been threatening. In fact, he'd lived in the United States for the past decade under an alias. The man even started a family. None of that showed malice to anyone.

It led Lee to assume Caleb Saunders was a threat to Winston himself. That worried and intrigued Lee.

As the senior analyst, she fell right under Winston in the chain of command. The Deputy Chief of Operational Security, though, had antiquated views about women, and Lee Hubbard assumed he only kept her around under the guise of control.

Her phone danced across the desk. The only other person in the office was Phillip, an analyst keeping tabs on a situation in Syria. Lee snatched it up, pausing only to read "Angie" on the screen.

"Hey," she answered.

"You're still at work, aren't you?" Angie complained.

"Yes," Lee groaned.

"I'm sitting in this hot tub completely naked with three glasses of chardonnay already in me. You need to join me soon," her girlfriend suggested.

"I'd like that," Lee acknowledged, "but give me another half hour. Nothing will come of it, but I have to double-check a few things."

"Is this still Winston's boy toy?" Angie quipped, no doubt thanks to the third glass of wine. When she got tipsy, she'd whine about how Winston was so repressed. Angie, who worked as a data retriever in a somewhat adjacent department, declared Carl Winston harbored some latent homosexual tendencies manifested by his homophobic behavior. Lee didn't agree. She knew Winston just happened to be an asshole. If Lee were to guess, he developed the characteristic to defend his complete lack of social skills and intelligence.

"Yes," Lee told her.

"The lab get back with their report?" Angie asked, slurring slightly. Her voice lilted up an octave as she spoke, signaling both her state of inebriation and the subsequent increased sexual drive. In other words, Lee thought, wine made her horny.

"Yeah," Lee said, ignoring her girlfriend's current condition. By the time she got home, either Angie would have drunk herself to sleep or sobered up enough to grow angry. No matter the situation, Lee wasn't expecting to get laid. "There's no evidence he was ever on the boat."

"He cleaned it," Angie suggested flatly.

"I know," Lee agreed. "It's a dead end. We aren't sure how long the cartel had it."

"From what I've heard, Corsair dumped it once he crossed the Gulf," Angie said. Then she crooned, "This already got you a bullet to the chest. You need to be careful."

"It wasn't Corsair who shot me," Lee reminded Angie. "It was my own partner."

"Yeah, who was working directly for Carl 'I Like to Bottom' Winston."

"Maybe," Lee remarked. "But he's too uptight for that."

Angie laughed, "True. Now, come home and fuck me."

"Soon," Lee promised.

"Ugh, I will just do it myself," Angie whined before hanging up.

Lee rolled her eyes. She hated this job, but it drove her. Angie was the same way. Lee wanted to be with her, but sometimes she couldn't stand it. Their relationship remained a secret at the office, although a poorly kept one. A handful of people knew, but the senior ones, including Winston, were clueless. Lee wondered how an agency devoted to intelligence missed something like this under its own nose.

Also, Lee never liked monogamy. She told Angie that initially, saying it's "a suckers' game." Neither of them wanted that type of relationship, but given Lee's heavy workload, it was the best she was going to get. If she was lucky, she'd hook up with that deputy again she met in South Florida. He didn't strike Lee as the marrying type either, but he confessed he had three ex-wives. So, perhaps he just wasn't the stay-married kind of guy.

Lee moved the mouse on the computer to reveal a map of Mexico. She'd highlighted where the agents found *L'étoile*. Her gut suggested Corsair was still in Mexico. He had a three-year-old girl with him, so he would have limitations on how and where he moved. She wondered if the bigger question was about his resources.

All bank accounts belonging to Audrey and Thomas Harrod, the alias Saunders adopted to start a family, had remained untouched after his disappearance. The Harrods had been traveling through Florida on vacation when a random carjacking left Audrey Harrod and her son, Jackson, murdered at a gas station. Their young daughter,

Amanda, was still in the car when the thieves made their escape. Had Thomas Harrod aka Caleb Saunders not been inside the store buying snacks for the road, the events of that day might have turned out differently.

Instead, Saunders left a swath of dead bodies across the Everglades until he supposedly retrieved his daughter and escaped on an airboat in the middle of a storm.

Lee thought it unlikely he had a stash of cash on him on that trip—probably what most families bring on vacation. After all, from what she learned once she dug deeper into Thomas Harrod, the man became domesticated. At least as tamed as a trained killer can be.

What did Corsair trade for *L'étoile*? Enough to survive a few months. That time would be ending soon. Winston voiced as much. He remained convinced Caleb Saunders would run out of money. However, Lee Hubbard didn't have that same optimism. Not once following the carjacking did Caleb Saunders flounder like a man who was out of practice. She suspected the part of him that operated as Corsair hid under the surface. As a rule, people don't change. Caleb Saunders found a reason to want to, though. When those carjackers took that away, he had nothing to lose.

She had a team digging through banks, trying to find the emergency funds Saunders had in place. That information has grown more difficult in recent years as digital currency rose in the world.

Of course, he had one avenue to generate income. He could kill for money. That could have been part of the trade he made with the Mondal Cartel. A gun for hire.

Lee leaned back in her chair, staring at the map of Mexico. If she gambled, her bet would be that Caleb Saunders was still in Mexico. If he was working for the Mondals, his handiwork would stand out.

She needed to track murders throughout the country. If they tied into the cartel, it might be the lead she was looking for.

The FBI and DEA worked closely with several Mexican agencies, and a database, similar to The National Crime Information Center, from the Executive Secretariat of the National Public Security System, gave her access to every crime reported.

She pulled up unsolved murders, eliminating anything that involved crimes of passion, children, women, and senior citizens. She considered leaving the women in the mix, wondering what Corsair's stance on that was. Based on her intuition, though, Caleb Saunders was a man with principles. After what he did to find his daughter, Lee fostered no doubts kids were off the table for him.

The results scrolled up in a spreadsheet—27,344 entries.

"Damn," she cursed. It would take a while to sort those and identify a pattern.

She took a few minutes to create headers for the page so she knew what the data actually meant. Now she could order by methods, location, and even a criminal record.

Lee faced the problem of distinguishing if Corsair killed the victim or not. It could easily be another hitman. The Mondal Cartel employed hundreds of men—most of them had no conviction against murder.

The computer screen stared back at her. She was getting hungry. It was midafternoon on a Saturday, and she'd skipped both lunch and breakfast. Unless the Starbucks Chai Latte this morning counted.

This could wait until Monday, she told herself. Corsair would not pop up today.

She saved the spreadsheet, moving it to a secure folder that was locked with a password. It would take one of the high-level IT guys to crack it, and that usually took weeks.

Once the icon indicated the file was updated, she closed the laptop. If she hurried, Angie would still have a good buzz. The hot tub would be a pleasant end to a Saturday.

6

The afternoon sun pierced through the canopy of green covering the gorge. Second Sergeant Eduardo Castillo stared down from the Puente de la Iguana into the ravine below the bridge. The trees growing from the rocky riverside didn't reach the concrete staircase connecting Isla Cuale to Gringo Gulch, the affluent neighborhood perched on the mountainside overlooking the Rio Cuale.

Gringo Gulch, whose name stemmed from its popularity for Americans coming to visit, might be most famous for the infamous pairing of Elizabeth Taylor and Richard Burton at the Casa Kimberly, the home Taylor and Burton lived in while Burton filmed the movie *The Night of the Iguana*.

The neighborhood resembled more of an Italian village with narrow cobblestone streets lined with houses, stacked side by side. Homes in the community still sold for large amounts, and it continued to house many Americans and other foreign expatriates.

Castillo received the report a few minutes earlier about a body in the gulch. With the height of the bridge over the river, Puente Iguana offered a few people a locale for their suicide. Castillo never answered a call here, but he knew every few years someone took a dramatic dive through the greenery below..

The report from headquarters indicated a couple of boys found the body. Unsurprisingly, they chose not to stick around. Castillo assumed they had to get to a phone to even call in the find. Like many communities, the distrust of state police, or any police, ran deep.

There was no easy trek to the riverbed, and Castillo put off the descent long enough. Until he confirmed the body existed, the secondary teams wouldn't show up. Kids were often calling in hoaxes, either to prank the police or divert their attention. A squad of officers scaling two hundred feet down the face of a mountain on a prank might easily amuse a couple of juveniles.

Castillo was used to trekking down mountain faces and inclines. In the army, his unit trained in the Sierra Madre del Sur range south of Puerto Vallarta. He completed some of those climbs freehand and clad in full tactical gear. While he donned the full gear today, he opted to descend with rappelling gear instead of by hand.

It took him a few minutes to crawl over the wall along Cuauhtémoc, the road running through the neighborhood at the top of the steps. He set his rope around a thick banyan tree trunk growing up between the bottom of the stone embankment and the rock face of the cliff. After securing a safety line, he attached the line through the harness buckled at his waist.

The edge of the gorge wasn't a completely perpendicular sheer, leaving Castillo to mostly walk backward down the incline. He stopped halfway to apply an extending connection around another tree. From here, the drop was straight down.

Castillo kicked off the rock, releasing the belay. With a *zip*, the line shot through the belay as he dropped fifty meters. The brake in his hand squeezed against the rope as he slowed himself down. After only a brief pause, the second sergeant shoved off the rock again, sliding toward the bottom.

Two more short rappels, and the police officer's feet touched the rocky riverbank. He tugged the rest of the rope free from his waist, letting it dangle along the wall.

In the shade of the trees, Castillo removed a bottle of water from his pack. Despite being lukewarm, the liquid refreshed the officer. He drained the entire thing, replacing the empty plastic container in his bag to carry out.

Born in Guadalajara, Castillo acclimated at birth to the hot Mexican climate. It didn't change the safety precautions he took to ensure he never overheated. The dangers were even greater for someone like him. He might not notice the signs of dehydration and heat exhaustion until it was too late.

His head turned to the sky, staring at the underside of El Puente de la Iguana. The white bridge remained visible despite the attempts of the foliage to mask it.

Golden pothos grew along the riverbank. Red leaves of the Ti shrub shot up like claws trying to rip through the thick layer of devil's ivy. Castillo waded through the growth. At first glance, there was no sign of a body.

Niños tontos, he thought to himself. It was nothing more than a prank.

Nonetheless, Castillo remained an efficient investigator. His strategy included a grid search. He lined up the edge of the bridge overhead, and in his mind, he traced a fifty-meter square box. As the cop walked the line, he let his feet shuffle instead of stepping. While he wore military issue combat boots, he didn't want to surprise a sleeping *cuatro narices* or rattlesnake. He knew it was unlikely to strike, but it was still wiser to avoid coming down on the rear of an escaping viper. The creature could launch at least half its body length, a distance that easily put its fangs well above Castillo's ankles.

No, he considered. Better to let the thing escape freely.

After twenty minutes, Castillo covered the area he'd mentally mapped out. Now, he moved to a different imaginary block of vegetation. The devil's ivy curled up knee high. Flowering lantana sprouted out around a strangler fig tree with its vast roots reaching out of the earth and seeming to wrap about the trunk.

Castillo stepped over an offshoot in the brush. The root jerked suddenly, causing the second sergeant to leap back in shock. He stared at the lump hidden in the growth. When it moved again, he stared intently.

A sigh, mixed with relief and embarrassment, escaped his chest as a juvenile iguana lumbered out of the greenery. The reptile offered Castillo barely a glance as it meandered up the strangler fig.

In the wake of the iguana's slithering tail, Castillo spotted a bright blue color peeking out from the ivy. He stepped closer, kneeling to inspect it. With his retractable baton, he nudged the object, revealing the lettering on the front—a bold lowercase "ny" in a field of blue. A circle around the letters read "New York Giants."

Castillo lifted the hat off the ground with the baton. It hadn't been down here long. The sun's ultraviolet rays and the moisture destroyed almost anything made of fabric. The colors fade in the sun and leach out in the water.

This one wasn't brand new, but Castillo guessed it hadn't been in the gulch long at all—a day at most. He turned his head up to look at the underside of the Puente Iguana. Pedestrians and runners constantly lost things over the side. Castillo set the cap down on top of the ivy, leaving it easily visible.

He returned to stepping off the grid he created. So far, the hat was the only find.

Twenty minutes, he decided. If he didn't see any sign of a corpse by then, he'd climb back to the top.

His feet continued to shuffle. On the third turn in his search pattern, he kicked something. The thud against the toe of his boot suggested it was heavy but not big. He snapped his wrist, extending the baton again. With a slow, sweeping motion, Castillo pushed back the greenery. A glint of metal reflected the afternoon sun.

Castillo squatted down for a better inspection. A chrome Ruger 22 revolver lay on the rocky soil. He leaned closer. His latex gloves were still in his pack. He should have pulled a pair out before he started, but he hadn't wanted to wear them yet. It simply didn't occur to him to put any in his pocket.

He straightened up. Perhaps the kids were onto something. He stared down the river. The flow from the mountain was about normal for this time of year. During the rainy season in the mountains the banks of the Cuale easily overflowed as the water rushed toward the Pacific Ocean.

If a body were in the stream, it likely would only travel a few hundred meters before snagging on a downed tree or a shallow sand bar. Castillo didn't see anything, and before he climbed back up the side of the mountain, he'd walk down the river's edge a ways.

He strained his head up again to examine the angle a body might fall. Given that the second sergeant had no reference for where the body might have fallen, he tried to consider every possible angle.

Castillo paused, seeing something in the crook of two limbs of the banyan tree. The broad leaves of the tree created a thick, lush barrier, nearly impossible to see through. It took moving around to glimpse through a gap in the leaves.

Despite the small clearing in the foliage, he couldn't distinguish what he was staring at. With a sigh of resignation, he grabbed the thick aerial roots snaking around the trunk and began to climb.

Similar to free climbing a cliff, Castillo pulled up with some ease. His feet struggled to find footholds on the mostly vertical roots, leaving him to pull up with his arms. The ascent was fast, and within a few minutes, Second Sergeant Eduardo Castillo reached the lowest branch. The cop threw his legs on either side of the limb, steadying himself as he took a short break.

Now that he was inside the shelter of the foliage, Castillo had a better view. Twenty meters above him a body bent backward over a thick branch. The man, who Castillo identified as Caucasian, struck the limb on his back. The impact broke his back, folding him unnaturally in half.

He removed his radio from his vest and called the dispatcher. This was no prank after all.

7

The keys in her hands jangled as she shook with pent-up anxiety. It took three tries to get the key into the keyhole. When she swung the front door of her apartment open, she retreated inside quickly, slamming the door before locking the knob and twisting the dead-bolt.

Her hand pressed against the wooden frame, and she leaned against it. Her breath came in staccato huffs. She'd run from the two men on the bridge all the way back to her small room in the *5 de Diciembre* neighborhood.

After several seconds, she pushed off the door. No one seemed to be coming after her. Her feet shuffled to the secondhand couch she'd picked up at a church sale just after she arrived.

Now that the excitement was over, she felt exhausted. Khloe hadn't run two miles since high school, and the dash she just made from Gringo Gulch took her through a hilly part of the city. Her legs ached along with everything else. The dress she'd just bought was wet with sweat, but Khloe was too exhausted to remove it.

Her brain was working hard now, and despite how tired she was, it wasn't going to stop worrying.

The second man came out of nowhere. He had an easy opportunity to grab or kill her. Instead, he warned her.

She'd stolen a look back before she was out of sight. The American—he was American, she thought—was fighting with the man in the blue hat.

Part of her wished she had stayed to find out what happened. Most of her, though, wanted to throw everything into a suitcase and get out of town.

That wouldn't work, she knew. She had nine hundred pesos left until the bank opened. That was around fifty bucks. Enough to eat on for a couple of days, but she certainly couldn't live on that.

Nic's parachute money was stacked up neatly in a safe deposit box at a bank not far from where she'd escaped the two men. But it was Saturday afternoon. The bank was closed until Monday.

Khloe considered the problem. Sonny might have tracked the passport to Puerto Vallarta, but he'd have no way of knowing where she was after that. The city was big, and she'd switched her identity up after she got here.

An image of her childhood home flashed through her mind. The single-story red-brick house sat at the end of a cove where she'd learned to ride her bicycle without training wheels for the first time. She'd lived in a quiet middle-class section of Kenwood, Ohio, where the majority of the people worked nine to five at the cereal factory. Kenwood was nothing more than a suburb of Cincinnati.

But it was home.

She longed to be there now. Her mom would be in the kitchen making her chili macaroni casserole while Khloe sat cross-legged in the overstuffed recliner in the den. Eventually her father would come in from outside, crack open a Miller High Life, and drop onto the sofa to watch the highlights of the Bengals game.

She hadn't talked to her mother or father in almost six months. Not because she didn't want to. Every day she missed them. If Sonny or Vincent wanted to find her, they'd be the first place to look.

What if they already had been there? Sonny was a bastard. Even if her father denied knowing where Khloe was, Sonny might take a perverse pleasure in torturing him to prove otherwise. The notion drove bile from her already anxious gut.

Khloe jumped off the couch, running into the bathroom. For two minutes, she retched up everything in her stomach. When that was gone, stomach acid spewed up her throat, burning her esophagus.

Exhausted, she collapsed on the white-tiled floor. The cool ceramic soothed her as she sprawled out.

Khloe missed her mother. Was she worried about her? Did she know about Nic's death? What would she think?

Maybe they think I did it, Khloe considered. What if the cops think I killed him?

She had never thought about that. After all, they would know she disappeared too, right? It might make sense. Isn't the spouse or partner the first suspect in a murder?

She straightened up on the bathroom floor. Khloe decided to make a plan. She'd have to wait until Monday to get her money, but then she'd head south. Maybe she could go to Rio or Chile. That might be far enough from Sonny Departi. Or she could get on a plane to Europe.

Of course, she only spoke English. After several months, she'd picked up her fair share of Spanish now. Though, she was far from fluent. At least she could order food and do some shopping.

Once she had her money and was ready to leave, she planned to find a phone and call her mother. If she could just hear her voice for a minute. By the time anyone traced the call to Puerto Vallarta, she'd be gone.

Maybe she'd arrange for a secret way to communicate with her parents so no one knew it was her. Something to keep them in contact.

Something to endanger them is more likely, she warned herself.

No, it would be enough to just talk to her for a minute, Khloe decided.

She pushed up off the floor, feeling some determination now. The simple act of putting a plan into motion boosted her confidence. There was no way Sonny knew where she lived. She'd leave first thing Monday.

The airport was out of the question. Most of her money was in US dollars. Airlines didn't let you pay with cash anymore. Buses and trains would though. She could take a bus out of town, then figure out how to get to South America.

Just as well, she thought. Sonny's guys might be watching the airport.

That might also be true for the bus.

"Shit!" she cursed aloud, walking back into her living room.

She had enough money to buy a car. Then, she could just drive all the way to Rio.

That made the most sense, she decided.

Khloe thought about Alejandro. He still owed her for this week's work. She'd go by and see him tomorrow. He deserved an explanation and a goodbye.

With this solidified plan, she started looking online for a cheap car.

8

Sonny Departi leaned back in the suede office chair. The seat came from a boutique in downtown Cincinnati that imported the chair from a small town outside of Rome. The handcrafted swivel chair might be mistaken for a nice one in any bank or law office. However, this chair had been carefully manufactured for Sonny Departi. After taking Sonny's measurements like he was being fitted for a suit, the craftsman molded the cushions to perfectly fit his shape. Furthermore, the artist—because Sonny considered this chair a work of art—selected the highest resilient acrylic foam to fill the seat and back. Underneath the soft leather, stripped and tanned from lambs, a mesh of thin wires offered the perfect temperature control. The thermostat was set to Sonny's own biorhythms. It would measure his temperature and match it according to his desired preference.

The chair, which some of Sonny's guys secretly referred to as "The Throne," set the man back $20,000. He was reluctant at first to buy such an extravagance, but in retrospect, he loved this chair.

The rest of Sonny's office matched his taste in chairs. The desk, also imported from Italy, was 125 years old, having been built for Count Ciano, a late nineteenth-century Italian aristocrat.

When Sonny stepped up to power, he held court in the T&T Construction building. The lavish furnishings he imported from overseas contrasted with the other offices. He demanded that his lieutenants improve their decor.

"It will tip our hands to the Feds," his first lieutenant, Vincent "Vinnie" Santoro, remarked.

"They fucking know who we are already," Sonny argued. "Let them know how well we do it."

Now, Sonny Departi sat behind the desk staring at Vinnie and the cell phone in his second-in-command's hand. The image on the screen was taken at a distance. Its subject was a twenty-something-year-old girl with dark brown hair walking down a busy street.

"It could be her," Sonny admitted. "Couldn't Vic get a better picture?"

"He was going to try," Vinnie told him. "He didn't want to spook her. His text said he was positive it was Khloe Evans."

"How would he even know?" Sonny asked curiously.

Vincent Santoro gave a half shrug. "He and Nic worked together a lot. I imagine he saw the girl a lot more than some of the rest of us."

"Victor's a perv," Sonny pointed out. "He probably jerked to her picture a time or two."

Vinnie chuckled. "He probably jerked it to a lot of folks."

Sonny let out an exaggerated shiver. "I don't want to think about it."

"None of us do."

The mob boss reached across the desk and took the phone again. "When is he getting back to you?"

"He said he'd confirm it and finish her off."

Sonny tossed the smart phone to Vinnie. "What are the odds?" Sonny mused. "Victor just happens to run into this girl in Mexico. Where did he say he was?"

"Puerto Vallarta," Santoro answered.

"Why the hell would Victor go there?" Sonny asked.

"It's supposed to be nice," Santoro suggested. "You know—beaches, girls, tequila."

"Victor needs to find a girl and settle down," Sonny remarked. "Grown men shouldn't go off on vacation alone."

"Maybe he's got some girl down there."

Sonny shrugged. "Let's hope. It's weird."

Sonny Departi never understood people. He considered himself a driven man, and if others didn't follow suit, he might as well be reading hieroglyphics. They made no sense to him. For Sonny Departi there was no work-life balance. As far as he was concerned, every day was a workday. He enjoyed that. Something about pushing the boulder up a hill everyday gave him satisfaction.

At least, he thought it did. Of course, even when he stepped into leadership, there were some who wondered how he got there. He wasn't quite good enough. Before his death, his father actually criticized the loudest. What more did the bastard want?

"Call him," Sonny demanded. "I want to know the bitch is dead."

Vinnie pressed a button at the top of the screen. Setting the phone to speaker mode, he laid it on the desk.

Four rings. Voicemail.

"Keep trying," Sonny ordered. "I want to know that the asshole didn't get picked up by the Mexican cops."

"Vic's good," Santoro assured him.

"I know, but this ain't the States. The Mexicans don't have the same rules that we do here."

"If I don't hear from him soon, I can send Jimmy and some guys down to follow up," Vinnie suggested.

"Hell, yeah," Sonny remarked. "Jimmy'll get the job done, for sure."

"I'll see if I can get them on a plane today," Vincent told his boss.

"If this bitch is in—where is it again?"

"Puerto Vallarta," Vinnie responded.

"If this bitch is in Puerto Vallarta, I want her taken out by the end of the weekend."

"Sonny, that's a little fast," Vinnie tried to explain. "We only have Vic down there now. The quickest I can get a crew in place would be tomorrow. That's if I can get Jimmy on a flight tonight."

"Besides," Vinnie continued. "We don't know that she knew everything that Nic knew."

"He really fucked us," Sonny bemoaned. "If we hadn't offed him, he'd have given all of us up."

"But if she'd have been talking to the Feds, she wouldn't have run."

"Would she not?" Sonny asked. "The Feds didn't protect Dominic now, did they? If the girl was smart, she'd realize they wouldn't protect her unless she had something to offer. Without Dominic, she probably had nothing. She'd just be dangling in the breeze, waiting on us."

Sonny nodded to himself, adding, "No, it makes sense she ran. I wish we'd have taken care of her when we did Dominic." The boss narrowed his eyes as he uttered the pointed statement.

"We never discussed killing her," Vinnie stated.

Sonny waved off the excuse. "We didn't know," he remarked. "Hindsight is twenty-twenty, ain't it?"

Vinnie nodded. "We been watching her folks' place," he told him. "According to their friends, they haven't heard from her since before I popped Nic."

"Or they ain't talking."

"They're old neighborhood folks," Vinnie pointed out.

Sonny curled his lip. It was the bane of his existence, trying to keep the local Italian population happy. Most of the work they did fell into the shadier side of business with gambling, loan sharking, and prostitution. Most of his men came from this community, and their families struggled with accepting the illicit activities. Goodwill went a long way, and Vinnie was correct: the girl's parents were part of the community. It wouldn't look good for his guys to go in and rough them up.

His head bobbed slowly as he realized that if the girl was in Mexico, this was the best situation. No one would ever know what happened to her. She'd be a statistic—another American female tourist that went missing abroad.

Vinnie sensed the change in Sonny's demeanor, and having become adept at surfing that wave, he interjected. "It's better to be sure and get her down there," Vinnie said.

"Safer," Sonny agreed.

"We'll fix it, Boss," Vincent Santoro promised. "If she's in Puerto Vallarta, she'll never leave."

9

The Olas Altas Bungalows were misnamed. The apartment building sat at the corner of Olas Altas and Pulpito, but there were no bungalows on the property. The three-story building shared a wall with the Palm Cabaret. Nearly every night about nine, the cabaret singers and dancers began belting out their covers of whatever star they were impersonating. Caleb noted that tonight was a montage, a tribute to Lady Gaga.

When he found the apartments, they were perfect for his needs. The units were divided up and sold like condominiums. Caleb found a local owner who was happy taking cash. An extra hundred ensured no real names were needed for the lease. There were only eighteen apartments, and from what Caleb could tell, they ranged only from one- to two-bedroom units.

The three levels formed a right angle overlooking a courtyard with a small pool and barbecue grill. A four-by-ten-foot plot was tended with vegetables for the occupants. Almost everyone spent at least a few hours a week maintaining the garden. It might have been the closest to a community Caleb had ever been a part of.

Caleb carried a bag filled with tomatoes, mangoes, and strawberries he'd just bought at the Farmers Market he'd dashed through an hour earlier. Since it was Saturday, he grabbed ten fresh tamales from the woman his daughter refers to as the "Tally Lady." He'd reheat them later for dinner.

"*Señor* Bryer," Miguel greeted Caleb using the fake name from his Canadian passport.

"*¿Miguel, cómo estás?*" Caleb asked him.

"I am very good, *Señor* Bryer," Miguel responded in staccato English.

"Roland," Caleb corrected, telling him his fake first name. "Call me Roland."

"Yes, Mister Roland."

Caleb shook his head at the young man. Miguel Vega was nearly thirty, but he had the goofy awkwardness of a teenager. Most of the day-to-day grind at the Olas Altas Bungalows was maintained by Miguel. He probably put in twelve-hour days, and most of the residents, who were foreigners, loved the man. Caleb guessed he got dinner delivered almost every night by the women, most of whom were married. His good nature and rugged good looks might have helped keep the kid fed.

Miguel swung open the metal gate leading up to the small flight of concrete steps. The one thing the Olas Altas Bungalows didn't have was handicap accessibility. Everything was up or down steps. Luckily, the apartment came furnished, and Caleb didn't have to bring anything in. Not that he owned anything worth bringing.

At the top of the steps was a portico wrapping around the second floor. Caleb paused at the railing to stare down at the two girls in the blue water. A giggle erupted from the water as the twenty-year-old woman tossed his three-year-old daughter in the air. Amanda came splashing down into the water. The water wings on her upper arms only allowed her to submerge for a second before they popped her up like a fishing bobber. The gleam of her smile never stopped even when she dunked under the surface.

"Trow me again, Angel!" Amanda squealed, dropping the digraph for a simple *T* sound.

"Once more," Angel told the girl.

Angel Rocha might be the one bind tying the father and daughter to Puerto Vallarta. The twenty-year-old woman baby-sat the girl for Caleb, bringing a feminine touch that Amanda desperately needed. Angel offered a normal aspect for the child. She was a playmate and caregiver. Even better though, Amanda loved the girl.

When Caleb arrived in the city, he couldn't take his daughter everywhere. In fact, it was important that the pair weren't identifiable just by their appearance.

He knew the OOC would be searching for a father and young daughter, and there was little he could do about that. For a split second, he considered sending Amanda to live with Audrey's parents in Georgia. It was probably the best decision, but it wasn't one that Caleb could do. Amanda was all he had.

It was the priest at Santa Cruz Catholic Church who steered him toward Angel, a young woman working to obtain a degree while caring for her mother who struggled with late-term Parkinson's. That circumstance made her an actual godsend.

Angel went to school at night, but most days from eight in the morning until the late afternoon, Angel stayed with Amanda. Between that time, she tended to her ailing mother. Despite that hectic life, the girl remained a beacon of joy. His daughter adored the young woman, and Caleb grew more grateful every day that he'd found someone like her to help him.

Angel leaned close to the little girl and whispered in her ear. Amanda's head turned up to see her father looking down at her.

"Daddy!" she squealed, pushing away from Angel to swim toward the edge.

Caleb smiled and descended the steps with the bags of food. He barely got the groceries on the ground before the soaking wet form of his daughter smacked into him. Her arms wrapped around his neck tightly, and her wet swimsuit soaked his shirt.

Amanda pulled her head back and puckered her lips until they resembled a soft, pink flower. Caleb kissed her back, relishing the childlike affection.

"Whatcha got?" Amanda asked, pointing at the bags of food.

"Stuff," Caleb responded playfully.

"What kinda stuff?"

"I went to the market and got some tongue."

"Eww," she spouted in a high-pitched tone. When she let it out, she asked, "Whose tongue?"

"Whose tongue?" Caleb repeated. "I got this one from an overweight jaguar."

"He won't be oberwhite anymore, will he?" she laughed gleefully at her own joke.

"He still has teeth though," Caleb warned, snarling to show off his incisors like a roaring cat. "He just can't lick you."

With that, he stuck his tongue out and licked his daughter's cheek. "Gwoss!" she cackled, her body rocking back and forth in the water as she laughed.

"Yeah, it's gross," Caleb confirmed. "You taste bad."

"Nuh-uh," Amanda denied.

"Yeah, you need a bath," Caleb retorted, pushing the girl away from his body until her grip loosened. He took a quick step forward and launched her up in the air.

A shrill echoed off the walls of the courtyard as the child flailed in the air for a second before splashing into the pool. Amanda's water wings jerked her back up to the surface instantly, and the girl continued laughing as she spewed chlorinated water from her nose and mouth.

"Daddy!" she screeched as if she was scolding her father. The broad gleam of teeth and her continued chortle indicated otherwise.

Caleb bent down, pulling three long-neck glass bottles out of the back. The outside of the soda bottle bubbled with condensation. He held the two bottles of mandarin Jarritos soda up.

"Who needs one?" he called.

The two girls rushed to the edge of the pool. Caleb popped the metal cap off each bottle, handing one to each of the girls before opening his own. He sat back on a wooden chaise lounger and turned the bottle up.

"Thank you, Señor Roland," Angel said graciously.

"How are your classes going?" he asked her.

"I'm finishing up the microbiology one," she told him. "I don't know if I'll be able to take the next one."

"Why not?" he questioned.

"Mama's not doing well, and I have to get the car fixed so I can take her to the doctor."

She wasn't asking for money. It was just a statement of fact. Caleb offered her a half smile. "Why don't I take a look at the car this week?" he suggested. Caleb wasn't a bad mechanic, but he'd actually take it somewhere to get it fixed.

"That would be great," Angel replied, beaming.

Angel smiled at the man. Caleb recognized the slight crush the girl had on him, but he wasn't about to jeopardize the relationship she had with Amanda.

In reality, he doubted he'd ever act on anything. The hole in his heart left by Audrey was too big for anyone to fill. She'd been perfect. He was grateful he realized that even before she died. It was a bittersweet condolence. Her loss hit him immediately.

It wasn't just that he lifted her to a pedestal. Caleb had the cold, studious eyes of a hunter, and Audrey fit with him like two puzzle pieces. She tempered him from himself.

Right after she died, he thought that it was nothing more than an exterior shell she'd molded over the hardened killer. But Amanda did much of the same thing. She softened Caleb, keeping Corsair from absorbing his soul.

But today he realized that life wasn't out of him yet. As Amanda squirted a spray of orange soda between her two front teeth, he wondered if it was adequately in check.

"I need to take this food up," he announced.

"Aww, Daddy," Amanda whined. "You can come swim with me."

His eyes shifted to Angel as he said, "Gotta put this away or you won't have any dinner."

"What's for dinner?" she asked in her sing-song tone.

"Tamales."

"Tallies?" Amanda exclaimed. "Can Angel eat with us?"

"Angel's always welcome to eat with us," Caleb assured both his daughter and her sitter.

"*Gracias, bebita,*" Angel told her. "I need to get home to Mama."

"Aww," Amanda complained.

"You guys play for a bit longer," Caleb suggested. "I'll get dinner ready in a bit."

He hoisted the bags of groceries up, carrying them back up the steps. Caleb and Amanda lived in apartment three which was on the level off the street, although since the city sat on a slope that ran down to sea level, the first floor and pool were below the entrance.

Their home was a simple studio apartment which worked for now. When Amanda got older, Caleb knew he'd need to find a place with two bedrooms. Likely two bathrooms, if his daughter was anything like her mother.

The split-second thought about Audrey hit him like a fist in the gut. He thought it might have been worse than a sucker punch.

Caleb repeated the same process every time her memory slapped him. He inhaled deeply, and he pictured her on their honeymoon. Her blond hair blowing in the wind on that beach just east of Panama City. He wanted to remember the smile she had and the gleam in her eyes. If he didn't focus on that, the image of her bloodied lifeless body, sprawled on the ground of a gas station, flooded into his mind.

Stepping into the small furnished apartment, Caleb set the bags of food on the small counter in the kitchen. Despite being somewhat sparse and sterile, Caleb enjoyed the place. A small balcony overlooked Pulpito Street where Garbo's Piano Bar sat. After the sun set, the little bar got busy. Like a lot of the old city, known more as the Romantic Zone, the establishment catered to gay men.

His two neighbors on either side often sat on their balconies. The couple on the left were French, and they barely acknowledged Caleb. He never let on that he spoke French, so when they conversed with each other his spy craft came out. They didn't say much about Caleb, but the wife remarked a few times about how much Amanda laughed. Caleb didn't know whether that was a good or bad thing. He assumed it was good, and anything to the contrary didn't matter to him as long as his daughter laughed.

The neighbors did have plenty to say about Frank, the Canadian ex-pat who lived on the other side of Caleb.

The sixty-year-old retired truck driver came down from Vancouver three months earlier. He loved to catch anyone, either on the balcony or by Miguel's desk, to talk—mostly about nothing. Frank never seemed to leave the building except to catch an Uber to Walmart on the other side of town. On exceptionally rare occasions, the man might walk down to the beach in the afternoon. Mostly, though, he sat on his balcony smoking cheap cigarettes and drinking Budweiser.

And he'd complain about how many gay men there were in the city. Of course, he'd temper every comment with how he didn't really mind. "I'm more of a live and let live kind of guy," he repeated to Caleb at least ten different times—always right after making some disparaging comment about how it wasn't his scene. For the most part, Caleb ignored him. To do anything else would have been tantamount to arguing with a rock.

Caleb placed most of the produce in a bowl on the counter. He didn't like to buy more than a few days' worth of food. Unwrapping the butcher paper around the tamales, he placed three in a skillet, leaving the corn husks in place. A little olive oil and water in the pan kept the husks from sticking to the cookware. As the water heated up to a boil, he sliced up a mango.

It was a simple dinner, but now it was a Saturday tradition—one of his favorites since coming to Puerto Vallarta.

As the tamales warmed, Caleb pulled the iPhone he'd picked up off the Giants fan. The man didn't have a case for the phone, and the edge of it sported a large chip from the corner. Caleb swiped the screen, avoiding the broken glass. There were three texts from someone labeled as Vinnie. All the messages asked the same thing, although with varying wording and increasing concern. "Is everything okay?"

Caleb scrolled back through the texts from Vinnie. There was a picture of a couple, and when he clicked the image to enlarge it, Caleb recognized the girl on the street. The man with her had his arm wrapped around her waist. He was about her age with black hair and a dark complexion. The pair gave off an intimate vibe.

The messages to Vinnie before the picture read, "Do you have any pictures of Nic's girl? Khloe, right?"

Vinnie responded, "Why?"

"I think I just saw her down here."

Vinnie asked, "Where?"

"Mexico. Puerto Vallarta. Girl looked just like her. Been a minute though. Wanted to make sure."

Vinnie said, "Here. Sonny says if it's her to take care of it."

Take care of it. Caleb didn't like those words.

It's not your problem, he reminded himself.

There was too much danger in sticking his neck out for this girl. His only concern was keeping his head down and protecting Amanda.

Still, he ran over those four words, "take care of it." He knew exactly what that meant. If it had been innocuous, this Sonny fellow wouldn't have referred to her as "it."

Khloe had a kill order on her.

Not your problem. You have a daughter to worry about.

But Khloe was someone's daughter, too. What would he want someone to do if she were his daughter?

Caleb relaxed a little. The immediate danger was over, and the man who intended to kill her was now dead. She might know that she was in trouble and already looking to make a run for it. Maybe if he just found her and warned her to take precautions that would be enough.

With an uneasy resolve, he flipped the tamales in the pan as the water sizzled around them.

10

The coffee tasted both weak and old, but Second Sergeant Eduardo Castillo poured a second cup. He stared at the computer in front of him, waiting on it to spit out an answer.

Once the crime scene team arrived on-site, he began the arduous task of collecting evidence. The gun and ball cap were gathered separately, as a crew from the coroner's office retrieved the body.

The afternoon turned into evening before Castillo made it back to the station. The forensic technician in the lab was Diego Navarro. He was a recent transplant from Mexico City. The man was more like a kid compared to Castillo, but he knew his way around the lab. Castillo reached for the phone as he took a sip of the coffee. His face twisted at the awful flavor, and he reminded himself for the hundredth time to bring in his own coffee in the future.

"Lab," Navarro responded on the phone.

"Have you pulled any prints from the scene?" Castillo asked the tech.

"Just finished them up," Navarro explained. "I'll email them to you. Do you want me to upload them to the system?"

"I'll do it," Castillo informed the man.

The system was the national database recently constructed by the Mexican Secretariat for Home Affairs. The program was an attempt to document the biometric identity of everyone in Mexico. While it fell short still on all the data, the program continued to grow, increasing the number of biometric identities regularly.

Castillo wanted to query the program in order to save time. If the forensic technician initiated the search, the results would go to Navarro. It would then take time for Navarro to forward that information to the second sergeant. This way, Castillo would be the one to get the results. Additionally, he'd send the prints through Interpol and the FBI for any international hits—something Castillo suspected would happen in this case.

That worried him, too. The victim appeared to be American, making him likely a visitor. Statistically, that increased the odds that the killer himself was a foreigner too. If the investigation didn't provide a suspect soon, the murderer might return to his home, making extradition difficult, if not impossible.

The Mexican government would file to bring the suspect back, but in places like America, lawyers could fight any extradition order for years. The proceedings would become a diplomatic nightmare, and the state attorneys might see it either as a mountain not worth climbing or, worse, as a bargaining chip.

Castillo couldn't think like that. He wasn't a political being. It mattered very little to him who was in charge, as long as he understood what the laws were. Eduardo Castillo wanted only to be a cop, and cops kept murderers from roaming the streets. At least, that was the idea.

Cartels and corruption had defied that goal. It wasn't as if Puerto Vallarta teemed with violence. In fact, the city remained something of a safe haven compared to other areas. The reason behind that came through the city in the pockets of its visitors. Officials wanted to keep the pesos flowing in on cruise ships and airplanes, so maintaining a certain level of safety was paramount.

Unfortunately, Castillo understood those measures hadn't removed the cartels. In fact, the Mondal Cartel remained extremely active. The police officer suspected there was an arrangement made between officials and the leader of the cartel—keep the violence out of the city, and the government would look the other way.

The idea of such a deal disgusted Castillo, however, he'd been in Juarez and other cities where there were executions on the streets. Puerto Vallarta didn't have that. It had its fair share of street crime—pickpockets or opportunistic thieves. Murders happened. They occurred in any populated area, but usually they were random or personal matters.

Of course, there was an issue with missing persons, something many suspected actually counted as murders. If there was no body, it was difficult to classify it as a murder.

What the city didn't get a lot of, though, were murders of Americans. Especially white Americans. Even the vilest cartels throughout Mexico knew that killing Americans drew unwanted attention. It was one thing to buy off corrupt Mexican officials, but once the US government started sticking their head into the cartel affairs, business became difficult to carry out.

If he hadn't found the Ruger, the death might be easy to chalk up to an accident or suicide. If those kids hadn't stumbled across the body, it might have been missed for a few days. Someone might have reported a smell, but in the gorge, it could have been overlooked. The breeze might have carried the odor out to sea.

Castillo hadn't decided yet if any of this had been a good thing. He could have been home hours ago, but if he could draw a swift conclusion to the case, he might be up for a promotion. The bump in pay would do more than the status change.

The computer in front of him sounded a shrill ding as a small box in the bottom right corner popped up, alerting Castillo to a new email. He clicked the box, and his email opened to an attachment from Navarro.

His fingerprints.

Castillo opened the file to see only three prints. One was smeared pretty badly, but there were a few ridges that could be made out. The other two were nice and clear. Textbook prints.

The officer opened up the link to the national database and found the upload image button. Once he dragged the prints over, he pushed the submit button with the little arrow.

Now it was a matter of waiting. The system generally scanned quickly. As Castillo understood it—and that was on the most rudimentary level—fingerprints were cataloged based on the different types of patterns. At least, that was the way one of the other technicians explained it to him. The computer broke the image up and searched each section.

Suddenly, a face popped up on the screen, faster than Castillo expected. He recognized the face immediately as the man he'd found in the bottom of the gorge.

Victor Alonzo Marino's name appeared under the image, which was a mug shot. The FBI logo appeared at the top of the window, indicating this information came from the US database. Castillo read the information in the file.

Victor Marino had a hefty criminal record. He was from Cincinnati, Ohio. Marino spent two years in prison for aggravated assault. While that was his only conviction, the list of charges levied against him indicated to a seasoned law enforcement officer like Castillo that Victor Marino was a veteran criminal. His lists of associates read like a mafia membership list.

Suddenly, Castillo worried that whatever peace was brokered with the cartel might have been broken. If Marino visited Puerto Vallarta on business, he would easily cross paths with someone from the Mondal Cartel.

Unless it was something worse, Castillo thought. What if he came to Mexico to align with the Mondal Cartel? Or maybe with another cartel trying to push its way into Mondal territory.

A shiver ran through Castillo. A cartel war was something every law enforcement agency in Mexico dreaded. Even corrupt officials didn't want that. They might maneuver behind the scenes for their respective side, but a full-on conflict disrupted the pattern and flow of things. It made it extremely difficult for cops on the take to cover for their bosses. That, in turn, brought the spotlight down on them.

The leaders of the different cartels didn't want war, either. That interrupted business. As it was, they were forced to work around both US and Mexican agencies. Adding another enemy made life more difficult.

That didn't mean there wasn't any animosity. The peace established was fragile, and given the way most cartel men thought, pride eventually became the impetus.

The last major cartel war claimed thousands of lives and was the result of a small traffic accident between two women in Mexico City. When the dust settled, it was discovered that one woman was the wife of the leader of *Los Cazadores del Sol.* The other was the daughter of a high-ranking member of the Tecati Cartel.

The real victim in that incident was the traffic cop who cited the wife. The man was kidnapped along with his wife and three-year-old son. When authorities found the trio, forensics determined the child and his mother were killed first—tortured for hours. The officer was beheaded, but it was assumed he was forced to watch his family's torment.

Castillo shook those thoughts from his head. He studied the forensic report. The two clear fingerprints belonged to Marino. Navarro lifted them off the grip and the trigger.

The smeared, partial third print came off the barrel. Navarro included a picture of the gun with the location of the prints. Castillo's eyes glued to the screen. His pupils seemed to flit about as he examined the image.

Castillo envisioned staring down the barrel of the twenty-two caliber Ruger. His right hand moved slowly as if he was going to parry the gun away. In Castillo's imagination, he saw the middle finger of the second man's right hand landing on the barrel as he pushed it aside.

No, not pushed it. The killer grabbed it and twisted it. The smeared print was made in a downward motion. Had he been simply shoving it away, the movement should have been in an upward swipe.

Explains how he disarmed the man, Castillo thought. *And the bullet hole in the step.*

They wouldn't have an autopsy until tomorrow, but the second sergeant saw Marino's face. It wasn't badly beaten, but there were some marks. A struggle. The way the American landed in the tree might account for some scratches. Perhaps even a bruise. But Castillo would bet there was more to it than that. After all, if someone tried to throw him off the Puente Iguana, he'd fight like hell to stop that.

The police officer checked the status of the third print. A notice flashed, and Castillo clicked his computer mouse.

In Spanish it read "Print Flagged For Consideration by Homeland Security."

Castillo had never seen that prompt. He tried to click the window, but it only flashed at him.

Strange.

He reached for the phone and pulled out a list of numbers for various agencies in both Mexico and the United States. He found the contact for Homeland Security and dialed the number.

It rang four times before going to a voicemail.

Of course, it was well into the evening in Washington, D.C. He'd need to wait until morning to try again. There was an emergency number, but he wondered if this would count. Likely not, and he might need to make an emergency call another time. If they tracked that sort of thing, he might burn a bridge.

Besides, he was exhausted. Tomorrow, he would make some big strides in his investigation. Finding the American's hotel would be a priority. Hopefully, he'd be able to match the partial print, too.

Eduardo Castillo closed his computer down before standing up. He carried the cold, weak coffee to the sink and washed it out.

11

Timothy Patterson stood in the parking lot of El Barril, waiting for the pickup. He was tired after a long day. Maddie and Jason fought against nodding off after starting early this morning, running from The Museum of Natural History where Jason ogled the bones of the Galeamopus and Allosaurus for several hours. After lunch, they spent a few hours trapped in an escape room, something Maddie assumed her father would be better at because of his job.

The maroon Chevrolet Tahoe pulled into the parking lot. The headlights washed across Patterson and his blue FBI-issued Dodge Charger.

"Dammit, Beth, brights," he cursed under his breath at his ex-wife.

The passenger door opened, and he realized Todd was driving. The prick likely left the LED headlights blaring on purpose. His ex-wife's new husband cared little for Patterson, in part because Patterson punched him in the face after discovering the man was sleeping with his wife. *Should have done more to him,* Patterson considered with regret.

"Sorry we're late," Beth offered. Her tone was the same apologetic one she always used with Patterson. When he found out about the affair, she told him she was leaving him, trying to temper it like an apology.

It pissed him off, but not because he wanted the marriage to go on. He recognized the demise before he ever caught Todd between his wife's legs. No, the anger came because he should have known better. Or, more accurately, he should have been the one who left. Instead, Beth had the control, and he ended up with the sympathetic stares from their friends. In this case, he'd have preferred to have been the asshole.

"It's fine, Beth," he assured her.

"We just have lunch at my mother's tomorrow," she explained.

Another reason to be grateful we're divorced, Patterson thought.

He said, "Really, hun, it's okay. We had a long day."

Beth strained her neck to peek in the back seat of the Charger at the two kids. "They look exhausted," she acknowledged before opening the door. "Maddie, Jason, c'mon."

Jason and Maddie popped up and started unbuckling their seatbelts. Slowly, they ambled out. Patterson glanced at the Tahoe's windshield. Todd steadily drummed his fingers on the steering wheel.

"Bye, kiddos," Patterson told his children.

"Bye, Dad," they responded in unison, each giving him a hug before running to the truck.

"Thanks, Tim," Beth said.

"Anytime," he replied, reaching out and hugging her. He knew she'd return the embrace; it was her thing. But he held it for a second longer than normal, and while he did so, his face shifted to stare directly at Todd.

He released her, catching her hand in his for another second. That would be enough to give Todd something to complain to her about. It might even garner a full-blown argument. Patterson almost smiled at the prospect, but he kept his expression impassive.

Timothy Patterson stood in the parking lot of a Tex-Mex restaurant waving at his kids and ex-wife until Todd got the truck onto the street. Even then, he waited a few seconds for the man to watch him in the rearview mirror.

The engine of the Tahoe roared as Todd hurried away from his wife's former life. Now, Patterson let a wry grin creep across his face. *Asshole.*

It was only half past seven, and he thought he might go back to the house and crack open a MadTree Gnarly Brown before dropping into the hot tub. Since the kids were gone tomorrow, he had nothing on his agenda. That meant he could drink himself to sleep without worrying about getting up the next morning. In fact, he could catch the Bengals game instead of entertaining his children. He knew it irritated Beth that his duties seemed to always include fun activities, but in his mind, she won the better end of the custody. The children were in school most of the day, and even when they got home in the evenings, it was dinner and homework with a side of television if the schoolwork was light. On the weekends, he had to keep them occupied. None of their toys or games were at his house. He kept a few things, but it was never what they wanted to have. So, that forced him to take them on excursions, and that got costly.

The cold can of Gnarly Brown now lingered on the outskirts of his thoughts, and his mouth salivated. While he'd had his fill of quesadillas and queso dip, Patterson thought tomorrow might be a good day to grab some wings from that place down the road. They even delivered, meaning he would not even need to get dressed.

As he pulled out onto Pavilion Street, his phone buzzed. A number appeared on the dash display, and he pushed the button on his steering wheel.

"Patterson, sorry to disturb your evening," Danielle Clifton told him on the other end of the line. Clifton was a special agent on Patterson's team. Recently divorced too, she often offered to work the weekends now. The duty wasn't difficult, but it involved manning any reports or updates the task force might require.

"No worries, Danielle," Patterson assured her. "I just dropped the kids off with Beth and the fuckhead. About to head home to a cold one."

"You'll want to hear this first," she suggested.

"What happened?" he asked, worried something broke during the routine surveillance his people were doing. It unnerved him when he got the news second or third hand. By then, he couldn't control the outflow of information.

"There was a request through AFIS from the Jalisco State Police earlier."

"Jalisco?" Patterson questioned. "Where's that?"

"It's in Mexico. On the southwest coast. I guess, that's southwest on Mexico. The request came from an officer in Puerto Vallarta."

"What did they want?" Patterson asked.

Clifton explained, "They sent in a set of fingerprints from a potential murder victim. They belonged to Victor Marino."

"Marino? What's he doing down there?"

"I can't say," Clifton answered.

"Have our guys seen Sonny move?"

"I thought you'd ask that," Clifton said. "He had dinner with his wife and mother-in-law an hour ago. They are still at Sotto as we speak. I believe they are on the dessert course, according to Jameson."

"Does Marino have any family?" Patterson asked.

"No, his mother died last year. The only person who probably gives a damn that Marino is dead is Sonny De-parti, and given that Marino wasn't one of his shining stars, Sonny won't shed a lot of tears for him."

"When was he killed, Danielle?"

"Earlier today. The officer requesting the information is quick. Guy's name is Second Sergeant Castillo. I talked to him before I called you."

Patterson sighed. So much for the beer and hot tub.

Clifton continued, "He told me Marino was discovered at the bottom of a gulch by a couple of kids. Castillo responded to the call to verify it wasn't a prank. He found a gun nearby with Marino's prints on it. Castillo said there was another print on the weapon, too."

"Do we know whose those belong to?" Patterson asked.

"No match yet," Clifton said. "It's one partial print, but no hits in AFIS. Castillo told me he'd contact me if he got an ID first."

"Doubt that," Patterson scoffed. Like most agents, Patterson assumed the United States had the premier software compared to other countries. "Wonder what Marino was doing down there?"

"Maybe he just wanted to take a vacation?" Clifton suggested.

"From beautiful Cincinnati?" Patterson joked.

"Nothing about Ohio is beautiful," Clifton quipped. "Unless you think a quarter inch of grime on everything is nice."

"Yeah, yeah, yeah," Patterson responded. "It's not as clean and crisp as Colorado."

"Hell, boss, no one wants to head for the mountains of Ohio," she remarked, referencing a popular beer slogan.

"I need to get down there," Patterson said.

"You just want out of the cold," Clifton commented.

"No, it's something else. Someone like Victor Marino doesn't get killed on vacation."

"People die on vacation all the time."

"Come on," Patterson argued. "Marino might not have been Sonny's top guy, but he's been around the block. We are pretty sure he's responsible for a few murders here. When a guy like that dies suspiciously, there is something to it."

"Yeah, probably true," Clifton conceded.

"What if Sonny had it done? Obviously, it wasn't him since he's working through a helping of tiramisu, but he could be behind it. Whoever did it might count on the inefficiency of the Mexican police."

"Castillo doesn't seem too inefficient," Clifton observed.

"But he also doesn't know the players. Any of Sonny's guys could be down there, and he wouldn't recognize what he was looking at."

Through the phone, he could hear Clifton tapping at her keyboard. "Okay, boss, there's a flight at nine fifteen out of CVG. You'll arrive at four twenty-five"

"Shit, book it. That will give me five minutes to pack a bag and get to the airport."

"Don't check anything," she suggested. "I'll call the guy over at TSA, see if he can expedite you to the gate."

"Thanks, Danielle. Can you call the State Department, and see about getting the Mexicans to let me bring my service piece."

"I'll set it up. Shouldn't be an issue if you're assisting them."

"Great, I'll call in the morning."

12

I t reminded her of a saw ripping through a piece of lumber. Lee pulled away from the sound, but the whirring
continued until her subconscious relented. The phone
buzzed on the nightstand.

"That's you," Angie murmured. The voice was muffled
by Lee's breasts where Angie nestled her head.

Slowly, Lee lifted her right arm off Angie's side. Her
girlfriend sucked in a breath of air as Lee rolled away from
her. Her hand reached for the vibrating phone.

"Hello," she rasped into the speaker.

"Agent Hubbard, this is J.W. Collins."

Lee's brain only struggled for a minute before piecing
the name with the face of the analyst toiling in what most
referred to as "The Basement," a term likely used by every
agency to denote the area where the banal grunt work
occurred. It wasn't technically in the basement, but the
small department remained isolated in the lower corner of
the building. The day-to-day operations in The Basement
comprised an intense amount of waiting. Manned by two
analysts at all times, the department's task required the
personnel to monitor all data traffic that might fall under
the OOC purview. Lee recognized the tasks The Basement

performed as thankless, and unlike her boss, she'd taken the time to meet and learn everyone's name down there.

That extra effort gave someone like J.W. Collins the initiative and foresight to reach out to Lee in the middle of the night instead of documenting whatever bit of traffic they highlighted for review the next day. It also meant that Lee Hubbard almost always got the information long before Carl Winston or anyone else in the OOC saw it.

"Sorry to bother you this late, ma'am," Collins told her.

"Don't worry about it," Lee assured him. "I'd rather hear about it now than on Monday."

"Yes, ma'am," the junior analyst acknowledged. "There was a fingerprint search earlier today through AFIS, and the system sent an alert to ours. The prints in question dinged our alerts."

"Who do they belong to?"

"The subject's name is Caleb Saunders."

Lee sat upright in her bed. The down comforter fell off her chest as she became fully alert.

Collins continued, "The file states it's classified, and the computer said to notify you or Mr. Winston immediately. I figured I should call you first. Mr. Winston doesn't enjoy being woken up."

"Might mean he has to work," Lee mused before realizing she'd voiced it out loud.

Collins didn't acknowledge her remark.

"Who requested the prints?" Lee asked, trying to recover a modicum of professionalism.

"An officer with the Jalisco State Police in Puerto Vallarta, Mexico."

"Mexico," Lee remarked with some satisfaction that her suspicions were correct. "Where did he get them?"

"It appears it was at a murder scene. I haven't reached out to the officer. Given the classification, you were the first call I made."

"Can you shoot the details to me in an email?" Lee asked.

Angie sat up, fully roused now. She stretched over and touched Lee's shoulder before getting out of the bed. Lee watched the naked figure of her girlfriend as she padded across the hardwood floor to the bathroom.

"Yes, ma'am," Collins agreed. Through the speaker, she heard him typing a few lines before he said, "It's on its way."

Her phone dinged as the email hit her inbox. Rather than struggle with the small screen, Lee pulled her laptop out of the bag next to the bed.

"I think I got it," she told him as she powered the computer. "Don't alert anyone yet, J.W. Let's monitor for any further information. If you can get a file on the victim, please send it along."

"Yes, ma'am."

"Good job, J.W.," she praised the analyst.

As soon as the call disconnected, she found the email on her computer to see what the Jalisco State Police were looking for.

When she opened the file, she stared at a typical police report. It never seemed to matter what country a document like this came from—they all appeared the same. If someone handed Lee an incident report in Mandarin, she thought she would still recognize it for what it was.

While she wasn't fluent in Spanish, Lee had an adequate reading comprehension in the language. However, in this case, the officer, a Second Sergeant Eduardo Castillo, sent the information in English. Lee noted the syntax was perfect.

Angie returned from the bathroom. Lee lifted her head to allow her gaze to follow the other woman's ample breasts.

"You like?" Angie teased.

"Always."

Angie slid back under the covers. "What is it?"

"Got a hit."

"Corsair?" Angie questioned.

"Yeah."

"Fuck, guess I might as well go to sleep," the other woman whined. "He'll keep you up all night."

"Sorry," Lee said with little meaning.

Like Collins said, details about Corsair remained classified, and while Angie worked in the same office with Lee, her clearance level wasn't nearly as high as Lee's. It was a risk to share anything with her, but Angie was also an ally against Carl Winston. Lee intended to take him down, and Angie would gather support from the other departments if need be.

Of course, that all depends on her relationship with Angie remaining secret, Lee reminded herself.

Angie rolled over, and Lee returned her attention to the computer screen.

Castillo appeared to be the responding officer to a dead body. While the official cause of death was pending, Castillo recorded that there were no visible injuries and death likely occurred as a result of the fall from the bridge, which he referred to as *Puente Iguana*.

Immediately, she searched the internet for the location. On a map, Lee located it on the map where it stretched across a river. It was impossible to determine how high the bridge was, but based on Castillo's observations, it was tall enough that the fall would kill a man.

I could slip off a toilet and die, Lee thought.

She returned to the report. Second Sergeant Castillo discovered a ball cap for the New York Giants and a Ruger SR22 pistol. The prints recovered were on the handgun.

Lee Hubbard leaned back against the headboard. Soft breathing came from the other side of the bed as Angie drifted deeper asleep.

A Ruger SR22 was a smaller pistol. It was lightweight, small, and perfect for target practice. All of which made it ideal for assassins. The Ruger even had a threaded barrel that enabled suppressors to be quickly added.

Lee scanned the report. Castillo wrote nothing about finding a suppressor either on the gun itself or nearby. She noted she needed to check that.

She switched back to the map of Puerto Vallarta. Was Corsair somewhere in the city? This was the first lead she'd gotten since he vanished on the *L'étoile* in the Everglades. If she reported this to Winston, he'd send her immediately with a termination agent. Lee recalled the last time she'd gone off with one of her boss's errand boys—she ended up in the hospital with a bullet in her.

Her fingers typed quickly. A straight flight from D.C. to Puerto Vallarta was almost seven hours. She'd gain an hour traveling from Eastern Standard Time to Pacific Standard Time, which was what Puerto Vallarta was on despite calling the time zone Mexican Pacific Standard Time. Considering that, if she could get on a plane in the next hour or two, then she would land in the early morning.

Lee grabbed the phone and dialed a number. The Office of Compliance had two Gulfstream G600 jets on standby in the D.C. area. They also employed ten pilots who rotated on-call duties. The goal was to have quick access for agents from the capital.

"Jacobson," a baritone voice answered.

"This is Lee Hubbard," she told the man, expecting him to recognize her as the Senior Intelligence Officer.

"Yes, Ms. Hubbard," he replied.

"How soon can we get the jet in the air?" she asked him.

Jacobson responded, "Where to?"

"Puerto Vallarta," Lee told him.

"I'd suggest we use the G600 at Potomac," he said, referring to the Potomac Airfield across the river.

"I can be there in half an hour," Lee said. "Is that enough time?"

"The flight plan will be filed within ten minutes," Jacobson informed her. "It's late, so air traffic will be down. I don't expect any problems, so maybe twenty minutes tops. I have two pilots twiddling their thumbs right now."

"Good. Just one passenger—me."

"Roger," he confirmed before she hung up.

"Where are you going?" Angie muttered, still half asleep.

"Puerto Vallarta," Lee answered as she set the laptop aside to dress.

13

Jimmy Agosti turned on the street that the voice on the car's GPS told him. The road was dark and steep, and the Nissan Versa he'd picked up at the airport whined as it climbed the bumpy street.

There were no numbers on any of the houses, and the voice on the GPS informed Jimmy he'd arrived. He looked out the driver's window at a wooded hill.

Damned computers.

It wasn't uncommon for the street numbers to be off outside of the United States, but Jimmy had never strayed outside of the continental states. The farthest south he'd ever traveled was Miami, and that seemed almost like a foreign country to him. He figured half the signs were in Spanish, something that he didn't see much of outside of the Hispanic areas of Cincinnati.

Jimmy turned right. A green street sign read "Pena." That was the road he was supposed to be on. He slowed the Versa to a near stop and stared at the yellow building. It looked like a two-story building, but with the way it sat on the hill, he thought there might be a bottom floor dug into the hill. It didn't look like much of a house. It was square with concrete steps that led up to an arched doorway with a wrought iron security door. There was a balcony on each of the levels, and a large rug hung over the black metal railing on the top floor.

What Jimmy still didn't see were the numbers "555" which would indicate it was the right house.

"Fuck it," he murmured, pulling to the yellow curb in front. Why did Vincent send him alone? He already knew the answer. He was the first to answer the damned phone.

Jimmy Agosti had been on Sonny Departi's payroll for twenty years. No, it was twenty-one. He had been fourteen years old when Vincent Santoro paid him $200 to watch a street corner for a guy to show up. He remembered the day. It was Tuesday, the ninth of July. Jimmy was supposed to be at the St. John the Evangelist's Teen Outreach Program. He'd gone the day before and knew if he had to sit through Father Carlos's diatribe about the impressionable youth and how they were the future failures of both the church and the country, he thought he'd go mad.

Instead, young Jimmy found himself at Italianette Pizza with a ten-inch Italian meat pizza and a Pepsi. When Jimmy saw Vincent Santoro come through the door, he knew exactly who the man was. Vincent was about ten years older than Jimmy, and he was idolized by the boys in the neighborhood. Vincent drove a Camaro, and he always escorted the neighborhood girls that all the boys fantasized about. On top of that, Jimmy's cousin reported that his older brother saw Vincent with a gun.

So, when Vincent asked Jimmy if he'd like to make a couple of hundred bucks, Jimmy jumped on the chance, leaving his half-finished pizza to run the three blocks. He sat on the corner for three hours before he saw the man Vincent asked him to watch. He didn't know the guy, but he went into the corner building. Before the door slammed behind the man, Jimmy dialed Vincent's number, reporting what he saw.

The news later reported that a man was killed on that block in a home evasion, but Jimmy never connected the dots. Not for several years, at least. But he liked the cash, and he loved the attention being connected to Vincent gave him. Jimmy offered his services anytime to Vincent, and two months later, the man asked him to deliver a package on his bike for another $200.

Thus began Jimmy's climb. He didn't officially meet Sonny Departi for three more years, and even then, it was in passing. Jimmy understood the hierarchy, but for all practical matters, Vincent was the only boss he knew.

Even now, when Vincent called, Jimmy jumped. If that landed him alone in Mexico looking for a safe house in the middle of the night, so be it.

He wouldn't be solo for long. Several of his guys—rather, Sonny's guys—were flying in first thing tomorrow morning. Vincent wanted someone down here fast, and Jimmy wasn't about to prove anything but dependable for Vincent. Besides, it gave him an opportunity to finally use the passport he got ten years ago. It was, after all, about to expire in three months, so it deserved to be used at least once in its lifetime.

Jimmy climbed out of the Nissan. The night air was cooler than he expected. At the airport, he'd only walked from the rental car stand to the curb where the Hertz people parked it for him. It was hard to tell if it was hot and sticky or the air was stifled with fumes from the lines of taxis waiting out front. Now, he felt like it wasn't nearly as miserable as he expected it to be.

His phone buzzed with a text from Vincent. "Are you there?"

Jimmy's fingers tapped away at the screen. "Just arrived, I think. No address on the house and GPS is fucked."

He climbed up the concrete steps to the front door. A combination key box like the kind realtors use hung on one of the bars of the iron security door. When the number sequence he got from the owner of the house unlocked the compartment, Jimmy let out a breath of relief. It was the correct house. He'd been worried that some angry homeowner would charge out at any second.

He unlocked the door and entered what the vacation rental website described as a villa. Jimmy had no idea what classified as a villa versus a house, but he didn't really care. The lights came on when he found the switch. Once he could see, Jimmy found himself staring at a tiled floor with a brick archway over the door. He moved through to the next room to find white and yellow alternating walls. Everything was either tiled, stuccoed, or bricked except the ceiling which was an almost mahogany-colored wood with exposed joists running from one side of the room to the other.

"House is good," Jimmy typed.

He continued through the rental, counting four bedrooms and three bathrooms. His stomach growled, but he ignored it. There wasn't likely to be any food in the house. He'd have to wait until morning.

Jimmy's phone buzzed again. "Package being delivered. Niza and Pablo Picasso Street. Park and leave your windows down."

He let out a groan. It was late or early depending on the perspective. He typed, "On way."

Jimmy left the carry-on he'd taken on the plane in the foyer and locked up the house.

Villa, he corrected himself as he got back into the Versa.

Jimmy drove through the dark streets, turning each time the voice on the phone's map app told him to. It took him twenty-five minutes to find the intersection Vincent told him.

On one side of the street was a condominium, and on the other, there was a small parking lot for La Martina Karaoke Bar.

Odd that it was in English and Spanish, Jimmy thought.

He pulled into the lot and left the windows on the Nissan down as he went into the bar. The crowd was thin, but two women were on stage singing a country song. Both were white, Jimmy noted, wondering if they were Americans. When they started in on the next verse, Jimmy recognized the Canadian accent coming through.

He sat at the bar and ordered a Modelo, thinking if he was going to be in Mexico he might as well try the beer. He didn't want to have too many. Tomorrow would prove to be a busy day for him. At least, he'd have a lot to do, searching for Victor or this Khloe girl.

After he finished his first beer, the girls on stage had left, and there were only three other people in the bar with him. The man who ran the karaoke machine started packing up, and Jimmy ordered another beer.

"Last call," the bartender, a Mexican man, said in what Jimmy thought was good English.

When Jimmy paid the man, he realized the two beers cost him about four bucks American. He shook his head in amazement.

He finished the second beer and left, hoping he could head back to the house now. The rushed travel was catching up to him. He stepped out into the night. The air tasted salty, and he remembered that the Pacific Ocean was not far to his left somewhere.

He opened the driver's door on the Versa and saw a black bag on the rear seat. He unzipped it, looking inside. Six Beretta 92s lay at the bottom of the bag next to a box of Winchester 9mm Luger bullets.

Jimmy grinned in the night as he rezipped the duffel and climbed behind the wheel. Half an hour later, he was back at the villa where he collapsed on the bed.

14

“I spy wiff my liddle eye somefing ’range,” Amanda stated flatly as she locked eyes with her father.

Caleb’s lips pursed to one side as he scanned around the room. He saw a turquoise-colored ceramic fountain molded like three pots pouring water from the top one to the next until the cascade splashed into a basin on the floor.

“Is it the fountain?” he asked his daughter.

“No!” she squealed, stretching the word out. “That’s blue.”

His head turned, and he stuck his finger toward a macaw that fluttered down from the tree growing in the middle of the courtyard of Coco’s Kitchen. “Is it that parrot over there?”

“No, Daddy, dat’s geen.”

Caleb smiled. “It has some blue on its tail too,” he pointed out.

“But not ’range,” she reminded him.

He nodded along. “No, not orange.”

“Do you gib up?” she questioned.

Caleb shook his head, twisting around in his chair to point at the lantana blooming from an old tin watering can. “Is it that flower there?”

"Yes, Daddy," Amanda exclaimed. "Good job."

"*Señor* Bryer, *buenas días*," Carlos, their regular server, greeted them.

Amanda straightened up in her seat. "*Benas días*," she tried to say.

The jovial waiter smiled at the girl as he knelt down in front of her. "*¿Cómo estás?*" he asked her.

The girl's face twisted in confusion, and both Caleb and Carlos grinned. Carlos explained, "It means, 'how are you?'"

"Good," she replied, beaming from ear to ear.

"In Spanish, you would reply, '*Bien.*'"

"*Ben*," she tried. Carlos nodded at her attempt before asking, "Juice?"

"We'll both take some orange juice," Caleb told him.

"*¿No quiere café?*"

"Not today, Carlos," Caleb answered.

The skinny Mexican server jotted down the two juices on his notepad.

"We can order too, if you're ready," Caleb informed him.

When Carlos nodded to him, Caleb said, "She'll have one churro pancake, and I'll have the *chilaquiles con huevos.*"

"*Sí. ¿Rojas o verdes?*" the waiter asked, referring to the red or green sauce that covered the fried tortilla shells and eggs.

"*Verde.*"

"*Bien*," Carlos acknowledged. "It won't take long."

Caleb watched the man hurry to the next table. Coco's Kitchen was always a popular breakfast spot with the foreigners. But on Sunday mornings, a perpetual crowd of people waited on the sidewalk as the tables in the open-air café remained full. Located only a block from their apartment, Coco's became Caleb and Amanda's Sunday morning habit, something Caleb realized might be dangerous. Despite that worry, it was a routine he thought Amanda needed.

He hadn't let his guard down since they entered the restaurant. Every fresh face that walked through the entrance registered inside his head. Caleb filed the images away. If any of them set off alarms, he'd react accordingly.

It was easy to fall into the trap of comfortability. But he'd learned that lesson, and while he wanted to give Amanda the most normal existence he could, the truth was he had to remain vigilant.

"Your turn, Daddy," Amanda said.

"Okay, I see something with my little eye, and the color is purple."

"Daddy! It's my dress!" The girl pulled the purple smock away from her chest proudly.

"Well, it's a pretty dress," Caleb replied. "On a beautiful girl."

The pit of his stomach tightened as he considered the Khloe woman. Would helping her put Amanda in danger? If it was just him, there'd be no doubts, but Caleb couldn't lose his girl, though.

Still, he thought about the girl.

How could he even find her again?

The question was moot, and Caleb knew that. He'd been in a business where he had to locate people before. Most of those were skilled, trained assets. This was a young woman with no real situational awareness. At least, he didn't think so. If she were smart, she'd have a go-bag ready. And twelve hours after the incident, she'd already be hundreds of miles from here.

However, nothing about her indicated to Caleb that she was that prepared. Likewise, little about the man in the Giants hat indicated he was an elusive hunter. His tail on the girl was amateurish. From the texts on the man's phone, he just happened to see her. Coincidence. Pure chance.

Caleb never liked coincidences. No one he ever worked with did either. Sure, they occurred, but the problem was there was no way to predict them. Next to poor planning, nothing blew an op like bad luck.

The same thing applied to people like Caleb and Khloe, who were running and hiding from their previous life. For Caleb, it took stopping for gas at the wrong place. For Khloe, it was crossing paths with someone that recognized her.

"*Aquí*," Carlos announced as he appeared with their food.

Amanda clapped her hands as a fluffy pancake coated in cinnamon and sugar touched down on the table in front of her. She ran her finger through the freshly whipped cream and stuck it in her mouth.

"Mmm!" she moaned.

"It's good?" Carlos questioned, and Amanda's head bobbed emphatically.

Caleb lifted his fork when his own plate arrived. He preferred the savory foods for breakfast, but the father also knew his daughter would never finish her food. He'd have ample opportunity to taste the churro pancake.

"Angel is coming to meet us here," he told Amanda.

"Goody!" she shouted, excitedly.

"She'll take you shopping today for a bit, and then you two can go back to the pool."

"Wha' are you doin', Daddy?"

"I have to find someone," he replied.

She threw her hands up, flinging a small glob of cream across the table. When it landed on Caleb's arm, the girl burst into laughter.

"You goofball," he snarled playfully at her. "Eat your food."

His daughter started tearing the pancake up and dipping it into the whipped cream while her father scooped fried *chilaquiles* into his mouth.

"Angel!" Amanda shouted with a mouthful of pancake.

"*Hola*," the young woman greeted her ward. "What are you eating?"

"A chairy pancake."

"Yum," Angel said, sitting in an empty chair.

"Do you need some breakfast?" Caleb asked her.

"No, maybe some coffee."

When Carlos came by, Caleb ordered her a cup. "Listen, I wanted to talk to you about your school."

"*Señor* Bryer..."

"No, don't start with me," he scolded her. "I couldn't survive without you, and Amanda adores you. That makes you family."

"*Gracias, pero*...but you don't need to do anything. You pay me already."

"I know I don't have to. Consider this a Christmas bonus."

"Daddy, it's not Christmas," Amanda interjected.

"It's almost Christmas though. I want to pay for your next semester. That should give you a little leeway to catch up on some bills."

"*Señor* Bryer, I don't know what to say." Her voice caught in her throat.

"Also, why don't I try to come have a look at your car," he suggested. "I'm pretty handy at those kinds of things." It wasn't untrue. Among some of the training he got with the OOC was mechanical engineering. Circumstances of an operation might force him to sabotage equipment, and the most effective way to do that was to know how the machine worked. It was basic training, but the principles of physics and mechanics applied across the board.

"*Gracias*," she replied demurely.

"You sure you don't want anything to eat?" he asked again, realizing he might push too much.

"No, thank you," Angel said. "I ate with Mama."

Caleb nodded and signaled Carlos to bring him the check. He'd already counted out what he figured the bill would be with a decent tip for their regular waiter. Again, he considered he was becoming too much of a fixture in the restaurant. The former OOC assassin wondered how long he and Amanda could stay in Puerto Vallarta before someone from his past showed up.

Unfortunately, he didn't think it would be long enough. Just the thought of that made him realize he needed to assure himself that his escape plan remained viable. He never intended to improvise a way out, and Caleb Saunders devised the best route out of the city if the time came. He even knew where he'd end up. As months passed, though, he would need to check those plans. Something as simple as road construction could derail everything.

"Here," he said, handing some money over to Angel. "If you find anything cute she needs."

Amanda shook from side to side, giddily. Caleb leaned over and kissed her head. "Be good for Angel."

"Yes, Daddy," she agreed.

"See you at home," he told them both, pinching off a bit of Amanda's pancake and stuffing it into his mouth.

"Daddy!" Amanda called as he walked away with a wave and a smile.

Caleb turned left as he came out the door for Coco's Kitchen. He paused at the hostess stand picking up a pack of matches as he smiled at the girl. While he pocketed the matches like hundreds of other customers, he counted twelve people waiting out front for tables. His instincts sensed nothing amiss, so he squeezed past the hungry crowd along the raised sidewalk past Eclecticos and 116 Pulpito. Neither restaurant had opened yet, and there were no crowds lingering around the doors. He stepped down onto the cobblestone road and continued toward the beach another block west.

The girl looked like she'd just gotten off work. Whatever the job that was, he was certain it wasn't waiting tables. Her attire struck him more as professional. Customer-facing, he guessed. A bank or retail position were possibilities.

Caleb strolled along the wooden walkway toward *Los Muertos* Pier. The white spire already attracted crowds as they snapped pictures of the structure. People lined up near the bottom for the water taxi to Yelapa, about fifteen miles south of Puerto Vallarta. The fare was around sixty to seventy pesos one way, which was less than five bucks American.

Caleb and Amanda took the boat ride to the small village a few weeks ago. The trip took a little over half an hour, and they found the beaches at Yelapa far more secluded. Caleb considered moving them down there except for the isolation. The only way out of the settlement was the water taxi or a three-hour drive through the mountains. He didn't like the lack of options for a quick escape, and he quickly abandoned the thought.

How long had she been off work? It had still been morning, so it couldn't have been long. She must work part-time somewhere.

Unless she was on her way to her job.

Caleb dismissed the idea. The woman—Khloe, he reminded himself—wasn't going anywhere in particular. When he first saw her, she was wandering through the crowd. He understood that. Being cut off from people leaves an individual somewhat lost. On more than one occasion, Caleb found himself on crowded streets where he could remain anonymous and still be near others. Somehow, it offered a substitute for a genuine connection, something he hadn't had since Audrey died.

He determined she'd gotten off work early. With the prospect of going home alone, the woman—Khloe—chose to meander along La Playa de los Muertos before cutting back. He was certain she hadn't made her tail until she reached the Isla Cuale Park. Maybe a few minutes before, but not while she was near the pier.

Caleb decided she'd come from the shops north of here along the Malecón. He followed the wooden path until it connected with a sidewalk. When he passed a popular seafood bar called *La Langosta Loca*, he paused and stared at the building opposite him.

She could work in a condo.

There were hundreds of them in the city, but he thought she had been close by. Caleb entered the modern white building with a sign reading Villas Vista Del Sol. It took him just a moment to find the front desk where he found a young, thin Latino man in a crisp black suit.

"Hi there. Is Khloe working today?" Caleb asked.

The concierge furrowed his brow. "There is no Khloe here."

"This woman," he clarified, showing the picture on the phone.

The man shook his head.

"Oh, thank you," Caleb replied.

Quietly, he left the building and moved north along the Malecón to the next condominium before the bricked pedestrian path crossed over the Rio Cuale. Again, he entered, located the front desk, and asked for Khloe.

The older Latina woman behind the counter answered, "I don't know any Khloe."

When he showed her the girl's face, she said, "She doesn't work here."

He nodded his appreciation before crossing the bridge.

After that he tried several restaurants, clothing stores, and an art gallery. None of them had an employee named Khloe, nor did they seem to register any recognition in the picture."

He continued along the path, stopping at every business.

A woman in a Kiosko convenience store paused. "I seen her," she told him in broken English. "She gets Diet Coke."

"When did you last see her?" he asked.

"Yesterday. Early, *antes de las ocho*. Before eight." She rotated between Spanish and English for Caleb's benefit.

Caleb nodded. Eight. Like a pre-shift drink. Diet Coke was her coffee, and perhaps she picked one up before work. That put her close to here.

He walked back onto the street and surveyed the stores. Several souvenir shops sold Mexican blankets and T-shirts, saying things like "This is the fun side of the wall" or "Tequila It's Not Just For Breakfast." Three doors down, though, was a sign reading "Silver Unicorn Jewelry."

Caleb entered the jewelry store. A short, older Latino man stood behind the counter talking to a young couple. He had several sets of earrings out, and the woman was examining them. The man leaned against the glass case, exhibiting all the signs of boredom. Caleb moved along the counters, studying the unique pieces. He was no expert on jewelry, but he'd seen his fair share. What the store carried appeared to be quality. The store owner catered to the cruise ship trade with prices in both pesos and dollars. Caleb noted that nothing in the store fell into the affordable category.

"We'll be back," the woman promised, having decided either to shop elsewhere or simply not to buy the baubles.

"Thank you," the dark-complected man behind the counter told them as the other man ushered his partner out of the shop before she could change her mind.

"Can I help you?" the clerk now asked him.

"Yes, I'm looking for this girl here," he said, showing the jeweler the picture.

"Uh, I don't know her," he lied, fumbling to put the earrings back in the glass case.

"No?" Caleb questioned. "It's just you that works here?"

"My wife too," he explained. "Sometimes we have help."

That made him the owner.

"But not this woman?" Caleb queried again.

The man shook his head a little too vigorously. "No."

Caleb nodded. "Thank you then."

He walked out of the jewelers and crossed the Malecón to the seawall, where several carts were setting up their shops. He found a spot along the wall with a clear view so he could watch the store without being easily seen from inside the shop. Caleb sat on the concrete wall and waited. If there was one thing he could do well, it was wait.

15

A floral-print duffel rolled out of the compartment to slam into Special Agent Patterson's face.

"Fuck me!" he grumbled, shoving the bag back into the bin.

A flight attendant's voice came over the loudspeaker. "Be careful when opening the overhead storage. Bags may shift during transit."

No shit.

"That was mine!" a stout white woman with a short bob haircut and a crooked beak of a nose complained. "I'd appreciate it if you wouldn't throw it around."

Patterson twisted his body toward her so that the lapel of his jacket fell open, revealing the Glock Gen 5 in its shoulder holster. The woman took in a gasp.

"I'm with the FBI," he assured her in his gruffest tone.

"I didn't think you could carry those on a plane," she said firmly.

Patterson sneered at her, turning back to pull his leather overnighter from the luggage compartment. The agent didn't want to clue her in to how big a hassle it was for even FBI personnel to bring their firearms into Mexico. It required several calls through the State Department and the Mexican State Police to get it approved.

He glanced forward to see the cluster of passengers clogging the aisle. It would be a few minutes before the flow started and everyone moved ahead to the exit. Until then, he could take his time getting out of the way of this entitled bitch.

"Could you hand me my bag, Officer?" she questioned in a demanding tone.

He glanced down at her stern, puckered face. "No."

"What?" she snapped, spinning her head to what Patterson assumed was her husband, a thinner man in his sixties with a receding hairline that seemed to match the tolerance he had for his wife. He was a browbeaten spouse serving out a life sentence, and he'd long ago succumbed to the circumstances.

"Did you hear him, Norman?" she demanded.

"Melanie, he's an FBI agent," Norman explained softly, as if that was enough of an excuse.

"I don't care," Melanie groused. "I want to see your badge number."

The corners of Patterson's mouth turned up slightly. "No," he responded as the passengers in the aisle began shifting forward. He locked eyes with Melanie, as if daring her to push him more.

"We aren't in the States," she remarked. "You don't have any authority here."

"No, but I can call and have your house searched because I suspect you are selling guns out of your back door."

"Melanie, please," Norman begged.

His wife slowly realized she might have bitten off more than she could chew. Instead of arguing, her lips pursed together as if they were holding in the next comment. Patterson smiled softly, reached into the overhead bin and retrieved the floral bag, handing it to Norman.

"You must be a saint," Patterson told the man.

Norman, quite smartly, didn't say a word. Melanie bit down on her tongue as the FBI agent turned with the flow of the crowd and funneled through the exit door and gangway.

Patterson hadn't really slept on the plane. He never found it feasible to do so in coach. At least in first class, the seats reclined, and the flight attendants offered real pillows. In the cheap seats, one only got to cuddle with the stranger next to them. The Federal Bureau of Investigation certainly didn't shovel out the extra money for their agents to fly first class, so Patterson felt like all the rest of the cattle shoved into the tight metal can.

Right now, the only thing Patterson wanted was a cup of coffee. However, he needed to get out of the airport, and he had to deal with Mexican immigration and customs. Luckily, he took Clifton's advice and compressed his clothes into the overnight bag, so Patterson didn't need to follow the crowd to baggage claim before pressing through to immigration.

The early morning arrival also meant the terminals were nearly empty of arriving passengers. Departing ones filed past him, but they were going to deal with immigration on the way back to the States or wherever their destinations took them.

He pulled both his passport and his FBI identification out as he approached a female officer, who he assumed was with the state police. He wasn't really positive who enforced the immigration down here. His goal was to keep his firearm, something that was usually common between agencies, but it was easier to accomplish when one wasn't rushing for a last-minute flight like Patterson did last night.

When she saw the FBI logo, the woman's brown eyes lifted to meet Patterson's. "Business or pleasure?" she questioned, sure of the answer.

"Business," he remarked. "I'm meeting with the police here about a murder."

Her thin eyebrow cocked up.

"I also have my service weapon," he told her.

The officer raised a finger and called to her supervisor, a slightly older female, who escorted Patterson to a private office where the woman made a phone call. Ten minutes later, the supervisor rubber-stamped his passport.

"Agent Patterson, you are ready. Can I take you to the taxi queue?"

"Thank you. I'm actually getting a rental car."

"Good," the lady replied, nodding. "Come along."

As they skirted the immigration lines, the supervisor pointed to rows of people with pamphlets stepping into the oncoming arrivals.

"Watch out for them," the supervisor advised.

Patterson furrowed his brow. "Why?"

"They'll try to sell you tours of the resorts, but the beaches are free."

The agent shrugged. "I don't have time for the beaches either," he explained.

"Here are the agents," the woman told him, directing him to the car rental stands.

"I probably need to exchange some money," he said.

"Not here," she recommended. "Rates too high. Go to a bank, much better."

He nodded his appreciation before departing from the woman. Twenty minutes later, he was pulling away from the curb in a yellow Nissan Versa. Patterson whispered some gratitude that the car came with an in-dash navigation system, and he tapped his finger on the touchscreen to input the address of the police station.

He cracked a grin when the feminine voice of the Versa informed him the drive would take *"veintidos minutos."* While his Spanish might pass for ordering a beer or finding the bathroom, he did piece together it meant "twenty-two minutes." That would put him there nearly forty-five minutes before he was to meet Second Sergeant Castillo. If he could find a cup of coffee, that would go a long way to refueling the agent.

Unfortunately, by the time he reached the station, he'd seen no drive-thru Starbucks. The closest he came was a Burger King, but he drove past after seeing the line of cars. Now he sat in the car attempting to order his thoughts and trying not to sleep. If he dozed off for a quick nap, he was certain that the light doze would do him more harm than good.

When the knuckles rapped on the window, he jerked up suddenly. A face peered through the glass at him, and he cursed silently for napping. Patterson opened the door.

"Agent Patterson?" the officer whose face woke him asked.

"Yes, sorry," Patterson mumbled, twisting his wrist to check the time. "I didn't mean to fall asleep."

"It's okay," the officer replied. "I'm Second Sergeant Eduardo Castillo."

"Tim," Patterson introduced, extending his hand.

"Call me Eduardo," Castillo offered. "Did you just arrive?"

"Yeah, I caught a red-eye last night."

"Red-eye?" Castillo questioned.

"An overnight flight," Patterson explained the colloquialism.

Castillo nodded. "Would you care to come inside? We have some *café*...coffee."

"I'd sell my mother for a cup," Patterson replied with a half grin.

The FBI agent followed Castillo into the building, a small white structure that could have been an old garage. A placard with block letters read "*Seguridad Policia de Jalisco*." Without the sign, the building resembled any other business in the area.

Inside, Patterson found, to his surprise, a police station like most he'd seen in the States. It might not have been the most updated, but it rivaled most mid-range city departments that he'd seen.

Castillo paused at a table where two Mr. Coffee coffeemakers sat. The two glass carafes were full of black liquid, and Patterson noted that just like every departmental coffeemaker he'd seen in the FBI offices and local police departments, the acrid coffee had long stained the clear glass to a muddy brown. He assumed that cleaning the pot might somehow screw with the flavor of the coffee. Castillo pulled two Styrofoam cups off a stack and handed one to Patterson, who filled it from the pot.

"*¿Crema?*" Castillo asked, lifting a container of powdered cream.

"Nah, I like it black."

The Second Sergeant nodded with approval as he took his cup and led Patterson to a desk. The officer motioned for him to take a seat. After he sat down, he passed a file over to the agent.

When he opened the file, he found several photos of a man's body. He recognized the lifeless face of Victor Marino from the mugshot photo on file with the FBI.

"That's Marino," Patterson acknowledged.

Castillo nodded. "The man is a criminal in the United States?"

"Marino's done some time, but not for anything significant. Both the Cincinnati PD and the FBI consider him a person of interest in several homicides, though. He's associated with a local gangster in the Cincinnati area."

"Like the mafia?" Castillo questioned.

"Yeah, definitely organized crime. They have their fingers in everything. Probably like your cartels." Patterson made the remark casually, judging Castillo's expression.

Rumors ran amok that the drug cartels compromised nearly all law enforcement in Mexico. Patterson didn't assume that to be a fact. No more than the idea that all American cops were good or bad. He understood the pull of organizations like Sonny Departi's or the many cartels' attempts to ensnare officers.

Castillo bristled at the mention of the cartels. He didn't respond, but Patterson sensed a revulsion from him. He wondered if that was because he was dirty and realized it classified him with murderous individuals in the cartel or if it was the opposite. The mere thought of the actions of the cartels soured the stomach of a good cop.

"Have you found anything else on him?" Patterson asked, trying to get back on track with the Mexican policeman.

"Now that I have his name, we'll locate his hotel. If this man is a criminal, maybe someone who came here with him was the killer."

Patterson nodded. "Did you have any witnesses?"

Castillo shook his head. "No, that area of the park was quiet."

"The best move is to find out where he came from," Patterson noted. "And who might have been with him. I'd like to see the body."

"Of course," Castillo agreed. "It is still in our little morgue here. He'll be moved to our central station today."

"You'll do the autopsy on him there?"

Castillo nodded. "But I think it will just confirm that he died from the fall. It might give us some other clues, though."

"Anything might be helpful," Patterson agreed. Most people might consider an autopsy on a victim whose cause of death was so obvious to be a waste of time. However, minor things, like the man's last meal or any chemical substances in his body, could lead an investigator to a more defined path.

Castillo rose, and Patterson followed him down a flight of stairs to a small morgue. There were only four cadaver lockers in the room. Castillo handed Patterson a pair of latex gloves, and both men donned them before Castillo opened the second drawer.

The cold, dead face of Victor Marino appeared to be sleeping. Patterson smelled the familiar scent of death. If asked to describe the aroma, he'd be unable to verbalize it. The best he might come up with was a lack of something. Like smelling distilled water.

Patterson leaned forward, studying the scratches on the man's face and neck.

Tree branches, he assumed.

There were no marks on the corpse's torso. His clothes protected him during the fall. Patterson assumed, since the man was naked, they were removed as evidence.

A female voice erupted through an old loudspeaker. "*Eduardo Castillo, teléfono, línea uno.*"

"*Perdón,*" the officer said, stepping to a phone on the wall.

While Castillo talked, Patterson lifted the man's hands, studying the fingers. Marino kept his nails trimmed but not manicured. He wasn't a man who thought getting a manicure was allowable.

The second sergeant reappeared at Patterson's side. "Would you like to see where we found the body?"

Patterson glanced up, nodding.

"This man must interest other people," Castillo remarked.

"What do you mean?" Patterson asked.

"That was another American agent who wants to meet us at the bridge."

"What?" Patterson exclaimed. "Who is it? An FBI agent?"

He wondered if the Bureau sent someone else along to shadow him. If so, why had no one told him.

Castillo shook his head. "I believe she said she was with Homeland Security."

Patterson cocked an eyebrow, frustrated, curious, and a little worried about what was treading into his case.

16

The Malecón had a crowd of Americans flowing down the middle of the pathway. The cruise ship offloaded its passengers about two hours earlier, and the taxis and rideshares began the back-and-forth trek from the cruise terminal to the shopping center. It was a near daily occurrence. Normally, the influx of fellow Americans comforted Khloe, reminding her of home.

Not today, though.

She was jittery, scanning every face as she walked toward a familiar one. Lying in bed last night, Khloe hadn't been able to sleep a wink. She ended up scrolling through the internet, searching for escape options. She was stuck until she got to the bank tomorrow, and she almost called Mr. Valdez to tell him she was sick. But they still owed her for her last check, and it was enough that she thought it would help.

Now she reconsidered that. It might amount to a thousand dollars. Was that worth it?

Hell, the store was right there, she realized.

Her eyes scanned around. Too many faces on the street, but most looked like the average tourist coming off a cruise ship. She stepped through the front door of the Silver Unicorn. Overhead, the bell rang out with her entry.

Alejandro Valdez talked softly with a woman who was inspecting the chains and pendants. Those were Mr. Valdez's bestsellers. It was pure silver, but the chain was cheap enough that the tourists loved grabbing them as souvenirs. The baubles were actually manufactured in Mexico City, allowing him to stamp them, figuratively, with the "*Hecho en México*" statement.

Valdez glanced up as Khloe moved through the store toward the back room. She should be safe in the store. Who would come after her in public? Plus, Mr. Valdez had security with a panic alarm that he could easily activate. The security company monitoring it assured the jeweler there would be a five-minute response time from the local police force.

Once the business day was over, Khloe would have to risk returning to her apartment. What if Mr. Valdez drove her? She'd have time to give him and his wife a good farewell. They'd been incredibly helpful to her, opening their home for dinner at least every couple of weeks. Mrs. Valdez expressed determination in finding Khloe a new boyfriend, and while Khloe had no desire to meet someone, she appreciated the woman's attention. It reminded her of her own mother.

Mr. Valdez's eyebrows crunched up when she stepped through the door. Worry washed over his face, and Khloe felt like a brick hit her stomach.

His wife came out of the back of the store and walked rapidly toward Khloe. For an instant, she thought the couple might be angry with her.

"Mrs. Valdez?" she stammered as the short, older woman neared.

"Khloe, we must talk," her boss demanded.

"What is it?" Khloe asked, her voice dipping softer as she tried to be demure to her boss.

"A man came in the store this morning," she informed the girl. "He was showing your photo and asking about you."

"My photo?" Khloe repeated. "What did he want?"

"He said he was looking for you. Alejandro told him he didn't know you."

"Thank you," the younger woman breathed. "What did he look like?"

"He was big. American. We have him on video," she explained to her. "Come, you can see."

Khloe followed Fernanda Valdez past the customer admiring the silver chains. Mrs. Valdez punched a number into a keypad next to the office door. A loud click and a buzz alerted them the lock disengaged.

When Khloe stepped through the door, her eyes took a second to adjust. The lights remained dimmed, so that whoever was in the office could look through the one-way mirror into the retail area. A thirty-two-inch monitor sat on a desk facing away from the large pane of glass. Six squares divided the screen, showing various angles of the inside of the store. Khloe knew there were two more cameras in the back office focused on the room itself and the vault where Mr. and Mrs. Valdez kept some of the high-end jewelry after business hours. Those weren't on the main screen because Mr. Valdez thought that if someone saw the monitor, they might not realize the back was being monitored as well. Khloe doubted that was the case, but she didn't tell him otherwise.

Fernanda Valdez touched the mouse on the computer and closed out the live images of the store. She selected an icon, and when a window came up asking for a time frame, Mrs. Valdez typed in 11:15 this morning. The screen opened up with six images of the interior of the Silver Unicorn that closely resembled the live ones she'd just minimized.

The cursor on the computer scrolled over the one showing the door, and the image exploded to fill the entire screen. Khloe sucked in some air suddenly as she stared at the man she saw yesterday. The one who threw the other man off the bridge.

"Shit!" she muttered.

"Who is it, Khloe?" Mrs. Valdez asked.

"I don't know," she admitted. "He and another man were following me yesterday."

Khloe's voice cracked as fear gripped her. Tears started rolling down her cheeks.

"Did he hurt you?" her boss questioned in a worried, motherly tone.

Khloe's head shook. "No, but he killed the other man."

"*¡Dios mío!*" the older woman gasped. "Why would he do this?"

Dropping her head, Khloe replied, "I think they are after me."

"But why?"

"I saw someone murder my boyfriend back in Cincinnati."

"*Oh, mi hija,*" Mrs. Valdez whispered.

"I've been hiding down here, but I think they found me."

"You must go!" Mrs. Valdez exclaimed.

"I can't leave until tomorrow."

"This man," the other woman said, pointing at the man on the screen. "He doesn't know where you live. That's why he's looking for you here."

Khloe paused, letting out a breath. She was right. If they were looking for her here, then they didn't know how else to find her.

"Did he seem to be checking all the stores?" she asked her boss.

The woman shrugged. She clicked the rewind button, forcing the American to walk backward out the store and to the left.

"He came from *la Zona Romántica*," Mrs. Valdez pointed out. "It was over an hour ago. You might have passed him."

Khloe swallowed hard. What if she had? Did he already see her? She'd been watching the people around her, but the streets were so crowded. It would have been easy to miss someone. This man could have been waiting in any one of the shops or bars along the Malecón, just observing everyone on the sidewalk.

"What do I do?" Khloe asked softly.

"Run away," the woman answered. "Why must you wait until tomorrow?"

Khloe explained about the money she had in a safe deposit box. "I can't get it until the bank opens tomorrow. I don't have enough to hide for long."

Mrs. Valdez nodded thoughtfully, and Khloe raised her hand in a stop motion.

"No, Mrs. Valdez, I can't take anything from you. My last check would be good." She paused before adding with a begging half smile, "Cash would be better."

"*Claro que sí*," the woman agreed. She turned and moved to the safe, opening it with another code on the keypad. Fernanda Valdez removed a small stack of pesos, handing it to Khloe.

"This is too much," Khloe insisted, counting fifty thousand pesos. It was almost three thousand dollars.

Mrs. Valdez retracted her hand, shaking her head. "Take it. You need to leave today."

Khloe stared at the colorful bills in her palm. It wasn't enough to live on, but she could get out of town for several days. Maybe lie low and slip back into the city later to visit the bank.

After some seconds of thought, she tightened the grip on the money. "Thank you so much, Mrs. Valdez."

"Here, you must change clothes," the woman insisted. She was smaller than Khloe in stature, but a little broader everywhere else. Still, the store owner stripped off her jacket and skirt, passing it to Khloe. "This way," she said, "he won't recognize you."

Khloe wasn't sure about that, but it was better than doing nothing. She wore a thin blouse with some black slacks. She kept the blouse on but slipped the blazer over it. Then she pulled the skirt on while Mrs. Valdez struggled to wriggle into the slacks.

With a smile, she told Khloe, "I'll have to make Alejandro do all the work today."

Khloe grinned. "Thank you so much."

"Get out of here," Fernanda Valdez ordered, but Khloe reached forward and hugged the older woman.

"*Cuidado, mi hija,*" Mrs. Valdez urged, pushing her gently toward the door.

Khloe stepped back into the lighted store, and Alejandro Valdez lifted his head to see his employee wearing his wife's clothes. The girl grinned sheepishly, grateful the customer was still talking to the man.

"Sorry, Mr. Valdez," Khloe apologized. "I have to go, and I wanted to tell you thank you."

"*¿Está bien?*" he asked.

She shrugged and stepped toward him to hug him. The sixty-three-year-old man squeezed her back. When he loosened his grip, Khloe pulled away and walked out the door without turning to look at the couple.

The bell dinged and buzzed at the same time as Khloe rushed through the exit. The Pacific Ocean glistened with the early afternoon sun overhead. Her hand lifted to shield her eyes as she turned north on the Malecón.

Mrs. Valdez was right; Khloe needed to get out of the city now. She pulled her phone out and started searching for the bus schedule. She could buy a cheap ticket for cash, get a few hundred miles away, and wait a week. How long would Sonny's guys search the area for her? They'd have to give up at some point.

There was a daily route from Puerto Vallarta to Guadalajara that made a round trip.

Damn, I missed it. Today's bus left at eleven in the morning. The only other way out of town was by car, and she didn't have one.

Khloe's heart started pounding.

Calm down, she urged herself. She could get to her apartment, grab some things, and find a cheap hotel somewhere until tomorrow.

That's it. I can even buy my ticket today, so all I have to do is get on the bus.

Something about having a plan soothed her. It wasn't a complicated strategy, but she just needed to do it.

She let out a sigh as she headed north on the Malecón, praying that she didn't cross paths with the man looking for her.

17

From his perch on the stone wall, Caleb watched as the dark-haired girl rushed out of the Silver Unicorn Jewelry's exit. The woman that was targeted by whoever Sonny was almost looked like anyone else, as she seemed to be scrolling through her phone as she walked hastily down the street. But it took half a second for Caleb to see the panic in her every move. Khloe's head popped up from the device to scan not just ahead of her but also all around. She was focusing on faces, something most people avoided. If he guessed, the owner of the Silver Unicorn warned her that some man came by searching for her.

He'd noticed the cameras when he entered the shop. There'd been no way to avoid all six of them, but he'd learned over time that although most faces were recorded hundreds, if not thousands, of times a day, that footage usually amounted to little. Video surveillance was only as good as the person monitoring it, so while he did his best to elude cameras, he wasn't too worried about being caught on most private ones. That didn't mean they were all safe—places like government buildings or airports networked those cameras. Facial recognition software had come a long way, and the computers could pinpoint features even at bad angles. But a jewelry store in a touristy section of Mexico only used the cameras as a deterrent. However, he guessed the owner showed her his image—and she recognized him from the bridge yesterday.

As he slid off the wall, an enormous wave crashed upon the shore behind him. Caleb paid no attention to the surf, absorbing the sound into the din of the marketplace as he drifted through the throngs of gawking cruisers trying to rush through the streets. He passed a man painted entirely in gray and posing on a chair motionless like Rodin's *The Thinker*.

Caleb walked along the wall, staying on the opposite side of the street from Khloe and lagging back about fifty yards. A sizeable crowd gathered ahead of him where several acrobatic artists ascended a pole about sixty feet up. The six men, known as the Flyers of Papantla, would perform precarious yet graceful aerial dances, held aloft by what seemed to be a strip of rope or cloth. Caleb suspected there was more to the act, but the couple of times he'd seen them do it was with Amanda. He didn't like tearing into the illusion as his daughter found the display fascinating.

Caleb used the growing group of onlookers to hide him as he waded through the crowd. Khloe was no longer staring at her phone. She still gripped it tightly, but her attention remained on the surrounding people.

A young child ran into his legs, and he glanced down for a split second to see a blond-haired girl just a little younger than Amanda turn her head up to stare into Caleb's eyes.

"Maggie!" a voice shouted desperately. Caleb lifted his gaze to spot a twenty-something-year-old woman who shared the same dirty blond hair and green eyes of the girl at his feet. Her face held terror in the creases of her forehead. The emerald-colored eyes narrowed as she squinted against the sun, trying to find the runaway girl.

He grabbed the child by the wrist as she began to spin in confusion. To her, the legs of the adults in the crowd were like thickets of corn stalks.

Caleb waved for the mother, and he lifted Maggie up in the air to hand her through the tourists to the young mother. The woman beamed as tears of relief welled out of her eyes. Her arms engulfed little Maggie, squeezing her as if she could never let the child go. Caleb's stomach tightened. He knew exactly how the mother felt.

His mind flashed on the image of Jackson's lifeless body sprawled on the concrete. The handle of the gas pump was still in his grip. Caleb forced his vision away from his son, trying to see only the background. That never worked. Instead, he saw the split-second glimpse he caught of his son's face, torn open by a nine-millimeter round.

"Thank you!" she gushed, but Caleb was already spinning from the duo.

Khloe wasn't in sight now, and he cursed to himself for a second as he quickened his pace, weaving through the crowd. She couldn't have gotten too far in those few seconds, but if she turned or stepped into a store, he might go past her trying to catch up.

Sentimental fool. That girl wasn't actually lost. Someone else could have moved in to help her.

But would they?

He slipped away from the audience, watching the acrobats, and crossed the cobblestoned Malecón. While the city designated the street only for pedestrians, there was still a sidewalk leftover from when the road accommodated vehicles. Caleb hurried along the walkway under the balconies of the colonial-style buildings looming overhead.

He released a sigh of relief when he spotted Khloe's dark head. She was still keeping it on a constant swivel, which was the only reason he could pick her out. The rest of the people on the street strolled along, unaware of anything else. Whatever she thought she was doing, it would not detect a tail very well. Her fear had her only watching the people in front of her. It would be tough to run any surveillance detection in this crowd. If he'd been in her position, the first thing would be to turn off the major thoroughfare and get out of sight. Of course, Caleb had years of training and instinct packed together. Poor Khloe was nothing but a scared little girl running for her life.

She passed the McDonald's on the right—technically the end of the Malecón—and crossed the next street, *Calle 31 de Octubre*. It was another of the many dated street names in Puerto Vallarta. Most seemed to relate to historical events. Khloe now entered a neighborhood known as *5 de Diciembre*, a reference to the date in 1929 when Puerto Vallarta established an ejido, removing land ownership from large landowners. This move infuriated the wealthy property owners, some of whom were foreign investors, and allowed the city to grow and develop out.

The differences between the touristy section of the Malecón and *5 de Diciembre* were stark. The area showed signs of locals with businesses catering to them like laundry, corner grocery stores, and general services. Restaurants and cafés along the streets began offering cheaper options. Caleb's favorite was the five *pastor tacos* for only ninety *pesos*. He would have to pass on the deal, but his brain cataloged the location for a future visit. Amanda loved the street tacos, and the girl would eat five in a single sitting.

Now that they were out of the crowded tourist area, he dropped back half a block. There was no shortage of pedestrians, as Puerto Vallarta remained a pedestrian city. Residents didn't drive anywhere unless they were heading across town to Walmart or Costco. Most of the time, they shopped within a few blocks of their homes.

As Khloe waded deeper into the streets of *5 de Diciembre*, Caleb found the walking traffic thinning, and he slowed his pace. If she turned around now, he'd have little to do but continue along as if he wasn't following her. Her manic searching of the crowds had lagged. She was getting close to her home. It was natural to grow more comfortable. All animals thought their nests or burrows offered safety. Unfortunately, that wasn't always the case.

So far, though, Caleb had detected no one else trailing the girl. That was a relief. He could get closer and approach her, but with her heightened fear, she might bolt, scream, or even attack. That wasn't the attention Caleb wanted. Best to wait until she settled.

She took a right on *Calle Venezuela,* and Caleb stopped at the intersection. Through the windows of a Kiosko corner store, he watched her turn to look up and down the avenue. Satisfied she was alone; she entered a three-story old colonial building. He ran around the corner, dashing across the street.

The door to the apartment was at the top of a six-step stoop, and he took the stairs two at a time. Slowly, he opened it, praying that the hinges didn't squeal his presence. The only sound was a slight creak, and he stood on the ground floor. Footsteps above caused the wooden planks on the steps to rub against each other, echoing squeaks off the plastered walls, and he calculated Khloe was on the third level. A jangle of keys came from above, followed by a loud click as she entered her apartment.

Caleb began up the steps, taking each step slowly to mitigate the sound of the wooden stairs. At the top of the three flights, Caleb faced a short hallway. Two apartments occupied this level on either side of the corridor. He stared along the walls, trying to figure which door led to Khloe.

He studied the wooden floors. The building was old, maybe fifty years at least. However, it was often hard to judge things like that in Puerto Vallarta. Really anywhere in Mexico. Not that the construction was shoddy, however, certain issues seemed overlooked. Like polishing hardwood floors. The residents of both apartments added a small mat outside of their entry. Only one had any words on it. "Love" curled out with flowers growing out of each letter.

English.

That wasn't much to go on, but given the limited choices, Caleb opted for the most obvious. He stepped onto the mat and knocked slightly.

"*¿Señorita, todo bien?*" he asked in a soft voice. *Miss, is everything okay?*

The knob turned, and Khloe pulled it open. It took her a second to register who was in the hallway, and as soon as her brain told her who Caleb was, the fear washed over her face, whitening her pallor.

18

"No!" Khloe shouted, swinging her left forearm to shut the door.

Caleb caught the edge before it slammed into the jamb. The corner of the frame pressed hard into the knuckles on his hand. Thankfully, she hadn't put enough force into it, as she was already moving back from the entrance.

He pushed the door open. "Khloe, I'm not here to hurt you," he offered calmly, attempting to reassure her.

"No, no, no, no!" she continued, repeating as she scrambled away from the door.

"Listen to me," he urged, keeping his volume low.

"I saw you—"

Caleb nodded. "Yes, that man wanted to kill you."

"How do I know that?" she asked.

"You do," he told her.

She backed herself up in what Caleb realized was a studio apartment, not too dissimilar to his own. Khloe pressed her back against a small range in the kitchenette area. Her arms pushed up from the countertop as if she were bracing for something.

"That man was going to kill you," he repeated to her.

"How can you be sure?"

Caleb pulled the dead man's phone from his pocket, handing it to her. "He was texting someone named Vinnie. Does that mean anything to you?"

Khloe's head made a quick curt movement that could have been a nod. She extended her right hand and took the iPhone gingerly from Caleb.

He added, "He said Sonny wanted the guy on the bridge to 'take care of' you."

"Shit, shit, shit!" she murmured.

Caleb stared at her as she scrolled through the texts. Her shoulders sank, and tears welled in her eyes.

"They're going to kill me," she whispered. Then she glanced up at Caleb. Fear filled her face. "Are you with them?"

"No."

"But—but, you could be after me too, for the money."

"I'm not," he reassured her.

She shook her head. "It doesn't matter, does it?"

He didn't respond.

"I mean, if you are, then I'm dead already, right?"

Caleb shrugged, as if to agree with her.

"There's no way I can get away from you."

He chuckled, almost to himself. "Not likely," he agreed before realizing how callous that sounded.

"Who are you?"

"Roland Byers," he replied, giving her his alias.

"How did he find me?" she muttered, ignoring the introduction.

"From the text, it looks like it was just your dumb luck. Guy was already down here and spotted you. Did you recognize him?"

"You said he called Sonny?" she asked.

"This Vinnie must have done it. He mentioned him."

"He must be one of Sonny's guys. If he knows I'm down here, he'll send more." Khloe was a ball of pent-up energy ready to explode. Caleb took a step back, so she had some room to move as she processed what was happening.

"Who are Sonny and Vinnie?" Caleb leaned against the stucco wall.

"Sonny Departi is the head of organized crime in Cincinnati. Vinnie is his number two guy. He also murdered my boyfriend."

"How do you know that?" Caleb asked warily.

"I pretty much watched him do it," she replied. "Nic—his real name is Dominic—was snitching to the feds. Apparently, he'd been gathering evidence of some kind, and they thought he had it at our place."

"And Vinnie killed him? You were there?"

She shook her head. "I was in the hall coming home when I heard the shot. Somehow, I realized what happened, and I hid. Vinnie came out of the apartment."

"But he didn't see you?"

Again, her head twisted back and forth. "I don't think so, but I ran."

"And ended up here?" Caleb asked.

She nodded. "I liked it here," she mused. "I figured they wouldn't hunt too hard for me."

"Probably not," Caleb agreed. "Until you accidentally walked past one of these gangsters."

"It's not fair," she groaned.

Caleb watched the young girl pace past him into the sitting area where she collapsed on an old green couch that should have been put on the street. Khloe started crying again. Caleb pulled out a chair from the table and sat on it backward. His forearms crossed on top of the backrest.

After several minutes, the flow of tears slowed, and she looked up at Caleb. "You saved me yesterday?"

"I didn't want anything bad to happen to you simply because no one chose to help."

Her bottom lip plumped up some. "Thank you," she whispered.

"Sonny knows you're in Puerto Vallarta by now, and I would assume he's either aware his guy is dead or, at least, that the dude's incommunicado. Will he send reinforcements?"

"If he thinks that I saw whatever evidence Nic has—or, er, had—yeah, he will."

"They don't know you saw Vinnie at your apartment, though?"

"I don't think so," she replied, pulling her knees up to her chest.

"You need a plan," Caleb told her. "Do you have a go-bag?"

"Not really, I have some money Nic squirreled away, but it's in a safe deposit box at the bank."

Realization dawned on Caleb. "That's why you haven't run yet," he remarked. "You want to hit the box when it opens?"

She nodded. "My boss gave me some cash this morning. I was going to catch a bus out of town. I figured the airports were too obvious."

"Yes, but buses will be the next thing these guys go for. Guys like this spend their lives circumventing surveillance. They'll think of anything you might."

"Doesn't matter," she explained, slumping her shoulders in defeat. "I missed the bus this morning. I'd have to wait until tomorrow, anyway."

"That won't work," Caleb remarked. "If you'd gotten on one today or yesterday, that would have been better. It would be enough of a head start. Now, though, the window closes. If they have the manpower, they can put people at any number of stops you might pass through, starting with the obvious—Guadalajara. Almost all routes would pass through there."

Khloe dropped her head into her hands. He didn't see the tears, but assumed they were there.

"Listen, in a case like this, you still have options. Running isn't always the only one."

"What can I do?" she begged, now showing her tear-stained cheeks.

"Your best option is to go to ground."

The girl shook her tear-stained face in confusion. "What? What does that mean?"

Caleb shrugged. "Do nothing. Stay out of sight for a while. This Sonny might send a team down to find you, but after a few weeks, he is going to give up. Then it will be easier to get out of town."

"You mean just lie low? Don't leave my apartment?"

The man pursed his lips with concern. "Ideally, yes. But I found you easily. That means one of them could do the same."

"Ugh!" Khloe let out a groan. "I need to stay, but I can't? What the fuck am I supposed to do? How did you find me?"

"Your job. Based on what you were wearing yesterday, I assumed you were leaving work. Obviously not a waitress-type career, you had a more professional appearance than that. I worked my way down the Malecón until I hit the jewelry store."

"Mrs. Valdez said they told you I didn't work there."

Caleb nodded. "He did. The man was trying to protect you, but I knew he was lying."

Her brow crinkled.

"I have a good read on people," Caleb explained. "As soon as I showed him your picture, he shifted gears into more of a protective father than an employer."

Khloe's face softened.

Caleb added, "If these guys coming after you find them though, they'll be the connection they need to get to you."

"You're telling me to stay put and hidden, but even that might not be good enough."

He shrugged. "There's no science to hiding from people. Too many variables in play. If the guy yesterday was alone, then it could take a day or two for them to respond.

Or they could have been on the plane yesterday afternoon, and they're walking along the Malecón looking for you."

"This is all too much," she moaned.

"Listen, Khloe, why don't you come with me? Nothing funny, I promise. But you can stay a couple of days in my apartment, keeping your head down. Then we can see about getting you out of town."

The girl's face twisted in doubt and suspicion, and Caleb realized how stupid that idea sounded. It was perfectly logical from his point of view, but Khloe was a frightened woman who suddenly saw an older man offering something that no female in her right mind would trust.

"Oh, shit, no," he stammered. "I don't mean it like that. You'd be staying with me and my daughter. If you want."

Leery, Khloe asked, "How old is your daughter?"

"Three."

"Where is your wife?" she questioned.

Caleb swallowed. He saw in her eyes the change he must have exhibited when she questioned that. "She's dead," he answered.

"I'm sorry," Khloe replied.

"Look, I understand if you don't want to go with me," Caleb offered. "I don't think you can stay here, and you can't run just yet. Anything you do is going to be risky at this point. The next best solution is a hotel off the beaten path."

"Why are you here?" Khloe wondered aloud. "Why help me?"

"I have a daughter. When I saw the guy following you yesterday, my thought was what if that were Aman—my daughter? I'd want someone to protect her."

"So, some kind of gallant chivalry."

"I think fathering a little girl probably fosters that," he admitted. "I could tell the man on the street intended to hurt you, too."

Khloe puckered her lips as she considered what Caleb said.

"I can help you gather whatever you want to go," he told her. "If that helps."

"Thank you," she acknowledged. "I need to get some stuff together."

"Try to get rid of anything that identifies you," he suggested. "If they make it to this apartment, you don't need to leave anything that will give them an idea of how to track you. Movie tickets, restaurants, anything."

"How could that help them?"

"If you want to find a person, it's a lot easier to know them. If they discover you like to eat Indian food, they'll circulate around those with your picture."

"That seems farfetched," she remarked. Her demeanor relaxed with Caleb.

"As farfetched as my finding where you worked based on your attire and the way you walked?"

She stared at him, now her eyes narrowed. "How did you know to do that?"

"I have some government training," he told her.

"Oh," was her only reply.

Khloe stood up and started going through her belongings, looking at each piece and wondering what piece of the puzzle that fit.

While he watched her fumble around, Caleb considered what he'd said. He decided to stop eating every Sunday at Coco's. In fact, he realized he was getting too comfortable here altogether. If the OOC found a trail that led to Puerto Vallarta, there were too many pieces he'd left around for them.

Poor Khloe was now in the crosshairs because of bad luck. He'd be foolish to ignore that.

The fight with the hitman yesterday replayed in his mind. Had he done anything that might trace back to him? The only thing he'd touched was the man's shirt, and it was nearly impossible to pull clean prints off of fabric. But that wasn't all. He'd swiped the gun away too. How did he touch it? It was unlikely he left a usable print on it. Other than the phone which he now carried, there should be no clues left behind. Somehow, that notion didn't comfort him.

19

The sun seemed to reflect off the white staircase as Lee cupped her hand over her forehead. From where she stood, she could see across the expansive gorge to the sea where the waves glittered like diamonds. She'd found the famous Gringo Gulch easily, and parked on the narrow cobblestone street, hoping that her car wasn't in the way. If the rental company had given her anything larger than a Toyota Prius, it would have been impossible for another vehicle to pass.

As Lee walked toward la Puente Iguana, she scanned the buildings for any cameras. There weren't any. Had this been any neighborhood in D.C., the homeowners on the street would have every conceivable angle of the road covered.

She stared down the steps that led to the park below. Lee wanted to visualize how Corsair was involved with this Marino's murder. She pictured the assassin on the stairs. What was he doing here? Could the former agent be freelancing? Or was he working for the cartels now? It might explain how a member of Cincinnati's organized crime family ended up dropped off the bridge.

A car door slammed behind her, and she turned to see two men exiting a red and white Mitsubishi pickup truck with "*Policía Municipal*" written on the side. One of the pair wore a uniform of the local police force—Eduardo Castillo. The officer towered over the other, an obvious American. FBI was Lee's guess from the cheap suit and swaggering demeanor. He was under six feet tall and over 215 pounds. The suit carried a worn look, and the tie's knot angled to the left at forty-five degrees as if he'd tied it on the go without the benefit of a mirror.

"Second Sergeant Castillo?" she asked the uniformed one.

"Yes," the officer replied, and Lee tried not to smirk at the deep, accented voice that came from the firm, attractive policeman. "Agent Hubbard?"

Lee took a broad step forward, extending her hand and gripping his with vise-like pressure. "Thank you for meeting me," she acknowledged.

"Agent Hubbard, this is Agent Patterson with the FBI."

Lee cocked her head as she examined the man's face. He was in his forties with gray flecks of facial hair stubbing out. The tear trough under Patterson's eyes sagged a bit. Matched with his slightly wrinkled suit, Lee guessed he took the red-eye to Puerto Vallarta as well.

It intrigued her. From what she learned last night from Jacobson, the other fingerprints belonged to Victor Marino, some low-rent thug from Cincinnati. But perhaps he wasn't as far down the totem pole as the rap sheet implied if the Bureau was going to overnight an agent.

"Nice to meet you, Agent Hubbard. You can call me Tim."

She took his hand, offering less squeeze so she could judge the man's own grip. His grip was firm but not strong. Either he was noncommittal, or Tim was worried about stomping over Lee's femininity.

"What is your interest in Victor Marino?" she asked Patterson.

"We've connected him to several crimes in Cincinnati," the FBI agent replied.

"You think someone offed him while he was on vacation?" Lee questioned.

"Well, I doubt he did it to himself," he pointed out.

"True," Lee acknowledged with faux bashfulness. "But was the killer from Cincinnati?"

"I'd like to lend my eyes to Eduardo here," Patterson told her. "Since I am familiar with the players."

Lee nodded and turned to Castillo. "Where did it take place?"

Patterson interrupted, "Agent Hubbard, you didn't tell us why you are here though? I am surprised Marino crossed into Homeland Security's sight."

"Tim, a lot of things pass under Homeland's scrutiny," she said flatly.

"How does this?" he asked bluntly. The man's brow furrowed. Lee had seen the Bureau in action. They had a way of swooping into an investigation, and the local law enforcement swooned at their bureaucratic muscles. Most times, especially organized crime ones, the FBI was top dog. National security agencies such as Homeland only stepped in for things like terrorist cells. However, Agent Tim Patterson likely never even heard of the Office of Compliance. It was a given he hadn't. The OOC might as well not exist. Only a few in the upper echelons of Homeland were aware of the department and the connective tissues linking it to the CIA.

"Unfortunately, Tim," Lee replied, placing a soft emphasis on his first name, "that is classified. Probably above your pay grade. No offense."

"Right, no offense," he murmured. She could see that the man didn't take it that way at all.

"What are you looking for then?" he asked, adding, "At the scene, I mean."

"I'd like to see how it played out."

Patterson cocked an eyebrow curiously. "Played out?"

"Yeah," she answered. "Same as you, I'm sure. Was Marino attacked here? Could someone have followed him? How does a person throw another guy off a bridge with no one seeing? You know, those kinds of questions."

"Puente Iguana is not always busy," Second Sergeant Castillo suggested. "On a Saturday, there is usually traffic, though. Pedestrians heading down to the park. Walking their dogs."

Lee nodded. "But did you have any witnesses?"

He shook his head. "No, we think it was around midday," he said. "Less people are out then."

"Fewer," Lee remarked without thinking.

The officer didn't notice her grammatical correction, and Lee silently chided herself for the rude comment.

"Where was the body found?" she asked.

"Come," Castillo ordered, and he trotted down the steps. At about a quarter length of La Puente Iguana, he paused at the edge. The second sergeant peered over the concrete railing below. The crime scene below was still marked off, but through the foliage, it was impossible to see the cordoned-off area.

"That tree there," Castillo told the pair, pointing down at the top of an immense banyan tree reaching up from the bottom of the gorge. "The body was caught in the limbs."

Lee nodded as she studied the canopy. It was difficult to tell from here, but the branches stretched wide from the massive trunk.

"How close was it to the center?" she wondered.

"A few meters," he replied.

Lee jogged up three steps and craned her head over. From here, an object would hit near the middle of the leafy barrier. She stepped back and stared intently at the concrete under her feet.

"You think it was here?" Patterson asked her.

"Makes sense to me," she answered. "If he fell from over here, the body would go through the middle of the foliage. Or at least close to it. Had he fallen farther out, the smaller branches might break as his mass fell through them. He'd be more likely to hit the ground."

"He could have pinballed off the higher limbs," Patterson suggested.

"Did he have broken bones?" she asked.

"*Sí*...yes," Castillo answered.

"His back?"

"His neck broke, and several vertebrae cracked."

She nodded. "He probably dove headfirst," she considered.

"I thought so," Castillo confirmed. "His hands had scratches on them as if he had them out to shield himself."

"Fat lot of good that would do," Patterson quipped.

"Instinct," Lee advised. "If he was headfirst, he'd bounce off a few branches, but his descent should still be straight down."

Patterson and Castillo both stretched over the edge to stare down into the greenery of the banyan's canopy. Each offered an agreeing nod without saying a word. Lee ignored them as they continued calculating in their heads if her assessment was correct.

She stepped back and stared down at the ground. For an assassination, the location was shit. It didn't track with any of the documented kills by Corsair. The stairwell was too open. If they'd come from the park, then Corsair would have trailed him to the middle before attacking. Logically, that made no sense.

Not that Corsair wasn't one to improvise. His recent run through Florida evidenced that. If he intended it to look like an accident, the bridge might work. But for Corsair to leave a print implied he fucked up.

That's if he planned it, she thought. The partial print was on the barrel of the gun. As if Victor Marino had the weapon up, and Corsair deflected it. Perhaps the motion was so quick and deadly that the result was Marino and his gun tumbled out of Corsair's reach.

Lee paused, kneeling down to the ground. A sliver of glass sat in the shadow of the next step. Carefully, Lee used her fingernails to lift the thin piece up. The shape curved an inch up like a saber coming to a point.

"What is it?" Patterson asked, stepping closer to see.

"Glass."

"What is it from?" Castillo questioned.

Lee's face lifted. "Cellphone," she suggested. "I bet Marino dropped his phone. Did he have one on him?"

Castillo shook his head. Lee shifted her eyes to Patterson. "Tim, I'm guessing the FBI has a little more in-depth information on Marino than what pops up in the system."

"What are you thinking?"

"That whoever tossed your gangster off the bridge took the man's phone. He might still be holding onto it."

"Why would he do that?" Patterson asked.

Lee didn't answer. She would not say that Marino could have seen Corsair or, even better, took a picture of the former assassin. That was something that the man she was hunting wouldn't want out there. She knew that there were other parties in the world gunning for Caleb Saunders, including Mahmoud Abbas, an arms dealer whose son Corsair killed a decade ago. It wasn't something she'd considered before. What if Abbas's contract on Corsair stretched as far as the mafia? Corsair already had dealings with the cartels. No doubt those connections reached criminal organizations in the States.

All of it was tenuous. If Abbas found Corsair, it would be luck.

Like the man leaving a print at a murder scene?

Corsair's fortune might be running out altogether. It suddenly seemed vital that she tracked down the operative before some other assassin got to him. That was if she wanted to find out what dirt he had on Carl Winston.

"What about cameras?" Lee asked. "Are there any on the streets?"

Castillo shook his head. "The park has some, but most are on the businesses." His right index finger pointed toward the top of the bridge. "Some of the houses might have security cameras, but it's hard to be sure."

"Do you have the manpower to check?" she asked hopefully.

His head swayed as if to say, "Maybe."

"I would just like to verify. If anything caught sight of Marino, we can follow him backward," she suggested.

"Good idea," Patterson agreed. "I'm going to see if my office can pull Marino's credit card information. If we could find what hotel he's staying at, then we have a place to start."

Lee gave Patterson a grin. "Might discover he was rooming with the guy who killed him."

The agent's face wrinkled, and Lee almost chuckled at the man's sudden displeasure. The mere thought of two men in the same room unnerved the agent.

She added, "Or his killer could have come with him from Cincinnati."

"Right," he replied, trying to regain his composure. He took his phone out of his pocket and walked three steps away as he dialed a number.

"It's Patterson," he said into the speaker. "I'm here in Puerto Vallarta with the local investigator and an agent with Homeland Security. Is there any way we can get access to Marino's cell records? We think the man who killed him might have it with him."

A pause.

Patterson responded, "Yeah, get that for us and we can track it."

Another few seconds as he listened.

"Thanks, as soon as possible," the agent said into the phone before disconnecting. To Lee and Castillo, he remarked, "Ball's rolling."

With a wicked smile, Lee announced, "Let's find the bastard then."

20

He already started hating Mexico. Tourists crowded the streets. Smelly, sweaty tourists with kids screaming and shouting. Jimmy didn't care for any of it.

Even worse, Jackie and WT tagged along at his heels. Both got in this morning, and Jimmy was back up early to get them at the airport. Between the run last night for the guns and the rush to meet these guys, Jimmy only slept about two and a half hours.

Now Jackie was whining about not having eaten anything except one of those Biscoff cookies the airplane gives out. The olive-skinned behemoth seemed intent on finding a "decent taco."

"This isn't a fucking vacation," Jimmy warned him.

"I hear ya, Jimmy, I'm just hungry. We gotta eat."

Luckily, WT complained little. Hell, the man barely talked. But he was a go-getter, and WT was Sonny's cousin or something. That unnerved Jimmy. What if WT came along to watch what Jimmy did? Report back to Sonny if he fucked up?

They were all three standing on the cobblestone road. The internet called it the Malecón. Jimmy thought it was nothing more than a row of souvenir shops, mostly. A few restaurants mixed in the bunch—all catering to people on the cruise ships with big-screen televisions playing the game. Why fly or sail halfway around the world to watch a sport anyone could catch at the corner pub?

"There's another one," Jackie suggested, pointing at the sign ahead.

They'd been to three different jewelry stores since they started this morning. It was at Sonny's suggestion. Apparently, Khloe Evans worked for a couple of years at Kenwood Diamonds before disappearing. He thought she might try doing similar work. Once they found the location where Victor had taken the picture he sent Vinnie, it gave them a starting point. Luckily, Victor caught a business sign, making it easier to identity. Not that it mattered yet. So far, it had been a complete waste of time. No one recognized the girl in the image.

The Silver Unicorn Jewelry sat back under an awning. The sign didn't have a unicorn on it, which Jimmy thought was odd. Why bother naming it something stupid like that if they would not put a unicorn on the front?

The door tickled a bell over the top, and a chime that reminded Jimmy of his grandmother's doorbell sounded. The three men filed through the opening into the cool shop, lined with glass cases. There were three customers in the store. A retired couple in their sixties conversed with the storekeeper, a short, stout Mexican clerk with graying hair. The clerk glanced up at the sound of the bell to see the three men. His eyes narrowed slightly before turning back to the man and his wife. The third customer was a younger woman with dark brown hair. Jimmy paused to study her longer, determining it wasn't Khloe.

How easy would that have been?

This woman carried a blue and red tote bag with the Carnival Cruise Line's logo on it. She twisted around and saw the three men. She inhaled quickly and turned back to push past them. The door's bell jangled as she exited.

Jimmy walked around the store. WT and Jackie spread out and meandered around as if they were looking at the wares. Jimmy wanted to wait until the older couple left. He wasn't sure how things worked in Mexico, and if he and his guys caused a scene, it might cause him trouble. There was no point in doing that unless they had the girl.

The Mexican clerk continued to lift his eyes up and follow the men around the room. He fidgeted with a bracelet he was showing the lady. Jimmy realized they didn't resemble the average jewelry customer. A single man might be searching for a gift for his girl. A guy and a girl could shop together. Three men, though, might set off mental alarms.

Jimmy scanned the room. There were at least six cameras he could see. While he wasn't sure how it worked in Mexico, the models he saw were all the type one bought privately, meaning the feeds were likely on property. Perhaps the video feeds uploaded to a cloud, but Jimmy bet they didn't connect to a security company somewhere off premises.

This would make a great smash and grab, he thought, staring at the baubles behind the glass. He was not an expert on jewelry, but he could spot the cheap from the expensive stuff. One thing Jimmy understood was what he could easily sell off. It wouldn't be hard to board a plane and carry most of this back to the States. Risky because he'd have to go through customs. But once he was home, what the hell could the Mexican authorities do to him?

But you gotta make it back first, he reminded himself. No, there were smarter ways to make money.

A door behind the Mexican opened, and a woman stepped through. Her black eyes swept across the room to the three men. She watched WT and Jackie near a case of watches before shifting her stare to Jimmy on the opposite side of the store. The other two men glanced at Jimmy, and the little woman strode along the counter to him.

"How are you?" she asked with a sharp edge on each enunciated syllable.

"Hiya," Jimmy greeted the woman, trying to appear cordial. "I'm looking for a friend of mine. She might work here, but I lost her number."

The Mexican lady stared at him.

Jimmy removed a picture of Khloe and Dominic. His index finger touched the female face. She turned her face up to stare at Jimmy.

"Why you want to find her?"

Jimmy smiled. "Me and my buddies were just on the cruise, and she used to live down the street from me in Cincinnati."

"I don't know her," she told him.

The man locked eyes with her. "I think you might," he suggested. "Take another look there."

She didn't shift her gaze. "No, I don't."

Jimmy raised up, turning to WT and Jackie. "Clear the place," he ordered them.

Both men moved to the couple talking to the man. Within seconds, they shooed them out of the store.

"What is the meaning of this?" the man behind the counter demanded.

Jimmy lifted the picture of Khloe and Dominic toward him. "Is this your wife?"

He nodded.

"Well, I asked her about this girl," Jimmy explained, letting his index finger tap at the photo under Khloe's face. "She said you knew her."

The man jerked his gaze toward his wife. "*¡Mentiroso!*" she shouted.

Jimmy reached across the counter and grabbed the older woman by the back of her neck as he pulled a Beretta from his pocket. "What did you call me?"

"I said you were a liar!" she blurted out defiantly.

"You got spunk, lady," Jimmy remarked. He turned to the woman's husband. "Who is the girl?"

Fear filled the eyes of the owner. "Her name is Khloe."

Jimmy grinned. "Yeah, we got that."

His neck rotated around to the woman. "Who is the liar?"

She snarled at him, and Jimmy released her nape and slapped her with the back of his hand. The gunman jumped over the counter and picked the woman up off the ground, ramming the barrel of the Beretta under her chin.

"Where is Khloe?" he demanded in a bitter voice.

"She doesn't work here anymore," her husband cried. "She quit."

"What is your name?" Jimmy asked her.

"Please!" the man begged.

The woman in his grip sneered at him, ignoring the question.

"She's a feisty bitch," Jimmy called to WT and Jackie.

"They make them mean down here," WT remarked, stepping toward the man. He had removed his own Beretta out and slammed the butt into the top of a glass case of watches. The shattering of the cabinet echoed through the empty store, and WT started pulling watches out.

"Ooh, a Rolex," he cried. "Want one, boss?"

"Wait!" the clerk shouted.

"We are waiting, jefe," Jackie told the man. "Waiting on you to get us Khloe's address."

The man gave a quick nod.

"Alejandro!" the woman snapped, and Jimmy snatched her by the hair, jerking her closer. The muzzle of his pistol pressed against her temple.

"Alejandro, I'd hurry," he advised.

"I don't know her address," he drawled. "But she lives over in *5 de Diciembre*."

"Why don't you have it?" WT asked, leaning across the counter to him.

"*¡Tonto estúpido!*" the woman hissed. "This isn't America."

Jimmy smirked at her. "You are quite spicy," he chuckled. "Go ahead, Alejandro. Where does she live?"

"I took her home sometimes. She lives in an apartment on *Calle Venezuela*. It's in the middle of the street. A three-story white building."

"Which unit is she in?" WT asked.

"One of the top ones, I'm not sure exactly."

Jimmy smiled. "See, that was easy, wasn't it?"

With a shove, he threw the woman to the floor and leveled the Beretta with her face.

"Jackie, WT, go there now. Find this bitch."

"What about us?" Alejandro asked.

"If it turns out you lied to us, we'll be back. If you try to call Khloe, we'll be back. If we even think you called the police, we'll be back." Jimmy's mouth widened into a broad smile. "When we return, there will be no niceties."

The American turned and aimed the Beretta at Alejandro. The Mexican jeweler trembled, and Jimmy walked toward the door. By the time the bell rang, the pistol disappeared into his pocket. Jimmy heard the click of the lock behind him as one of them ran to secure the store from the three men. The Silver Unicorn would likely be closed for the rest of the day.

21

Khloe almost seemed to ricochet around the small flat. Caleb sat on the ratty sofa, watching the girl move from one section of the room to another. Anything that resembled paper, she examined, crumpled, and deposited in a trash can. The former OOC agent considered he might have sent her spiraling when he suggested she make sure there was nothing to link her to the apartment. But it was second nature to him to remain free of those things. Caleb removed every bit of refuse from his place each day. Even receipts from the Kiosko where he paid cash found themselves shredded and flushed. The only thing he'd take out to the communal garbage was the cardboard toilet paper rolls and empty dish soap containers. If something contained writing of any kind, it was burned or ripped to pieces before finding its way into Puerto Vallarta's sewer system. Larger items or even foodstuff took more time, but he bagged and discarded those things in a street can somewhere as he walked through the Romantic Zone. It was unlikely anyone would track him from a used egg carton, but Caleb liked the old habits. Besides, it kept rotting food out of the trash, which he hoped prevented rats.

Now, Khloe rooted under the bed. How the girl had settled into the apartment in what Caleb guessed was such a short time period, he'd never understand.

"I don't think you have to worry about food containers," he pointed out as she pulled several McDonald's wrappers from the table.

"You said they could track me by what I ate," she retorted.

"Yes, but McDonald's isn't going to lead them anywhere."

"There's only one around here," she reminded him.

"Then don't go there," he advised.

"What else do I need?" she asked.

"Not much," he answered. "You'll want to travel light."

She stared at a blue Nike duffel stuffed with a couple of changes of clothes. "I guess this will do," she replied. Khloe handed Caleb the bag of refuse she'd accumulated. "Can you run this trash out? There's a can on the street."

"Fine, but we need to get moving," Caleb told her, pulling the bag out of her hand.

He headed back to the entry leading to the stairwell. As he opened the door, a voice sounded from below.

"He said third floor. Where's the damned elevator?"

"You lazy fuck, just get up the stairs."

Caleb stepped back over the threshold and closed the door softly. He latched the deadbolt and locked the knob as he dropped the bag of refuse on the floor. When he turned to find something to block the door, Khloe stared at him.

"We have trouble," he stated, grabbing a chair and propping it under the knob.

"What?"

"Just get out on the balcony. Quick!" he ordered.

Caleb backed away from the entry and studied the door's construction. It was a hollow-core model which offered a little more protection than a curtain. One well-placed kick would splinter the wood around the knob and swing it wide. Hopefully, these guys wouldn't jump straight to that.

Khloe squeezed out the raised window onto a small balcony. Or, at least, it's what passed as one. The concrete railing surrounded a two-and-a-half-foot square platform that only comfortably fit Khloe. When Caleb climbed through the opening, he pushed her against the balustrade.

"You need to get to the next window," Caleb ordered.

"Are you kidding?" she snapped.

"There are a couple of guys coming up the steps as we speak. If you would rather receive them at the front door, we can head back inside."

"Shit!" she blurted out. "I don't know if I can do it."

The gap between the railings was about three feet. Caleb pointed toward the next one. "It's a small hop, Khloe," he suggested. "I'm right here with you."

The girl looped the strap of the Nike bag over her neck, letting it hang off her shoulder before climbing on top of the rail. Caleb put his hand on the small of her back, steadying her. Behind him, a knocking on the door called out a warning.

"Go!" he urged in a hushed tone.

She hesitated for a second. A loud banging came from inside, and she glanced behind her at the open window. Her eyes widened at the sound, and she turned and leaped forward. Her feet stumbled over the next railing, and Caleb sucked in a breath, afraid she might tumble headfirst off the terrace. Instead, she hit the concrete platform on one knee.

Caleb jumped up on the balustrade and took an enormous step, pushing off the top of the balcony rail with his left foot. His right touched the narrow concrete barrier, and he caught his balance on top of it by grabbing a ceramic drainpipe running down the building.

There was a small ledge that extended from the balcony around to the corner of Khloe's apartment building. From the lip, they could drop about a story to the roof of the neighboring structure.

"Follow me," he ordered, slipping past the girl and climbing out on to the shelf. His feet filled the lip, and his toes jutted over the edge an inch. "Keep your back to the wall," he explained, demonstrating it by pressing against the stucco surface and sliding his feet along the rim.

Khloe looked at her window again before following Caleb off the safety of the balcony.

"I don't know about this," she groaned.

Caleb stretched his right arm back and took her hand. "Just stay with me," he told her as he crept along the shelf.

No sounds came from the apartment, but he guessed the men at the door wouldn't wait much longer before bursting into Khloe's home.

When he reached the corner, Caleb looked back at Khloe. "I'm going to let go of you for a second so I can make the turn. I'll help you around after that, okay?"

She nodded, more than a little nervous. Caleb released his grip on her fingers, and carefully, he sidled his left foot around the corner. It didn't matter that the ledge was the same width, even at that spot. The way he had to flex his body made it feel like his narrow path was shrinking more. His left hand touched the ninety-degree angle, and the man inhaled sharply as he swung his right leg out and around in one swift motion.

With a breath of relief, he faced the building now. It was a little discomforting. People want to move away from danger. Humans carry that instinct inside them, and if that drive kicked in now, he might step back off the ledge. However, he knew he could help Khloe around the corner easier if he was facing her direction.

"Take my hand again," he said, sticking his left hand past the side of the building for her.

He couldn't see her, but when her fingers slid into his palm, he tightened the grip.

"Just inch around," he explained. "I have you."

Their hands moved toward him, and he scooted along the edge as she made it to the corner. "Just follow it around. You're almost there," he promised.

A few seconds later, the girl made it to the side of the building. Her heavy breathing sounded like she was fighting panic. For the moment, Caleb thought they were at least hidden from the men coming into her apartment.

"What do we do now?" she asked, after catching her breath.

Caleb's head motioned behind them at the next roofline below them.

"Seriously?" she questioned. "It's not even flat."

Over his shoulder, he examined the gabled roof below. Traditional clay shingles covered the top of the building, which pitched at about a thirty-five-degree angle. It wasn't ideal, but they would drop far enough up the roof to give them about fifteen feet to slide before they would slip off the edge and plummet two stories to the ground.

"We don't have a lot of choice," he explained.

"Can't we just wait until they leave?" Khloe asked.

"We can't stay here long before we attract attention. Probably not even long enough for whoever is in your place to leave. They'd just walk out on the street to a crowd gawking at us."

"Damn," Khloe muttered.

"I'll go first," he assured her. "When you jump, I can catch you."

"Who's going to catch you?"

Caleb shrugged. "I'm relying on luck and good fortune."

"How does that normally work out for you?" she asked.

He didn't tell her that for the most part it, combined with the trained skills he'd acquired, kept him alive for at least ten years longer than he probably should be. Instead, he took another glance over his shoulder and stepped back into nothing.

He landed in a crouch, absorbing the drop in his knees. A shingle under his left foot shifted out from the others and skittered down the slope until it vanished off the side. The tinkle of breaking ceramic echoed up from the sidewalk.

Caleb tested his footing and judged it secure before turning his head up to Khloe. He extended his hands up to her, and she silently shook her head. He couldn't blame her. No sane person would willingly jump off a building into a stranger's arms.

"C'mon," he whispered.

She leaned forward before pulling back against the wall. Her cheeks brightened as her mouth clenched.

A voice reverberated off the buildings across the street. Caleb couldn't make out what it said, but the words sounded like English. American English. If he were getting specific, they probably had a very guttural dialect.

Whatever the regional accent was, it spurred Khloe, who seemed to understand the voices clearer from her perch. Caleb watched the girl jump out from the building rather than drop. She came down almost on top of him, and he twisted around, pivoting on his left foot as his hands tried to catch the girl.

Mostly they slowed her descent, but not enough. Her feet hit in front of Caleb, and three rows of barrel shingles displaced, sliding toward the street. Khloe's feet whipped out from underneath her as they rode the loose ceramic tiles down the incline. Caleb extended a hand to grab her as her body slammed down on the roof. The impact loosened an entire swath of shingles, and the girl slid along the slope out of his grasp. The Nike bag dragged after her.

Caleb dove forward. His hand caught the canvas duffel as he hit the surface in his own tumble toward the drop. Both of them, riding loose tiles, raced toward the end of the slope.

Khloe let out a scream as she slipped off the roof. Caleb grabbed a gutter spout with his left forearm. The right hand, still gripping the gym bag, caught the weight of it and Khloe, who hung on the Nike bag's shoulder strap. Both girl and duffel swung back toward the building like a pendulum. Khloe struck the wall and slipped out of the band.

Caleb chanced a glimpse to see the girl fall face first onto a terrace below. He pushed off the concrete side and leapt to the balcony below. He landed in a roll that carried him away from her.

Khloe groaned behind him, and Caleb bounced to his feet. "You okay?" he asked, giving her a quick examination. Scratches covered her legs and arms, but the rapid darkening of her face indicated she took the bulk of the fall on her right cheek.

"We need to move, Khloe," he told her.

"I need a second," she retorted through a swelling lip.

He was about to point out they didn't have a second when the gunshot reverberated between the buildings.

"Get down!" Caleb shouted.

22

Khloe let out a piercing scream as Caleb shoved her against the sliding glass door leading into the apartment. Caleb craned his neck to see a man on Khloe's balcony aiming a handgun toward them. The gun bucked with a shot, and Caleb pulled back. The bullet shook the metal railing on the balcony as it glanced off the wrought iron.

A searing ferrous chunk burned his cheek—shrapnel from the round's impact with the iron. More gunfire peppered the railing, and Caleb buried his face over Khloe, shielding her from any flying debris. From where the men were shooting on Khloe's balcony, they couldn't get a clear shot, but they would prevent them from sticking their head out to get a clearer view. It also limited Caleb's initial thought of dropping from the terrace to the ground. It was only one flight, and the quicker they reached the street, the better of an advantage the two would have on their attackers.

"Inside," Caleb demanded, pulling Khloe to her feet. The girl grabbed the handle, jerking it to the side. With a swoosh, the sliding glass door opened, and Caleb shoved the girl through the gap. He followed her inside to see a young mother staring at them. Two toddlers, a boy and a girl, gazed up at the intruders.

"*Lo siento,*" Caleb apologized to the family. The mother leapt to her feet, corralling the two children behind her. She shouted something at them in Spanish.

"*¡Fuera!*" she screamed at Caleb. Then to the children, "*¡Niños, pónganse detrás de mí!*"

The toddlers obeyed, cowering behind their mother's dress. The boy, though, slid his eyes around the fabric to see Caleb.

"*Lo siento, Señora. Estamos en peligro. Hay hombres malos disparándonos.*"

"*¡Fuera!*"

"Door, Khloe." He urged the young woman to the exit as the mother lifted a green-colored bottle of cooking oil like a baseball bat. Emboldened by her weapon and in full mama-bear mode, the young woman lunged at Caleb, who stepped out of the path of the swinging bottle.

"Go!" he shouted at Khloe, who dashed for the front door of the small apartment. She stumbled over a secondhand dollhouse the kids had been playing with on the floor. The pieces scattered across the floor. Khloe grabbed the handle and jerked open the door.

Caleb raced behind her, and before he reached the second step, the door behind him slammed with such force that the gust of wind rushed at his back. Khloe shoved through the security entrance leading to the sidewalk.

The sunlight blinded Caleb for a split second as he came out of the interior into the daylight.

"Where do we go?" Khloe cried as she stepped out onto the ridged and cobblestoned street.

"That way!" Caleb exclaimed, pointing east up the hill, away from Khloe's building. The two charged up the incline along *Calle Venezuela*. Steps raised the sidewalk as they passed each building. Caleb took the first small flight of steps two at a time, trying to urge Khloe to move faster. She tripped on a jagged piece of concrete, and Caleb extended his hand to catch and steady her.

Luckily, the street seemed almost empty, giving them plenty of room to run. Only one elderly woman with gray hair pushed a wire cart filled with potted plants downhill on the other side of the road. When they passed her, Caleb turned to see two men dash out of Khloe's apartment building onto Calle Venezuela. Both men doubled over for a second, catching their breath, before they peered up and down *Calle Venezuela*. A third followed out the door, joining the other. One pointed his finger up the slope at the fleeing pair, and Caleb wasted no time in continuing after Khloe.

"Wall!" Khloe shouted, and Caleb turned to see the pavement end at a four-foot wall. At the top of the wall was a railing where someone added a small portico to their home, blocking the road completely.

"Cross the street!" he ordered, and the two dashed across the empty road. Caleb expected to hear more gunshots as they ran through the open area. He let out a little "thank you" as the streets were silent. Behind them, the starter of a car turned over for a split second before the whine of an engine sounded.

We should have gone the other way.

The direction they were running grew less populated, and Caleb cursed himself for not heading back toward the heavier trafficked areas. It would have been easier to get lost in a crowd. Now, they had to rely on outrunning the trio of killers.

"Right!" Caleb shouted to Khloe, who was about fifteen paces ahead. Without responding, she turned on *Calle Bolivia*. Caleb crossed the road behind her as the shouts from the men downhill chased after him. Private homes lined the street, and there were no pedestrians out. It was Sunday, and most businesses in *5 de Diciembre* were closed. The residents were off enjoying the afternoon.

"Pick up the pace," Caleb prodded at Khloe, whose run had slowed to a jog.

"Where do we go?" she asked as they reached the end of the street.

"Damn!" Caleb cursed, staring at the narrowing road that turned into a driveway, dead-ending at a garage. The sidewalk on the east edge of the street turned into a stone staircase that crested the hill and presumably fed out on the other side of the driveway. Caleb scanned his memory to recall if he'd ever been this way. He didn't remember.

Tires squealed behind them as a Nissan Versa turned onto *Calle Bolivia* in a haste.

"They're here!" Khloe screamed.

"Stairs," Caleb said, hoping they'd lead them somewhere.

The pair ran up the stone steps as the Versa slammed on its brakes.

At least the car can't get up here, Caleb thought as he reached the top of the stairs.

"Get them!" someone behind the two shouted.

When he came off the steps, Caleb stared down the road ahead of him. The narrow road stretched about a quarter of a mile to the next intersection. A small Toyota Tacoma from the early 2000s sat on the top of the hill. On the right side of the street, a garage door stood open where a 1960s model Volkswagen Beetle sat lifted at the front onto jack stands. Precariously dangling, a motor hung over the opened trunk from a makeshift engine hoist constructed from two I-beams welded together. The top beam was bolted into the concrete ceiling for stability, and a thick chain and block held the weight of the Volkswagen's engine aloft. The chain ran back along the ceiling of the garage to a series of anchored into the concrete wall. Two separate hooks secured two links about a foot apart—a jury-rigged safety catch to secure the chain on the pulley.

Footsteps clambered up the steps, and Caleb spun around with nowhere to run.

"In here," he snapped at Khloe. He grabbed her arm, pulling her into the opened garage.

23

Jimmy wheezed as he led WT and Jackie up the steps. His lungs burned, and he hadn't run all the way up the hill like the girl and whoever this guy was.

I gotta stop smoking, Jimmy scolded himself as he pulled out the Beretta.

He'd never seen such a fucked-up road. All the streets were like a mash-up of patches. Cement and stones covered part of the road. Then strips of concrete filled in a stretch. Now, he found a wall in the middle of the street with stairs to the top. How the hell did anyone get around in this town?

Jackie gasped behind them as they reached the summit. The pair they were chasing were gone. Jimmy paused, catching his breath as he searched for his quarry.

The street rolled downhill for a long distance before it leveled off in a valley. No one was on the road, though.

"No way they got that far," WT remarked. He sounded like the least winded of the three.

Jackie just shook his head and bent over at the waist again. He sucked in as much oxygen as he could. The air was too hot and sticky, though. Sweat poured off his forehead, and he used the back of his hand to wipe away the droplets before they flooded his eyes.

"Where the hell are they?" Jackie muttered between breaths.

Jimmy stared at the open overhead garage door a hundred feet down the road. He pointed at WT, directing him to the old Toyota truck. "Check it," he ordered as he moved toward the garage.

WT had his own Beretta out but down next to his leg. Carrying a piece in another country made him nervous. It was one thing back home. Cops are a little more hesitant to shoot someone holding a gun, but this was a different world. He saw the police at the airport. Decked out like they were ready to invade Grenada, the guys carried heavy firepower that made his Beretta feel like a popgun.

He circled the truck. It was unlocked, but empty. Jimmy glanced his way, and WT gave him a nod, indicating it was all clear. Jimmy pointed at the garage.

"Watch the street," he warned, in case the two wanted to make a run.

"Jimmy, what if they're armed?" Jackie suggested.

"They'd've shot back, don't ya think?" Jimmy responded. "It's just a fucking girl and her boyfriend."

Corsair squatted on his haunches behind the old Volkswagen Bug. He gripped an ancient monkey wrench. The numbers, etched into the metal when it was manufactured many decades earlier, were illegible after years of use. Corsair's hand wrapped around the handle of the almost nine-inch tool. A thin layer of oil covered the metal, and he tightened his grasp on it.

From where he crouched, he could see a piece of Khloe's shirt sticking out of the steel toolbox sitting under the crude worktable. Calling it a toolbox was a stretch. The cabinet reminded Caleb of an old military locker, only this one appeared to be homemade. Bulbous welds coursed along each corner, and the repurposed hinges were the thick heavy-duty kind used on thicker steel security doors. She'd just dropped into the box before the men outside started talking.

Without being able to see the three men from where he sheltered, the former agent hoped the guys after Khloe had the right level of confidence with caution. He heard one remark they thought he and Khloe were unarmed. The garage offered hiding places, but it was also glaringly obvious. They would suspect it was a feint, designed to lead them into the garage while the pair made an escape. If they showed enough savvy, at least one would stay on the street watching for them.

The shuffle of feet on the rough concrete floor drew closer. Corsair smiled. It was only a single set of footsteps. He could take down one target with ease, and the other two would hold their fire—at least for a few seconds—while their compatriot was in the combat zone.

The scrape of shoe soles came around the driver's side of the Beetle. Carefully, Corsair shifted the angle of his feet. His lungs dragged a long, slow breath in. He felt the beats of his heart increase in anticipation. The oxygen in his chest immediately grabbed hold of the hemoglobin coursing through the capillaries. A second deep breath added more as he sensed the figure loom closer.

Like a rocket, he launched up from his haunches. His right hand whipped around with the open end of the wrench swinging like a mace. Metal collided with flesh and bone, and the Beretta in the man's hand jerked away as it fired. Glass exploded as the twenty-two-caliber bullet skipped off the windshield of the Volkswagen. Corsair twisted back, bringing the flat side of the tool across the man's jaw. The wiseguy's head snapped around, and Corsair drove his left fist into the man's face.

"Shit!" someone outside shouted. "Jimmy!"

"Jackie, don't!" another called.

Corsair didn't have time to focus on them. Jimmy still held the Beretta, and if the former OOC agent faltered, gun usually beat wrench.

Jimmy stumbled back, clearly dazed from the one-two strike of tool, then fist. Corsair brought the improvised weapon back around. His aim lifted, and the antique tool slammed into Jimmy's temple. The man's legs failed him, and before he hit the floor, his body was limp.

Metal clanged against concrete as the wrench dropped from Corsair's grip. He swooped down, scooping up the Beretta 92. He came up with the barrel out, firing at the two men framed in the doorway. The first round went wilder than Corsair intended. The glare of the sun beaming into the dark garage caused his eyes to take half a second longer to focus than he realized. Both men separated, and as they took cover, their guns opened fire on Corsair.

He dropped in front of the Beetle as bullets tore through the garage. The sounds of glass breaking and metal pinging echoed through the garage. Shards of what had been the vintage Bug's windows rained down on Corsair.

He hadn't counted the shots, but each Beretta held at least fifteen rounds. When the gunfire ceased, he heard the clicks of release as both men dropped the magazines from the emptied guns. Corsair popped up, firing four bullets in a sweep across the door. He had hit nothing, but for the moment, he wanted to keep the two men from charging into the garage.

As he ducked back down, another barrage of bullets slammed into the cinderblock walls and shelves of tools. Metal and dust shrapnel spewed around the room.

How many more magazines did they have?

Corsair glanced at the figure of Jimmy, sprawled on the floor. He likely had more ammo if the two outside did. But to get to him, Corsair would be in the open. He still had about seven rounds before the Beretta ran dry.

The gunfire stopped again.

"Brother, give it up!" one of them called. "You can't get out of there."

"Well, you can't get in either," he shouted back.

"We've got you outnumbered," the voice responded. He sounded older than Caleb, and if the two outside were comparable to Jimmy, they'd be in their late forties. It was the one who shouted for Jackie to stop.

"You do," Corsair acknowledged, twisting his head to shout over the Beetle. He strained his ears to listen for both where the man was speaking from and if either were trying to approach. "Why don't you just come on in?"

The other one laughed sardonically. "Yeah, why don't we all die? Did you kill our buddy?"

"You mean Jimmy?"

There was a murmur of an exchange, but Corsair couldn't make it out. Likely an admonishment about protocols like using real names in the field. Although these guys didn't think like actual soldiers. He had to distinguish that they were soldiers of a sort. In retrospect, while they lacked training, they displayed skills learned and developed in some sort of real-life scenario. They split up almost instinctively, and they were keeping him pinned down.

I shouldn't have missed the first shot. It was a stupid mistake, and Caleb realized the last ten years might have left him rustier than he initially thought.

"He's still breathing," Caleb called out.

Another blur of words. Then, "We just want the girl. You can get out of this alive."

Corsair studied the man on the ground. He'd be out of commission for a bit. Even when he woke up, Jimmy couldn't put up much fight.

If he woke up. The blow to the guy's head was strong, and a wrench made a perfect blunt-force weapon.

Jimmy's long-term condition mattered little to Corsair. Right now, he needed to extricate himself and Khloe from the garage. Without getting shot.

How long could they continue shooting up some random stranger's garage before the police were called? Corsair knew he could wait them out until the cops arrived, but he'd be entangled with the police at that point. That wasn't an option.

He needed out now. Caleb reached over and grabbed the wrench off the floor. He tossed it at the toolbox where Khloe was hiding.

"Khloe!" he rasped in a hushed voice.

The lid lifted, and the girl peered out. Her eyes were red, and Caleb guessed she'd been crying in the box as the gunfire filled the small room.

"I'm going to try to get us out of here," he explained to her.

"How?" she mouthed without speaking.

"I don't know yet," he told her. "Just be ready to move when I tell you to."

She nodded.

One man outside shouted, "You're out of options, man."

Corsair lifted his head over the hood of the VW. Both men were on either side of the open door. Neither stuck more than an eye around the corner.

They're low on ammo.

Not that it helped much. So was he. If either popped out much more, he could get a clean shot. But he'd expose himself just as much while he took aim.

Corsair scanned his surroundings. He almost smiled. An old metal gas can sat on the workbench. A freshly made round hole dribbled fuel out the side. He rose fast, firing two shots to either side of the door, pushing both men back for cover. He took two steps, grabbed the can, and returned for his cover.

"Khloe, be ready to get in the car!" he ordered. "On my mark."

The girl gave him a nod. Corsair released the magazine. Without unloading it, he counted the shells he could see before slamming it back into place. It looked like three plus one in the chamber. Hopefully, enough.

"Now!" he hollered at Khloe as he turned and rolled the round gas can out the door like a bowling ball. The container wobbled as it traveled past the car, flinging gasoline out of the bullet hole. He fumbled in his pocket, producing the matches he'd lifted earlier at Coco's Kitchen. Without tearing one of the cardboard sticks out, he folded several down over the back and as he snapped his fingers against them, six or seven scraped across the strike strip, igniting the flammable tips.

Khloe scrambled out of the box and started toward the passenger's door as Corsair dropped the ball of flame on into the small puddle of fuel.

Whoomph. A line of fire chased after the rolling gas can. It seemed like a delay before the tongues of flames caught up to the container.

It wasn't like in the movies where a little gas causes an enormous explosion. Instead, the fuel in the can ignited, and the pressure blew the top off. Liquid flames spewed out, and both shooters took cover.

Khloe slid into the passenger seat, as Corsair, halfway into the driver's door, leveled his Beretta at the two hooks on the wall. The first round glanced off the hook.

"Shit!" he cursed. He didn't have enough bullets if this didn't work.

The second twenty-two-caliber bullet obliterated the cheap metal hook. The weight of the motor plummeted as he tried to shoot the next hook. But the sudden drop of nearly three hundred pounds snapped the curved end. He dropped into the seat as the chair zipped through the pulley like a whip.

The front of the car lurched up as the Beetle's engine dropped down in the empty space. Corsair's hand checked the gear shift, finding it in neutral. When the front end crashed down, the hood jerked open, swinging up into the busted windshield and spewing more tempered glass onto the passengers. When the car slammed down, the jack stands previously holding it up fell back as the car lifted, so when the tires hit the ground, momentum sent the Bug rolling back.

The house attached to the garage sat at the top of the hill. With an assist from gravity, the car rolled quickly into the street where flames spread out across the cobblestones. Corsair fired out his window, hitting the man on his side as he spun the wheel hard. He caught sight of the figure jerking back against the wall as the round hit him in the chest.

The other gunman started firing as the Beetle bounced downhill, picking up speed. Bullets pinged off the rounded hood as it flopped up and down.

Khloe screamed.

"Stay down!" Corsair demanded. The metal on the Volkswagen was thick enough to stop a twenty-two-caliber, but it only took one slipping past to hit them. He stuck the Beretta out the driver's window. Firing blindly up the hill, he steered the car as it raced down the street.

The road behind them stretched a long two blocks as it sloped steeply toward the valley. Caleb jerked his arm back in as the left side of the Bug ricocheted off an old Mazda truck.

The speedometer wasn't registering how fast they were going, but Corsair guessed it was close to forty-five or fifty miles per hour. As the car passed the first intersection, he tapped the brakes to slow their descent. His foot pressed to the floor with no effect. Again, he shoved the pedal down, but the Volkswagen didn't react. Instead, it picked up speed.

"Slow it down!" Khloe shouted.

Caleb turned his head to watch out the back window as he told her, "No brakes."

24

Her feet were getting tired, but Lee wasn't about to complain. In fact, she could tell Patterson was wearing out faster than she was. Some innate pride drove her to push harder than he did. There was something about his demeanor that irked her. Of course, she was more than aware Carl Winston and a few others soured her perception of men in government bureaucracies.

Eduardo Castillo, on the other hand, gave her an entirely different perspective. Besides the rugged handsomeness he exuded, the second sergeant moved like the Energizer Bunny. The Jalisco State police officer carried a professionalism she didn't see in her agency. The man remained dedicated to his task. Perhaps, she considered, he wanted to springboard off a successful investigation, but his willingness to work with the pair of Americans suggested to her he was just a good cop.

After leaving the gulch, the trio worked their way through the park at the bottom of the steps of Puente Iguana. Following the trail amongst the trees, they visited several shops searching for security cameras that might have caught the victim and, hopefully for Lee, Corsair. This was the fourth shop with surveillance. The three crowded around the young woman who was selling dresses in the little stand. She had an iPad where the footage replayed.

As they studied the screen, a man in a blue cap walked past. Castillo made a note of the timestamp on the image. They watched for a few more minutes, and no sign of Corsair or anyone else who could be Marino's murderer appeared.

"He might have been waiting for Marino," Patterson suggested.

Lee considered that. It was possible. Corsair didn't use any particular MO when he carried out missions. He'd as likely pick off a target with a sniper rifle from two hundred yards as walk up behind him with a knife.

"Let's rewatch that," Lee recommended. "I'd like to see the few minutes before Marino passes."

Castillo translated the request to the girl, who dragged her finger along the line at the bottom of the screen. The video jumped back, showing several people moving slowly past the camera.

"Wait!" Lee announced. "There."

The shopgirl paused the video without Castillo translating. The frozen image was of a woman in her twenties.

"Shit!" Patterson mumbled.

"Do you know her?" Castillo asked the FBI agent.

"I think so," he said. "It's hard to be certain, but she looks like a witness named Khloe Evans. Her boyfriend was a low-level goon for Sonny Departi, but he got himself murdered several months back. The girl went missing."

"Did she kill him?" Lee wondered.

Patterson shook his head. "No, I'm pretty certain Vinnie, Sonny's right-hand man, did that, but she disappeared the same day. Some speculated she was in a shallow grave somewhere."

"Looks like she's alive," Lee pointed out. "But I'm guessing you already assumed that. What do we know about her?"

"The Bureau suspects she witnessed Dominic Tratora's murder."

Lee straightened up. "That would explain why his guy was down here then," she suggested.

"I've been looking for her too," Patterson admitted. "If it hadn't been so obvious she'd packed a bag and run, I might suspect Vinnie killed her, too."

Lee Hubbard folded her arms. "The Bureau didn't know she was here?"

He shook his head. "No, we have a flag on her passport, but nothing registered when she crossed the border."

"It is much easier to cross into Mexico than the United States," Castillo pointed out.

Lee snickered. "Tell that to half the politicians in Washington."

Castillo grinned. "The brown devils can walk through concrete walls."

"That's what some would make us believe," she agreed. "Plus, you're only going to steal our children, take our jobs, and burn our crops."

Castillo gave out a belly laugh. "Look around this city," he suggested. "*Gringos* almost line up to come down and live here."

Lee shrugged. "Honestly, most of the people screaming about it don't even buy it. But Washington needs to make everyone afraid of something."

Castillo bowed his head. "It's not much better here. We let criminals run rampant, and most of our politicians don't know how to stop them. The cartels employ your neighbors and family members. How can the police turn on them?"

Patterson nodded. "Same thing up north with the organized crime families. Sonny Departi is one small section of the country. Even the city, but the cops don't touch him because they all go to the same church."

"We need to find this girl," Lee interjected.

Castillo stood up and stared out from the stand of dresses. The camera aimed northwest.

"She would have come from that direction. There are at least four paths she could take to get into the park. It's too centralized."

"She looked dressed for work," Lee pointed out.

Castillo nodded. "Not something outside, either. Her hair wouldn't have been so neat if she was out in the wind and sun all morning."

"Probably a shop?" Patterson wondered aloud.

"I'm betting that doesn't narrow it down at all for us," Lee commented. She turned to the second sergeant. "Can you see if there's an address for this—what was her name?"

Patterson replied, "Khloe Evans."

Castillo nodded. "Let me make a phone call."

The Mexican officer stepped away from the pair of American agents as he pulled his cell out.

"Who are you after?" Patterson questioned. "Not someone in Departi's crowd."

"I can't say," she said again.

"Homeland Security, though?" he asked.

Instead of answering, she just turned to stare at him.

"A terrorist?" Patterson mused. "Connected to Sonny Departi? That doesn't make a lot of sense. I wouldn't have put Sonny in with those people."

"I really can't say. It is all classified."

Patterson's eyebrow furrowed. "The other print," he stated flatly. "The partial we couldn't identify. Somehow you did, and that got you on a plane."

Lee didn't respond.

"Homeland's intent has always been a bit more vague than the other agencies. That was one of the smart moves George W. did post-9/11. You guys don't get your hands tied nearly as much as the rest of us."

Again, Lee said nothing. There was little point in arguing the merits of things like the Patriot Act with people. Everyone had an opinion or else they didn't think. Nothing ever said changed that thought process, so why waste the energy? Besides, anything she said might come across as either complicit or denial. That was tantamount to confirming Patterson's suspicions, even if they weren't accurate.

Castillo reappeared without the phone to his ear.

"Any luck?" Patterson asked.

"My office will look for *Señorita* Evans, but they have another report we should investigate."

"What is it?" Lee asked.

"A woman reported that two Americans just entered her apartment."

Patterson's eyes widened. "Are they still there?"

Castillo shook his head. "They left without causing any real problems, but the woman said they came through the balcony door from the roof. She also reported hearing gunshots."

"The Americans were shooting?"

"No, the woman said the two were a male and a female, but they were unarmed. She reported they were being shot at."

"We need to get there," Patterson exclaimed.

Lee didn't speak, but she agreed. Her thoughts were mulling over if the man might be Corsair. If he was, how would she approach him?

Let's get to that point first.

25

"Stay down!" Corsair urged Khloe, who lifted her head as the Volkswagen continued backward down the rough road. Gunshots echoed between the buildings, and without the loud drone of an engine, the reports were clear. The plink of twenty-two-caliber bullets against the raised hood also gave an audible reminder of the threat at the top of the hill.

Corsair offered some silent gratitude to the Volkswagen manufacturers in the late sixties who opted to use heavier steel in the Beetle's construction.

"Can you stop?" Khloe cried out. Her voice came up from the floorboard where she stuck her head.

Corsair knew the answer to that. It was easy. Yes. He could stop the car. Just not with the brakes. Likely, the master cylinder plus plenty of other components were removed, along with the engine. Whatever was done rendered the braking system useless. That meant he'd need to slow the Volkswagen using good old-fashioned physics. Newton's first law of motion, to be exact.

An object in motion stays in motion—unless acted on by an external force.

The problem with that was what force would be required. Anything in the path would stop it with jarring and likely somewhat disastrous results. The Beetle itself wasn't a relatively safe vehicle. Despite the thicker steel, VW Bugs were notorious for crushing on impact—especially in front-end collisions. Since the engine was in the rear compartment, there wasn't much support in the front to fend off the pulverizing metal. But the motor in this particular Bug rattled loosely around the trunk, so how it would react was anyone's guess.

Corsair's torso twisted around with his right arm on the passenger seat as he steered the runaway vehicle down the hill. The next block remained mostly empty, with only two cars on opposite sides of the street and raised sidewalks about two feet above the cobblestones. The biggest problem was that the road looked like it terminated at a dead end. He veered the rear toward the nearest car, double-checking to ensure no one was in or around it.

"Hang tight!" he warned Khloe just before the driver's side scraped the nineties model Peugeot. A screech of metal on metal reverberated through the Beetle, but he felt the impact slow the vehicle.

In one quick motion, Corsair brought his right hand over to the wheel, spinning to the left. The rear of the Volkswagen spun ninety degrees until they were perpendicular with the street. Both hands tried to hold the steering wheel straight, but inertia drove the car around until the nose continued down the hill.

He's slowed down to a near stop before their speed increased. Now the speedometer registered, and the little

Bug passed thirty kilometers per hour. Like a pendulum, the hood bounced down and up, slamming into the windshield with each pass and leaving Corsair only a second to view the road ahead when it descended.

The left fender struck a white car that Caleb didn't have time to identify. That impact jarred the VW like a pinball, spiraling it back around at an angle. The entire vehicle lurched with a crunch of metal as the rear end of the Beetle slammed into the raised concrete sidewalk. Both Corsair and Khloe jerked against their seats as their momentum ceased.

"Get out!" Corsair shouted, not having the time to check Khloe for injuries. He needed to reassess the situation. Where were the gunmen? How much of a lead did they have?

Corsair shoved the driver's door out only for nothing to happen. The latch released, but the door only moved a millimeter. Either the crushed front fender or clipping the Peugeot earlier bound it closed. Khloe's side had no problem, and the girl scrambled out of the car.

At the top of the hill, Corsair saw the older of the two gunmen jogging down the slope. The man stopped and fired at them, but at that distance he hit nothing. Corsair pushed himself over the gear shift and tumbled out the passenger's door. He turned and grabbed the Beretta off the driver's seat, checked the chamber to see a round still ready to fire, and lifted to his feet, grabbing Khloe by the hand.

"Are you okay?" he finally asked.

She nodded warily.

"Good, let's move," he urged her, pulling her up.

The road ended only fifty feet past where the Beetle crashed. The pavement morphed into a driveway that stopped at a flight of red concrete steps.

"Go up," he ordered the girl, pushing her toward the drive. She started running, and he turned to see the gunman pausing halfway up the hill. The other man gasped, and he leaned against the wall, watching the pair as they climbed the stairs into a copse of trees seemingly in the middle of a group of buildings.

Without looking back, Caleb ran after Khloe. She was already nearly a hundred feet ahead of him, and the foliage now hid her from him. He didn't stop as they hit the top of the steps. They were running through a residential courtyard between several houses. Khloe pushed through some palm trees and vanished again. When Caleb followed her through the barrier, he stood in a driveway. They jogged down to the street, passing a silver BMW. The house where they found themselves had a hand-painted sign over a large wooden arched door. The name of the house was *Casa San Antonio Del Mar*. A blue dolphin porpoised over the words.

"Let's keep on," Caleb ordered Khloe, who slowed as they reached the street. If he allowed her to stop, she might go into shock. While he'd dropped the number of assailants from three to one, he still only had one round left in his Beretta.

"Where are we going?" she begged.

"Up into the hills," he explained. "We need to lose them."

Khloe sucked in some air and nodded. Caleb took her by the hand and led her up a set of stairs on an empty lot. Whatever house or building the flight once went to had long since been demolished, leaving only the rock foundation now overgrown with dry, flowering shrubs and sprouts of green-leafed plants forcing their way through the cracks in the concrete. When they reached the top of the steps, the two climbed through the rubble until they reached the top of the vacant lot.

Ahead of them, the mountain continued to rise, and the yellowed grass grew away from the paths forged by others cutting through the growth. Caleb guided Khloe to a trail that curved to the southeast. He glanced back at the street, searching for the third gunman. The man hadn't emerged from trees at the end of the road. Caleb guessed with both of his buddies down that any further pursuit might not be high on his agenda.

That didn't comfort Caleb yet. He needed to be miles away from the scene before he would completely come off the adrenaline high of battle. Even then, he worried there might be reinforcements coming. These three arrived on scene faster than he expected.

A slight worry filled his gut. There was nothing to identify him. When Jimmy came around, he'd never be able to identify Caleb's face. Unless the man he shot was wearing body armor, that guy would not get up, period. The third gunman never got a good enough look at him.

Even knowing all that, he worried that somehow this might blow his cover. It wasn't possible. He assured himself of that. But the visions of Jackson, lying in a puddle of his own blood, still filled his mind. Was Amanda safe? That was all that mattered.

Stay on task.

The order came from his subconscious, reminding him that his only objective at the moment was get Khloe to safety. Sweat dripped down his cheek, and he ignored the perspiration. Khloe, though, struggled in the heat. With the midday sun scorching them, the only breeze hitting them felt like a convection oven. She gasped as she pulled herself up over the rocks.

"Shit!" she screamed, jumping back as the grass moved around.

Caleb raised the Beretta as a *ch-ch-ch* came from the grass.

"Is that—"

"Rattler," Caleb replied, stepping around the girl. The coiled viper stared up through the blades of dried brush. The brown and gray scales blended into the vegetation and dirt, and if Caleb wasn't locking eyes with it, the damned thing might have been invisible.

"He's huge," Khloe exclaimed. "Are there more?"

"Probably not," he assured her, although he wasn't certain. The snake's body was thicker than any rattlesnake he'd ever seen. It probably found a healthy supply of vermin along the streets here.

Caleb kept the Beretta aimed at the reptile.

"Shoot it," Khloe urged.

"Why?" he asked softly. "We're intruding in his home."

"Yeah, well, he looks like he's ready to strike," she suggested.

"That he does," Caleb agreed. "But we're in his territory. I bet he has free range of this area, and we're intruding."

"I'm okay with leaving then," she replied.

"Carefully, work your way up that direction," Caleb instructed, pointing away from the rattlesnake. "Then you can cut back across behind him."

"What about you?" she asked.

"He and I are going to hopefully just sit here until you get around. After that, I'll back away and let him have his rock back."

"How can you tell it's a boy?" she asked.

Caleb shook his head. "I can't, and there's very little chance of me picking the bastard up to check."

Rocks creaked and tumbled down the hill as Khloe moved off the path. She made very slow progress, checking before she put her foot down anywhere. Three minutes later, she was thirty feet to the other side of the snake.

The rattlesnake remained tensed, but his tail didn't rattle off any warnings. Caleb stepped back, still aiming the barrel at the snake. He guessed the snake was at least four feet long, but coiled as it was, another foot or two of the reptile might hide beneath it. His movements were slow, but Caleb held the viper's gaze until he was several feet away. Even then, he watched the snake to be sure it remained where it had been. He'd hate to trip over it as it made a run in the same direction he was going.

"I've never seen a rattlesnake before," Khloe admitted when he reached her.

"They are dangerous," he told her, as if she wasn't aware of the fact. He pointed down the hill to a road. "Let's get down there."

"What if those guys are driving around looking for us?" she asked.

"I don't plan to stay on the street long, but it will take them a bit to regroup."

Caleb actually assumed they were done for a bit. The best case the remaining guy could do would be scoop up Jimmy and get the hell away from there. Caleb was all but certain that his partner was dead. They were smart enough to get out before the Mexican police showed up. In fact, the local cops worried Caleb right now more. There had to be a witness who would identify an American couple—like the mother whose apartment they ran through.

By the time they reached the street, Caleb knew staying in public wasn't a viable option. He stared up the street at the mountain overlooking the city. A white cross peeked above the greenery.

Caleb crossed the street as some Chinese-manufactured three-wheel cargo trucks rambled up the street. He waited until the beige truck passed before jogging across. Pointing up the next road running south, Caleb hurried along the sidewalk. This piece of road was only one block before it ended at *Calle Allende.*

When they reached the intersection, Caleb paused, staring at a wooden cross planted in another vacant lot. A worn trail led up past a chain-link fence into the woods.

"Really?" Khloe asked. "There might be more snakes."

"Snakes are better than guys with guns," he pointed out, although Caleb guessed they'd run into another snake before they met any more of the Cincinnati underworld today. At least for now.

"I'll take the lead if you want," he assured her. When she nodded her agreement, he began his climb.

"Where does this go?" she asked.

"Top of the mountain. It's *Mirador el Cerro de la Cruz.*"

Realization sounded in her voice as she replied, "Oh, the cross."

Caleb grunted an affirmative. The Hill of the Cross was an observation point set over the city. The site offered no parking, so the only access was to hike the trails up the side of the mountain. Most people stuck to the maintained ones, but Caleb figured as long as he reached the top, they could take the easier path down after dark. It would be an easy hike in the dark, especially since Caleb often ran the trails when he was training.

Khloe slowed down behind him, and he stopped to see her leaning against a tree. Her chest heaved as she tried to get more oxygen.

"Tell me about this Sonny," Caleb said while the girl caught her breath.

"I don't know what to tell," she replied. "He's the boss, really. According to Nicky, he runs everything in town—Cincinnati. Except maybe the gangbangers, but they steer clear of him."

"What did Nicky—Nic do for him?"

She shook her head. "I don't know exactly. Nic didn't talk about what he did. It's a thing with these guys. They all act like they just go to work. Like it's no big deal. I think Nicky killed people, though. Or, at least, he was there when it happened."

"But he was snitching?" Caleb asked.

She shrugged. "Yeah. Or he planned to do it."

"Did he want out?" Caleb asked.

"I don't know," Khloe replied. "I don't think so. What I think he thought was that he could rip Sonny off and report him somehow. It was the kind of stupid idea that Nic would think of."

Caleb remained quiet.

"Nicky was an entitled shit. I didn't want him dead, but—" Her pause was interminable. Tears welled in her eyes. "I didn't want him dead. He wouldn't let me leave, and when he—"

"It's okay, Khloe," he told her.

"But," she mumbled. "But, I was relieved."

He nodded. "You didn't kill him."

"It feels like it," she told him.

Caleb watched her, but he thought about Audrey. Nothing he said to Khloe would make her feel better, because there was nothing anyone could say to him to make him feel better. He should have been pumping gas. Better yet, he should have filled up at a different station. As far as Caleb was concerned, he might as well have pulled the trigger to kill both his wife and his son.

"We need to keep moving," he finally said.

She nodded.

"Why does Sonny want you dead, then?" Caleb asked as they climbed higher. "Do you know what evidence Nic had?"

"The only thing I know is who killed Nicky."

"Vinnie?"

"Yeah. I suppose if they get Vinnie, it might tie to Sonny."

There seemed little chance of that scenario happening. In that world, if a guy got busted and sent to prison, he didn't talk. Vinnie would just do his time.

"How did you meet Nic?" Caleb asked.

"He came into the jewelry store where I worked to buy a bracelet."

"For whom?"

"Huh?" she asked.

"Who was the bracelet for?"

Khloe shrugged. "I don't know."

Caleb thought about pointing out the glaring red flag there, but valor reminded him to keep his opinion to himself.

A few hundred feet ahead of them, the slope leveled off. They were standing on the edge of the woods, staring across the summit of the mountain. An orange cell tower raised off the peak, reaching up into the sky. Alongside the structure sat an array of satellite dishes. A raised white and maroon-colored multi-leveled platform rose in the middle. A stone crucifix prominently displayed on the top tier stared out across the city and the Pacific Ocean.

"I haven't been up here," Khloe told him.

"It's quite a view," Caleb assured her as he marched across the grass to the deck. When he reached the metal railing, he ducked between the two pipes.

The peak of the observation deck was accessible by no less than five different sets of stairs, not counting the ones leading up from the base of the mountain. Caleb began ascending them as Khloe came up behind him.

"What are we doing?" she asked.

"We're going to have a look," he replied. "I think we need to wait until the sun goes down before we start back down. Besides, you may never get to see this again."

She nodded compliantly, following him up the steps.

An older couple in jogging attire descended toward them. As they approached, Caleb heard the woman ask what her husband wanted for dinner.

Before the man responded, Caleb interjected, "Excuse me, I lost my phone back on the trail. Would you have one I could borrow? We were supposed to call my wife when we started back down so she can meet us."

"Oh dear," the silver-haired lady responded. "What happened?"

Caleb faked a sheepish grin. "I slipped on a rock. Luckily, I'm fine, but my iPhone took a skydive."

The woman glanced at her husband, who offered her a slight but wary nod.

"Thank you so much," Caleb said as she handed him her phone.

Caleb took two steps away, dialing a number.

"Hey, Angel, we're going to be late. Do you mind making sure our girl is in bed?"

When he finished, he returned the phone to the couple with a quick, "Thank you."

The married tourists continued down the steps as Khloe and Caleb climbed the rest of the way up.

"I thought you said your wife was dead," Khloe pointed out.

"She is. That was the girl watching my daughter. I should have been home by now, and I wanted to touch base with them."

Khloe studied his face. "Why wouldn't you just tell that couple that?"

Caleb turned to look at her. "Right now, we're running from men who want to gun you down, and they don't mind doing the same to me if I'm in their way. I'd prefer that if those friendly folks get asked, they can't give away anything that would help them find us."

Khloe nodded before turning to stare out across the sea. The sun was dropping to the horizon, turning into a bright red ball. Caleb leaned against the black pipe railing and watched the day end.

26

The mother guarded the two children who stared from around the woman's legs at the three. Lee gave the little girl a smile, and the child waved three fingers cautiously at the agent.

Second Sergeant Castillo asked a question in Spanish, and the woman responded.

He translated, "She says the man and woman came through that door." He pointed at the sliding glass door leading out to the balcony. "They dropped off the roof," Castillo added.

Patterson walked toward the balcony and stared through the glass. He pulled the door open with a squeal as the wheels inside the frame rolled across the metal track. The FBI agent stepped out onto the balcony. He stretched out to see the street below him before turning his neck to study the distance to the roof.

"That's about twelve feet," he told the others. "Quite a drop."

The mother rattled something else. "*Corrieron directamente a la puerta.*"

Castillo asked her, "*¿Han dicho algo?*"

"*En inglés. No los entendí.*"

"*Gracias*," he replied to her.

The police officer looked at Lee. "She said they only spoke in English."

"Look at this," Patterson called from the terrace.

Lee and Castillo stepped out, and the agent pointed at a fresh gouge in the stucco coating the railing.

"What's that look like?"

"Could be anything," Lee suggested.

"Yeah, but it could be where a bullet struck. It's about the right size."

Castillo leaned closer. "There isn't a bullet there."

"No, but it could be where it glanced off the building."

Castillo's phone vibrated, and he went back inside.

"You think someone was shooting at them?" Lee questioned.

"It makes sense. Why climb down from the roof?"

"Could the FBI check flights?" Lee asked. "Might be good to see if someone from your neck of the woods flew in yesterday or this morning."

Patterson nodded. "They got here quick if they did."

"So did we," she pointed out.

"True," the agent agreed.

"Agent Patterson, Agent Hubbard, there's been a shooting nearby," Castillo explained when he returned to the balcony.

"How close?" Patterson asked.

"Just up the road a bit. We can walk it."

The FBI agent grunted, but turned to follow the officer. As they left, Castillo thanked the mother again.

"I'll be right behind you," Lee told the two men who started down the stairs.

"*Señora, ¿es éste el hombre que entró en su apartamento?*" Lee asked the woman, showing her Caleb Saunders's file photo on her phone.

"*Sí, pero parecía mayor.*"

"*Gracias.*"

The young woman confirmed that Corsair was the man who came through her apartment. While she said he appeared older than his picture, it was still a solid confirmation. After all, the photo was over ten years old.

Lee hurried down the steps to catch up to the men as they started up the hill.

"Did anyone see the shooting?" Patterson asked Castillo as he tried to quicken his pace to stay in stride with the younger, lankier officer.

"I am not sure. The report is that there is a dead body, and the person who called the police said his car was stolen and men shot up his garage."

The trio reached the top of the hill, and Patterson wheezed slightly. He attempted to cover the gasp with a cough, but Lee could see he was struggling with the climb. When Castillo turned right, the FBI agent almost let out a sigh of relief that the road ahead ran level.

"It's a dead end," Patterson moaned when they reached the end of the street.

"We can take the steps," Castillo assured him.

Lee smirked when Patterson paused to stare up at the flight of stone stairs curving to the top.

"Hell," he muttered as he stepped in behind the second sergeant, who jogged up the stairs. Lee wondered if the Mexican officer was enjoying running the FBI agent around. As for herself, the hike wasn't strenuous, but she ran five miles most days.

When they reached the other side of the wall, four police trucks identical to Castillo's sat on the narrow street. Flashing red lights grew brighter as the shadows of the buildings darkened. The last remnants of the sunset stretched overhead, reddening the sky to the color of a cherry.

Six armed police officers formed a cordon around a black tarp. It took Lee a second to realize the tarp covered a mound that she surmised was a figure underneath it. Castillo marched up to an officer on the scene who appeared to be in charge and spoke to him. As he did, the others parted to allow Lee and Patterson to pass.

Behind the policemen was a garage. The shelves on the back wall appeared at first glance to be in disarray, but as Lee studied the scene closer, she realized the tools and equipment had been destroyed. Chunks were torn from the homemade wooden table under the shelves, and the concrete wall displayed pecks and holes similar to the one Patterson found on the balcony a few minutes earlier.

Lee glanced at the ground, counting at least two dozen twenty-two-caliber brass shells littering the road.

"Damn!" Patterson commented with a whistle. "Someone got their ass shot off, didn't they?"

Lee stared at the damage in the garage as Castillo stepped up.

"Did the victim have a gun?" she asked the second sergeant.

"Yes," he replied before looking over at the officer he spoke to and saying, "*¿Dónde está su pistola?*"

"*Javier, la pistola*," the policeman called to another man who walked over to a police truck and opened the door. He returned hold in a plastic bag with a silenced Beretta pistol inside it. The officer passed Castillo the gun.

"I don't think this guy was alone," Lee remarked wryly.

"Not with that peashooter," Patterson replied.

Castillo pointed at the tarp. "He was shot in the chest with a small caliber, too."

"Can we see him?" Lee asked, and Castillo nodded, moving over to the black canvas. He pulled it back, and Lee studied the man beneath it. Not Caleb Saunders.

"I know him," Patterson admitted. "William Thomas Valera. He goes by WT."

"He one of Sonny's guys?" Lee asked.

"His cousin."

"Hope they weren't too close," Lee quipped.

"I doubt Sonny sheds tears for many folks," Patterson considered.

Lee noticed an older Mexican man squatting across the street. The man could have been in his fifties or sixties, but his age was hard to determine. Years in the sun leathered his skin, and Lee wondered if he might be ten years younger than his features suggested.

"Is that the owner?" she asked Castillo.

He nodded. "He told my officer that they stole his car."

Lee turned back to the garage, envisioning Corsair fighting his way out of the shop.

"Can you put out a call for your officers to be on the lookout for it?" she asked.

"No need," Castillo replied. "It's down the hill."

Both Patterson and Lee turned their heads to follow the road down the slope. At the end of the street, two more police trucks blocked the road. Their red lights bouncing red glows off the buildings.

"Is anyone down there?" Patterson asked.

"No, but do you want to take a look?" Castillo asked with a half smile.

"If one of your guys will drive us down there," Patterson answered.

Castillo asked the other policeman something in Spanish. "*¿Puede uno de tus hombres llevarnos hasta allí?*"

"*Javier, lleva al sargento segundo en tu camión.*"

The officer who gave Castillo the Beretta motioned for the three to get into the older model Dodge truck. Castillo opened the rear door, allowing Lee and Patterson to slide into the back seat before he climbed into the passenger's seat. In less than a minute, Javier stopped the truck in front of a yellow Volkswagen Beetle. The front fenders bent inward with gouges and scratches. The rear bumper hung from the back, having been torn away during impact with the concrete wall.

The three exited the police truck and walked around the Beetle. As they got closer, they could see the dents from the bullets fired at the car. A spiderweb of cracks spread over the entire windshield.

Patterson let out another whistle, similar to the one he did when he saw the garage. Lee said nothing, but her brain was working out how Corsair escaped. She chalked up the one dead man to him. While the Beetle took a beating, it was obvious the passengers walked away.

"Who is with Khloe?" Patterson asked, directing his question at Lee.

She regarded the FBI agent, and he said, "I know. It's classified. But he got away from the garage, and I'm guessing he killed old WT."

"Look at this," Castillo suggested, walking to the back of the car. He lifted the trunk, revealing the loose engine awkwardly wedged into the space.

"He knocked the motor out?" Patterson questioned with a note of incredulity.

Castillo shook his head. "The owner said the motor wasn't in the car."

"What?" Patterson exclaimed.

A smile drew up on Lee's mouth.

Patterson continued, "They escaped Sonny's guys in a car with no fucking motor?"

Lee laughed out loud.

27

There was a pounding in his head that only seemed to pale compared to the pressure he swore his brain was making against his skull. Jimmy stretched out on the bed. Jackie paced back and forth in the next room. Despite the excruciating pain, Jimmy had enough of his wits to know how much trouble he was in. WT was dead, shot with Jimmy's own gun.

It wasn't supposed to happen this way. Once they found this girl, it should have been easy. Who the hell was this guy running around with her? He didn't get much of a look at the guy before he clobbered Jimmy. It was a blur. Jimmy vaguely remembered going into the garage. Then nothing.

Jackie got him out of there. When he finally came around, they were in the little rental car racing away from the garage.

He'd already taken too many aspirins. Whatever he did, his head didn't register a difference. If he opened his eyes, the room tilted. Jimmy was worried. He thought he might be dying. A hospital was out of the question. By now, the local police would be all over the garage. They'd find WT. Luckily, Jackie said he took the man's passport and identification. That should slow the cops down some. Back home, they'd run his prints, but even if they did, Jimmy didn't think Mexico could get the records from the US.

He heard a gentle knock. "Jimmy, you all right?" Jackie asked softly.

"No," he growled at the door. There was nothing about what happened that was all right. His body begged sleep, but Jimmy feared he might not wake up.

"Vinnie texted me," Jackie whispered.

"Did you answer?" Jimmy asked.

"Not yet," he replied. "He said you weren't answering. WT's phone is buzzing too."

"Shit! Shit! Shit!" Jimmy moaned. He needed to tell Vinnie what happened. With WT dead, Sonny would be mad. Or worse.

Jimmy rolled to his side slowly. The lights were all off in his room, but the glow under the door cast enough light for him to find the phone next to the bed. When he touched the screen, the phone illuminated. It felt like a spotlight burning into his retinas. He fumbled with the phone until he got to the settings and dragged the brightness control down. Even the dimmed screen hurt Jimmy's head, but at least he could somewhat focus on the words.

Jimmy opened WhatsApp on his phone.

"Bad day," he typed in the message box when it appeared.

"What happened?" Vinnie responded.

"We lost WT."

"WTF?" Vinnie said.

"She had company."

"Who?"

"IDK. Some guy. He surprised me. Clocked me with something. I think he cracked my skull."

"Fuck."

Before Jimmy countered, Vinnie typed, "Jackie okay?"

"Yeah, he got me out of there. Took WT's ID and phone."

"Good," Vinnie replied.

"What now?"

"Wait."

Jimmy stared at the phone for several minutes. When it went dark, he leaned back on the bed. How long did Vinnie want him to wait?

Somewhere in his brain, it occurred to him that Vinnie or, more likely, Sonny, might want Jimmy to pay for WT. Would they send Jackie in to finish him?

Jimmy didn't care. At least, not at the moment. If Jackie came in to kill him, there wasn't much to do about it.

Hell, it might make him hurt less.

He leaned back on the bed, closing his eyes as he tried to block out any light. When the phone buzzed a few minutes later, he didn't move.

Once Jimmy finally sat up, he fumbled for the phone. He'd been asleep for almost three hours, but he swore it had only been a minute.

"Sonny called a Cortez guy. His people will find the girl," Vinnie's first message read.

Four more followed it.

"Jimmy?"

"Where the fuck are you?"

"This is taking too long."

"Sonny and I are coming down."

Jimmy read the last text.

"Dammit," he whispered. The last thing he needed was Sonny down here.

And the Cortez Cartel? Those were some heavy hitters. The cartel carried a certain notoriety of violence. Even among the other cartels in Mexico. Jimmy didn't know Sonny had any connections down here, but that didn't surprise him either. Sonny's business included a hefty drug trade. Jimmy just hadn't known where it came from.

He stared at the messages.

How much shit am I in?

It took him another fifteen minutes to tap out a response. "Sorry, Vinnie. When will you get here?"

He waited ten minutes with no reply before he lay back on the bed and fell asleep.

28

"Daddy!" an urgent hushed voice called.

Caleb opened his eyes to see Amanda staring at him on the couch. Her face was only a couple of inches from his, and she blinked her long lashes at him. The girl was wearing a nightgown with Belle from *Beauty and the Beast* and the words, "Every girl needs her beauty sleep."

"Daddy," the child repeated.

"Yeah, baby," Caleb responded, matching his tone to her own whispered speech.

"Who is in your bed?"

Caleb sat up and glanced at the mound of blankets on the bed he normally slept in. Khloe was still asleep.

"It's my friend," he explained. "She needed a place to stay."

"Is she your gulfwiend?"

Caleb shook his head. "Why don't you go put on some clothes?" he asked her.

She nodded, turning to a green plastic storage bin where Caleb stored her clothes. She dug through the clean laundry, coming out with a t-shirt with a yellow smiley face on it and a pair of pink shorts. Normally, Caleb would brush her hair before they left the apartment. He didn't want her to give off the vibe that she had a single father. Besides, she was a girl, and while he'd never be able to replace his wife, he wanted her to feel like a little girl should. Of course, he wasn't sure what that would be. Raising a daughter by himself scared him more than facing down the three men yesterday.

Caleb watched the child struggle to get her head through the opening in the shirt, and when she pulled it down, the grinning face was on her back. Her chin touched her chest, and she threw both fists to her side in frustration. He smiled and motioned for her to come over. When she obeyed, Caleb lifted the shirt off her torso, keeping her head poking out of the neck hole. Then he spun the girl around. Amanda let out a giggle as he slid the cotton fabric back over her shoulders so she could jut her arms out of the sleeves.

Caleb stood up and grabbed a pair of shorts and a plain black shirt he picked up from Walmart. He didn't wear anything too flashy. The last thing he wanted was someone noticing a logo on his clothes. Most people didn't think about that, but even a shirt one bought on vacation might give away details about the person.

He stepped into the tiny bathroom and changed out of the running shorts he put on last night. Once he dressed, he brushed his teeth and washed off his face before coming out and picking his daughter up. The two slipped out into the early morning sun, leaving Khloe to sleep off yesterday's excitement.

"Who is she?" Amanda asked again as he carried her to the steps.

"*Buenas días, Señor Rowland,*" Miguel said to Caleb as he passed the front desk.

"Mornin' Migill," Amanda told the young man.

He smiled at her, offering her a wink. She tried to return the gesture, but the best she could muster was a hard, tight blink.

"All right pumpkin," Caleb announced when he reached the bottom step. "You get to walk."

He dropped the girl from his arms, catching her wrist in the air just inches before her feet touched the ground. She let out a squeal, clasping her hand in her father's at the same time.

"Wanna go to the beach?" he asked.

"Will you Yoda me?" Her face turned up to his.

"Yoda you?" He questioned with a grin. The girl loved to ride his back while he jogged, and when she watched The Empire Strikes Back one night, the term "Yoda" became synonymous with the action.

She nodded ferociously.

"Hmm," he mused. "I guess. But not until we get to the sand."

She grinned. "Yay!"

The pair ambled along the sidewalk, turning right at the corner onto Pulpito. From the intersection with Olas Altas, the road rolled downhill all the way to the ocean, and Caleb and Amanda walked slowly down the curb. Early morning kept the streets quiet. Most people didn't get out until at least seven, and that was still half an hour away.

The time meant the beach crowd hadn't arrived. When they reached it, Caleb spotted a single jogger heading toward the pier.

"Ready?" he asked the girl.

"Yeah, Daddy!"

With a sweeping motion, he swung his daughter up by one arm. His other hand caught her, depositing the girl firmly on his shoulders. Amanda's hands grabbed both sides of his head. She was careful not to pull his hair. Caleb warned her it hurt if she did that, and the girl struggled for a bit to avoid reflexively grabbing handfuls of hair when she got scared. His ears were fair game, though.

With Amanda comfortable on his shoulders, Caleb broke into a slow jog. Normally, he'd run faster, but every time Amanda came along for a ride, he slowed his pace without thought. From the walkway, he ran around the umbrellas and chairs set up on the beach. When he jumped from the dune down to the waterline, Amanda gripped his ears and released a high-pitched howl.

The surf slammed onto the sand, and sea water reached up toward the dunes. Caleb's feet switched up and down the sand, avoiding the foamy sea. Each time the waves almost touched his feet, Amanda would shriek, "It's gonna get you!" When he avoided the water, she shouted, "Good job, Daddy!"

Caleb continued down the quiet beach. The empty chairs would fill soon with the boys in their bikinis. For now, most of them were sleeping off the tequila and dancing that kept them going on the streets until the early morning.

As he neared the end of the beach, the pair ran past a few locals trying to beat the rush of the crowds. The surf increased as they neared the bluff, blocking passage. Waves rolled toward the rocks, climbing to astounding heights before slamming into the jagged stones. At least twice since Caleb moved here, someone ventured out into the waves only to be smashed unceremoniously into the outcropping. Their bodies resembled meat run through the grinder, and the prevailing question was whether they died on impact or drowned.

Cut into the stone cliff were steps that traversed up the side of the crag to Mirador Punto Muerto. From there, pedestrians could continue down the other side to the neighboring beach, or they could take in the view toward La Playa de los Muertos. In the evening, the pier to the north glowed on the surface of the Pacific Ocean. Music blared from below at all hours, and plenty of teens hiked to the top with pizza and cold beer to watch the night from above.

Caleb grabbed Amanda's ankles, steadying her as he ran up the stairs. The wet stone was slick, but he maneuvered up them quickly. When he reached the peak, he lifted Amanda off his shoulders. He sat back on a rock, smoothed by decades—maybe centuries—of butts rubbing against it. Now a perfectly smooth curve formed on the stone. Amanda sat astride his legs and stared back at the beach.

His daughter stretched her hand over her head, wrapping her little fingers around his throat. She'd done that to

Audrey when she was nursing as a baby. Now, it was still a reflex for her, usually when she settled into contentment.

"It's nice up here, Daddy," she mumbled, speaking into the wind.

"Yes, it is," he affirmed.

The panoramic view of Puerto Vallarta was something to behold. From where they sat, he could gaze around the bay to the Marina District, where the cruise ships docked every day. He liked the city so far. But was it the place for his daughter to grow up?

Would he even be able to hide long enough for that to happen? After last year, he doubted it. Somehow he'd fooled the Office of Compliance and the rest of the world that he was dead. That entire deception folded on itself when those shitheads shot Audrey and Jackson. He announced to the world that Corsair was still alive. But he did it for Amanda. Without a doubt, he would do it again.

But he already knew the OOC was searching for him. What kind of life was he offering Amanda by running?

He considered what it would take to go back to the OOC. Somehow, Caleb knew that would never happen. Not while Carl Winston was there. To Winston, Caleb was a threat. He was too. At least a threat to Winston. Once Caleb realized the jobs Winston sent him on were unsanctioned, it didn't take him long to compile a list of hits that only benefited Winston. That kind of information, even if unsubstantiated, would wreak havoc on a career. It might cause an Oversight Committee to dig deeper into other dealings in the OOC.

For Corsair, he almost wanted to dare Winston to come after him. But for Caleb Saunders, he was fully aware of what he had to lose. She was bouncing on his lap right now.

Was helping Khloe a mistake? He might draw undue attention to himself. Caleb still worried he left some piece of evidence on the man at the bridge. There was a part of his brain set up for survival that warned him. It begged him to take Amanda and leave today—before it was too late.

What would Khloe do? She could easily stay at Caleb's until Sonny exhausted his search. How many men could the man bring down from Cincinnati? At some point, he'd find the endeavor more trouble than it was worth.

Just run.

He was sacrificing his safety for this girl he just met. Worse, he was putting Amanda in danger. For what, a girl who tangled with the wrong people in a different life? She was nice enough, but was it worth it?

Audrey, what do I do?

There was no answer. Never was. Caleb knew Audrey would have an answer. In fact, he knew what she'd tell him to do. There was one thing about his wife he loved—her certainty in the face of doubt.

I miss you.

Caleb didn't believe in much. What happened after death wasn't some mystery to him. He just didn't consider it. In his line of work, he couldn't. If there was some giant scale waiting to weigh out the good and the bad, he didn't want to ponder how askew his karma was. If there was some great judge preparing to decide whether Caleb deserved heaven or hell, he doubted he trusted that decision.

Besides, what could he do except what he thought was right?

That's exactly what Audrey would say. She'd ask him, "What do you think you should do?"

Damn you, woman.

Why did she have to go? What was it that let Caleb get so lax? Ten years ago, those guys wouldn't have been able to cross the street without Caleb catching a scent of death on them. Yet, he walked into that convenience store without regarding them at all.

Damn you, Saunders.

The waves rose nearly twenty feet from the sea before thrashing the rocks below them. Amanda's fingers stroked the skin around Caleb's neck.

He let out a long, heavy sigh.

29

"I'm hungry, Daddy," Amanda told him as they walked to their apartment door.

"Do you want some *chilaquiles*?"

She nodded her head. Amanda loved the Mexican breakfast of fried tortillas, although she preferred hers covered with butter and honey, while Caleb liked some eggs and chorizo mixed into the shells.

He unlocked the door as the toilet flushed. Khloe stepped out of the bathroom.

"Hi!" Amanda greeted the woman.

"Hello," Khloe replied with a smile. "You must be Amanda."

The little girl extended her hand to Khloe, who took with a grin. "I'm Khloe," she told the child.

"Are you hungry?" Amanda asked.

Khloe seemed to consider it before saying, "Yes. I haven't eaten since yesterday morning."

"We're gonna get chilly killys."

Khloe arched an eyebrow.

"*Chilaquiles,*" Caleb clarified.

"Oh, that sounds delicious."

"There's a place about a block from here," he explained. "Come on."

The three of them walked out of the apartment onto the walkway overlooking the shimmering blue water of the pool. Miguel was picking bugs and leaves off the surface with a long-handled skimmer. He glanced up from his work, offering them a furrowed brow before he waved. Caleb gestured back to the kid. He only ever saw Angel with Caleb and Amanda, so a new person might raise some questions. Hopefully, the boy would just assume Khloe and Caleb had a romantic connection. Those types of things happened. At least, Caleb assumed they did.

When they reached the street, Caleb led them to the left. Khloe gave the sidewalk bar of The Palm Cabaret a confused look. The theater added a tented seating area with a couple of plush couches that remained full of people every evening. From their apartment, Caleb could hear the music playing all night in the building. It was usually good—covers from classic rock bands or the occasional show tune. Most of the crowd out front comprised performers or their friends, and all of them greeted Amanda with a flourish when she and Caleb took an evening stroll. Now, like the rest of the bars, The Palm was dead quiet.

Two blocks north, Caleb stopped at a corner café. A weathered old man Caleb recognized as the owner stood at the entrance watching the street. The sign next to him read, "*Las Tres Huastecas*."

"*¿Quieren desayuno?*" the gray-haired man asked.

Caleb nodded. "*Mesa para tres.*"

The elder owner picked up three menus from a wooden podium pushed up against the wall. He motioned for them to follow. The dining room was empty, but it always seemed to Caleb to be slow. It was a simple eatery, nowhere near as trendy as Coco's Kitchen. The flatware and dishes were utilitarian, probably from a restaurant supply company that stocked thousands of restaurants in Mexico. Even the decor made Caleb think they had undergone no major remodeling since the old man opened the restaurant. Based on that, Caleb guessed the diner started in the late seventies or early eighties.

None of that mattered, though. No one in the business spoke English—an unusual occurrence in Puerto Vallarta. Even the food wasn't fancy. Instead, it was basic Mexican fare. However, it was delicious.

As soon as the owner showed them to their table, Caleb ordered a coffee for himself and an apple juice for Amanda. Khloe piped up, asking for a coffee, too.

"How did you sleep?" Caleb asked the girl.

"Gah, more than I thought I would. Didn't think I'd ever wake up."

"It's the stress," he explained. "Your body was so hyped up that when it came down, you crashed. Like coming off a sugar high."

"You know those aren't real?" Khloe claimed.

Caleb shrugged. "Thousands of mothers before us believed it."

"That's why they call them old wives' tales."

The man returned with the drinks. In Spanish, Caleb ordered the *chilaquiles* with honey for Amanda and some *juevos rancheros* for himself. Khloe ordered the *chilaquiles con juevos.*

"Where is your family?" Amanda asked Khloe.

"They live in the United States," she replied.

"Have you talked to them?" Caleb asked.

She shook her head. "Not since I left Cincinnati."

"Why not?" Amanda pressed her.

Khloe donned a sad smile. "It would be bad for them."

"Oh, like Mimi," Amanda remarked. "We can't talk to Mimi because bad people would hurt her."

Khloe's eyes shifted to Caleb warily.

"Amanda, drink your juice," he chided the girl.

She bobbed her head as she slipped the straw in her mouth. Khloe studied Caleb's face, and he gave her a knowing smile.

"The bank opens at nine," Khloe told him. "I think I can get there and make it to the bus before it leaves at eleven."

"The bus might be dangerous," Caleb suggested.

She shrugged. "What else can I do? Hitchhike?"

"You're welcome to stay with us for a few days," he offered. "It will be a little crowded, but after a bit, Sonny will give up. If he gets no sign of you, then he will think you already left the city."

"I'm not sure," she replied. "I'd like to at least get to the bank, so I have some freedom to decide."

Caleb didn't like the idea of going to the bank. The gunmen yesterday found Khloe's apartment a lot faster than he expected. Her bank made another ideal target.

"You know, if you are leaving town, it might be safe to make a phone call before you go."

Khloe's brow crinkled. "What do you mean?"

"Sonny already knows you are in Puerto Vallarta, so it won't give anything away. You could call your family. By the time they track down where you are calling from, you'll be long gone."

"I don't know," she said with some concern in her voice.

"Are both of your parents still alive?" he asked.

She nodded.

"Let me assure you they want to hear from you. No matter what."

"Sonny might be watching them," she pointed out.

"Sonny's a gangster," Caleb told her. "He isn't a shadowy government agency capable of listening to your parents' every phone call. A ten-minute conversation won't risk much, but it will make them—and you—feel better."

She fell silent. A young boy came out of the kitchen carrying two plates. He placed the dishes in front of Amanda and Khloe before running back to the kitchen to retrieve Caleb's eggs.

"Chilly killys!" Amanda shouted excitedly as she took up her fork tightly in her hand and stabbed at the shells.

"Eat up," Caleb told the girl. "You get to swim with Angel today."

Amanda smiled. "Are you going to swim too?" she asked Khloe.

"No," Caleb answered. "Khloe and I are going to go run some errands."

Amanda twisted her lips into a grimace for a split second before her lips parted wide to stuff some honey-sweetened tortillas into her mouth.

30

Banco Azteca, the branch Khloe used, was on the other side of Rio Cuale, a few blocks from the Malecón. After Caleb left Amanda back at the apartment with Angel, he and Khloe caught a taxi. The cab dropped them close to the river. They had about ten minutes until the bank opened. He wanted to make sure they were in and out as expediently as possible.

They crossed the Rio Cuale Pedestrian Bridge, a part of the famed Malecón. The city had definitely woken up by now, and the people filed along the span in both directions. Caleb ran this way occasionally, but he wondered what the designer of the bridge thought when he planned it. Bricks created a ridged surface that made crossing the overpass somewhat uncomfortable on the soles of the feet. It seemed like something that worked better in the planning stages than the execution ones.

They took the steps down and crossed under the structure. A pixelated mural covered the abutment under the bridge. The image was the likeness of Maria Félix, a famed Mexican actress from the middle of the twentieth century.

When they came out from under the overpass, the walkway carried them into a strip filled with vendor stalls similar to the ones on Isla Cuale. The goods being sold were the same souvenir-quality items hocked everywhere.

The passage between the small shops narrowed as they moved through them. Vendors waved and cajoled them in attempts to entice them to peruse their stores. A short stone wall created a barrier from the sidewalk to the riverbank. Carts filled nearly every available space. Between one of the few gaps, two men leaned against the fence.

Alarms sounded in his head, and he smiled at Khloe casually while he took another look. Both men were locals with rugged features. Neither was over thirty, but they each had scarred knuckles notable even from thirty feet away. Fighters. That didn't mean anything necessarily.

Caleb wished he still had the Beretta on him. Granted, with only one bullet, it might be less of an asset. Both of them remained relatively still as they walked by, and Caleb almost let out a sigh of relief—until he saw a third man stationed against a stand of candles. Like the other two, this man carried himself like a threat.

As they drifted past the man, Caleb noted the bulge at the man's waist. He was carrying. Caleb placed his hand at the small of Khloe's back, guiding her through the maze of clothes, toys, and souvenirs.

"What are you doing?" she muttered.

"Just looking," he replied. Caleb didn't want to scare her yet. Even more important, he wanted to avoid drawing the attention of the men who were watching the bazaar. Whatever their intent, a couple of freaked-out Americans could spur them into action.

"What is it?" she asked, a hint of worry creeping into her voice.

"It might be nothing," he assured her.

"Is it them?" Her head started twisting around as she searched the crowd,

Caleb spurt out a fake laugh and caught her cheeks in his hands as if he intended to kiss her. His face remained soft and jovial.

"Remain calm," he ordered in a sing-song tone. "If you draw attention, it might be worse."

"What is it?" she repeated.

"Look at this dress," he said, directing her to a rack of smock-style sundresses.

"There are three guys looking for something" he explained in her ear. "They're locals, but at least one has a gun."

"They wouldn't have locals, would they?" She referred to Sonny and his men.

Caleb shrugged. He could see a justification for it. After all, he knew for certain he killed one of the men yesterday. Jimmy, the one in the garage, might not be dead, but the blow to his head probably left him at the very least badly injured. Local thugs were cheap, and they would know the area, but there were inherent issues with temporary talent like this. They were hard to manage, and often their skills were lacking. That the mafia encountered the same staffing problems that an accounting firm did almost made him chuckle.

"Stay here," he warned. "Act casual."

"Act casual?" she questioned.

"Yeah," he replied, cocking his head to the side. "Be cool."

He stepped away from her, moving around the cart like a bored husband waiting on his wife. Caleb picked up a tri-colored maraca. As he shook the instrument, he turned slowly, counting two more men milling around somewhat aimlessly. He scanned the crowd, relieved to see he wasn't the only Caucasian male in the market. Unfortunately, he was the only one under sixty, which meant if they were looking for Khloe and him, he fit the description better than anyone else.

He caught one man watching him, and he put the maraca back. The Mexican had tattoos covering his arms and shoulders. Most were images of women, some words in Spanish, written in a fanciful script that Caleb wasn't close enough to distinguish. However, one tattoo stood out to Caleb. On his neck were the Greek letters kappa and zeta—KZ.

Shit.

The Cortez Cartel.

When Corsair entered Mexico last year, he parlayed some jobs for the Mondal Cartel in northeast Mexico in exchange for travel documents. While the work was necessary, it wasn't something he wanted to do, and before he started, he did some research in to the different cartels. Knowing the players provided him with some security and peace of mind.

The Cortez Cartel worked mostly out of Guadalajara, but their region stretched to the coast and covered most of the state of Jalisco. Puerto Vallarta would be the logical export port for the cartel's products, so their presence was logical, if not expected. However, in the last six months, Caleb hadn't run across any of them—certainly not working like they were obviously doing now.

Average people accept coincidence as a regularly occurring event. And, one had to admit, they happen all the time. In Corsair's world, coincidences were never to be trusted. They were impossible to plan for. Since they remained unpredictable, they were equally impossible to ignore them.

Caleb moved to the next booth, scanning nonchalantly ahead for more members of the cartel. He counted only the five. If they were here for them, how did they know?

It wasn't a matter of "if," Caleb decided. The Cortez Cartel was working with Sonny Departi, and Sonny found out Khloe banked at Banco Azteca. Not only that, but he knew she used this specific location. That impressed Caleb, since the bank had only opened fifteen minutes earlier. Caleb considered that for a bit. What connections would Sonny need to get bank information in a different country before banking hours?

Suddenly, that changed things. It made everything even more dangerous. Not just for Khloe, but also for Caleb and Amanda.

31

Caleb slipped through a narrow path bordered by rows of logoed shirts. A woman in her twenties smiled at him, expecting him to buy a shirt with three overturned shot glasses and the words, "One tequila, two tequila, three tequila, floor."

"Excuse me," he mumbled in English as he pushed by her. She turned and stared at him, annoyed by the American's rudeness. Without paying her any more attention, he came out behind her tent. Quickly, he walked along the edge of the booths and carts until he reached the entrance of the bazaar. He ducked into a booth filled with traditional wrestling masks. He had slipped past the men, and now watched them from their flank, hidden in the racks of souvenirs.

The five members of the Cortez Cartel had huddled together, seemingly in discussion. All of them had matching KZ tattoos. Most were around their necks or face, but all were prominent enough to be seen like a badge. Locals would recognize the symbol and give the goons a wide berth.

One man had a cellphone to his ear. He gestured toward the bazaar, as if directing the others to spread out.

Caleb understood their plan immediately. They would span across and move systematically through the market, searching for their prey. Of course, that would only work if another team came from the opposite direction. Otherwise, Caleb and Khloe could get through the marketplace and exit the other end. Now the gang would pinch him and Khloe in the middle with no place to go.

It was still early. And a Monday. Many of the shops just opened nine, and the tourists were in bed, sleeping off the drinks from last night, or enjoying their breakfasts somewhere. Caleb couldn't count on a crowd to hide in.

The five men spread out. Two remained in the pathway as the other three picked their way through each stall. They'd be out of sight of each other for a few seconds. If he didn't do something soon though, they'd find Khloe hiding in the booth where he left her.

Caleb stepped out from behind the racks of masks and scudded along the stone barrier to the next booth. He couldn't see the men now, but he hoped he calculated correctly.

A second later, one of the cartel crew repositioned himself to the rear of the tent. Caleb stepped up to the man and wrapped his elbow around his neck, jerking him back. The thug, surprised, flailed about, knocking a shelf of carved wooden figures over with a crash. Caleb twisted the man around in a swift motion, driving his head toward the wooden counter.

The crack of the man's skull against the table toppled the merchandise on the pavement. Another cartel man charged into the tent, searching for the sound of the noise.

The man pulled a Glock 22 from his waistband. Caleb grabbed a painted bull skull by one horn, swinging it around. Bone and keratin smashed into the man. The point of the horn ripped into the man's neck, and he jerked around. The Glock tumbled to the ground, and Caleb scooped it up without a glance at the fallen man.

He charged out of the tent as the other three men turned. All three had guns out, and Caleb's right hand flew up as the Glock bucked three times. Surprise didn't even register on their faces before each dropped consecutively.

Some woman shrieked at the gunfire, and Caleb sprinted toward the booth where he left Khloe. She cowered in the back, and he caught her by the hand.

"We need to go!" he shouted, pulling her to her feet.

They ran in the direction of the entrance when a figure blurred from the side, tackling Caleb. The two fell sideways into a stall, where they collapsed into a table filled with colorful ceramic *calaveras*. Bright *Día de los Muertos* skulls shattered as they crashed to the concrete. Caleb rolled away from the massive form rising from the sidewalk.

The man in front of him was over six feet tall and outweighed Caleb by a hundred pounds. Unfortunately, none of that appeared to be fat. He was a giant brutish muscle, and he let out a low growl.

Caleb lost the Glock in the fall, and he scanned the ground for it as he moved away from the gargantuan hands, clenched to strike.

The goliath charged at him, and Caleb leaped back out of his reach. Three hundred pounds of muscle pressed

Caleb against the stone wall, and he stole a glance over it to see the drop from the top of the wall to the river below was about twenty-five feet. Too far to jump, and if he did, that would leave Khloe alone to fend for herself.

The giant swung at him, and Corsair deftly dodged the first swing, coming up with a quick double jab to the titan's abdomen. He might as well be slamming his knuckles into the stone wall. Caleb barely had time to register how ineffective his blows were before the back of the brute's hand struck him across the face. The impact jolted him off his feet, and before he could recover, the other man drove a fist toward his head. Caleb twisted to the side, narrowly avoiding what would have been a killing blow. Instead, he felt the man's other balled hand hammer on his chest. The air in his lungs blew out, and Corsair gasped for a breath.

A gunshot exploded somewhere, and Caleb saw the surprise in the man's face. He straightened up, turning to see Khloe standing behind him with the Glock 22. The giant's back reddened from the gunshot, but he didn't drop.

What the hell?

Khloe squeezed the trigger again, and Caleb watched the man jerk as a bullet hit his chest.

He didn't fall, but instead took another step toward Khloe. Corsair drew back his right foot and shot it forward into the man's left knee. The joint bent sideways, and the brute dropped to one knee with a snarling cry.

Caleb climbed to his feet, slower than he intended. His chest burned, but he pushed the thought back in his mind as he stepped around and took the Glock.

The giant struggled to straighten his knee, and in a second, he was back on both feet, although to Caleb's relief, his kick weakened the big man's stance. As the behemoth lumbered toward them, Corsair lifted the Glock and fired a single shot into the man's forehead. His legs were still stumbling forward, and the man face-planted into the sidewalk.

"Are you okay?" Khloe asked.

Caleb slowly nodded as he grabbed her wrist, pulling her to the stone wall.

"We need to jump," he told her.

She looked over the edge. "You're kidding?"

"It's better than another round with them," he pointed out. "Just bend your knees and let them take the fall. It won't kill you."

"It might break my leg."

"There are more of them, and they'll do a hell of a lot more than break your bones."

"Fuck," she moaned as she climbed over.

"I'll lower you as far as I can. If something happens to me, just keep running."

She nodded, and Caleb grasped her by the arm. The girl let go of the stone wall, and Caleb stretched over the barrier as her weight dragged against him. His chest pressed against the top, and anguish flooded his body. He gritted his teeth and reached as far down as he could.

"Go!" he groaned, and the girl dropped.

As soon as the weight was gone, he got ready to climb over the wall.

He felt the impact on his arm before he heard the shot. Neither sound nor pain registered, though, before he rolled over the top of the wall and fell.

32

Caleb crashed down along the face of the wall. Small trees taking root on the bluff whipped him as he fell. Despite the thrashing the saplings gave him, they might have slowed him. Not enough to prevent the wet thud he made when he hit the rocky riverbank. The air rushed out of his lungs, and for a split second, Caleb couldn't breathe.

Khloe screamed in fright, and the high-pitched noise broke through the shock of the fall. From his back, he raised the Glock in his hand just as a face appeared over the ledge. Before the man at the top had a chance to review his handiwork, the gun in Corsair's hand barked. The face staring down vanished in a spurt of blood and bone as the forty-caliber round tore through the man's cheek, just right of his nose, and out the back of his head.

The man slipped back like a wet noodle sliding off the edge of the pot. Caleb sucked in a painful breath and rolled to his side. Every bit of exposed skin on his arms and legs was cut from the sharp bits of granite on the riverbank His upper left arm wouldn't move. Khloe reached down, putting her hand under his arm. The pressure sent waves of pain through that arm, and Caleb groaned as he pulled himself to his feet.

"Are you okay?" she asked, holding him steady.

"We have to go," was all he said.

He stumbled for a second before his legs remembered how to work. He pushed her forward with his right hand, still gripping the Glock. Without a word, she started splashing through the shallow water as they ran downstream toward the beach.

Caleb tested his left arm as they ran. It began to respond. Judging from the blood dripping down his arm, the bullet passed through him or grazed him. He thought the latter more likely. If the brachial artery had been hit, the blood loss would have slowed him down—if it hadn't already rendered him unconscious. It was even possible the bullet was still in him, but he didn't think so. That was a completely different kind of pain. Although until the adrenaline in him subsided, he might not be able to judge the pain correctly. He needed to get away from here and inspect the wound.

And wrap his chest. He still struggled to get a deep breath, and Caleb bet that the less-than-jolly giant might have broken a rib or two. Maybe all of them considering how badly he hurt.

At least his legs were working. The two continued jogging through the water. If they could reach the beach before any of the Cortez Cartel reorganized or found reinforcements, then they might be able to disappear in the maze of streets in the Romantic Zone.

Shouts behind him deflated that hope. He stole a look to see three men climbing over the wall. They'd chosen a wiser entry point with only about an eight-foot slope.

Khloe heard them too, and she almost froze in her tracks as she turned back.

"Keep going!" Corsair ordered, waving her forward with the Glock.

Above them on the Rio Cuale Pedestrian Bridge, a few people noticed the commotion in the river. The first few likely thought it was something diverting to watch, but when one of the Cortez men raised a gun and fired, the scene became inexorably macabre, drawing more of the crowd as the beginnings of the audience shouted out to those around them.

Caleb spun around, firing once. Unlike the men charging after him, Corsair only needed the microsecond to lock onto the first target and fire. The bullet's intended destination was the middle of the closest man's chest. In his haste, the round went high, catching the lead in the neck.

The forty-caliber bullet weighed no more than eleven grams with a diameter of ten millimeters. That same round left the barrel of the Glock 22 at roughly 1200 feet per second, or a little over 800 miles per hour. The resulting impact almost lifted the man from his feet as the mushroomed round tore through the soft flesh.

The other two men both skidded to a stop in the river as their friend's head nearly tore off his shoulders. Dumbfounded, they stared as the body splashed into the waters of Rio Cuale.

Caleb was already running again before the pair regained their composure. Both lifted their weapons, firing after Corsair.

He already rounded the piers of the pedestrian bridge, and their shots only peppered the concrete pylons. The soft white sand shifted as Caleb ran. Each foot sprayed back grains in an arc as they pushed Caleb forward.

As he ran out from under the bridge Corsair tightened his grip on the Glock 22, but he didn't turn to fire despite the two men coming fast around the corner. He caught a glimpse of the crowd forming on the edge of the bridge, and the shouts from the people above carried down to him. In this day and age, it was expected that right now someone was filming Caleb and Khloe's life-and-death race as they ran for their lives. In fact, it was safe to assume that footage might be streamed live on a social media outlet somewhere. If he turned back to fire, there was a strong possibility his face might be captured on that video. He didn't know how far facial recognition software had come since he worked for the Office of Compliance, but given the abilities it had over a decade ago, he assumed there were improvements. Hell, artificial intelligence could search the trillions of bytes of data uploaded daily with very little human interaction. The OOC could have a positive identification on him within hours, if not minutes.

Luckily, the two men in pursuit must have considered the same thing as they chased them. Perhaps being caught on film shooting at two Americans might not be the publicity the Cortez leadership desired. Whatever the reason they hadn't fired again, Caleb remained grateful.

Somewhere above them, the faint sounds of sirens echoed off the buildings as they grew closer. He didn't want to find himself in police custody, but if the sirens dissuaded the goons behind them, Caleb was more than content with that.

He urged Khloe toward the restaurant ahead. La Langosta Loca was one of the popular beachfront restaurants with twenty or thirty tables on the sand, allowing diners an opportunity to eat and drink near the crashing sea. The morning crowd was still thin, but several tables were occupied. A few showed signs of use but the customers were taking advantage of the nearby water for a quick swim.

Caleb passed Khloe as they ran through the tables. Without stopping, he grabbed a floppy oversized beach hat and a large towel draped over the chair.

The sirens were now closer, and Caleb saw blue lights flashing in his periphery. They must have been on the Malecón, and it wouldn't take them long to converge on the beach.

"This way!" he called to Khloe as they ran through the building. A vendor carrying an array of classic Mexican *serapes* sidestepped out of Caleb's way. Fumbling in his pocket, Caleb produced a hundred-dollar bill. He smashed it in the man's hand, grabbed the *serape* on the top of the man's stack, and pointed to the two men in pursuit.

The vendor stared confused at Caleb who mumbled, "*Lo siento*," and jerked the pile of blankets out of his hand. With a twist, he flung the stack of blankets at the two men. The motion sent a stabbing pain down his arm, and Caleb doubled over as the movement felt like he'd just been clobbered in the chest again. However, the stack of clothes spread out in the air, disorienting the Cortez goons, and sending the poor man scampering after his loose capes.

Caleb recovered and took off after Khloe. As they ran out the restaurant, he slipped the *serape* over his head and plopped the big hat onto Khloe.

"Wrap up!" he ordered, handing her the beach towel. As soon as they hit the street, Caleb rounded the corner of La Langosta Loca, cutting down an alley back to the beach. The pair reached the wooden walkway running behind the row of restaurants and slowed to a casual walk. When they'd gone a hundred feet, he glanced back. There was no sign of the Cortez thugs. They moved past three more restaurants before stepping up past a vacant hostess stand. Caleb grabbed two menus from the table and led her to a corner table. The pair sat down, and Caleb shielded his bloody arm with the menu.

"We need to split up," he told her.

"What?" she exclaimed. "But you're hurt."

He nodded. "I think I'll be okay, but I can't do a lot more to protect you."

"What do we do?"

"They're looking for a man and a woman."

She nodded in agreement.

Caleb pointed to a table of three women in their forties. They were currently paying their check.

"When they leave, go with them. Follow as closely as you can. Hell, talk to them if possible, but get a few blocks away from here."

"Where do I go?"

"Head back to the restaurant we had breakfast. I'll make my way that way too."

Khloe took a deep breath. "Are you going to be all right?"

"As long as I don't have to do any major lifting," he assured her. "Now, go. They're leaving."

Khloe swallowed, stood up, and walked up behind the women as they walked toward the front door. Caleb watched as she inched along with them. One of the ladies glanced at her for a second, and Khloe said something to her with a smile. The woman returned the smile as the four women appeared to walk out together.

Caleb unrolled the silverware on the table, wadded the napkin up in his pocket, and rose to leave. He found the restroom, and he was relieved to find it empty. He wet the cloth napkin and stepped into the stall. After rolling the short sleeve up, he examined the bullet wound. It wasn't merely a graze. The round was through and through, but it was shallow, having only torn a hole in his skin. The exit wound felt like it was an inch or two from the entry point. He cleaned the blood off and wrapped the cloth around his arm.

There wasn't much he could do for his ribs right now. He'd been right though. As the rush of the fight died away, the pain in his arm and chest intensified. He needed to get out of the restaurant and make sure the Cortez Cartel wasn't waiting around. With a sigh, he pushed up to his feet with a grunt and exited the bathroom.

33

Second Sergeant Eduardo Castillo sipped the scalding coffee from the stainless-steel cup his wife bought him last year for Christmas. Inside the container was half a liter of black Oaxaca coffee that he brewed first thing this morning. After leaving the crime scene last night, Castillo barely made it to bed by half past midnight. Even then he'd be unable to sleep. His mind raced with curiosity about the incident at the garage.

Why wouldn't it though? That had been a major shootout. The second sergeant had seen a few cartel hits over the years, but most were a little neater. Perhaps a better term was efficient. The cartel didn't waste bullets the same way these *gringos* did. Who were they shooting at anyway? A girl and a guy who managed to not only escape, but they did so by killing one of the gunmen and getting away in a vehicle without a functioning engine.

That stumped Castillo. Logically, it made sense. The physics worked. After all the garage was at the top of a hill, but they still had to get the vehicle out of its parking spot while being shot at. According to the owner, the vehicle was on jack stands, and the motor had been hoisted out of its compartment.

Castillo took another drink of steaming coffee from his cup as he waited in front of the Marriott. Both Agents Hubbard and Patterson chose to stay at the chain hotel. Castillo assumed it was the one their agencies chose, but it was inconvenient. The hotel was across town in the Marina District.

It was his own fault for offering to pick them up. Patterson was quick to agree, saying he'd just as soon not drive around in a city he wasn't familiar with. Hubbard offered more reluctance. Castillo liked her. She wanted a degree of independence, and being ferried around the city by the local police didn't fit that bill. Plus, she was holding her cards tight to her chest. He understood what Agent Patterson and the FBI wanted, but Lee Hubbard answered evasively about what she wanted.

Castillo had a theory. Hubbard didn't care one bit about the girl. He could see that when this Khloe Evans name came up. It was inconsequential to her. But she didn't say as much. However, she perked up at the mention of Evans's male companion. Lee Hubbard wanted him.

The partial print must have been his. That was the only logical reason Castillo could come up with for Hubbard's appearance.

That left him wondering who this man was. Castillo suspected it was the male companion who shot the American. He probably drove the car. If one could call that driving. It reminded him of his son's favorite Pixar movie *Toy Story* where Woody tells Buzz Lightyear that he can't fly and he's only "falling with style."

His phone vibrated in the console of his truck, and Castillo answered it as he watched Lee Hubbard come out of the Marriott. He hung up as she opened the front door. Yesterday, Patterson made an extra effort to beat her to the truck each time so he could sit in the front seat. Castillo noticed a smugness in her as she took the roomier seat.

"I just got a call," Castillo told her. "There's been another shootout just off the Malecón near Isla Cuale."

"That's where Marino was killed, right?" she asked.

The police officer nodded. "This is a big one. We have seven dead."

"Shit!" she whistled. "Let's go then."

"But Agent Patterson?" Castillo asked.

Agent Hubbard twisted her watch to check the time. "Agent Patterson is now a minute late," she advised.

Castillo gave her a soft and silent reprimand with her eyes. She smiled back at him.

"No matter," he remarked. "Here is Agent Patterson."

The FBI agent stalked out to the truck. As he neared the vehicle, his face twisted when he saw Hubbard sitting in the front seat. His visage soured with resignation as he opened the rear door.

Patterson grunted a "Good morning" as he settled into the back.

"*Buenas días*, Tim," Castillo greeted the man. He repeated what he'd just shared with Agent Hubbard as he shifted the truck into gear and pulled out of the Marriott's parking lot.

It took them nearly half an hour to traverse from the Marina District to Isla Cuale. When they arrived, Castillo counted eight marked Jalisco police vehicles, two National Guard vehicles, and two more unmarked cars he suspected belonged to the Ministerial Federal Police.

"Let me speak with the officer in charge," Castillo suggested as he exited the vehicle.

The two agents got out of the truck and waited as the second sergeant moved past a small pizza place called Pinocchio's. Several local cops were directing gawkers along the Malecón to move away, and as Castillo rounded the corner to the Calle Encino shops he almost froze when he saw the results of the mayhem.

Three lifeless bodies lay sprawled in the street. Before he could move closer, a chief inspector wearing a mask across his face straightened from the where he'd be inspecting the three men.

"Who are you?" the inspector asked in Spanish.

"Second Sergeant Eduardo Castillo," he responded. "I'm escorting two American agents investigating the murder in Isla Cuale Saturday."

"What do they want?" the inspector questioned languidly.

Castillo raised his eyebrows with an expression that almost said, "Who knows?" However, the officer verbally answered, diplomatically, "They are looking into connections to the mafia in the States."

"Hell," the inspector remarked. "They can take a look as long as they don't touch anything. They are your responsibility, Sergeant."

Castillo gave a curt nod to the man before heading back to the vehicle to get the agents.

"Holy shit!" Patterson muttered under his breath as the three walked down Calle Encino. The chief inspector was now walking through a vendor stand. He stared down at a figure on the concrete.

"Is that a fucking skull?" Patterson asked. The chief inspector turned to survey the FBI agent.

"*Sí*," the inspector acknowledged. "It's a bull's."

"Damn!" Patterson replied with some astonishment in his voice. "I've seen some crazy shit, but that's something."

The FBI agent turned to Hubbard. "This must be your guy," he suggested.

The female agent didn't say anything but stepped closer to the body. One horn from the painted bull skull penetrated the man's neck. The point drove through the soft tissue. Castillo thought at least four or five centimeters of the horn were inside the man. Sticky brown blood pooled under the man's head where the carotid artery had been torn open from the impact.

"He's cartel?" Agent Hubbard asked but with a tone that implied she was stating the fact rather than questioning it.

The chief inspector responded, "Cortez. They all are."

"Tim Patterson. FBI." Patterson stepped up to the inspector, extending a hand.

The ministerial officer reached out and grasped the agent's palm. "Chief Inspector Gomez," he introduced himself.

"What happened here?" Patterson questioned as Hubbard continued to move slowly around the stall.

"We have witnesses who claim a single man killed these men. More have come out claiming that a man and a woman were running from them."

Patterson cut his eyes to Hubbard who ignored the FBI agent. Castillo noted how her face barely registered anything but impassive ambivalence, but he recognized that drive. Lee Hubbard was hunting the man with Khloe Evans. Even Patterson could see that.

Who was he? An undercover agent?

No, Castillo decided. Even if he was deep undercover, she'd wait for contact first rather than jeopardize his safety with an investigation. Although it was a small one considering she was the only Homeland officer here.

A former agent, then. Disavowed. Or worse?

The police officer stared at the skull protruding from the neck of the Cortez Cartel member. Whoever Hubbard was after, he was a stone-cold deadly motherfucker. Seven members of the deadly Cortez clan were dead, and it wasn't an ambush. On the contrary, it appeared the locals intended to ambush them.

Gomez approached him, motioning with his head for Castillo to step to the side. In Spanish, the chief inspector asked, "Who are these Americans?"

Castillo responded in his native tongue, "The FBI agent is searching for a witness. We had a murder on Puente Iguana Saturday. The man who was killed was with the mob."

"Seriously?" Gomez snapped. "Was it an assassination?"

Castillo shook his head. "I don't think so. The murdered man might have been trying to kill the witness, and this other man was with her."

"Who is he?"

Castillo cast a wary stare at Hubbard. "Not sure. The woman is with Homeland Security, but she is very interested in the man."

"Some of the tourists on the walkway got videos of the pair running away," Gomez explained. "We can let them take a look, if they will identify them for us."

Castillo nodded, and Gomez pointed toward one of his officers who was standing with a small group of tourists.

"Who is this guy?" Agent Patterson questioned Hubbard as Castillo approached the two Americans.

Hubbard didn't respond.

"C'mon, Hubbard. This bastard just killed seven men." Patterson squatted down next to one of the men lying on the street. The man's white tank top was beginning to turn brown as the circular stain of red blood dried in the heat. A round hole in the center of the man's chest likely blew his heart apart on impact. "Hell of a shot," Patterson remarked. "These weren't regular guys either."

"I can't really say," Hubbard explained.

"Lemme guess," Patterson suggested. "National security."

She shrugged.

"Bullshit," Patterson spat. "Is he one of yours or something?"

"No, he isn't."

"Aha, you do know who he is," Patterson blurt out excitedly.

Lee Hubbard's face smoothed out as she stared back at the arrogant man. "I do not," she clarified.

Patterson's left eyebrow lifted, and Castillo stepped forward.

"Agents Hubbard and Patterson," he addressed the two, "we have some video of the incident if you'd like to review it."

"Abso-fucking-lutely," Patterson rasped.

"The chief inspector asks only that you help identify the couple in the video."

"No problem," the FBI agent remarked quickly.

Castillo watched as Hubbard offered a half-hearted nod in agreement. The woman was keeping everything close to her chest, but he waved them over to the officer with the tourists.

The man in full tactical attire spoke softly to a Latina woman who was showing him her phone screen. Castillo stepped up to the man.

In Spanish, Castillo said, "Chief Inspector Gomez told me we could review their videos."

The officer nodded before pointing the woman in front of him toward Second Sergeant Castillo. She handed an older iPhone to the officer who rotated the screen to face himself. Hubbard and Patterson crowded around to see the screen.

On the phone, a frozen image of the river basin displayed with a large triangle icon indicating it was ready to play.

Castillo's index finger touched the triangle, and the video started.

Wind and scraping came from the speakers as the scene began. Two figures splashed through the ankle-deep water below. Three men chased them. All three of the pursuers carried pistols. As the man being chased turned and fired a gun, the lead man in pursuit dropped.

"That's definitely Khloe Evans," Patterson blurted out.

The man with Khloe twisted back around, and his face dropped. Castillo stared at the screen watching him run. He kept his head down, resisting any urge to glance up at the camera.

Castillo admired the man's marksmanship as well. He had turned and fired in a swift motion. The bullet found its mark too. That kind of shooting was difficult to train. It didn't require a strain on Castillo's investigative mind to draw the obvious conclusion—the man was an operative.

Hubbard didn't flinch as she watched the iPhone video. Castillo no longer wondered what her interest was. The man was a wanted fugitive, and if Castillo were a gambling man, he'd wager he was trained by the United States government.

Agent Hubbard straightened up and pulled out an iPad from her shoulder bag. In seconds, she opened up the map on the screen. The image zoomed down on the satellite photo of Puerto Vallarta. The green swatch of land indicated where the river ran.

"What were they doing here?" she wondered.

"Khloe and your guy?" Patterson clarified.

Hubbard ignored the remark. She touched the screen where the first murder was. A small, inverted teardrop shape marked the location. Then she followed up by marking the garage and Khloe's apartment. Finally, she added one where they stood. A trapezoid perimeter appeared on the map.

Hubbard magnified the image. Landmarks, street names, and business names appeared on the screen.

"I think they had a reason for being over here, and these cartel guys were lying in wait for them."

"It's early," Castillo pointed out.

"Exactly," Hubbard acknowledged. Her index finger and thumb increased the size of the map, and the tip of her finger touched a business name only a block from the bazaar—Banco Azteca.

"The bank?" Patterson questioned. Then, he added, "She needed to get running money."

"That's my theory," Hubbard suggested. "Marino died on Saturday, and we think he was after Ms. Evans. She didn't have enough cash to run. Maybe she kept it all in the bank here. But she thought she could get in first thing."

"How did the Cortez Cartel find her?" Patterson asked.

"The cartel will have contacts throughout the banks," Castillo offered.

Hubbard added, "It seems your Sonny Departi has some heavy connections."

Patterson folded his arms. Castillo wondered more about who was helping Khloe Evans now.

34

The sun glinted off the driver's rearview mirror in a blinding flare. Jimmy squinted even through the polarized sunglasses. He swallowed again, trying to force the bile back down to his stomach. The nausea rivaled the pain in his head. Jackie thought his skull might be fractured—something Jimmy didn't want to consider. If that were true, he could have a brain bleed or risk some serious brain damage. But he couldn't get away to even think about going to the hospital.

Not while Tomás stewed next to him.

The Mexican just hung up from another phone call. Jimmy couldn't understand a word of it, but even without knowing any Spanish, he recognized what a pissed-off tone sounded like. And Tomás exuded pissed.

Jackie sat behind him in the back seat, and Jimmy hoped the lout held his tongue. He didn't want to feed any fuel to Tomás's fire. All Jimmy knew at the moment was Tomás lost seven men this morning. Of course it was all in an effort to solve Sonny's problem with Khloe Evans.

"Who is this man?" Tomas asked for the third time. "*¡Siete muertos!*"

Jimmy just shook his head.

"Is he FBI?" Tomás asked. "CIA?"

"We don't have any clue," he admitted. The man wanted to point to his own caved-in head as reassurance that neither he nor Jackie knew anything. The only consolation to Jimmy was that if the guy killed seven men from the Cortez Cartel, he didn't feel nearly as stupid for letting him clobber him with a wrench. Even with potential brain damage though, Jimmy didn't voice that thought. He doubted Tomás was one to empathize with anyone, particularly minutes after being dealt such a defeat.

"He's American," Tomás declared as if somehow Jimmy would know who he was.

No shit, Jimmy thought. But he kept his mouth tightly shut.

"I've been told we have people on all the bridges. We know they crossed into Old Town. If they try to go back across, we'll see them."

Jimmy doubted that. Although, he didn't expect to catch sight of them at the bank. That seemed to him like a long shot, but it had paid off. Well, maybe not paid off at all. They were back at square one.

Not really, he reminded himself. They did know they were on the run. It wouldn't take long for them to resurface, and now that the Cortez Cartel had a vested interested in meting out revenge, they'd have people on every street. It almost frightened Jimmy how integrated into the city the cartel seemed to be. Sonny's crew ran Cincinnati, but Jimmy didn't think he could flood the streets the way Cortez did. He wasn't even certain where in the hierarchy Tomás landed.

"We know the girl lives back on this side of the river," Jackie pointed out. "But she ain't going back there. Maybe this guy has a place somewhere on that side of town."

Tomás shook his head. "*La Zona Romantica* is mostly tourists. *Gringos* everywhere. It will be *difícil*—difficult—to find them on the streets."

Jimmy tapped his finger on the door. He didn't like the guy. Hell, he didn't care for any of the cartel people. They scared him a little, and Jimmy wasn't one to frighten easily. However, he had the unnerving sensation that Tomás had no regard for anyone's life. And what Jimmy worried about was if something went south between Sonny and the cartel, he and Jackie would be the ones left out to swing.

"How many men do you have out there?" Jackie asked from the back seat. The question almost made Jimmy cringe. Jackie either didn't have the same worries as Jimmy or he didn't care. Although, Jimmy really guessed that Jackie was just too stupid to grasp the ever-tightening situation they found themselves in.

"Plenty," Tomás answered, glancing up in the rearview mirror at Jackie. The Mexican's eye flitted toward Jimmy. "It's gonna cost your boss though."

Jimmy pursed his lips. His temple throbbed, and he just wanted to close his eyes.

"I'm sure we can work something out," he finally assured Tomás. He didn't want to mention that those decisions were well above his pay grade. Jimmy wondered what Tomás considered plenty of guys, and if there were plenty, then why was he so worried about finding him in—what did he call it? *Zona Romántica*?

Tomás grunted in response. Jimmy's phone erupted in a shrill ring, breaking the tension for a second.

"Hello," Jimmy said.

"It's me," Vinnie told him through the phone. "Sonny and I just landed at the airport."

"What?" Jimmy asked. "Where? Here?"

"Yes, in Puerto Vallarta," Vinnie rasped into the phone.

"What are you doing here?" Jimmy asked, realizing too late he should have kept the thought to himself.

"Coming to make sure the fucking job is actually done," Vinnie snapped.

"Vinnie—" Jimmy began to say.

"Sonny rented a house in some place called Gringo Gulch," Vinnie told him. "Do you know where that is?"

Jimmy had no idea. He pulled the phone down and asked Tomás, "Where is Gringo Gulch?"

Tomás stared at him. "Up the hill," he explained. "Overlooking the river."

Jimmy put the phone back to his mouth. "Yeah, we can get there."

"Good. Bring Jackie and this wetback fucker with you," Vinnie growled.

"Got it," he responded, thinking it might be less wise to let Tomás hear the racial slur Vinnie threw out there. He might not like the guy, but he certainly wasn't going to sidle up against him either.

"What happened this morning?" Vinnie asked.

"The guy that killed WT yesterday, killed seven of Tomás's men. They got away."

"Holy shit!" Vinnie muttered. On the other end of the line, Jimmy heard Sonny ask a question. "That asshole killed a bunch of the Mexicans," Vinnie said to Sonny.

Jimmy just sat on the phone waiting for Vinnie to come back to the conversation. "Do we know anything about this fucker?" he finally asked Jimmy.

"Nothing," he answered. *He's a deadly bastard*, Jimmy thought. But at this point, if no one realized that, they weren't paying attention.

"Damn," Vinnie complained. "Just meet us in an hour."

Before Jimmy answered, Vinnie hung up. He stared at the phone before looking up at the narrow eyes of Tomás. His life just got more complicated.

35

Khloe ducked her head low as she ran across the street. The women that she had left the restaurant with were cordial when she asked if she could walk along with them. They immediately closed ranks around her. She'd mentioned a man on the beach harassed her, and the ladies herded her to the middle. It worked out better than she'd have considered as they started south toward the heart of the Romantic Zone.

After several blocks, Khloe decided she needed to get farther from this group, too. Not that she had any logical reasoning behind the thought. More like a fear that somehow they'd recognize her or someone from the market might see a crowd of females shielding another. Khloe told herself that was too obvious.

In truth, though, it was because they did what all friendly people do—asked her questions. When they questioned where she was from, she lied, saying Seattle. It was the biggest city she could think of that was the farthest from Cincinnati. It seemed like a boring place to her, and really, the only things she ever heard about the place involved Starbucks and Nirvana. At least, that's what she thought. But the women tried to grill her with questions. One lady had been in Seattle the year before, and she inquired about a specific restaurant that Khloe didn't know and from the woman's reaction, she expected a native of the city to know the place. That freaked her out, and she made a quick excuse to head a different direction.

Now, she slipped into a boutique. Roland told her the men in the marketplace were part of the cartel. Did Sonny send them after her? Her stomach twisted, churning up the *chilaquiles* she ate for breakfast and threatening to hurl them over the racks of clothes she riffled through.

The cartel?

Her mind swirled at the thought. She should be dead right now. Hell, if Roland hadn't intervened on the bridge, that guy would have murdered her there. Here, several days later, she still pumped blood through her veins, but only because of Roland. This morning made—was it four times he'd kept her from being killed? He'd even warned her about the bank, but it seemed unlikely that Sonny could find her there.

She needed to meet him at his apartment, but a nagging concern tugged at the recesses of her consciousness. Should she go back to him? It was dangerous, and Roland handled himself well. It scared her how easily he'd killed so many people.

Her fingers trembled. She had shot that big guy, too. He didn't die, at least not right away. But she'd still pulled the trigger. Khloe didn't remember if she'd ever held a gun before, let alone fired one.

Roland was hiding, too. That was obvious. Khloe assumed he was using a fake name.

Maybe I need to do that.

What was she doing by letting him be involved? It might put him, or worse, Amanda, in danger. That didn't seem fair to her. Why couldn't she survive without having to put that little girl in harm's way?

She just needed to leave town. It was too dangerous to stay any longer. After this morning, the police would be looking for her too. Plenty of people were on their phones, videoing them on the beach. By now, the cops would have those videos. They'd probably end up on the internet too.

What if her mom saw that?

Khloe's knees wobbled, and she grabbed a rack of sundresses as she tried to steady herself. If she could slide to the floor, she would. But that would only draw attention to her. Instead, the girl straightened her spine before turning to look out the large pane of glass at the busy avenue. Across the street, a small boutique hotel rose a few stories. The sign read "Hotel Mercurio" and judging from the many Pride flags flapping off the building, it catered to the gay community.

At that moment, the hotel seemed like the safest place. If the rest of Sonny's crew were like Nic, they wouldn't get caught anywhere near anyone who was gay. Those guys worried they'd catch homosexuality; they didn't want to get close to them.

Khloe crossed the street, entering Hotel Mercurio. A muscular, mustachioed man stood behind the front desk, a counter with blue and white tiles around the bottom. He watched her for a second, and she realized how out of place she was.

"Do you have a phone?" she asked.

"Yeah, it's down the hall," he told her skeptically.

Surely, I'm not the only woman he's ever seen here.

Khloe found an older pay phone. Not so old it took actual coins, but it had the slot for a calling card. She lifted the receiver and dialed a string of numbers.

"If you'd like to make a collect call, press one or insert a method of payment," an automated voice informed her. She pressed the one button.

"Who is the call from?" the voice asked.

"Khloe."

Through the handset, the line rang. Her stomach tightened into a ball as if it were floating. What if no one was home?

"Hello."

"There is a collect call from Jalisco, Mexico, from Khloe." The name "Khloe" was her own voice recorded and played back. "If you will accept the charges for this call, please press one."

A tone sounded, then her mother said, "Khloe?"

"Mama," Khloe uttered before her eyes welled up and tears streamed down her cheeks.

"Oh, baby, thank God you are okay," her mother cried. "Anthony! It's Khloe!" She hadn't pulled the phone from her mouth before shouting for Khloe's father.

"Where are you?" Haley Evans asked.

"Mexico."

"Yeah, I guess the operator said that," Haley remarked.

The phone clicked, and another voice came over the line. "Khloe?" Anthony Evans questioned.

"Yes, Daddy," Khloe replied.

"Where the hell are you?" he demanded.

"She's in Mexico," her mother answered.

"You had us worried sick?" Evans spouted. "What were you thinking? Your shithead boyfriend gets murdered and you vanish. We thought you were dead, too."

"I would be," Khloe told him. "Vinnie Santoro murdered Nic. He would have killed me, too."

"Why the hell would Vinnie kill Nic?" Evans asked. Khloe's father grew up in the neighborhood with Vinnie and Sonny, but he often excused the rumors spread about their criminal involvement. Like most people in the neighborhood, he knew Sonny ran the numbers and gambling, but anything that involved drugs or murder was something most people close to Sonny never believed. "He's another Italian the system wants to step on," was a common excuse.

"Nic planned to rat on them," she answered.

"Of course he was a fucking rat," Evans spat. "Good riddance."

"Anthony!" his wife scolded.

"Daddy, I saw Vinnie leave the apartment that day. I heard him shoot Nic. If he'd have seen me, he'd have killed me then too."

"Honey, we can work it out with Vinnie," he told her.

"No, Daddy, Sonny sent guys down here to kill me."

"What?!" Haley Evans exclaimed.

"I recognized the first one, but someone saved me. Now, there are lots of people looking for me."

Her father's throat cleared, but he said nothing.

"You need to call Vinnie," Haley ordered her husband. "Explain to him. Tell him Khloe won't cause any problems."

"No!" Khloe shouted into the phone. "He'll just kill you too, Daddy."

There was a moment of silence.

Finally, Anthony Evans asked, "What are you going to do, sweetie?"

"I can't call you again," she told them.

"No, Khloe!" her mother blurted out.

"Mama, I can't. They might come after you trying to find me. Right now, they already know at least where I am in Mexico. But I can't stay here."

"Khloe," her dad's gruff voice came over the speaker in a softer tone.

"Yes, Daddy," she answered dutifully.

"Be careful." His articulation cracked, and Khloe let out a gasp along with a sudden flow of tears. Khloe sobbed into the receiver for several minutes.

"*Señorita*, are you okay?" the desk clerk asked as he stuck his head around the corner.

She nodded to him. He returned the gesture before vanishing from sight again.

Great, I'm drawing attention to myself.

"I'm sorry," she blubbered into the speaker. Now that her crying slowed, she could hear her mother crying as well. "Mama, I'm so sorry."

Her mother continued to cry. Her dad instructed, "Khloe, if you can, email your Aunt Lee. Just to let us know you're safe."

Khloe understood what he was asking. Lee wasn't her actual aunt but an old friend of her dad's. She also lived in Phoenix. *Smart move, Dad.*

"Yes, Daddy."

"I *sniff* love *sniff* you," her mother eventually said.

"I love you too, Mama."

"Bye, squirt," her dad told her, using the name he'd called her throughout her childhood.

"Bye, Daddy." She sucked in a deep breath and pressed the receiver down, disconnecting the call.

Khloe ran back out of the hotel. She dashed down the street toward Olas Altas. Realizing how awkward that appeared, she pulled back to a slow walk, but her feet moved only from rote memory. Her brain continued to order her not to cry anymore. No one wanted to see a tearful girl sobbing on the street. People would stare, and some of those might be the wrong people.

The morning traffic on the streets had picked up, and tourists filled the sidewalks, milling along after their late breakfast. The crowds comforted her, but at the same time, they concerned her. How could she spot someone among all these people?

What if some stranger slipped up behind her in the street with a knife? She'd never be able to tell her parents she was alive. Would the Mexican police even notify them? She didn't have her passport on her. The cops might regard her as a nameless victim of a crime, labeling her as a Jane Doe or whatever name the local cops gave people like that.

Would Roland know? It should be a relief for him. He had enough on his plate.

Khloe's feet climbed the steps on the sidewalk next to the small corner shop. As she stumbled past The Palm Cabaret, she felt exhaustion hit her. The outside bar area was empty since the club was closed, and Khloe sank into the leather couch under the tent. She wasn't visible to anyone on the street, and only if someone passed her on the walkway between the tent and the building would they be able to see her. She pulled her body into the corner of the couch and drew her knees up to her chest.

Then she cried. It wasn't a loud sobbing, but her head sank between her legs. With her face hidden, she bawled.

36

After Khloe had enough time to get out of the restaurant, Caleb got to his feet.

"Excuse me, sir," a waiter stepped up to him.

"Sorry, I have to go," he insisted, pushing past him.

The server glanced back at the table where Caleb had just come from. He turned to a man that resembled a manager, offering a frustrated shrug.

Caleb's right arm wrapped around his side. Every move he made shot pain through his nerves, especially now that the adrenaline subsided. He had at least a cracked rib, but from the way it moved, there was likely a broken one. If he didn't want to double over at the wrong time, he needed to wrap his torso.

In his years in the field, Caleb found that, next to a Walmart, most restaurants had nearly anything one required for quick medical attention. Need a surgery table? There was often a prep station complete with carving knives. Need antiseptic? The bar offered all sorts of varieties. The cleaning closet had an ample supply of bleach as well.

Caleb walked through a swinging door into the kitchen. The most common thing about restaurant kitchens was how no matter how unusual something was, over half the people just moved around it to do their job. Servers and line cooks tended to remain focused on their task to the detriment of their surroundings. Caleb sidestepped a food runner carrying a large tray filled with six plates of food. Two servers glanced up from their tasks of grabbing plated dishes from the expo line. Both women seemed to acknowledge him, but their food would get cold if they waited to check what he was doing. With their hands burdened with the meals, they exited the kitchen.

Caleb lifted a roll of clear plastic wrap, stuffing it under his arm. He picked up two fresh, still-white towels from a bin. As he marched toward the back of the kitchen, the sounds of spatulas scrapping the griddle and something bubbling in the fryer filled the room. He grabbed a serrated knife, likely used for slicing bread, and turned the corner.

The walk-in freezer was in the rear, and like in every restaurant, it was the last bastion of sanity in the busy establishment. When he stepped inside, white vapor curled around his warm skin. Carefully, he removed his shirt. Even without a mirror, he noted the subcutaneous tissue blackening from the brutal beating. Some places reminded him of a purple fried egg.

Caleb stretched the two towels around his chest before unwinding the wrap around him. The rags would keep the plastic from cutting off all oxygen to the area. It would become a sweaty, uncomfortable mess if he'd let the plastic sit directly on the skin.

He spent five minutes winding the plastic wrap around himself as tight as he could do it. Once it was taut, he took a deep breath. The pain in his chest hadn't gone away, but at least he could breathe easier. Now that he'd bound his torso, the constriction should keep the ribs from moving too much.

Suddenly, the walk-in door opened, and a cook in a white smock stood dumbfounded in the doorway. A look of confusion crossed his face as he stared at the shirtless man wrapped in clear plastic wrap.

"Who are you?" he demanded, and then his eyes drew to the serrated knife lying on the box next to Caleb. With a swift motion, Caleb grabbed the handle and used the blade to rip the plastic.

"I'm leaving," he stated in explanation.

"You're bleeding," the cook announced, pointing to Caleb's arm.

"Shit, yeah," he acknowledged, wrapping a towel around the graze left by one of the cartel bullets. He slipped into his shirt and marched past the man.

"You can't do that," the cook called, but mostly he just stared after the man as he exited the kitchen.

"He can't do that," the cook called. "Chef!"

By the time the chef responded to the alert from the panicked employee, Caleb pushed through the front doors and stepped out onto the sidewalk.

He spotted two of the men who followed him and Khloe on the street. Corsair stepped across the street, where the two men would have no trouble spotting him. He climbed the steps into Cárdenas Park again. On Mondays there was no Farmers Market, but the park still functioned as a gathering zone. Small crowds or friends gathered around in clusters with their coffee or breakfasts.

Corsair stole a glance to verify the two guys continued to follow behind. They were talking to each other while searching the crowd—looking for Khloe.

He cut across the park, taking an almost identical path that Khloe had taken the first day. If he led this pair away from the touristy areas, he could zigzag through the side streets, avoiding cameras along the way. In the months since he'd been in Puerto Vallarta, he learned to spot and avoid most surveillance.

He headed east on a small, bricked street. The mountains loomed up above the city from there, and Caleb sped up his pace to a trot. He didn't want to risk losing them, but he needed to put out a sense of urgency on his part. Hopefully, they'd pick up on that and try to keep up.

A voice echoed between the buildings, and when Caleb checked, one tried to speak into a phone through ragged breaths.

Caleb turned a corner as a white taxicab pulled onto the street a block ahead. A couple climbed out of the vehicle, dragging shopping bags out with them. They were in their seventies, and Caleb guessed they leased a nearby apartment based on the bags of groceries in their hands. He broke into a sprint as the woman was about to close the rear door.

"Hold that cab, please," he called.

Instinctively, the woman stepped out of the way as Caleb slid into the empty back seat.

"Thank you," he offered as he pulled the door closed.

"*Basilio Badillo y doscientos, por favor.*"

"Of course," the man responded in English as he shifted into first gear.

Caleb watched the two men standing on the street curb as the taxi passed them. He kept his eyes on the one still on the phone. He'd report that they lost him. For now. It wouldn't take them long to reach out to the taxi company and find out where the cabbie took him.

The cab came to a sudden stop behind a Volkswagen box truck attempting to climb the steep hill. The city engineers chose the top of the cobblestoned road to be the ideal place to put a stop sign. For most vehicles, it was a minor annoyance, but today the building across from the intersection was running its sprinkler system and subsequently sending streams of excess water running over the slick stones. The box truck's tires spun furiously and futilely as the driver tried to get the loaded freight truck up the hill.

Two guys were behind the vehicle, shouting instructions to the driver, who shouted curses back when no traction could be attained. The taxi driver muttered something in Spanish, and Caleb tossed a thousand pesos into the front seat before slipping out the back door. By the time the driver realized what was happening, he turned to stop Caleb. The wad of bills distracted him for a second, and when he finally looked back for his passenger, Caleb vanished on the street.

By the time the rear door slammed and the driver had time to look back, Caleb was nowhere to be seen.

Caleb headed south on whatever street he stopped on. It wouldn't take him long to get his bearings, but for the moment, he wanted to blend in.

He wondered if the two men still after him was a good sign that Khloe got away. That might not be true, though. He'd killed several of the cartel members this morning, and the machismo pride the cartel attempted to carry meant he'd made a very dangerous enemy. Puerto Vallarta couldn't be home anymore, he realized.

Drug cartels weren't much different from intelligence agencies across the globe. They paid a great deal of money and instilled a large dose of fear by creating a vast network. The Cortez Cartel would broadcast across the streets, looking for an American man and woman. He'd seen information channels work like that with incredible speed. It left him no choice. He would escort Khloe out of the city today with Amanda.

Caleb quickened his pace up the slope. He should be able to weave between a couple of condominium buildings to the gondola that traveled up and down the slope from Pulpito, only half a block from his apartment.

Behind him, he heard a horn blare before a deafening crunch. He guessed the truck didn't make it up the hill.

37

Lee Hubbard waited in the center of the street, where the pedestrian pathway known as the Malecón intersected with Aquiles Serdán. Castillo stood by the host stand at La Langosta Loca, talking to a short, stocky Latino man in a cheap suit. The restaurant manager reminded her of the maître d' at the French place Angie loved to go to. His brow remained furrowed in frustration as he spoke to the second sergeant.

Castillo received the radio call while they were reviewing the phone footage several of the tourists on the pedestrian bridge took. The chef at the beachside establishment called in that an injured man was hiding in the walk-in cooler. When a cook confronted him, the man fled into the street.

Lee glanced up at the building. The closed-circuit cameras on the exterior were newer models, and she wondered if they had similar ones in the dining room. When Castillo finished the initial interview with the manager, she intended to ask him.

She walked toward the alley, and Patterson, realizing she was moving away, hurried to catch up.

"You're looking at the cameras," he pointed out.

"Yeah," she acknowledged.

"Hoping your guy actually showed his face here?" he questioned.

It was frustrating to find that of the four videos from the bridge they watched, none of them offered a clear view of the man's face. To Lee, that was confirmation enough. Only someone as skilled in countersurveillance as Corsair could successfully avoid the cameras every time.

Lee had mixed feelings about it, too. As long as Corsair remained at large, she might get to him first. If he set off alarms back at the Office of Compliance, then Winston would send out an entire posse. That might mean Lee wasn't the first to find Caleb Saunders. It could also result in a much bloodier outcome.

As she looked between La Langosta Loca and the neighboring restaurant, a bar called La Maquina, two men shrank away from the street.

"Hey!" she called to the two, but they scurried toward the back of the opening.

Lee sidled into the small space that was too small to be called an alley. At best, it was a gap.

"Stop!" she shouted again.

"What is it?" Patterson asked behind her as he followed her. "This is fucking tight!"

When Lee reached the back of the building, she stepped out onto a sandy spot. The beach was already busy, and her head turned up and down the sand, searching for the two men.

Patterson popped out behind her, gasping for air.

"Damn, that was too much," he declared. "What was it?"

"Two men hiding there. I think they were watching us."

Patterson took a second to stare up and down the beach. "Where did they go?"

Lee shook her head.

"They might have just been some local street punks, and you scared them."

"I don't think so," she insisted. Her instinct told her it was more. "They were watching us."

"What did they look like?" Patterson asked.

"Hard to say. They weren't old—maybe in their twenties. Young twenties, at that."

"That would make sense," Patterson agreed. "That's a job for someone down the food chain. But why?"

"I'm thinking they want to know if we catch up to the girl before they do."

"Good point," Patterson conceded. "But do they want my girl or your guy?"

Lee glanced at him. "I doubt it matters much now."

Patterson nodded. "After what this guy did by the river, I doubt it. The cartel will want his head, for no other reason than to remind people not to fuck with them. The last thing they want is someone to think they can get one over on them. It's a sign of weakness."

"Is the FBI aware of what Sonny Departi's cartel connections might be?" she asked Patterson. "If we went straight to the source, we might protect Khloe from them."

"Looks like your guy is doing a decent enough job of that," Patterson suggested.

"Until his luck runs out," Lee remarked. "If we don't get ahead of this, we'll just be chasing. We need to be proactive now instead of reactive."

Patterson shrugged. "I'll contact the office. If there's anything in the files, we'll find it."

Lee sighed. The idea seemed fruitless to her, but she was worrying that Corsair was about to take flight. If he bolted from the city now, it might take months to get a bead on him again.

"Let's go see if we can check the cameras," she suggested.

"Not sure what the point is," Patterson said. "We know who we're tracking, and I'm willing to wager your guy didn't look at a single one."

Lee didn't reply.

"I'm curious," Patterson commented. "Why is this guy helping Khloe at all?"

Lee looked up at him without a word.

"I mean, I get he's a rogue agent, right?" he asked nonchalantly. "What's the benefit to him helping her? It's only drawing attention to himself, right?"

Lee couldn't explain to him what she knew about Caleb Saunders. She wasn't sure herself, but over the last year, the profile she was building on him continued to expand. Caleb Saunders wasn't the same man that disappeared in Turkey over a decade earlier. Marriage must have softened him. Well, not softened, because a gentle man didn't kill seven people in the street, even if they were dangerous cartel members. No, Lee thought his wife gave him a more solid base—a moral guideline. Plus, Corsair was a father now. That skewed his outlook. For the better, Lee considered.

However, Patterson was right. Corsair's involvement with Khloe Evans drew undue attention to him, and she knew that meant her time was running out. Hell, if Winston didn't call her today to find out why she was in Mexico, it would shock her.

"Where did you go?" Castillo inquired when the pair of agents returned to the front entrance.

"Hubbard saw two guys on the side of the building," Patterson explained. "They took off."

Castillo raised an eyebrow. The manager asked, "Were they dangerous? What were they doing?"

"They ran off," Lee offered.

Castillo's face hardened. "We have some footage, but none of it gives us anything new," he told them.

"Big fucking surprise," Patterson quipped.

38

Jimmy walked up to the door, an ornate, red, wooden one with a large brass knocker in the shape of a lion. The whole thing reminded Jimmy of Scrooge's door in *A Christmas Carol*. As he reached up to pull back the smooth ring hanging in the jaws of the predator, he worried the feline mouth would open up to snap at his fingers. He let the brass thud against the wood.

Clunk. Clunk. Clunk.

"Jimmy!" Vinnie exclaimed when he opened the door. His tone was congenial, as if they were a pair of friends reuniting after a long time. "Come on in."

Cautiously, the man stepped into the foyer of the villa. He turned back to catch the view from the entrance before Vinnie closed it. From the front step, one could gaze across the rooftops opposite the house to see only the tops of the trees in the Isla Cuale Park before the terraced city stretched down to the sea.

"Your head looks terrible," Vinnie remarked, peering at the gash on his temple.

"It feels that way, too."

"What the hell did he hit you with?" Vinnie asked.

"A giant fucking wrench," Jimmy explained. "I didn't see it coming."

"Damn, better watch out next time."

Better watch out next time? Better not be a next time.

"Sonny's on the patio." The statement came out like a host inviting a guest to join them, however, Jimmy recognized the faux sentiment for what it was. He not only didn't trust Vinnie but also he feared the man.

"Jimmy!" Sonny called as he passed through the French doors to a quaint courtyard at the center of the home. The stone walls reached up toward the blue sky. Green ivy-like vines crept up the sides of the house with small tendrils extending from the stalk to grip the porous rock.

"Sonny," Jimmy greeted his boss.

"Quite a place, ain't it?" the man marveled, gesturing up at the courtyard. He sat a wrought-iron table with a glass of red wine and a plate of cheese. "I should get down here more often. It seems like a pleasant city."

"Yeah, I guess so," Jimmy agreed. "How was your flight?"

"How was my flight?" Sonny repeated. "Vinnie, look at this guy. His head looks like a fucking cantaloupe and he's concerned about how my trip was. You're a good guy, Jimmy."

"Uh, thank you."

Sonny crossed his arms. "You seem worried, Jimmy."

"I...uh..."

The boss let out a sigh. "You aren't in trouble," he assured him.

"Really?"

Sonny turned his face to Vinnie. "Tell him as much."

"You ain't," Vinnie promised.

"But WT..." Jimmy stammered.

"Oh, the situation is fucked," Sonny responded. "No doubt about it. I had to tell WT's mother that some fucker killed him. She's my aunt, you know?"

"Yeah, Sonny. I know."

"She didn't take it too well, for sure. But it's part of it. What I want now is to find this bastard and put him in the ground. For WT."

"Me too," Jimmy replied, a hint of relief escaped into his voice.

"Vinnie, you hear from that spic?"

"Two guys spotted the guy on the street, but no Khloe."

Sonny nodded along. "Must've split up," he commented.

"They lost him, though," Vinnie explained. "Jumped in a cab. Tomás has a guy going to the cabbie to find out where he took him."

"Good," Sonny answered. "Jimmy, you met Tomás, yes?"

Jimmy nodded.

"Whatcha think of him?"

"He's pissed that seven of his guys were killed this morning."

Vinnie let out a soft whistle under his breath.

"Seven. How the hell did one guy take out seven on the streets?"

Jimmy shrugged. "They don't think he had a gun, either. At least not at first."

"Wait a minute," Vinnie interjected. "The guy didn't have a gun at all?"

Shaking his head, Jimmy answered, "Not from what Tomás said. He took one off his man."

"Is this guy a Fed?" Vinnie questioned. "Or what? Who the hell can do that?"

"From what I've heard," Sonny responded, "this guy ain't a Fed. At least, not sanctioned that anyone can tell."

"What does that mean?" Vinnie asked.

"It seems vague, but so far, no one knows who he is."

"We should hire him," Vinnie joked.

Jimmy instinctively drew his finger up to his temple, thinking that would be an insult.

Sonny eyed Jimmy. "No, it might be better if we put this one in the ground."

"Tomás is already gunning for him," Jimmy told them. "He's pissed about it."

A groan came from Sonny. "If he's already going after him, why are we paying the bastards so much?"

"It's their turf, Sonny," Vinnie reminded his boss.

"Don't they get the best end of the bargain?" Sonny growled. "We give the exclusivity into our market, and I still have to drop a million on Tomás."

A million? That shocked Jimmy.

"We can call the whole thing off," Vinnie suggested. "It's up to you, Sonny."

"No kidding," the man muttered. "Of course it's up to me."

Vinnie shook his head. "I'm just saying we don't have to chase the bitch. She hasn't said anything so far. Maybe she didn't know anything."

"No, that little prick, Nic, knew enough to put me away. Why wouldn't he tell his girl?"

Vinnie said nothing, but Jimmy wanted to cancel the entire thing. If he didn't have to run around after Khloe Evans and her boyfriend, he might survive.

"What do you want, then?"

"Vinnie, drop a bounty on her head. Half a million. Put one on this asshole too," Sonny demanded.

"We'll be in two mil between Cortez and this."

Sonny shrugged. "I'd rather sleep at night. We'll make it up along the way."

Jimmy wanted to shrink away. If they dropped an open hit on these two, it would muddy the waters, with everyone gunning for them. Hell, people would come out of the woodwork to take a potshot at a million bucks. Somehow, Jimmy didn't care. Whoever killed this bastard could have it all.

39

Caleb spent several minutes of looping back and forth along the streets, ensuring that no one was following him. He'd been certain, but years in the field taught him to never trust the initial feelings. If someone trailed him, they were invisible, a feat he hadn't seen happen before. He worked to search for drones. That technology had advanced over the last decade, and it was an area that would make countersurveillance challenging. Spotting a dot half a mile in the sky was difficult, and sometimes impossible. The best course of action was to slip through buildings where the cameras on the drones couldn't see him. In lieu of that, narrow alleys forced the drones to get closer in order to maintain a simple line of sight.

It wouldn't surprise him if the cartels employed those measures. They'd have the budget to purchase military-grade equipment. There was no doubt that the OOC had access to them, and if they could limit their search to a small section of Puerto Vallarta, like the Romantic Zone, it might take them some time, but eventually they'd catch sight of him.

Time to leave, he reminded himself.

With deliberate steps and a swiveling head, he walked down Pulpito in the shadow of a condominium. The wrapping around his torso was loosening. Probably the sweat under the plastic caused it to slide. As the tension lessened, the ache in his chest increased.

He turned his attention to his surroundings as he walked. The logo above the door read "Signature by Pinnacle" with a mountaintop behind the words. Given that the building sat atop a hill so steep that it created a gap in the road, he thought the name made sense. He passed a construction crew shuttling bags of dry concrete mix up to a higher floor using a wooden pallet along with a rope and pulley as an elevator.

At the crest of the hill, the condominium board constructed a small gondola to ferry residents down to the street below. The ride was gratis to anyone, and Caleb often took Amanda up it just for fun. When he got in the cart, the operator, an old man who actually pulled the lever to carry passengers up and down the slope, gave him a smile.

"*Buenas tarde*," he offered.

Caleb nodded to him as he slid the gate closed in the small gondola, which amounted to little more than a four-person cage with two wooden bench seats facing each other. The car jerked as the cable carrying it popped and snapped over the large pulleys at the top of the hill. The operator just smiled as if the quick motions were normal. When they reached the bottom of the hill, the old man pulled the metal gate back so Caleb could step out. Caleb slipped twenty pesos into the tip bucket attached to the inside wall.

"*Gracias*," the operated replied.

"*De nada*," Caleb responded as he climbed down the steps to the sidewalk running across the street from the Olas Altas Apartments.

A line of cars rumbled past, and when the last one rolled by, Caleb stepped onto Olas Altas and crossed the road. Despite having run a constant surveillance check since jumping out of the taxi, Caleb scanned the sidewalks for anyone who might be watching. Nothing set off any mental alarms, and he climbed the stairs to the apartment.

"Good afternoon, Mr. Roland," Miguel greeted Caleb as they passed on the steps. "How are you today?"

"Afternoon, Miguel. Doing good. You?"

"Just working," he sighed. "Mr. Roland, I have to ask, though. The girl staying with you—is she a friend?" The man smiled a sheepish grin as he lowered his face.

Caleb bristled for a second before answering. "My sister. She's only here a few days."

"Is she single?" he asked, glancing up with a conniving expression.

"No," Caleb snapped.

"Oh, I'm sorry, Mr. Roland," Miguel stammered like a kid caught in the middle of some misbehavior. "She seemed nice, is all."

"*Es bien*," Caleb assured him. "She's a very private person, though."

Miguel nodded as Caleb walked the rest of the way up the steps to the second level. He didn't look back, hoping that Miguel took the rebuke to heart and didn't press the issue. He couldn't blame the guy. After all, Khloe was an attractive and smart girl. At a glance, she seemed exactly what a young man Miguel's age would want. Of course, the mobsters gunning for her detracted some from the appeal. It might be more than Miguel could handle.

"Daddy!"

Caleb glanced into the courtyard where Amanda and Angel were splashing in the pool.

"Are you having fun?" he asked his daughter.

She responded with an almost violent nod, followed by a toothy grin. Angel gave him a reassuring smile that the pair were doing great. He realized how much he'd miss having Angel around when they left. Not as much as Amanda would, though, and he regretted that they needed to flee.

I need to set Angel's school up, he thought, remembering his promise to help the girl. It would take some financial finagling once he got settled, but he'd ensure that she could go to the university without worrying about tuition. He worried that if they had to leave without an official farewell, it might be traumatic for Amanda. After all, she'd already had that happen when Audrey died. It wouldn't be fair to do it to her again. Unfortunately, fair had little to do with it.

He unlocked the apartment door, and when he entered, Caleb found Khloe on the bed, asleep. He didn't want to wake her. The stress from the day spiraled her into exhaustion. People who aren't used to the ebbs and flows of adrenaline might not handle the chemical imbalance. The result was usually sleep—hard and fast sleep.

Caleb slipped into the bathroom, gently closing the door with. He turned on the shower before stripping his clothes and then peeling the clear plastic wrap from his torso. When the air hit his sweaty skin, it felt cool, but the loosening of the binding sent an ache through him. He stepped into the steaming stream, rinsing himself off in the hot water.

When he got out of the shower, he found the first-aid kid under the sink. Years in the field taught him to have something on hand for emergencies, and within a day of settling into the apartment, he stocked a kit with enough medical supplies to perform minor surgery in his new home. He removed a roll of elastic bandage that he wound around himself with a little more care than he'd done with the plastic wrap in the restaurant. Once he ensured he'd secured his chest, he dressed.

Without making a sound, Caleb pulled a bottle of Pacifico from the refrigerator and slipped past the sleeping Khloe to the sliding glass door leading out to the balcony. He stepped out and settled into the plastic chair. The afternoon sun remained shielded by the building, and the ocean breeze came straight up the street from the beach. He popped the top off the beer and turned it up as the door on the neighboring balcony opened.

Crap.

Frank, whose last name Caleb had never gotten, walked out onto the terrace. The retired truck driver from Toronto had been living next door for the past three months. So far, Caleb thought he'd only gone to walk on the beach one day a week. Beyond that, he only left his apartment to go across town to Walmart for his groceries. Frank did little, and it was clear from the gut hanging over his waist.

"Hey neighbor," Frank greeted as his lighter snapped.

"How's it going, Frank?" Caleb said. The ocean breeze suddenly smelled of Camel cigarettes.

"Another Monday," Frank moaned as the plastic lawn chair creaked when he sat down.

Caleb resisted the urge to roll his eyes. How did someone living in paradise with no job worry about what day it was?

"You hear them last night?" Frank asked.

"Them" referred to the people that gathered across the street from their balconies at Garbo's Piano Bar. It took half a conversation with Frank for Caleb to realize when he said "them" he meant "the homosexuals," a clarification Frank offered in case Caleb wasn't astute enough to recognize the blatant bigotry.

Caleb admonished Frank on the spot, but he was greeted with his neighbor's statement, "Oh, I don't care what people do. They just shouldn't do it in front of others."

"They shouldn't just live their life?" Caleb countered.

"I mean live and let live," Frank retorted, and Caleb did not know how the Canadian worked that thought into his sentence.

After that conversation, Caleb attempted to avoid engaging in words with Frank. The man said he planned to leave at the end of the month, and Caleb had looked forward to being able to sit on his balcony in peace. Now that he knew his own time in Puerto Vallarta was short, it didn't seem to matter.

"They were singing all night," Frank moaned.

"It's a piano bar, Frank."

"Yeah, I know. But those people get so rowdy."

"'Those people'?" Caleb questioned without looking toward the man.

"You know what I mean."

"Mmm," Caleb groaned, opting to take a drink from his Pacifico rather than respond to the comment.

Then he repeated his catchphrase. "You know, I'm all about letting people live and let live."

"Uh-huh," Caleb remarked. At first, he wondered why someone with such potent feelings about gays would bother moving for several months to the center of a gay tourist spot. It seemed like the self-avowed bachelor might be in denial. Until today, Caleb had just been counting down the days until the man left.

He drained the rest of the Pacifico. "I'm getting another beer, Frank," he told his neighbor as if he should expect him back. However, when he returned to the apartment, he had no intention of listening to Frank's inane drivel.

Khloe sat up on the bed. Her eyes looked dazed as she tried to riddle out where she was.

"You're awake," he remarked, and the girl blinked three times before looking at him.

"Yes, sorry," she muttered. "I must have fallen asleep."

"It's the adrenaline rush," he told her. "You crashed after."

"I'm sorry," she repeated.

"Don't be. That response is normal human nature."

"No one followed you?" she wondered, drawing her knees up to her chest.

Caleb shook his head. "No, I lost them. For now."

"For now?"

Nodding, he replied, "They were everywhere."

"They were Mexican," she stated. "That's not Sonny's people?"

"It's the Cortez Cartel."

"Cartel?" she repeated. "Why are they involved?"

"If you never crossed paths with them, my guess is that Sonny hired some extra help," Caleb explained.

"What do I do?"

"We have to leave town," he told her.

"But I don't have any money," she responded. "Can't we wait until they forget about me? You know, like you said?"

He shook his head. "Not anymore. They can drop a low-level guy to sit outside your bank for weeks."

"Wait, you said 'we,'" she pointed out.

"I just killed several members of the Cortez Cartel. They don't strike me as the forgiving type, and while I think we're safe for the moment, it won't take long for them to scour the streets for both of us. I can't risk my daughter."

"Sonny won't stop, though," Khloe pointed out.

"We could kill him," Caleb suggested.

Khloe stared at the man. Slowly, her face changed as the idea settled inside her. "You mean it?"

He nodded.

"Are you some kind of secret agent?" she asked.

Caleb lifted an eyebrow.

"You know how to do things," she suggested. "Plus, I think you're hiding from someone, too."

Caleb sat on the sofa opposite the bed and stared at her. "I'm not a secret agent," he said. "Not really."

"What are you?"

"Right now, I'm nothing," he answered.

"But you were. CIA? Are you here on some secret mission?"

"Not CIA, and it's best if you don't know," he stated.

"Is your name Roland Bryers?"

He shook his head. "And I can't tell you what it is."

"I would never tell anyone," she blurted out, sounding offended. "Not after all you've done for me."

"Khloe, I don't doubt you at all, but I have to protect someone besides myself."

The girl glanced over at the corner where a small pile of stuffed animals sat. Khloe nodded. "I get it."

Caleb crossed his legs and looked at the woman. She turned to him again. "Can you really kill him?" she asked.

"We'd have to get him to come here," he suggested. "That would be the easiest thing. But, yes. I can kill Sonny. No problem."

Khloe watched the man, trying to gauge if he would do what he said. The impassive stare he offered sent a chill over her.

"How would we do it?" she wondered, grasping the idea now.

"He wants you. So we offer him—well, you."

"Like bait?"

"Exactly," Caleb answered with a grin. "I get word to him that I'll trade you to him for cash. Probably a lot of cash. But the caveat is, I'll only deliver you directly to him."

"Would he do that?"

He shook his head. "Not likely, but it might get him down here, at least. Men like Sonny can't get where they are in life without a hefty ego. He will blame everyone under him for failing, and when he thinks he can outmaneuver me, he'll agree."

"What if he does? Outmaneuver you?"

"Then we'll die."

40

The plan itself was simple. Step one was to find a cartel member.

They did just that on the other side of Lázaro Cárdenas Park. The man, sitting in a newer model Toyota Tacoma, was in his forties—a higher-ranking associate of the cartel given his nice truck and the cushy job.

Too close to home, Caleb thought. They were only three blocks from the apartment, and this park was often a walking destination for either him or Angel to take Amanda. Caleb resisted the urge to bolt right then. It wasn't fear that spurred that call to action, but prudence.

Caleb and Khloe sat at a bar sipping a margarita. Rather than try to disguise both of them, Khloe used a cap and some men's clothes, albeit colorful and bright, to transform into a young man. The restaurant itself was a cantina-style establishment that, similar to Garbo's, catered to the gay tourist trade. Caleb suspected that the machismo the cartel exhibited might cause them to avoid places like that.

It was stupid and careless, but Caleb, long ago, learned to understand the nuances of humanity. Almost every man he targeted was predictable in their own way. Their life up to that moment defined them, and humans don't stray too far from their definitions. The drug world was cutthroat, and in order to survive, the members in that society needed to be just as vicious. They only trusted what they understood, and based on most of their upbringing, they had no grasp on the people who differed from them. It scared them—as if being near a gay man might somehow convert them.

While Caleb found the ideology ignorant, he had no qualms about using it against them. Khloe and he sat at the bar watching the Tacoma.

"There's another one," Khloe remarked as a skinny late teens or early twenties kid walked past the truck. He made a signal with his hand, and the cartel man behind the wheel nodded. The spy craft was obvious. These guys were amateurs, something which made it easy for Caleb. After all, if they had been professional, one of the men giving updates would have checked the local bars.

Cartels, perhaps more than a lot of organized crime, developed a complacency, thinking that the fear they've instilled in the people, coupled with the officials on their payroll, provided them a layer of security. Much of that changed a few years back when the Mexican government reformed the state police, but corruption crept into every police department in the world. It would be no different here.

But that ego made them stupid.

"Another one," Khloe pointed out, taking a sip of her margarita. She was developing a good eye for surveillance. Caleb figured it was the high level of anxiety from months on the run mixed with common sense and necessity. "How many do they have?" she wondered.

"Kids like that?" Caleb asked. "Probably hundreds of teens out there being groomed to do jobs just like this. They flood the street with them, and whoever spots us first gets rewarded."

"Geez," she sighed.

Since sitting at the bar, they'd counted seven young men—boys—pass the Tacoma and give a signal that Caleb assumed meant nothing to report.

"Those kids are going to do anything they can to get their foot in the door," Caleb explained. "And they will endure all sorts of shit to do so."

"Same with the Sonny," Khloe reported. "Nic busted his ass running errands just to get to where he was. Fat lotta good that did him, huh?"

Caleb shrugged. "Some guys make it. More don't. Those kids are interchangeable to the man at the top. If the cops bust one of them, the most he can do is give up Mr. Tacoma there."

"Couldn't the police just climb the ladder until they get to the top?" she asked.

"Theoretically, yes, but realistically, no. Once those guys graduate to sitting in trucks, they start to understand the repercussions and benefits. If Mr. Tacoma talks or anyone even suspects him of talking, he becomes a liability to someone. Maybe they kill his boss in some gruesome fashion, so that by the time he squeals, there is no one to squeal about."

"Ugh," she groaned.

"Works that way where you come from too," he pointed out.

Khloe nodded. "That's why they want me," she assumed.

"Likely. Or it might be more sinister than that. Perhaps they want to kill you just to spite Nic."

"But he's dead," she retorted. "What does that help?"

"It reminds the next Nic that his actions go beyond himself."

She shivered. "That asshole."

The corner of Caleb's mouth lifted.

"What's the plan, then?"

"You're going to slip out the back and head to the apartment. Stay out of sight, but don't look like you're staying out of sight."

She cocked her head sideways.

"Just be careful," he advised.

"What are you going to do?"

"I'm going to send Sonny a message," Caleb explained.

"Think he'll come?"

"I'll try to be convincing and simple. He can have you if he brings me half a million dollars."

"Half a million?" Her face grew ashen as she worried for a brief second that he might go through with it. "Why so much?"

"Trust me," he assured her. "He will not want to pay me. Sonny'll agree to it, but he isn't going to bring the money. This will be a double cross where he'll probably give me over to the cartel for killing their guys."

"But that's a terrible plan," she muttered.

"Not if it gets him here," Caleb promised. "Go, now. I want you gone for a bit before I go into action."

Khloe stood up and walked to the rear of the cantina. When they first arrived, he had her slip to the back under the guise of looking for a bathroom. She found a door propped open in the kitchen to keep the heat to a minimum. Fifteen seconds after she got off the barstool, she should have been in the alley and heading away from the park. They took a circuitous route here during which he gave her an abbreviated lesson on running countersurveillance, and he ordered her to follow it on her return while putting that training into practice,

Caleb folded his hands on the counter. His angle allowed him to stare into the Tecate mirror hanging over the bar for a perfect line of sight to the Tacoma. He waited six minutes until another watcher signaled the driver. How long would the guy stay here before he got bored, or they changed tactics?

Now was as good a time as any. When the bartender walked to the back for a second, Caleb stood on the rails on his barstool, raising himself up another foot. He reached across the bar and picked up a sharp knife the bartender had been using to slice limes. Caleb sat back down, swiveling around and sliding the handle of the knife up his right sleeve.

He walked out of the cantina, crossing behind the Tacoma. While the truck had a back seat, the rear doors only opened when the front one did. Ideally, Caleb would slide into the rear before the driver could react. Now, he'd play it out differently.

In three long strides, he shifted directions toward the passenger door. His right hand wrenched it open, sliding into the seat. The driver, surprised, twisted around to find the blade of the bar knife at his throat.

In Spanish, Corsair rasped, "If you flinch, I'll bleed you out right here."

The driver, a thick man in his late thirties, flicked his eyes at the intruder. His pupils widened as his situation struck him. This was the man he was supposed to be looking for, and the bastard just got into his car.

"Both hands on the wheel," Corsair ordered. "Very slow."

As the driver complied, Caleb slipped his hand behind the driver's back and retrieved a black Glock G48. He moved the palm of his hand over the driver, checking for any more weapons. He found a spare magazine he took from the man's front pocket.

"What do you want?" the driver asked.

"A conversation," he answered, lifting the cellphone from the console between the front seats. "I want you to call the man in charge of you. As high as you can get."

He gave a curt nod as Corsair swapped the knife in his hand for the nine-millimeter Glock, checking that a round was chambered. The barrel pressed against the man's ribs as Corsair thumbed the safety off. If he pulled the trigger, the bullet in the chamber would exit the barrel at an upward angle through the man's ribs, tearing a tunnel through most of the organs in his body starting with the liver and gall bladder before blowing through the heart and lungs. If no bones stopped its trajectory and velocity, the bullet could exit through the man's upper left back.

No matter what happened, he'd be dead in an instant.

The driver understood that. He took the phone from Corsair's right hand and opened the screen. He dialed a number.

"Tomás, I—"

Corsair grabbed the phone from his ear and ordered, "Grab the wheel."

He put the phone to his ear and said, "Tomás, I'm sitting here with your man. I want to speak with Sonny Departi."

"Who is this?" the man named Tomás asked in Spanish.

"I'm the one who killed a bunch of your guys earlier today."

"Ah, I see," Tomás replied after a momentary pause. "What makes you think I can let you talk with Sonny Departi? Better yet, why would I even let you?"

"Because I'll kill this guy right here."

"Eh, I don't care," Tomás replied.

Caleb assumed that in less than a minute, any cartel force in the area would descend on his location. He needed to move this along.

"I'll trade the girl, but I want to talk to Sonny."

Tomás chuckled. "Hold on."

Corsair counted the seconds. Twenty-seven passed since he took the phone. He was going to bolt before a minute lapsed.

An American voice came over the phone, saying in English, "This must be Mr. Roland Bryer."

Caleb froze.

"Mr. Bryer, I thought you wanted to speak with me?" Sonny Departi asked over the phone.

Caleb swallowed, shoved the barrel of the G48 against the man's ribs, and pulled the trigger.

41

The gunshot echoed through the car despite being muffled by the driver's body. Corsair threw the door open, and his feet hit the street in a sprint. As he ran, he noted two younger men crossing from Cárdenas Park in a hurry. Caleb still gripped the Glock G48 in his hand as his feet thudded against the sidewalk. Aware that it might draw attention, he shoved the weapon into his waistband.

If Sonny Departi identified his alias, he either had already found the Olas Altas Apartments or would soon. Caleb already knew which one it was—Sonny tipped his hand intentionally.

Someone lunged at him from behind a car, and Corsair skidded to a stop. A kid no older than twenty swung a knife at him. He blocked the kid's arm with his left before wrapping his hand around the thug's wrist. With a snap toward him, he jerked the boy forward. The action surprised his attacker, who expected his quarry to leap back. Stumbling ahead, the kid couldn't slow himself as Corsair jerked him around into a blue Nissan on the curb. Before the cartel's initiate rebounded, Corsair caught the back of his head and shoved him forward again. The impact of the guy's face on the rear passenger window shattered the glass.

As he dropped the unconscious figure, the assassin spun toward the other two, who had been running up behind him. Both of them were only a little older than the boy, who was bleeding at Corsair's feet. The closest, a skinny, mustachioed man wearing a dirty, white, sleeveless shirt, stopped, shocked to witness what Caleb did to the other kid.

The other passed his friend, almost unable to stop. Caleb recognized the small revolver in his hand, and the Glock came from behind him, firing before the guy realized he should raise his own gun. The bullet hit the man in the face, jerking his head back and stopping all forward momentum. As the dead kid still stumbled a few feet; his leg muscles took a microsecond to learn that the brain was already gone.

Corsair shifted the direction of the barrel and fired. The other man twisted around as the round struck him in the shoulder. Alive, the cartel member toppled to the sidewalk as Caleb turned to run.

Had this been a Saturday afternoon instead of a Monday, people would have filled the streets. As it was, once the gunfire started, the few pedestrians ran for the nearest cover, either taking shelter behind cars or inside open stores.

The police would be here soon, and if Caleb didn't get far enough away, the cops would surround him. He ran a block before slowing to a walk and turning down an alley. The one-way access ended at a loading dock, and Caleb jumped up on the concrete platform and tried the door. It opened, and Corsair passed through, finding himself in the receiving area of a hotel.

As the back of his hand wiped the sweat from his forehead, he strolled through the service corridors until he found an elevator. Two hotel employees strolled by him without giving him much notice. As expected, he discovered a stairwell ten feet from the elevator, and Corsair walked casually up a flight to the next level, where he exited out of the back of the house into the guest area.

Two minutes later, he ambled out the opposite side of the hotel onto the street. His pace quickened without launching into a run. If he drew any more attention to himself, he might not reach the apartment at all.

Each step tightened his stomach more, and when he came to Olas Altas, he turned the corner. A figure stepped out of a t-shirt shop toward him, and his left hand shot out as his right reached back for the Glock. He caught himself before he struck Khloe.

"They were here," she gasped, and Caleb saw the reddened eyes.

"Where?"

"Three guys came out of the building," she stammered. "They had Amanda."

Caleb took off in a run, dodging a man on a bicycle. He ran up the steps to the second level before he stopped. The door to his apartment was open, and he pushed it.

Bare feet stuck out from the opposite side of the bed, and Caleb sprinted toward them. Angel lay on the floor. A rip split across her t-shirt, revealing bruised ribs. Caleb dropped to his knees, rolling her to her back with care. He cringed when he looked at her face, beaten and bloody.

"Angel, can you hear me?"

A groan came from her lips.

"Is she okay?" Khloe asked behind me.

"No, she's hurt bad."

"Is she—"

"She needs medical attention," Caleb answered.

"I'm sorry," Angel whispered. "I couldn't stop them."

"Shh, Angel. It's okay," he replied. "I'm going to get you help."

"Amanda," she said.

"Shit," Khloe moaned.

"What's going on, Roland?"

Caleb turned to see Frank, his neighbor, standing in the doorway with three Walmart bags in his hand.

"Frank, come here!" he ordered.

His neighbor obeyed, and the man dropped his groceries when he saw Angel on the floor. "What the hell?"

"She needs help," Caleb stated.

"I'll call the cops," he replied.

"No!" Caleb countered. "No cops. I need you to get a taxi. You can take her to the hospital."

"Why not get an ambulance here?" he asked.

Caleb gave Khloe a look, silently ordering her to take his place at Angel's side. He stood up and locked eyes with the retired trucker. "The cartel did this."

"What?" the Canadian retorted. "You don't mean 'The Cartel'?"

"I do, and if they find out she's still alive, they might come after her."

Frank's face paled, and after a second, he nodded. "Okay, we take her to the hospital."

"No, you take her," Caleb countered. "They took my daughter."

"Oh shit," Frank muttered. "I'm sorry."

"Save it Frank. Just go get a cab. Remember no cops."

He dipped his head and ran out of the apartment, heading for the street.

"What do I do?" Khloe asked, cradling Angel's head.

"You have to help him get her to the cab. Then you need to get as far from here as you can."

"But—"

"I can't protect you anymore," Caleb explained.

"How can I get in touch with you?" she asked.

He grabbed a pen off the table and jotted down an email address and password. "This is a dead drop email. You can log onto it. If you want to send me a message, type an email and don't send it. It will show up in the drafts. I'll respond the same way. Never hit send, and the email doesn't go anywhere."

She nodded.

"After you get her to the cab, run. You can check it in a few hours. Then, just check it regularly during the day."

"I'm sorry, Roland."

"Whatever you do, don't tell me where you are until I show you that Amanda is safe."

"Why not?" she asked.

"Because they'll want me to trade you for her."

Khloe stared at him, knowing right then that he'd make that trade if he had to. She swallowed, and Caleb turned to walk out the door.

42

Caleb fumed as he stormed out the door. He didn't have any clue where to start, but he figured there was at least one cartel member standing watch over the apartment building. If he caught him, he'd rip his way up the food chain.

Why did I put her in danger again?

When those motorcycle thugs killed his family, they kidnapped Amanda, and Caleb fought to get her back. He swore to himself that he'd protect her from this. Now, because he stepped in to save Khloe, his daughter was in trouble.

Miguel came up the steps as Caleb hurried past. The kid dropped his head as they passed each other. Corsair stopped, turning around to face the man.

"Miguel, where have you been?" he demanded.

"Uh, *Señor* Bryer. I went to the hardware store."

"What for?" Caleb inquired, staring at his empty hands.

"Just some stuff," Miguel replied.

Corsair's eyes narrowed, and he grabbed Miguel by the front of his shirt, dragging him toward the railing that overlooked the pool deck and courtyard.

"Where's your fucking 'stuff'?" he growled, throwing the young man into the railing.

"I—uh—" he stuttered.

"I need to see the cameras," Caleb told him.

Miguel's eyes widened. "They aren't working."

Corsair cocked his head. "I saw the screen this morning," he countered, pointing at the monitor behind the front desk.

Miguel shrugged, not seeming to know how to answer the man.

"What did you do, Miguel?" Caleb shouted as he pushed the kid back so his torso stretched over the drop.

"Nothing. I didn't do nothing." His voice strained as he tried to respond to Caleb.

The assassin reached down with his right hand and caught Miguel in the crotch, hoisting him up over the balustrade.

"Please! *¡Por favor!*" Miguel begged. "*Señor* Bryer, please."

"Where is my daughter?" Caleb almost screamed at the man as he let him dangle over the fifteen-foot drop.

"I don't understand," Miguel responded, grasping out with both hands as he searched for anything to hold onto and failed to do so.

"They took Amanda."

"No, they weren't supposed to take her," he cried.

"What?" Caleb jerked him back over the bar, throwing him to the ground. "What do you mean?"

Footsteps came up the stairs, and Caleb spun around on instinct, ready to attack the person running. Frank wheezed as he reached the top.

"Cab's out front," he gasped before studying the scene unfolding before him. Caleb stood over the prone figure of Miguel, who lay sprawled on the floor. "What's going on?" Frank asked, concerned.

"I'm about to find out," Caleb grunted. "Get Angel to the hospital."

Frank didn't move. Instead, his eyes flicked from Miguel to his neighbor. "Go, Frank. She needs help."

The former truck driver gathered his wits and hurried to Caleb's apartment. A minute later, he and Khloe carried Angel out the front.

"Angel?" Miguel whispered.

Caleb stepped toward the man. "What did you do?"

"They made me," he stated.

Bending over, he pulled Miguel to his feet. "What did you do?"

"I told my cousin about you. He wanted to know if the girl was here?"

"Amanda?" Caleb questioned.

"No, not her," Miguel explained. "Your sister."

"But they took Amanda."

Miguel nodded without thinking. "But they weren't supposed to."

"They might have killed Angel," he snapped at the handyman.

"It wasn't supposed to be like that. They said they just wanted the other girl."

"Why?" Caleb shouted. His voice crackled with rage.

"If they ask, you do it. My cousin—he's a wicked man. He'd hurt me or *mi madre*."

"So he asked, and you allowed them in?"

Miguel shook his head. "I didn't. They told me to leave for an hour or so."

"But, let me guess, you gave them my apartment number."

"He'd hurt me if I didn't," Miguel argued.

"What the fuck do you think I plan to do to you?"

His head whipped side to side. "It wasn't supposed to be Amanda."

"But it was," Caleb growled.

"I'm sorry." The young man cried. Tears streamed down his face. Whether they were from fear or sorrow, Caleb neither knew nor cared.

"Here's what is about to happen," Caleb said in a flat tone. "There are two choices here. I kill you or you tell me who your cousin is and where to find him. Then, your only job from now on is to make certain that Khl—my sister—gets out of here. If anything happens to her, I will come back and cut you from here"—he stuck his index finger just below Miguel's Adam's apple—"to here." Caleb dragged the tip of finger down the man's torso to below his navel.

"I promise you for damned sure that you won't die right away, either. If you think the Cortez bastards are bad, you haven't seen shit."

Miguel's head jerked up and down. "I'll make sure she gets away," he vowed with some relief in his response.

"Now, where the hell is your cousin?"

43

C aleb found the address that Miguel gave him was still in the Romantic Zone of Puerto Vallarta, but it was on the eastern side, far from the entertainment and beach area. He stood in front of an apartment building that rose five stories above Aquiles Serdán. Balconies lined the white exterior all around, a typical architectural feature throughout the city. Each unit had its own terrace with double doors leading from inside to the outside where a small iron railing enclosed the balcony.

Like many buildings in Puerto Vallarta, this one appeared to have some renovations going on. Three laborers were working late. They used a rigged elevator similar to the one Caleb saw earlier. At first glance, Caleb thought they were hauling cement up the line, but he realized it was smaller bags of grout. Two men hauled on the rope, pulling it up through a block anchored at the peak of the structure. As the sun was setting, the three men worked to finish before night fell. It was the end of their day, and this must have been the last task they needed to finish.

Antonio Ortega, Miguel's violent cousin, lived on the top floor of the building. Miguel didn't know the number, but he swore it was the southwest corner apartment. Caleb let his eyes trace up the face of the white edifice until he located Ortega's unit. Being on the corner offered a bigger balcony that extended from one side to the other. It might not have more square footage on the inside, but the added outdoor space likely garnered a higher rent, and some perceived prestige over the other residents.

From the street opposite the apartments, Caleb scanned for sentries. Nothing was amiss. This wasn't a cartel stronghold or even a high-ranking leader in the gang. It was the home of an underling, albeit a pleasant home. That implied that Ortega had enough clout to benefit from the cartel's business.

He entered the building, careful to watch for any straggling friends of Ortega's. There was no elevator, an obvious observation given the construction crew's makeshift version. Instead, a single flight of stairs zigzagged up the center of the structure. The landing at each level split the building in half. Caleb climbed the five flights. There were eight apartments on each floor.

From his waistband, Caleb removed the Glock he'd taken off the driver earlier. He swapped the fresh magazine for the partial one, pocketing the almost full one into his back pocket. He rapped on the wooden door for apartment 503.

The handle rattled, and the door swung open to reveal a thirty-year-old man with a thin Zorro-style mustache. His eyes widened as Caleb pressed the barrel of the Glock against the man's forehead. Before Ortega moved, Caleb struck the man in the throat. A gasp escaped his lips as he struggled to get air down his trachea. Corsair pulled the

G48 back and cracked the base of the pistol's grip into the man's temple. Ortega's eyes rolled up in his head as his body went limp.

Caleb stepped over the form on the floor and dragged him away from the entrance before shutting the front door. With the Glock at the ready, Caleb moved through the apartment, searching for Amanda or anyone else hiding. It took him two minutes, and he found Ortega's place empty. The man decorated his home with gaudy, expensive junk. It was the decor of someone who acquired an excess of money not too long ago. Most of the furniture and decorations were new, a recent purchase made when Ortega advanced in the organization.

Corsair returned to the unconscious Ortega, and the assassin hooked his arms under the man's armpits, dragging him into the bathroom. He shoved Ortega's head into the toilet until the man jerked around, inhaling some water. Caleb pulled him out, letting Ortega cough and spit until his lungs cleared.

"Antonio, do you speak English?"

Ortega didn't respond, and Caleb slammed his face back into the bowl. This time Ortega struggled, trying to push away from the rim.

"Let me repeat: do you speak English?"

"Yes," he shouted, spewing toilet water from his mouth as he spoke the words.

"You fucked up," Caleb told him. "Where is my daughter?"

"I don't know," he answered, and Caleb drove his head back into the water, holding him for a few seconds longer.

He jerked him out, allowing him to cough up the fluid before Caleb dunked him again. Corsair repeated the treatment for over a minute, not giving Ortega any time to suck in a breath. It wasn't dissimilar to waterboarding. Ortega would be desperate for air, and each time he came up, his body thought it was a reprieve only to find Caleb wouldn't allow him to have the much-desired oxygen.

After that minute passed, Caleb dragged him out of the bowl. The man vomited water over the floor.

"Want to try again?" Caleb asked.

"I wasn't there," Ortega lied, and Caleb gripped the back of his head.

"No! Wait!" he cried, tears streaming down his face. "Tomás took her."

Tomás, the same man the driver called earlier. The one who handed the phone to Sonny Departi.

"Where is Tomás?"

"I don't know," Ortega wailed. Caleb thought about dunking him again, but he believed the man. "He's taking her to the American."

"Sonny Departi?" Caleb inquired.

"I don't know the man's name," Ortega declared.

"Where does Tomás live?" Caleb asked.

Ortega froze. His brain worked on the logic of his situation. He found himself in a very compromising position. If he gave up Tomás's address, he was just like a rat. That might as well be a death sentence, but the man in front of him was, without a doubt, going to kill him if he didn't give him the information. Once Tomás or any of his fellow members saw the bruises and cuts on Ortega, they'd realize he told the man where to find Tomás. He would be just as dead.

Before he could finish the thought, he found himself face down in the toilet again. When Caleb pulled him up, he seemed to realize that the immediate danger outweighed future threats.

"He has a house in *Las Mojoneras*," Ortega told him. He rattled off the address in the upscale neighborhood.

"*¡Antonio! ¿Va todo bien?*" a voice called from the corridor outside the apartment. "*¿A qué gritas?*" What are you screaming at?

"*¡Ayúdame!*" Ortega bellowed.

Corsair gritted his teeth and shot Ortega in the head. More voices shouted from the hallway, and a crash sounded as the door splintered open.

44

Lee paced around the substation, picking off small chunks of the Styrofoam coffee cup that she'd emptied minutes earlier. They'd had no action on Khloe Evans or Corsair in hours, and she couldn't help but worry that the former OOC agent had gone to ground with the girl. That was his training, and after the incident this morning in the market, Corsair would regroup and evaluate his situation. The smart thing to do was to lie low.

Almost every fugitive who got away did so because they stayed out of sight. Manhunts can't last forever. Once any leads thin out, those heading the hunts have to decide how much manpower to give it.

It also meant she knew she made a mistake in coming down here with no one else from the OOC. Once she called an updated Carl Winston, that trigger couldn't be unpulled, and he'd have a response team on the ground in hours. Her flying to Mexico alone to find nothing would piss him off if he got wind of it. She'd need to craft her report to him with some care.

Lee had put off the call long enough. Castillo offered her and Patterson an empty office to make calls from, and she closed the door.

The phone rang.

"Winston," her boss answered.

"It's Hubbard."

"Where've you been, Lee?" The question wasn't accusatory. After all, Lee worked out of the office on a regular basis.

"I'm in Mexico," she informed the head of the Office of Compliance.

"What are you doing there?" Now his tone grew curious and frustrated.

"Following up on a potential Corsair sighting here."

Lee almost heard Winston sit up and come to attention. "What do you have? Is he located?"

"Not yet," she responded. "Local police recovered a gun with a partial print belonging to Caleb Saunders last weekend."

"You're there alone?" Winston demanded.

"Carl, the call came through late Saturday, and I wanted to study the evidence before putting a fugitive response team in the field. It was barely a hit on a partial, and we know Corsair came through Mexico already. It could have been months old. I wanted to give it a preliminary investigation first."

"Dammit, Lee, we need to be down there analyzing anything. Our people need to scan the CCTV networks."

"I agree now, but before today I didn't have confirmation," she explained.

"You have it? Corsair is there?"

"I don't have a confirmed sighting," she stated. "However, I have seven dead members of the Cortez Cartel."

"What the hell is Corsair doing?" Winston demanded. "Where in Mexico?"

"Puerto Vallarta."

"I'm sending a response team immediately. They'll be there in the morning."

"Carl, I suspect Corsair isn't going to show."

"Doesn't matter. We'll find where he's been hiding. Obviously, he's still entangled with that other cartel. That's something."

"I don't think so," Lee told her boss. "If it's him down here, he is with a woman who has the Cincinnati mob after her."

"Typical Corsair," Winston groaned. "Who is the woman?"

"Her name's Khloe Evans. She seems to be a witness that the FBI wants to get and this Sonny Departi out of Cincinnati wants to kill."

"And Corsair is in the mix?" Winston remarked. "Perhaps one of these other parties will remove the asshole for us."

"Perhaps," Lee repeated without any enthusiasm.

"I want confirmation, though," Winston demanded.

"I'll be sure to bag his head," Lee quipped.

"Damn straight." She could almost hear the bastard smiling into the phone at the thought. "But I'll take photographic proof."

The door to the office opened, and Patterson stepped inside with his phone to the side of his face. His eyes registered surprise that Lee was already in the empty room.

With a quick nod, he backed out, shifting his eyes to the woman and closing the door.

"We'll get a surveillance team on the ground," Winston assured her again. "I'll send Carlos down to coordinate with you. You stay on the locals while they run surveillance."

Lee knew what that meant. Carlos would update Winston before he ever talked to Lee. She'd be a step behind if they found something.

"Roger," she agreed, because there was little else to do about it.

"Good," Winston replied before hanging up without offering her a farewell.

Her head shook at the idiot she called a boss. She walked back out of the office to tell Patterson he was welcome to use if for some privacy. The FBI agent wasn't in the hallway, and Lee wandered back toward Castillo's desk. Neither Castillo nor Patterson was around. She strolled back to the front door.

"Agent Hubbard," a voice called, and she turned to see Second Sergeant Castillo. "Agent Patterson wanted to go back to his hotel. Do you want an officer to drive you as well?"

"Yeah, we hit a wall for the night," she stated.

His face twisted in confusion, and she realized her colloquial phrase might not make sense to the man. "I just mean, I think it is going to be quiet for now."

He nodded. "If anything happens, I'll be called at home. You and Agent Patterson will be my first phone calls."

"Thank you," Lee offered with a genuine smile. She liked the man. Castillo struck her as an honest, hardworking law enforcement officer, determined to fight for justice in a culture that might not believe in the benefit.

"I have an officer out front to take you," he told her before heading back to his desk for what Lee guessed was a few more hours of work. She recognized the dedication in his eye, and it was another reason her admiration for him grew.

On the curb in front of the substation, a Toyota truck, identical to Castillo's, idled. Patterson paced half a block away on the phone. His staccato gait increased in rapidity as he spoke in the speaker. Lee passed a cursory glance over him before claiming the front seat again. The driver gave her a nod but didn't say a thing.

Doesn't speak English.

Two minutes later, the rear door opened as Patterson slid into the truck.

"*¿Estan listo?*" the officer asked. Ready?

"*Sí,*" Lee replied.

Patterson remained quiet in the back during the twenty-minute ride back to the Marriott. When the driver pulled into the circular drive of the hotel, he said, "*Buenas noches.*"

"*Y usted,*" Lee responded as she exited the front of the Toyota.

"Night," Patterson told both her and the driver as he started toward the lobby.

Lee paused by the front desk, considering ordering something from the bar as Patterson continued toward the elevator. She walked over to the Ceviche and Tequila Bar, where several hotel guests were crowding. Lee thought some light seafood and a cold beer might help her sleep. At the bar, she sat at the corner and picked up a menu. When the bartender came by, she ordered a Modelo Dark and a small shrimp ceviche.

In a mirror hanging on the opposite wall, Lee saw Patterson trot back out the front door. He cast a wary glance at her back, unaware she watched him in the reflection.

"Sorry, can you hold that order for a minute?" she told the bartender before he opened the bottle of beer.

Lee walked out the front doors to see Patterson getting into a white car that pulled up at the valet entrance. A white man in his forties drove the vehicle, and Lee watched it pull away.

She spun around to wave at a cab parked on the side where it waited for its next rider. Lee hurried over and slipped into the rear seat.

"Can you follow that car?" she asked.

The cabbie gave her a suspicious look. "He's my husband," she lied.

A dawning realization crossed his face. "*Sí*," he replied. "I will keep away?"

Lee nodded. "Please, don't let him know we're back here."

The driver remained silent as he cruised along the streets of Puerto Vallarta. Doubtless, he felt sympathy for the woman in his cab whose husband was so obvious about his running around on her.

Wherever Patterson was going, it was taking him back toward the south side of town. He drove up into the hills, and Lee recognized it as the area called Gringo Gulch, overlooking the river valley where Castillo found Marino's body.

What is he doing?

Patterson and his driver turned into a small street.

"Slow down," she suggested, afraid if they got closer, Patterson might spot them.

The driver let the cab decelerate to a crawl as they inched along the streets. The cobblestone road curved between the tall villas on either side.

"Can you stop here?" she asked.

The man complied, and Lee handed him a handful of bills. "If you can wait, I'll need a ride back."

"*Sí,*" he said with a nod.

Lee got out of the rear door and walked down the dark road. Ahead, she saw the white car Patterson rode in parked in front of a villa. A red real estate sign read "*Se Renta.*" No one was visible, and Lee backed into an alcove between two houses and watched the front of the house.

Forty-five minutes passed before the front door opened. Patterson stepped out with two men. They talked for several minutes before Patterson extended his hand to the older of the two men. The man turned back into the villa, ignoring the proffered handshake.

Patterson followed the other man to the car. A minute later, the headlights of the car washed over the nook where Lee hid.

After the car was gone from her sight, she pulled out her phone, opening up the search engine. After a quick search, she let out a slow breath. The image on the screen was the latest photo taken of Sonny Departi, and she'd just seen the man with the FBI agent.

45

Corsair lowered his head, crouching as he ran down the passageway. The Glock, extended in his grip, fired twice. Wood exploded into splinters as the rounds smashed into the door frame. A figure jumped back out of the doorway. The loosely hung door, almost ripped from its hinges, swung back.

"*¡Aquí arriba!*" someone shouted in the corridor.

Caleb couldn't make out a response, but he heard the pounding of footsteps on the wooden stairs. He backed up, training the iron sights of the nine-millimeter on the door. He was only down three rounds in the magazine. That left him fourteen shots before he had to swap to the partial magazine. Enough to stop anyone entering the apartment, but he still needed to get out.

He jerked his neck around to study the balcony. His feet shuffled backward as he held the gun on the door. Voices outside filtered through the cracked door. They were arguing in Spanish about who would come through the door next.

Caleb slid the sliding-glass door open. The crack in the front door darkened, and Caleb fired a round. The bullet slammed into the busted door, banging it against the jamb.

"*¡Mierda!*"

Caleb stepped onto the balcony and glimpsed over the edge. There was no easy way to drop to the next floor from here. He squinted along the balustrade as it turned the corner. Antonio had the larger, more expensive corner apartment. Caleb ran to the edge. The best chance he had was to move to the next platform. It was a four-foot gap between the railings on each terrace.

I have to find better ways to get out of these buildings, he thought as he stepped onto the top rail and vaulted to the next one. His right sole touched the top of the balustrade as he continued forward, landing on his left foot and stepping forward with his right to stop his momentum.

He stretched over the side again, hoping for a better place to drop. Unfortunately, it appeared the architect designed the uppermost floor balconies to extend out farther than the rest. It would require at least a five- to eight-foot swing back toward the building to get to the fourth floor.

Only one way to go.

Caleb wasted no time climbing on the railing to leap to the adjacent balcony. If he could get around the building before anyone came through Antonio's apartment, he might have a head start.

He jumped to the neighboring balcony, turning just as a Latino man around thirty-years old appeared at the corner. Caleb dropped as the man fired at him. Three shots echoed between the buildings, and Corsair straightened up to return fire. The gun exploded with two shots, sending the man back around the corner for cover. Caleb didn't wait, jumping up to the railing and leaping to the next balcony.

He dove forward, gliding over the railing and landing in a somersault on the terrace.

The door was wide open, and Caleb glanced up to see two construction workers standing inside the apartment. The laborers stared at him with gaping mouths. He rolled to his back, hearing shouting from Antonio's friends on the other balcony. It wouldn't take them long to head down the hall to the correct apartment. Caleb sat up, aiming the Glock back in the direction he'd come. No one was on the balcony.

He straightened up and looked at the two workers. Behind them, a stack of dry grout stood in the room. Caleb spun around to see a half-full pallet of dry grout dangling from a block secured to the corner of the building's roof.

Oh shit.

A banging came from inside the building as the men from Antonio's apartment pounded on the door. One man turned to the door.

"Your gloves," Caleb demanded, pointing his finger at the man who wore leather gloves.

The man didn't understand him, and only stared at him, confused.

"*¡Sus guantes!*" Caleb translated. His index finger jabbed at the man. "*¡Dámelos!*"

Somewhat confused, the man peeled the gloves off, tossing one at a time to Caleb. The other worker shuffled toward the door. Corsair donned them after sliding the Glock into his waistband. Then he hoisted himself over the rail, landing on the pallet.

"*No, ¡espera!*" The worker begged Caleb to "wait" when he realized what he was doing.

"*No tengo tiempo,*" Caleb explained as he grabbed the end of the rope tied off on the railing. With a quick pull, he released the bowline knot as the door to the apartment flew open and two men raced into the room, firing.

While there were only four bags of grout left on the pallet, each weighed just over twenty-two kilograms. Add that to Caleb's 190 pounds and about thirty pounds of wood that made up the pallet. The resulting weight of 420 or so pounds plummeted toward the sidewalk with only Caleb's grip to slow it down.

Even with the leather gloves, his palms felt the heat as the rope whipped through his hands. Caleb paid no attention to the man leaning over the railing. The gunshots went wild, and he ignored the thump of bullets into the grout beneath his feet.

He tightened his grip. The result was an abrupt stop where the weight of the pallet pulled down on the line. Caleb's feet came off the pallet as he started back up. Beneath him, the sudden shift of both weight and speed tipped the wood platform sideways. Three bags of powder slid off, and had Caleb been paying attention, he'd have heard the successive explosions as each bag smashed into the concrete below. But Caleb, who was initially jerked upward by the pallet which, when fully loaded outweighed him by about forty pounds, now found himself heavier than the empty thirty-pound platform. He dropped, and the wooden platform crashed into him as it shot upward.

The time it takes for a human to fall four stories is somewhere between one second and 1.1 seconds. If Caleb had been counting by "Mississippis" as he remembered from his childhood, he'd only have made it to the second "iss" before the pallet slammed against the block and tackle at the top of the building.

Caleb still hung onto the rope. Only he was about eight feet above the concrete curb. The rest of the line dangled below him, coiling on the sidewalk. He slid down the rope, glancing up and down the road before releasing the rope and diving away. A full "Mississippi" later, the pallet shattered on the sidewalk and street.

Caleb almost didn't move, realizing he'd just landed on his broken ribs.

Get up!

He pushed up off the ground, wincing at the throbbing in his hands and the stabbing pain in his chest.

At least my feet work.

He took off in a half run and a hobble before Antonio's friends made it down the stairs to the street. Caleb pulled off the leather gloves and threw them behind him on a pile of gray dust left from the busted bags of grout.

46

Despite the head start that Patterson had, Lee made it to the cab, who happily waited for her and was even happier when she slipped a wad of cash to him, and caught up with the white vehicle. With a great deal of skill, the cabbie stayed a decent distance behind them. Red taillights glowed four car lengths up.

I knew I didn't trust him, Lee considered.

He was working the other side, trying to ensure that if Castillo or the Jalisco State Police found Khloe Evans first, he could pass that along to Sonny Departi. Or he would finish the job himself.

Granted, Lee was playing a similar game. Although she could justify it. If she located Corsair before the team from the Office of Compliance did, then she had a chance to uncover whatever information Caleb Saunders had that frightened Carl Winston so much. Lee could argue that what she was doing wasn't counter to the United States of America, in that she hoped to expose Winston. Plus, her plan didn't involve murdering an innocent woman.

The drive to the hotel took a little longer. The man returning Patterson didn't seem to be in the same rush.

Now that Sonny Departi had his word with Patterson, the urgency was gone.

Lee wondered what Patterson's agenda was. If he'd come down here to find Khloe, then why did Sonny come too? Or maybe Patterson hired himself out once he thought he had an edge. On the other hand, he could just be going along and selling whatever information he came across.

Bastard.

When the white car turned into the Marriott's lot, Lee watched Patterson exit the vehicle without so much as a cordial farewell before the driver headed left out of the drive. She bet he didn't even take the transmission out of gear. That might not mean much to most, but it clued Lee to the hierarchy—or at least the perceived hierarchy. Whoever was driving didn't enjoy having to fetch and return the FBI agent.

"*Gracias,*" she told the cabbie, handing him more bills.

He counted the money and smiled at the added gratuity she included for his trouble. This trip had been a profitable one at what was likely a slow time of the night.

By the time she reached the lobby, Patterson stepped into the elevator. Lee strode over and pressed the up button. The second elevator dinged a few seconds later as it opened for her.

Patterson's room was on the same level as Lee's—five. The elevator whirred as it climbed to the fifth floor. When the doors opened, she swallowed and walked down the carpeted corridor.

At room 1547, she rapped on the door. The peephole darkened for a split second before the chain rattled.

"Hubbard?" Patterson questioned through the cracked door. "What are you doing here? Is something up?"

"Yeah, I tried to call, but you didn't answer," she lied, knowing he hadn't been in the room.

"Oh, right. I walked down to the lobby." He had stripped his jacket and shirt off, donning a Cincinnati Reds t-shirt.

"Can I come in?" she asked, surveying him with a sweep of her eyes. His service weapon wasn't on him, but she realized that didn't make him safe.

The FBI agent opened the door, and Lee walked inside.

"What is it?" Patterson wondered as he closed the door. "Did Castillo call?"

Lee turned to face him, drawing her Kel Tec PF 9 and leveling it at the agent.

"What the fuck?" Patterson remarked. Surprise coated his words.

"Hands up high and grab the door," she ordered.

The FBI agent rotated on one foot and leaned against the jamb. "What are you doing here, Lee?" He switched to her first name. It was typical Bureau tactics—relate to the perp. It was a technique that only worked with people out of their element. People who committed crimes of passion or impulse might be talked down by that maneuver, but any hardcore criminal wouldn't buy into that.

Lee ignored him as she closed the space between them. She ran her hand over his front and lower back before working down each leg. On his right ankle, she removed a small Smith & Wesson thirty-eight snub nose. Once she pocketed the revolver, she took the handcuffs from the leather pouch on his belt.

"Put them on," she ordered. "Just the right wrist."

Patterson complied, and when the shackles snapped around his wrist, Lee pulled the right over, securing the other cuff to his left.

"Now, find a seat," she commanded.

"What the hell do you want?" Patterson demanded.

"I want to know how long you've been on Departi's payroll."

"What are you talking about?" he blurted out with the appropriate amount of indignation.

"I'm sorry," Lee retorted. "Was that not Sonny Departi I just watched you meeting with?"

"Look, Hubbard, it's not like that."

"Let me guess," she suggested. "You're working under-cover as a dirty cop? That's not a hard stretch, huh?"

"It's true," he claimed.

"No, it isn't," she refuted. "You're dirty."

"You can't prove anything, Hubbard."

She smiled. "You know the thing about working for a shadowy government agency?"

He stared back at her. "You work for Homeland," he said.

"Only on paper," she admitted. "In truth, I work for a branch that has such a benign name that no one looks into us. But we topple governments, assassinate leaders. And sometimes annoying government agents who get in the way."

"Bullshit!" Patterson spat.

"Right now, you are in the way," she declared. "And you picked a dangerous place to do it. I'll kill you and have my team clean it up inside of half an hour."

"I don't believe you."

Her grin widened. "Except you really do, don't you? You've seen the video of the guy I'm hunting. He killed seven people in the city today, and I'm the bitch they tasked with bringing him down. You think that's because I'm too dainty?"

He considered that for a second before shaking his head.

"Listen, Patterson, I don't give a shit if you're on the take. Hell, the US Government doesn't pay enough, does it?"

The FBI agent didn't move. His eyes remained locked on Lee's.

"Sit down already," she ordered again, grabbing his Reds shirt to drag him toward an armchair next to the bathroom. The man dropped back into the seat at an angle to allow his cuffed wrists some room behind his back.

"Now, are you ready to talk?"

"What do you want to know?" Patterson asked.

"What did Sonny want?"

Patterson squirmed as he shifted in the seat. "He said they found the guy's apartment."

Lee tried not to show any surprise, but she straightened a little. "The guy with Khloe?"

Patterson nodded. "But they weren't there. At least that's what Sonny was saying."

"Are they watching it?" Lee asked, the hopefulness in her tone betrayed her.

Patterson shook his head. "No, the cartel found it, and they took the man's daughter."

"You're shitting me?" Lee gasped. "Sonny took his daughter?"

"Yeah, that wasn't anything to do with me," Patterson explained. "Kids are off limits."

"Aren't you quite the saint?" Lee quipped. "I'd stay as far away from Sonny Departi as you can now."

"What do you mean?"

"Do you think Sonny considered this through?" Lee asked.

"He's going to trade the girl for Khloe Evans."

"No, he isn't," Lee countered. "Even if it worked for him, he'd end up killing the kid because witnesses are bad for business."

Patterson didn't answer.

"Of course you knew that," Lee pointed out. "You aren't an idiot. Sonny Departi had no doubt, when he took the girl, that she'd never survive."

He shook his head. "He did it without talking to me."

"Right. That I'll believe," Lee acknowledged. "But I'd stay away from Sonny now. You don't have a clue what he stirred up."

"What?" Patterson inquired.

"This guy killed seven people this morning just walking on the street. What do you think he'll do to get his kid back?"

"Sonny's got the cartel backing him," Patterson argued.

"This isn't the first time someone kidnapped his girl," Lee explained. "Last time, he killed an entire motorcycle gang, almost single-handedly, to get her back."

"Who the hell is he?" Patterson asked.

"He's a guy that you don't want to get in the way of," she answered. "You don't want to be between him and his daughter."

"I don't believe it," Patterson stated.

"Trust me," Lee assured him. "Sonny signed his own death warrant. Now lean forward."

The FBI agent obeyed, and Lee unfastened the left cuff and hooked it through the arm of the chair before snapping it back closed around Patterson's wrist. She found his cell phone, his passport, and his service weapon. Before she left, she took the cord from the phone's receiver.

"If you stay here, either I'll rescue you in the morning or the maid will. One way or the other, you'll thank me because tonight will probably be bloody for the boys from Cincinnati."

"C'mon, Lee," Patterson called as she walked out of the room.

Lee almost smiled as she strolled down the corridor. She knew where Corsair was going to show himself, and she intended on getting back to Gringo Gulch for a front-row seat.

47

The house stood out on the hill. Lights glowed from the upper floors, giving the building a set of glowing eyes peering out into the night. On either side, the house shared walls with the neighboring homes. Gutted and undergoing renovations, the one on the north side appeared like a skeleton on the hillside. A chain-link fence stretched around the site—an attempt to secure the vacant home from trespassers.

Corsair clung to the shadows as he approached from up the street. He checked his pockets. The Glock rested against the small of his back. In his front pocket was a spool of paracord and about twenty zip ties Caleb had bought at a hardware store on the way here. Both items might come in handy, and neither raised a lot of questions when he purchased them.

Only eight feet tall, the fence would have been easy to scale if the crown hadn't been lined with razor wire, twisting around the upper rail. When he reached the top, Caleb put one hand on the upmost wire in a small space between two-inch-long razors. He hung on the fence as he studied the upper wires. The salty sea air had corroded the sharp edges—an ironic two-edged sword. At least the razors had lost their edge, but any cut he received wouldn't be a clean slice. Instead, it might rip through the skin.

Screw it. He pressed his weight down on the top wire and attempted to vault over. From where he hung, there wasn't much of a vault. Instead, he pushed up and rolled on his back across the wire before dropping to the ground.

Warmth oozed over his back as blood seeped from the tears in his skin. His cotton shirt stuck to the wounds, and he'd take the time to inspect them later.

A homemade ladder, built from two twenty-foot pieces of lumber, leaned against the outside of the house. Caleb tested the bottom rung, and finding it secure, he ascended slowly. Whoever had been using the ladder left it next to an open window. When Caleb reached the top of his climb, he found the opening was being prepped for a window installation. He swung one leg onto the sill and hoisted himself into the hole.

Inside the dark house, he saw the new window resting against the wall. It was going to be the first thing the crew worked on in the morning, and Caleb almost grinned at his luck. But it wasn't a time for grinning. Even that small amount of self-satisfaction sent waves of guilt through him. Amanda was in dire danger, and it seemed it was his fault again. How can he be a good father if just being her father put her in danger?

He could always send her to live with Audrey's parents. After all, they were great grandparents, and it would give her a sense of stability. However, it meant never seeing her again. On top of that, he knew his cover as Tom Harrod blew the day those gangbangers killed Audrey and Jackson. That meant the OOC and any of the enemies Caleb made in the past would know that the Lyles were Audrey's parents. It didn't get Amanda out of danger if that put her back in the sights of those out to kill Caleb.

The interior of the home was ripped down to concrete and wood. He moved through the dark, straining to see his surroundings and making each step with care. A staircase led up to the next level. At least it was the skeleton of a staircase. In time, the builders would cover it in tile or carpet, but for now it was only risers nailed to two stringer boards that angled up to the landing above him. He didn't bother to test the steps, trusting that the contractor constructed them to be weight-bearing.

At the top floor, he found a rooftop terrace or, at least, what would soon be a rooftop terrace. From there, he could see the Pacific Ocean glowing under the moonlight. He stood for a moment at the edge. His head swept sideways to the next house, where Antonio told him he could find Tomás.

From the balustrade of the rooftop, there was only a five-foot drop to the next parapet. Caleb climbed atop the railing and leaped down. He landed on the ceramic-tiled roof. The overlapping shingles shifted an inch when his feet hit, but he dropped into a crouch to keep his center of gravity low and ran up the slope to a gabled window facing the ocean.

Caleb looked through the glass into a dark, empty room. He pushed up on the window, hoping it would budge. But the latch inside held it shut. With two quick blows, he used his elbow to break the pane. Careful not to cut his arm, he reached inside and slid the latch over so he could open the window.

As he crawled through the opening, his shirt shifted on his back, peeling the dried scab to allow fresh blood to dribble out. Caleb ignored the burning sensation caused by the cuts as he waited in the dark. After a few blinks, his eyes adjusted to the darkness. He found he was in an attic with only enough head space to stand in the center of the room. The roof on either side of the room took a sharp angle down, leaving anyone over five feet tall hunched. More importantly, he discovered there was no door in or out.

Shit, it's a dead space, he thought.

No, that wasn't correct. He could make out boxes stacked on one side of the room. They didn't wall those up, so there had to be a way in from below. He lowered himself to the floor to search for an opening or door. On the far side of the room, he found a hatch that swung up into the attic. He heaved up on it, feeling the door catch on something. Caleb tugged harder, and the hatch moved only a quarter of an inch.

It's padlocked, he guessed.

Caleb took the Glock G48 in his grip and yanked up on the handle again. He lowered the barrel of the nine-millimeter to an inch above the thin wood, then squeezed the trigger. The gunshot exploded in the cramped space, and a hole appeared in the hatch. Caleb jerked up on the door, and the hasp holding the padlock ripped free of the wood.

Someone was shouting below, no doubt stirred to excitement by the gunshot. However, coming from the upper level of the house and muffled by at least one floor, more likely two, determining who was shooting or where they were would be difficult.

Caleb grabbed either side of the opening and dropped to the floor below. He estimated about three people were running around downstairs.

"Quiet!" someone called in Spanish. The movement stopped. Caleb envisioned them standing stock still, listening for anything. For all they knew, it could have been a backfiring car. Caleb didn't move.

Thirty seconds passed before any voices sounded below.

When they did, he couldn't make out the words. However, they seemed calmer. There is an innate deficiency in the human brain. When the flight-or-fight instinct fires off, the body reacts, either with the urge to flee from danger or charge into it. If, as with the men downstairs, there is no obvious risk, the natural tendency is to relax. Another half a minute went by and someone laughed, perhaps at themselves for jumping at a random noise. By now they'd explain away the sound. It wasn't quite a gunshot. During that time, no one thought to check the house for intruders. That was an error that came from a lack of training.

More laughter and talking commenced, and Caleb took a moment to examine the room. It was a hallway with tile floors—a plus for moving across. If the substructure of the dwelling had been wood, the tile would limit the flexibility in the wood and, in turn, reduce the chance of squeaky wood alerting anyone below. However, the builder constructed the house of concrete in order to endure in the tropical weather, and Caleb could do jumping jacks up here without shaking the ceiling. He moved with deliberation toward the steps.

As he made his way down the stairs, Corsair attuned his ears to the voices. What they were saying didn't matter. In fact, he ignored the inane chatter. Instead, he pinpointed how many he heard and where they might be located. It was important to determine which one was Tomás. The others didn't matter, and, in fact, anyone else was a liability if he left them alive.

Then he heard what he wanted to hear.

"Tomás, do you want another beer?" someone asked.

"Yeah, and bring the tequila back."

There you are. Corsair almost grinned. He didn't, instead he took the final two steps in a single stride, coming around the corner into a den with three large, soft, leather sofas and a glass coffee table. The remnants of someone's coke lines were still on the clear top, and a young girl lifted her head from the drugs in time to see Corsair raise his Glock.

The gun fired, and the man heading toward the kitchen for a beer and tequila fell forward as the bullet tore through his brain. With a sweep of his arm, Corsair carried the nine-millimeter around as an angry man in his twenties popped up. His bloodshot eyes blinked as he pulled a Beretta nine-millimeter from his waistband. His barrel never cleared the man's belt before the Glock fired a round into his chest.

The girl screamed and dove under the legs of the table. An acrid smell of urine flooded Caleb's nostrils as he leveled the Glock at the older man still seated on the couch.

Tomás blinked, and Caleb could tell from the man's pupils he'd been hitting the lines on the table, too.

The girl under the table cried and begged in Spanish, "My God." Caleb ignored her, pulling several bag ties from his pocket and tossing them onto the table.

"*Sus manos,*" he ordered. Your hands.

Tomás stared with a blank expression at the Caleb for a few seconds before wrapping the plastic around his thick wrists. When he had the ends around, Tomás looked up, feigning a helpless countenance. He offered the wrists toward Caleb to secure, but the assassin sidestepped toward the couch and nudged the urine-soaked girl with his toe. She sat up, and he motioned for her to secure Tomás's wrists.

"Who are you?" Tomás asked after the girl pulled the plastic tight.

"Come on," Caleb prodded, sitting on the table in front of him. "Who do you think I am?"

The cartel member shook his head, although he didn't do so with a lot of conviction.

"You're going to tell me where my daughter is," Caleb stated in a flat, emotionless tone.

Tomás didn't answer. His pupils were still tiny pinpoints, and Caleb saw the man set his jaw in determination. Corsair popped to his feet. His left hand shot out, catching a handful of black hair. With a sudden yank, Corsair yanked Tomás by his hair. The man let out a high-pitched howl and thrashed. Corsair's fingers twisted to get a tighter grip as he jerked the other man forward.

Tomás tumbled into the glass-topped table, shattering it into hundreds of small pebble-size shards of glass.

Corsair jerked the man up again, pulling him into the kitchen. Tomás had what Caleb considered a fancy kitchen, but Caleb was currently living in an apartment with an old two-burner gas range, a micro-fridge, and an old microwave. In comparison, Tomás had stainless-steel appliances with a commercial-grade gas stove and oven. He threw the man into a wooden chair. Tomás whimpered, and Caleb realized he was still holding a clump of the man's hair that he'd pulled out of the scalp. Before Tomás could recover any composure, Corsair struck him in the nose. The sharp crack indicated Caleb broke the cartilage. Subsequent streams of blood from both nostrils confirmed the trauma.

His head lolled to the side for a moment, and Corsair removed the coil of cord, binding Tomás to the chair.

"You with me?" Caleb asked the man. He glanced in the other room to the see the girl still cowering on the couch. He strode into the den and pulled her to her feet.

"How old are you?" he inquired in Spanish.

It took her a few seconds to say, "Thirteen."

He shook his head. "You need to leave here and never talk about this. Do you understand me?"

She nodded.

"Go!" he ordered, pointing toward the front door.

The girl sprinted out the door, and Caleb followed to see her running down the street before he secured the lock. It was about even odds she'd go tell someone about what was happening, but the question was how long. While not intending to do so, Caleb traumatized her, and it would take a few minutes for the shock to wear off. By the time that happened, Caleb intended to be long gone from here.

He returned to the kitchen to find Tomás more alert now. "I'm back," he replied in a sing-song tone as he walked to a rack of hanging knives. Caleb picked up a butcher knife, inspected the blade, and smiled.

"Nice," he remarked with some admiration. "You keep some sharp tools."

Tomás continued to glare at him with the tough-guy face.

"Wait, this is better," Caleb whispered, removing a cleaver that hung from a rack under the cabinets. He studied the edge of it as well.

"What do you want?" Tomás asked.

"My daughter."

The man shook his head. "I don't have her."

Caleb lit the front burner of the range by turning it to ignite. The self-lighting stove popped and a blue tongue of fire leaped up. He adjusted the flame to high and turned back to Tomás.

"You can answer my question or I'll cut off a finger every time I don't get the answer I want. Do you understand me?"

"Fuck you," Tomás cursed.

Corsair grabbed the man's arms, still bound with zip ties. He shoved the man's arms on the table, and while Tomás attempted to pull away, the binds held his upper body in place.

"Last chance," Corsair warned.

"Fuck—aaaaa!"

The cleaver drove down, slicing through the man's bones and severing the left hand from the wrist. Blood spurted out as Tomás screamed. Corsair grabbed the man, shoved him toward the stove, and placed his wrist in the blue flame. The assassin felt Tomás go limp as he passed out, and Caleb dragged him back to the table.

While he waited, Caleb sat across from Tomás and nudged the lifeless hand. The muscles in the hand twitched when the blunt end of the cleaver pushed it around. It took another two minutes before Tomás regained consciousness.

"Oh, that was my bad," Corsair remarked, as if apologizing. "I think we stopped the bleeding, though."

Tomás groaned. A few seconds later, and the man whispered through gritted teeth, "You're a dead man."

Corsair pulled back the blade to bring it down on the man's right hand.

"No, wait," Tomás howled. "She's at Departi's place. In the Gulch."

Caleb held the cleaver aloft and waited. "Where?"

"It's on *Farolito*. In Gringo Gulch."

Caleb held the blade up still. "Which one?"

"It's on the right. Against the hill. I don't know the number."

"You're sure she's there?" he asked.

"Yes, please!"

"What's his plan? Sonny?"

Tomás shook his head despite answering, "He wants to kill you and the girl."

"Then he'll kill my daughter?"

Tomás gave a small wag of his chin.

"My daughter was off-limits," Corsair growled.

"I'm sorry," Tomás said, but his eyes widened as the cleaver swiped across his throat. The next sound coming from him was air escaping up his trachea as the blade severed the head from the man's neck.

48

Patterson sat in the chair for much longer than he wanted to admit. For the first ten to fifteen minutes, he stewed in rage. Hubbard had the gall to come up against him. Eventually, he realized that not only did she have the balls to do it, but she'd succeeded. When tonight was over, she'd report him to the FBI, and his career and his life would be over. That led to twenty minutes of worry and regret. He'd end up doing time. Hell, Beth would take his custody of Jason and Maddie.

Then, he decided he'd stay in Mexico. He could disappear down here.

With what? Was Sonny going to pony up enough money to support him? Not likely. Once he wasn't an agent, he'd be of no use to Sonny, anyway. More than likely, Sonny would judge him to be a liability, and considering the effort he was putting out for Khloe, who Patterson was certain knew nothing, then he'd be in for big trouble.

Once the self-deprecation ended, Patterson plotted how to get out of it. There was a simple answer. Lee Hubbard needed to die. He glanced at the phone. If he called Sonny, he could send Vinnie outside to find her and put a bullet in her head.

That would mean telling Sonny that Hubbard compromised him. They might kill him just because the threat was there. Would they know Hubbard hadn't reported him already? Patterson didn't think so. She was too single-minded. Right now, she knew she had one shot at getting this guy, and if she reported him, that might bring agents from the Guadalajara consulate down. That would muddy the water for her.

He was certain she had called no one about him yet. That meant if he got to her first, then he'd clean it up before anyone—Sonny or the FBI—ever knew about it.

The bitch took his key to the cuffs, but he had a spare one in his bag. He stood up and dragged the chair across the room. His overnight bag was on the shelf in the closet, and Patterson stared up at it. With his hands through the arm of the chair, he'd have a hard time reaching it.

His brain was already working out how to get to her. She'd be waiting within sight of the villa, but in that area, the houses were wedged together on the narrow, winding streets. It would leave very few places to watch. If she was correct, and this man intended to come after his daughter, then the only way into the house was through the front. The rear of the house had been built into the stone mountain behind it.

Patterson grabbed both hands onto the arm of the chair and lifted it up. He tried to squeeze the legs into the closet door to reach the bag, but the gap wasn't wide enough. Two legs struck the door no matter what way he rotated the chair. After a few minutes, he set the legs down to rest his arms.

He considered smashing the chair. Maybe. That seemed like something done in the movies.

Not smash. He needed to pry the arm off. If he could get some leverage, that might do it. After all, the wood was only about three inches thick, and it had to be attached to the seat under the cushion.

He carried the seat to the bathroom door, and he rolled the chair to its side and sat on the floor with it. Hooking the arm on the inside of the door frame, Patterson placed one foot on the wall and the other on the arm of the chair. His back hunched forward as he tried to hold everything in place. The position was awkward and uncomfortable, but he applied pressure to both feet while he heaved back with his arms.

It took a second, but an audible crack sounded. He redoubled his efforts, pushing with his feet and pulling with his upper body.

Whatever cracked snapped after several seconds of straining against the frame, and Patterson rolled onto his ass. The arm hadn't wrenched free from the back, but it gave him an opening only a few inches wide to slide the restraints through. Free from the chair, he jumped to his feet and dragged the overnight bag down. The spare cuff key was in a side pocket, and when he removed the cuffs, he rubbed both wrists where the metal had cut into the skin.

No time for that, he reminded himself.

Hubbard took his gun, but if he got close enough, he thought he could overpower her. All it took was surprise, and he didn't think she'd be expecting him to get free.

As he headed for the lobby, he realized if what she said about this guy was true, then he might well kill Sonny Departi, too. That didn't break Patterson's heart. He never liked the man, and the only reason he worked for him was because Sonny backed him into a corner.

Wouldn't that be a treat? If Hubbard's target killed Sonny Departi. Hell, it would be easy to kill Hubbard during the turmoil. She'd be in the crossfire.

No matter what, Patterson hoped tonight turned just bloody enough for him to solve his key problem. Once Agent Hubbard was out of the way, he would have no problems.

49

Her feet burned. She knew she should have switched shoes at the hotel. Well, she realized that after she'd left the Marriott. By that point, Lee didn't have enough time to go back. Corsair would show up at any time, and she assumed every minute counted. He might have already been watching the house earlier when she followed Patterson. It depended on how long ago Sonny Departi and the local cartel kidnapped Amanda Harrod.

Lee struggled, trying to keep straight all the names in her head. Lee did not know what alias Caleb Saunders currently used. However, she had no trouble thinking of him by either Caleb Saunders or Corsair—his birth name and code name, respectively. His daughter was born Amanda Harrod, since Corsair's identity at the time was Thomas Harrod. Did he force the girl to change her name? At her age, adapting to a new name would be easier, but Hubbard wondered what effects that would have on her growing up.

She thought it curious at first that Saunders bothered to bring his young child with him. As her father, logic said that he wanted to be with her, but the danger it put her in seemed too high. Why not leave her with his wife's parents?

Of course, it was obvious why that was a bad idea. Not only was the Office of Compliance after Caleb Saunders, but Corsair made enemies around the world. Any of them would not hesitate to grab a little girl if it would draw her father out.

Lee Hubbard felt sorry for Caleb Saunders. He'd escaped the agency, faking his death and finding a degree of happiness. Two thugs snatched that away when they shot his wife and son. Bad luck and chance. That's how she viewed it. He was in the wrong place.

She shifted on her feet, trying to relieve the pressure on her right foot for a few minutes. It had been a couple hours since she settled into the shadows across from Sonny Departi's rented villa. So far, there had been no sign of Corsair. No sign of anything. The last car, driven by an old man in a pickup truck collecting scrap metal on the side of the road, passed by forty-five minutes earlier.

Sonny Departi wasn't stupid. He had a small contingent of guards around the house. All of them appeared to be Latino, and she suspected their allegiance belonged to the Cortez Cartel. Did he suspect trouble from Corsair? Or did Sonny only want the show of strength?

Six men made the rounds in three pairs. Two would stand on the portico for twenty minutes until another pair came out. Those two moved to the street, where they relieved two more who returned inside the house. It was methodical, and the discipline and structure of the guard duty surprised Lee. These sentries might have had some military training. Or, at least, someone who deployed them did. But they still maintained more professionalism than she expected.

Their performance was better than she had seen in the motorcycle gang Corsair chewed through in South Florida. She remembered the rampage she'd witnessed when those gang members kidnapped his daughter. Corsair was merciless, and somehow she doubted he'd mellowed since then. Six patrols would not stop him. It was just a matter of time.

All she had to do was wait. But for what? Her official objective was to capture or kill Corsair.

That's insane, she considered.

Lee had no illusions that she could accomplish either on her own. Caleb Saunders was a killing machine. The very best had trained him, and perhaps only the very best could bring him down.

However, if she could talk to him. Just meet him face-to-face, and she might assure him she was on his side.

Not officially, of course. She'd need to take Carl Winston down in order to facilitate that. Was that even a viable option? She might not like Winston—hell, she hated the bastard. But did that make him wrong?

Based on Saunders's previous record and deployments, it didn't seem conceivable that he'd turn traitor. In fact, there wasn't much in the files to indicate what broke. If he could explain to her what scared Winston, then she might help him. And herself at the same time.

Her instinct assured her that Caleb Saunders, while a highly efficient killer, was not an evil bogeyman. Those same gut feelings didn't offer the same assurances about her boss. Carl Winston had something in play. Or at least he did when Saunders walked away. Whatever it was, she wanted to know.

She felt a shiver run over her body despite the warm night air. Lee looked up at the sky. Most of the stars weren't visible, washed out by the light pollution from the city. Lee wrapped her hands around her upper arms as she shifted to the other foot for a bit.

50

From the top of the mountain, Caleb could stare over the city. A half-moon hung in the sky, but low-hanging clouds drifted in front of it. Still, the night remained bright, and he turned back to see the path he'd marched to the peak.

It had taken him over an hour to trek across the elevation to this point. Once he left Tomás's house, he worked his way up a different set of trails to the *Mirador el Cerro de la Cruz* than the one he and Khloe had traversed yesterday. Or rather, two days ago, since it was now just after midnight on Tuesday.

By scaling the mountain, Caleb could come up north of Gringo Gulch. It had only taken a look at Google Maps to find the house where Sonny Departi was staying. The villa had been built into the side of the cliff, and in theory, that would offer a natural barrier. Anyone who approached from that direction would have to cross over the peak through undeveloped forests in the dark over steep, rocky, and precarious trails.

But it wasn't anything Corsair hadn't undertaken in the past, and now he stood atop a rock face overlooking the top of Sonny's temporary home. He began his descent, free climbing down about thirty feet to the roof.

His right foot slipped down first as he searched for a foothold. Every body length took him ten minutes to traverse as he made his way down. Free hand climbing without a rope up a rocky cliff, even in the dark, was easier than descending. Each movement must be careful, as his toes scraped along the rock for any outcropping or cut to support his weight. Those moves were slower still because of the broken ribs and bruising he'd sustained in his drop from Antonio's building.

When the roofline lay only a few feet below him, he stepped back and settled on to the top of the villa. He turned to survey his path. Sonny's house had multiple levels of roof. The builder attempted to construct it so that it appeared to be a part of the mountain behind it. From the front, the lines of the villa disappeared among the background of stone. It also made transitioning from level to level easy, and Caleb did just that as he moved to forward atop the building.

On the edge, he stared down at the street below. When Caleb squinted his eyes he discerned the cobblestones from this height. He counted two men pacing along the street. Neither carried an obvious weapon, but he assumed they had handguns. A glint of light caught his eye across the road. He squinted to study the shadows. After a minute, his eyes distinguished what or, rather, who sheltered in the darkness. Once he saw it, the shape was easily identifiable. A woman leaned against the wall, watching the front of the villa. Corsair admired her craft.

From ground level, she'd be almost invisible in the ruins of the demolished house where she took refuge. One man patrolling the street had passed her twice without spotting her. Her location was ideal for observing the residence. In fact, even a few feet back from where she stood would take her out of the line of sight of Sonny's home.

Who the hell was she?

Caleb knelt down and staring at her for several minutes. When both patrols moved far enough from her, she checked her phone. The light from the screen illuminated her face, and even from this distance, Caleb recognized her features.

She was in Florida, and she worked for the OOC.

Son of a bitch!

He stared down at the darkness after her phone went off. They'd found him. It didn't matter what happened after tonight. He had to leave. Not that he hadn't already figured on that. He assumed that after the damage he'd inflicted, he would make it to the top of the Cortez Cartel's list. Even if all they knew was his Bryer identity, Puerto Vallarta was too dangerous for him. Hell, if the OOC arrived, he assumed that they identified his apartment too. Everything he'd attempted to do just to give Amanda a stable life just evaporated.

If only he had ignored that little voice inside him when he saw the threat to Khloe. He could still shuck oysters on the beach. Amanda could grow up a little more, spending her time in the pool with Angel.

And poor Angel. They almost killed her because of him. That wasn't fair.

What is fair, though? In his life, he'd seen the good. He'd seen the bad. None of it was fair.

Did he deserve it? In retrospect, Caleb had done some terrible things. That he'd only done so at the behest of his country didn't matter. Especially after he discovered that some of those actions he carried out were not for the sake of his government but because a career bureaucrat deemed those deaths necessary. Maybe even profitable.

For those actions, Caleb felt he needed to serve penance. How many lives did he take for Carl Winston's benefit? He didn't see an excuse for being misled by his superior. Caleb blamed himself for following those orders without question.

When it all came down to it, he knew he had no way to ignore that little voice, no more than he could allow harm to come to Amanda. He thought he was serving penance, but it was more than that. Caleb Saunders wasn't the same man he'd been a decade earlier. He wasn't the same one who joined the Office of Compliance when he wasn't even twenty years old yet. That part of him was still there. Corsair was as much a part of Caleb Saunders as Thomas Harrod was.

Was this OOC woman alone? It didn't seem likely. They would bring out a full surveillance team. He scanned the streets below. No one else hid in the shadows. That meant little, though. He trusted he could remain undetected, and any new assets in the OOC underwent the same, if not better, training that he did.

None of that mattered now, though. Amanda remained his only concern, and once he assured himself there was no more threat to her, he'd focus on Carl Winston's team.

Caleb leaned forward, inspecting the house below him. A balcony jutted out about ten feet below the roof's edge, and the assassin grabbed the ledge and swung out and back in, releasing as his legs whipped toward the house. Caleb landed on his feet, allowing his knees to bend and absorb his weight.

He stood in an arched passage recessed into the house. Giant wooden shutters hung on either side of the span. A gas lantern flickered on the voussoir stones that gave the opening its curved shape.

Caleb stared into the darkened room as his eyes adjusted to the lighting. In a few seconds, he made out the shapes of furniture and the soft glow of an accent lamp. Caleb removed the Glock G48 from his waist and checked to see a round was chambered. He'd found two more magazines at Tomás's home after his interrogation ended. He had sixty-three rounds in four magazines.

Corsair lifted the Glock and stepped into the dark room.

51

S he was nowhere to be seen, but caution warned him not to step out onto the street yet. Once Hubbard spotted him, Patterson didn't know what would happen. He needed to find her first. Especially since she had his weapon. That part worked for him, though. Patterson couldn't kill her with his own gun. Even in Mexico, that wouldn't work.

He had a burner phone in his bag, and right now, he was studying the satellite image of Gringo Gulch. There was one logical spot for Hubbard to be, and he saw the outline of the building. A house across the street and to the south of Sonny's place. From the map it wasn't obvious, but now that he was closer, he realized the house was not only vacant, but it was in ruins. Patterson figured it was a fire that ravaged the villa, and whoever owned it never went about rebuilding it. Now the home occupied a lot, and anyone wishing to buy it would have to demolish the rest of it before beginning construction—an expense that far outweighed the return. Eventually, someone with more money than sense would come along and build on it. They'd want the only thing that this section had little of—space. It wouldn't matter that they could build up in the hills for a fraction of the cost. This house would be around the corner from Elizabeth Taylor's famous home. Prestige like that was worth it to the foolish rich.

Patterson never expected to be that kind of rich. But a small cabin cruiser in the Bahamas would be enough for him.

He crossed the street and crept up the sidewalk. If Hubbard was in the house, she was watching Sonny's place. That would mean Patterson could come up from the other side without drawing her attention.

The more he thought as he walked, the better his plan would be. He just had to disarm her first. After that, he could march her inside and present her to Sonny. He'd ensure the bitch was dead, and it would score Patterson some points with the man. He'd respect Patterson a bit more for protecting him.

Not that Sonny Departi's opinion mattered to Patterson. His money did, though, and if he had to be in bed with the asshole, he might as well make it worthwhile. If Hubbard's target showed up, Patterson could duck out of the way. Or maybe let Sonny and Vinnie gun the man down. If he played this all correctly, it would benefit Patterson no matter how it ended. As long as Patterson avoided getting shot during the mayhem. That was the key through the whole thing.

He stepped up to the house. Only the concrete walls remained, and the FBI agent crawled through what had once been a window. Even the pane was gone. The neighbors didn't want to stare at burnt cinder or shattered glass, so someone cleaned it all up.

Patterson shuffled his feet. The last thing he wanted to do was step on something that made a noise.

A faint glow appeared, and Patterson froze. Odd shadows danced around, and it took him a second to realize the woman was looking at her phone. Was she checking the time? It was a mistake. Now Patterson had a good idea where she was. If he was right, she was on the opposite side of the wall beside him. He moved slower, taking almost a minute to go ten feet to the edge of the wall.

Patterson sucked in a deep, slow breath and waited. Fifteen minutes passed, and the FBI agent never flinched. He had been in stakeouts before, where he endured hours without a pee break. This would not be that long.

The glow of her phone screen came on again, and he sprinted around the corner. It was her mistake. The bright light screwed up her night vision for a second, and in that moment, Patterson closed on her fast.

Hubbard must have heard or sensed something in the dark. She flinched toward him, but Patterson charged at her with a balled-up fist that hit on the side of her head. The agent tumbled to the ground as Patterson landed on top of her, delivering blow after blow onto her face.

He stopped after several seconds, and he found himself stretched across the unconscious form. Without wasting a second, he frisked her, removing a Kel Tec handgun and his own Glock Gen 5. With a smug sense of pride, he slapped the cuffs on her wrists, binding them behind her back before rolling her over.

It took her several minutes to move, and when she opened her swelling eyes, Patterson stared at her.

"Get up," he ordered.

The OOC agent rolled to her side, trying to get her feet under her without the aid of her arms. After several seconds, she stood up. Hubbard started coughing and blood spewed out of her mouth. Patterson stepped back as a clot of blood landed on the floor at his feet.

"Let's go," he told her.

"Where?" she asked, but it came out like marbles through her busted lips.

"I'm getting my just rewards," he remarked.

"Corsair is coming," she warned him.

"Who? Corsair? Is that his call sign?"

"He's going to kill everyone," she said.

Patterson shrugged. "That solves a lot of my problems," he admitted.

Hubbard leaned against the wall and cast a scornful look at Patterson. "You're out of your element, Patterson," she informed him.

"Let me deal with that," he assured her. "Now move."

Hubbard allowed Patterson to direct her across the street. Her body ached from the beating he'd just dealt her, but she climbed the stairs at a slower than normal pace. Two men on the front portico stepped toward the pair. Patterson recognized them from earlier.

"I need to talk to Sonny," the FBI agent demanded.

The two men shared a concerned glance, but one walked to the door and entered. A few seconds later, Vincent Santoro appeared in the doorway.

"What the hell are you doing back here?" Vinnie asked Patterson with an irritated tone.

"Your guys are dropping the ball here," Patterson told the man. "She's been watching the place."

With that, Patterson pushed Hubbard into the house. Vinnie led them to the den where about ten men, comprising both Americans and Mexicans, sat around.

52

Corsair remained motionless. His ears tuned to the sound coming from the stairwell. Voices raised as the commotion caused by the new guests' arrival came to a crescendo. From what he could understand, they discovered the woman from the OOC watching the villa.

Not my problem.

His only concern was finding Amanda and getting her out of the house. Once he located his daughter, he'd have to come up with a plan to escape. There was no way to go back out the way he entered. Caleb didn't think he could make the jump from the balcony to the roof alone, much less carrying Amanda. If he could get over that hurdle, the free climb would be easier, but it would require Amanda to hold on to her father as he ascended the wall. All of it was far too precarious to be the best option.

He was standing in a hallway with three doors—two on the right and one on the left. When Corsair was training for covert incursions, the first rule his mentor, Marcus Davids—codenamed Hood—taught him was to take everything slow. Most operations became compromised when the operative reacted too quickly or attempted to rush through an operation. "Slow is good; slower is bet-ter," Hood instructed frequently.

There were, of course, instances when speed mattered, but, in those cases, he accepted the dangers accompanied by swift actions. In all other times, the number one rule was to take it a breath at a time.

Despite the urge to find his daughter first, Corsair re-mained motionless, allowing his ears to do the work. He could still pick up the voices downstairs, but they'd calmed down. His brain filtered that sound out, separating it into a little room in his mind, and allowed only the sounds from the top floor to register.

Corsair guessed Sonny's plan. He'd think that forcing Caleb to worry all night would spur him to give up Khloe faster. It was a logical move. After all, many people allow panic to escalate, and in turn, they decide to ease that fright despite the consequences. Only Caleb Saunders wasn't among most people. He'd faced this fear before, and then grief compounded it. Today differed little from that day all those months ago when *Las Serpientes*, the motorcycle gang that murdered his wife and son, kidnapped Aman-da. Except for that now, Corsair was awake. Caleb knew either he would find his only child or die trying. No other options existed.

He could hear breathing. Slow, rhythmic breaths punc-tuated with deep huffs. Sounds of sleeping. Not his daughter, though. Amanda made nothing more than a whimper when she slept. This was an adult.

He touched the doorknob. It felt warm to him, al-though the logic center of his mind warned him that meant nothing. He cracked the door. The slight click of the latch was barely audible. He stepped into the room. A small lamp glowed on a bedside table.

He resisted the sigh of relief that wanted to escape his lips when he saw the soft angelic face nestled against the pillow. In a chair next to the bed, a man leaned back with his arms crossed. The source of the breathing sounds. He dozed deeper than just a nap. Tasked with watching over the girl, the boredom of the guard duty wore on him. His lack of discipline allowed him to justify closing his eyelids for a short period. Only the man had no training, and to him, sleep was sleep. Despite sitting up, he slipped into REM sleep.

Or so Corsair thought. Two eyes opened, and the confused guard assumed for the briefest of seconds that Corsair was one of his comrades from downstairs. The dozer sat up as he realized he wasn't supposed to be asleep.

Corsair rushed him, and in that instant, the man in the chair recognized this newcomer wasn't supposed to be there. He lunged out of his seated position toward Corsair, who sidestepped the attack. Caleb's fist drove into the man's head with enough force to send him to the floor. The guard rolled across the room, toppling a table and pulling a gun. In the dark, Corsair couldn't distinguish the make, but he ignored that fact, leaping to knock it from his grip before he had it around.

A high-pitched cry sounded behind him as Amanda, jolted awake by the sound of the scuffle, wailed in fear. Caleb wanted to comfort her, but for the moment, he was helpless to soothe his daughter.

Corsair struck the man again as he tried to get to his feet. His opponent launched his foot out, sweeping Caleb's legs out from under him. The assassin hit the tile, and his hands pushed himself up off the floor.

He felt the blade before he ever saw it. Corsair jerked away when the stabbing sensation ripped through his left shoulder. As he pulled out of the man's grasp, he extended his right arm and struck him in the neck with a knife hand.

A gasp escaped the guard's lips as his throat closed up after the blow. The knife, still embedded in him, cut through more flesh as he moved. Corsair shoved the pain aside and wrapped his right forearm around the man's neck. With a sudden jerk down and an audible crack, he separated his vertebrae. His body slumped lifelessly on the tile floor.

The bedroom door swung open, and instinct sent Caleb's hand around the gun the other man dropped a few seconds earlier. As the barrel came up, he aimed and fired. Two shots hit the silhouette in the doorway.

Before the body fell, he turned to scoop up Amanda.

"It's Daddy," he assured her.

"Daddy?"

"We have to go," he told her. "Close your eyes."

Adrenaline coursed through him, but the pain in his shoulder increased despite the surge of biochemistry designed to keep him moving. It didn't help that he held Amanda on his left side and her weight pressed against the muscle, driving more flesh against the blade.

Corsair ran into the hall as a Mexican man appeared at the top of the staircase holding a small nine-millimeter Uzi. He hesitated when he saw Corsair carrying the little girl. It was a pause that would end his life as the gun in Corsair's grip fired twice. If the cartel member had been a target, both rounds would have been in the center ring. He fell backward down the stairs.

Caleb entered the farthest bedroom, dropping Amanda to the floor. He turned to cover the door with his weapon.

"Sweetie, I need you to hide," he told her.

"Daddy, he hurt you," she said, pointing to the knife handle.

"It's going to be okay," he promised. He reached over his shoulder and pulled the knife out. His face winced as the pressure of the blade increased for the split second before it came free. Blood dripped down his back.

He blinked hard as the intense pain threatened to black him out. But he regained his composure, breathing through the agony.

Standing up, he motioned for Amanda to hide. "Don't come out for anyone except me," he ordered, praying to himself that he hoped he could return for her.

There was no way to get out of the house without going through the street entrance. Even if he'd been able to jump to the roof before taking a knife in his back, now there was little chance he could scale the cliff face alone. With Amanda attached to him, the task became impossible.

If he planned to walk her out the front, then Corsair had to clear the way. He stepped into the hallway, watching the only access to this level—the staircase. It also meant it was the only exit.

Apparently, the men downstairs were now considering their options. No one else charged up the stairs after the last man went back down with two bullets in his chest.

Corsair closed his eyes for a second, trying to will the pain in his back away. For the first time, he looked at the gun in his hand. A Beretta APX that its owner had not cleaned in a while. He pulled the magazine. A quick count told him he had about ten shots remaining.

He switched the Beretta to his left hand, worrying that the wound on his back would weaken that side. His right hand raised the Glock. He took a deep breath and started for the stairwell.

53

The stairs leading down to the main level of Sonny Departi's leased villa curved with a plaster wall on one side. A black iron banister wound along the opposite edge, beginning twelve steps from the landing. It allowed Corsair to descend halfway before exposing himself to the men below.

Again, he took each step while listening below. The time that passed as he walked ten steps was over a minute. On the next level, an eerie silence hung in the air. If he'd been able to peer around the corner, he would see ten men aiming various weapons at the stairs.

"Is that Mr. Bryers?" someone called. "How did you get up there?"

A feminine voice muttered something. Then a shout from her. "Corsair, count ten men!"

The OOC woman.

"Shut up," a gruff American man shouted, and the sound of flesh slapping flesh echoed.

Corsair considered his options. He felt the sticky warmth of blood dripping down his back. Not so much that it was arterial blood, but enough that he would need to stop the bleeding soon.

"What is this Corsair?" Sonny asked. "Who are you?"

He leaned against the wall and raised the Glock. "Why don't you ask her?" he called down.

Corsair stepped down and fired a single shot. He had taken the split second he came into view to sight on the nearest target and hit him in the face. By the time the nine remaining men returned fire, Corsair was back around the corner.

"I fucking told you!" the woman shouted. Satisfaction coated her words.

"Who the hell is he?" Sonny demanded.

"He's going to kill all of you," she blurted out. Another sound as someone struck her.

"Mr. Bryers," Sonny called up. "That was an impressive shot."

"I have plenty of bullets here," Corsair assured the man.

"But do you have enough time?" Sonny asked. "I'm guessing this lady is the first wave coming after you. She's what? Homeland Security? Does that mean you are a terrorist?"

Corsair didn't reply.

"Someone like you could earn a lot of money working for me."

"Oh, what do I have to do? Give you an innocent girl?"

"I get it," Sonny remarked. "You got a little girlfriend, and you're playing house. But let's be real, there are better girls out there. I can offer you safety. Hell, we'll start with killing this bitch here."

"And my daughter?" Corsair asked.

"She'll be safe, I promise."

Caleb straightened up. "Let's talk," he suggested.

"Come on out," Sonny said.

"Everyone lowers their weapons first," Corsair demanded. "You saw what I can do. The next round will drop you. After that, it's fair game."

"That's reasonable," Sonny agreed.

Corsair counted off ten seconds before he moved down one step. He descended one more stair before he was around the corner. He had his second, longer look at the den. The man he'd shot lay sprawled on the floor in front of a sofa. Behind the couch, two Mexican men stared. Their weapons remained drawn, but the barrels were down. Four men, divided into groups of two, stood ready on either side of the room. Neither group had much cover, but they all waited. Standing at the rear were two older Americans. Another American squatted over a limp female, the Office of Compliance agent.

Both the Glock and the Beretta hung in each of Corsair's hands. He stared at the two older men, deciding which was Sonny.

His choice spoke. "So, what were you?" Sonny wondered.

Caleb didn't answer. "What are you offering?"

Sonny watched the guns in the assassin's hands. "Why don't you put down your weapons, and we can talk?" he asked.

"Hmm, that seems like I'd lose my bargaining position."

Sonny shrugged. "I can't blame you, but I'm guessing you are a professional, right?"

Caleb offered a gesture that seemed to say, "Of course."

"I just want Khloe Evans."

"What's in it for me?" Corsair questioned. His eyes darted between the nine targets.

"We can make whatever arrangement you consider fair," Sonny answered.

The stream of blood continued down his back. The flow was strong enough that most of the blood didn't congeal on the skin, but still some had thickened, sticking to his shirt. He let a part of his brain focus on sensing the blood-soaked cloth clinging to him so that he didn't think about the screaming pain in his shoulder.

"I want the woman," Caleb stated.

Patterson flinched, saying, "She's a liability."

Sonny cast a scowl at the FBI agent.

Caleb added, "She and I have some unfinished business."

Sonny shrugged, indicating it was an amenable accord. He looked at the woman on the ground. "I don't think she's able to get up right now."

Caleb barely cocked his head.

"Where is Khloe?"

"She is probably gone," the man on the stairs replied.

"Where did she go?" Sonny asked. His brow furrowed as the words came out.

"Hell if I know."

"That seems to reduce your bargaining power," Sonny pointed out.

"I never intended to bargain for her life," Corsair told him as both guns in his hands raised. The Glock and the Beretta discharged within a second of each other. His first round from the Glock struck Patterson in the face. Unfortunately, the Beretta, fired from Caleb's left hand, didn't make it on the mark. Instead, the bullet clipped the Cortez Cartel member on the far left side of the room. The man took the shot in his left arm where it gouged the biceps. It took half a second for Corsair to correct his aim, but at that point the Mexican man spun about from the impact. The Beretta fired two more rounds, neither finding a target.

Seven guns opened fire on the stairwell as Corsair dove back around the corner. Something threw him into the wall, and he scrambled up the stairs despite the burning sensation in his hip. Corsair stopped two steps up and out of the line of fire. His right hand touched his side where blood soaked through his pants. He tested the weight on the leg and found it held. Corsair couldn't tell if the bone broke. However, he could feel the bullet still under the skin. It wasn't deep, but with every movement, he felt the piece of lead in his body.

Gotta keep moving.

"He's hit," Sonny announced. "Jimmy, take Jackie and Carlos there up and finish the fucker."

"Hell no," Jimmy retorted. "Ain't no way I'm going up there."

"What?" Sonny shouted.

"That asshole almost killed me once. I'm not getting close to him."

A gunshot echoed up the staircase, and Caleb moved to the next level. He crawled to the bathroom, where he wrenched open the drawers, searching for anything to slow his bleeding. A bottle of generic acetaminophen stared up at him. As he swallowed four of them, he realized they wouldn't kick in before he was either dead or gone from the house. In the drawer was a butane lighter used for igniting the candles decorating the bathroom. Under the sink, he found three cans of aerosol air freshener. Corsair pulled them out, testing to find them all brand new.

Caleb stuck his head out the door, looking down the hallway at the stairwell. Whatever transpired downstairs must have encouraged the others to venture up the steps. Corsair lowered himself to the ground, a brief reprieve on his him. Prostrate on the tile, he steadied the Glock. The Beretta lay next to him, ready for him to take it up when he needed it.

The hallway was dark, and he counted on the amateurs coming after him to look for him at eye level. He waited as the first figure climbed the stairs. It took them almost a full minute to brave steps. Three shapes now appeared at the landing, and Caleb worried he hadn't located the light switch. If they flipped it and turned on the lights, they would spot his position right away.

Whatever logic they were using seemed to think there was some safety in leaving the hall darkened. Corsair lined up the iron sights of the Glock on the first man. He took a deep breath and applied the five pounds of pressure on the trigger as he squeezed. The brass ejected from the chamber as he fired the second and then third shots. The last two casings were still in the air by the time the last round found its target. Each bullet struck the chests of the respective targets. Even wounded, Corsair's marksmanship was incredible. It had been an innate talent of Caleb's and the thing that attracted Carl Winston to him during his brief stint at Parris Island.

But now wasn't the time to admire his shooting. He estimated there were three combatants downstairs, and he still had to go down the stairs to reach them. He tried to push up to his feet, but his leg buckled under him.

Maybe the bullet fractured something after all.

He picked up the Beretta and fired a single shot into the concrete wall before pushing himself back in to the darkened bathroom.

Then he waited.

On the first floor, he could hear the discussion, but couldn't make out the mumbled words. Although, he guessed what they were debating—four shots, and no one had come down the stairs. Who remained alive?

His leg ached and throbbed all the way down to his knee. He'd need to move, but at the moment, he didn't think his nervous system could handle the pain. If he had to fight the last three guys, he worried he would lose right off the bat.

He realized he had belly crawled back through the puddles of blood he left on the floor. Blood covered his entire front. It was a lot, but not quite to a point of being life-threatening. Of course, that's a superfine line to walk down. Once he went too far, he might not recover.

He tore a swath of toilet tissue off the roll hanging on the wall. As he gritted his teeth, Caleb stuffed the paper in a wad against the bullet wound in his hip. The pressure on the raw flesh sent rivulets of pain coursing through him.

Bile forced itself up his throat, and Caleb swallowed back the vomit. There was no time for that.

"Damn," someone whispered with a near whistle in their voice. He peered out from the dark as the light in the corridor came on. Caleb had no line of sight on whoever was out there, but from his angle he saw two corpses lying halfway off the landing. Their torsos splayed down the stairs like a dropped cloth.

"Is he dead?" Sonny called from downstairs.

"No sign of him," the man outside the bathroom responded. "But there's a metric shit-ton of blood. If he ain't yet, he will be."

"Over here, Vinnie," another man said in the hallway. He was closer to the bathroom door, following the smear of a trail that Caleb left.

Caleb leaned his back against the toilet, allowing the fixture to support his weight.

"Wait," Vinnie ordered. He snaked his hand around the corner and found the switch. He jerked it back before their prey tried to shoot it off.

Neither man stuck their head around the door jamb yet, and Caleb went limp, attempting to appear lifeless.

It took ten seconds before the first man looked around the door jamb, and Caleb prayed they didn't unload their weapons at him.

"Shit," the man whispered, and the other, Vinnie, appeared behind him.

Both men relaxed for a second. One second. Corsair fired two shots from the Glock. Surprise registered in their eyes when the realization that the dead man, covered in blood, just killed them.

"Vinnie!" Sonny called from downstairs.

In a muffled voice, Caleb shouted, "We got'im," trying to run the syllables together to be indistinguishable.

"About fucking time," Sonny responded.

Caleb pushed up on the toilet until he sat on the lid. Once he steadied himself, he grabbed the sink basin and pulled himself to his feet. The initial pain raced through him, and he tested the leg. It would hold—for now.

He struggled to lift his leg enough to crawl over the bodies, both in the bathroom's doorway and again at the staircase landing. He waddled down the stairs to see Sonny Departi holding a gun on the OCC woman.

"Nice try," he remarked. "You are a tough bastard."

Sonny tightened his grip on the woman, pulling her in front of his entire body. He left a small area of his head open, but Caleb worried he was too shaky to attempt that shot.

"What makes you think I won't shoot you through her?" Corsair asked.

"I'm taking a gamble, I suppose," Sonny answered.

"He will want me dead," the woman muttered.

"No, he doesn't," Sonny replied. "This guy might not want you to catch him, but the asshole's got a fucking Lancelot syndrome. He wants to be the good guy."

"He's an assassin," she spouted.

Sonny watched Caleb with unblinking eyes. "We can work out a deal," Sonny told him.

"Yeah, I think your bargaining position has weakened."

"Fellow, you're bleeding pretty bad," Sonny pointed out. "I doubt you have all that much time to wait."

The OOC agent still had her hands behind her back, leaving her with no moves to fight. Caleb kept one eye on her and the other trained on Sonny. He inhaled a breath. The gangster was correct. He needed to get Amanda and leave so he could tend to his wounds. The longer this dragged out, the worse his chance of doing that was.

"Let's come to an arrangement," Sonny suggested.

The woman blinked at him before she went limp. Her weight dropped, and Sonny, surprised, let her slip down in his arms.

Caleb squeezed the trigger, and Sonny's head snapped back, spraying blood and brains behind him before he fell to the floor.

The woman scrambled on her backside toward another body. Caleb struggled to stride after her. He reached her and leveled the weapon at her head.

"I'll kill you if you don't stop moving," he warned.

She froze and stared up at him. "I don't want to hurt you," she said. "I just want—"

Caleb hit her across the temple. It was a glancing blow, delivered with enough force to render her unconscious without killing her—he hoped. He knelt down and felt for a pulse. Steady.

He stood up and turned to attempt to make it up the stairs to retrieve his daughter.

54

Lee sat on the front steps of the villa as the Jalisco State Police and the Federal Police swarmed the house. She'd lost track of time, and so far, neither she nor the police recovered her phone. Lee assumed it was in one of Patterson's pockets, but once she found the handcuff key, she didn't bother digging around for it.

Now, she alternated between rubbing her wrists where the cuffs chafed the skin and feeling the knot on her head where Corsair clobbered her. That pissed her off, too. But there was a logical portion of her brain working too, and it pointed out that, with about ten corpses littering the villa behind her, she was lucky he didn't add her to that number. It would have eased the pressure on him somewhat. Not really, she decided. Winston wouldn't have stopped, but at least Corsair wouldn't have a witness to identify him.

If only I'd had the chance to talk to him, she wished. Two minutes would have been enough to argue her case. Just to let him know she wanted his help to get Winston. Instead, he knocked her out, leaving her with a concussion and a massive headache.

It could have been worse.

Considering how most of Corsair's encounters left the other side dead, she had to agree with that assessment. It gave her some confirmation of his character too. After all, she was an easy target, but he didn't kill her. Even when Sonny Departi held her as a human shield, he refused to take the shot.

Caleb Saunders had a moral stance. She admitted it was an ambiguous one, but considering how he'd stepped in to help Khloe Evans and chose to—not protect Lee, but at least value her life. It indicated he had his own rules, and that was important. In the future, it would allow Lee to predict his behavior better.

She needed to get in contact with the surveillance team. Lee lost track of time, but she realized it was in the early morning. The team should arrive within a few hours, and by then, Lee assumed Corsair would be out of the city.

If he wasn't already...

Corsair left his bloody clothes in the upstairs bathroom, where it appeared he treated his wounds. When he appeared on the steps, he looked like he could barely stand. He'd need to seek some kind of real medical treatment soon. That might be her team's best chance to locate him.

"Agent Hubbard," Second Sergeant Eduardo Castillo said as he came from behind her. "How are you feeling?"

"A throbbing headache, but otherwise, I'm okay."

"This is—what is the American term?"

"A clusterfuck," she suggested.

"*Sí*," he conceded. "What happened?"

Lee explained, starting with her discovery that Patterson worked for Sonny Departi. "I would say the FBI will be tearing Patterson's life apart now."

"It is bad," he agreed. "What can you tell me about the suspect who killed everyone?

"Not a lot," she lied. "I saw the man, so I can give you a description."

"Was he the one you were searching for?" Castillo asked.

Lee shook her head. "No," she lied again. "That man wouldn't have left me alive. I'm not sure who this one was."

"What was his nationality? American?"

"Maybe, but he spoke with an accent. It seemed European. Of course, I wasn't as alert as normal."

Castillo nodded, and Lee suspected the officer didn't believe her whole story. She couldn't give the Mexican authorities Corsair's description. If they somehow found him before her, then it might cause more trouble. Lee didn't know what Corsair would do if the Mexican police cornered him, but she thought—at least now—that he wouldn't kill indiscriminately. In fact, he might use what he knew to trade for his freedom, and a former OOC assassin killing in a foreign country would cause an international incident.

"I suspect," she offered, "that he was working either against the cartel or the Cincinnati mob. A third party."

"We think there were some cartel people outside the house," Castillo explained.

Lee nodded. "I saw four. Patrolling on the street and in the front."

"Did they come in during the gunfight?" he asked.

"Not that I saw," she replied, trying to remember.

Castillo's head bobbed. "While the walls are thick, it seems unlikely that they wouldn't have heard the gunfire."

Lee lifted an eyebrow. "What do you think happened?"

"Two incidents occurred last evening. Both involved members of the Cortez Cartel, including a high-ranking leader."

"What?" Lee asked, straightening her back.

"Several people were killed by a single man who escaped rather incredibly. This was at the apartment of a person we've identified as a street-level—you might call him an officer. The other was Tomás Gonzales, a man we know is the head of the Cortezes in Puerto Vallarta. We found him beheaded."

"Oh shit," Lee breathed.

"It is indicative of an attack on the cartel," he admitted.

Lee nodded. "Were the ones outside involved?" she asked.

"Or they were smart enough to flee rather than fight."

She wondered if he believed any of that. It was true, though. Corsair was, no doubt, the one responsible for those other attacks, and while they were assaults on the cartel, it wasn't for the reason that Castillo assumed. Lee saw how Corsair worked in Florida. It was the same thing here. He started at the bottom and climbed his way up the ladder until he found where his daughter was.

"Did they find my phone on Patterson?" she asked.

"I'll check and see," he assured her.

"I'd like to reach out to my boss so he can facilitate a conversation with the FBI about Patterson."

Castillo nodded. "It appears the suspect came through the roof," he explained. "And he was wounded."

"He came from upstairs. Is there no way in that direction?"

The second sergeant shook his head.

"How did he leave?" Lee asked.

"We assume he went through the front. However, we haven't established yet if he took a vehicle. We found a rental car parked in the property's garage. With this many people in the house, it would seem likely there was more than one vehicle."

Lee considered that. She could have the team search for abandoned cars. Corsair wouldn't keep anything too long. In today's world, that information was too accessible. As late as it was, the best move Corsair could make would be to ditch the car soon and steal another. The owner of the second car wouldn't notice their vehicle's theft until morning. That gave Corsair several hours of travel time before the victim ever reported it.

"Let me send one of my men to get a description so I can get you back to your hotel. You will need some rest."

Lee nodded, knowing that she had no rest in her future. Even if it was a futile search, she'd be combing Puerto Vallarta for Corsair. She'd want to search for the smartest routes out of the city, too. He'd waste no time trying to get out of the country.

If he hadn't already escaped.

Corsair was a professional, and whatever identity he had when he came into this house died in there, too. Whatever that identity was, Lee Hubbard knew Saunders established it months ago. Hell, he could be at the airport waiting on the first flight out of Mexico. By the time the team landed and scoured any CCTV footage, he'd land in another country, ready to vanish for good.

Castillo rose to his feet, leaving Hubbard on the steps. She reached up and touched her temple, wincing as she did so.

55

The café bubbled with activity. Caleb sat in the corner with a laptop. The computer was brand new or, rather; it was new to him. He'd purchased it months ago, leaving it in his go-bag. Now, he was scanning the news out of Puerto Vallarta while searching for transportation out of Mexico. The reports read that police were hunting for a European male person of interest involved in a systematic attack on suspected members of the Cortez crime organization. Many of the pundits speculated more than reported on the situation. The consensus with two former government officials who now consulted with the press was that a faction of the Cortez Cartel seeking to take over orchestrated the attack. One opinionated correspondent suggested it was the beginnings of a war between the cartels. Although they didn't know what other cartel was involved. As yet, none had taken responsibility.

The suspect's description was not a match for Caleb. In fact, it was far enough from him to be purposefully false. The woman from the Office of Compliance didn't want the *Federales* to get to Corsair first. He wondered if leaving her alive was the smartest move. At the time, it felt wrong. Besides, he barely had the strength to climb the stairs to Amanda. Not that it mattered, because it still seemed like he made the right decision. Audrey would never have approved of murdering a defenseless woman in handcuffs, even if she presented a future threat.

Caleb decided he would deal with her and Carl Winston down the road. For now, he needed to get out of Mexico. He wasn't sure he would survive the drive to Mexico City, but now, two days later, he found himself ready to move. Not fast, though. His wounds, while tended to, hadn't received proper medical attention. He'd broken into a veterinary clinic in the town of Compostela, where he extracted the bullet from his hip and cleaned the wound. The knife wound proved to be more difficult, but he'd managed to clean it and tape it closed. Amanda, despite her age, was helpful in applying a bandage, which helped slow the bleeding down until he got to Mexico City.

He glanced up from the computer to see the two girls approaching. Khloe held Amanda's hand, and the pair sat down at the corner table.

"Well?" Khloe asked. She'd insisted on finding him when she got the message he sent from the veterinarian clinic's computer.

"We can't go back to Puerto Vallarta yet," he assured her. "That will be months, if we're lucky."

"But can we get out of Mexico?"

"I think so. Obviously, for us, going south is the only option. However, you can decide what you want to do."

Khloe let out a sigh. "Do you think it's safe for me to go home?"

Caleb didn't respond at first. After several moments, he replied, "No. Even if Sonny's organization has no hit out on you, we have to assume the cartel does. They only have my alias, I hope." Although, he was almost certain of that.

"My parents?" she asked, worried.

"I don't know," he admitted. "If it were my folks, I'd suggest they disappear. It seems like a lot of trouble for the Mexicans to go after them, but I would lean toward being cautious."

Khloe nodded.

"Is Koey going to stay wid us?" Amanda asked.

Caleb gave the woman a smile. "You are welcome to," he offered.

"I don't think I can handle being on the run alone," she confessed. "I don't even have a passport I could use."

"We can work on that," Caleb promised. "I worked with a guy down in Belize City that makes beautiful documents. Hopefully, he's still around."

"We still have to get across the border," she pointed out.

"We hoof it," he explained. "There are plenty of ways across. It's just not getting caught while doing it."

"I don't have any money, either," she reminded him.

"Well, we're in luck," he said. "Sonny Departi didn't travel light. I have about twenty thousand dollars in cash. Unfortunately, I couldn't risk taking his credit cards."

"Thank you so much," Khloe told him for the countless time. "I'd be dead without you."

He just smiled a half smile. Angel's beaten body flashed through his mind. Caleb wanted to check on her, but even that much contact might give him away. Whatever it took, though, he'd come through on his promise to fund her education. It would require a couple of bank transfers that he could only accomplish in person, but it was something manageable.

"We're sitting too long," Caleb warned. "We need to get a car. Anything more public will be obvious with three Americans."

Khloe glanced at her hands. "You never told me your real name," she reminded him.

"I guess that's fair," he admitted. "You're in for the long haul."

She nodded.

"It's Caleb."

Khloe Evans gave him an approving nod. "Thank you."

"And I'm 'manda," the girl blurted out proudly.

"I know who you are," she joked with the girl.

Caleb closed the laptop. "C'mon ladies, we have a long way to go," he stated.

Read the bonus chapter here.

www.ingramcontent.com/pod-product-compliance
Lightning Source LLC
Chambersburg PA
CBHW031834310726
48972CB00005B/1276